GW00676297

LEGACY

OF

TEMPTATION

Also From Larissa Ione

~ DEMONICA/LORDS OF DELIVERANCE SERIES ~
Pleasure Unbound (Book 1)
Desire Unchained (Book 2)
Passion Unleashed (Book 3)
Ecstasy Unveiled (Book 4)
Eternity Embraced ebook (Book 4.5) (NOVELLA)
Sin Undone August (Book 5)
Eternal Rider (Book 6)
Supernatural Anthology (Book 6.5) (NOVELLA)
Immortal Rider (Book 7)
Lethal Rider (Book 8)
Rogue Rider (Book 9)
Reaver (Book 10)
Azagoth (Book 11)
Revenant (Book 12)
Hades (Book 13)
Base Instincts (Book 13.5)
Z (Book 14)
Razr (Book 15)
Hawkyn (Book 16)
Her Guardian Angel (Book 17)
Dining With Angels (Book 17.5)
Cipher (Book 18)
Reaper (Book 19)
Bond of Destiny (Book 20)
Bond of Passion (Book 21)

~ MOONBOUND CLAN VAMPIRES SERIES ~
Bound By Night (book 1)
Chained By Night (book 2)
Blood Red Kiss Anthology (book 2.5)

~CONTEMPORARY/WOMEN'S FICTION ~
Snowbound
The Escape Club

LEGACY
OF
TEMPTATION

NEW YORK TIMES BESTSELLING AUTHOR
LARISSA IONE

Legacy of Temptation
A Demonica Birthright Novel
By Larissa Ione

Copyright 2024 Larissa Ione
ISBN: 978-1-957568-71-3

Published by Blue Box Press, an imprint of Evil Eye Concepts, Incorporated

Author's Acknowledgements

When I was little and adults asked what I wanted to be when I grew up, I told them, depending on my age at the time, about hoping to be a veterinarian, or an astronaut, or maybe a police officer who worked with K-9s. I never mentioned wanting to be an author, even though, deep down, I dreamed of becoming one from the day I learned to read.

It just seemed silly. An unachievable fantasy.

So I went to college. Goofed around getting a Criminal Justice degree I would never use because I truly didn't know what I wanted to be besides a writer. Instead of a Criminal Justice career, I waitressed. Did security work. Trained dogs. I was really kind of lost.

Finally, I joined the U.S. Air Force and went through the meteorology program, which I loved. After I got out of the military, I worked for the National Weather Service and the FAA for fifteen years.

But you know what I never stopped thinking about?

Becoming an author.

I wrote in my spare time, and eventually I started submitting manuscripts. When I sold my first book (which is a whole other story), I finally felt like I was where I was supposed to be. All those years of being lost finally made sense.

Now, here I am, fortunate to have seen my dream come true. I've worked with incredible publishers, editors, and agents over the years. I've been starstruck by authors I read long before I got published, and I've made so many friends of my readers. This career has handed me a life full of incredible opportunities, experiences, and friends, for which I am so very grateful.

I can't list everyone who has touched my life or this book would be twice as long, and it's already a monster. But please know that I love and appreciate you all.

I do want to express my deepest gratitude to Liz Berry, Jillian Stein, and M.J. Rose for giving this series the best home it could have. What you've done with Evil Eye has been incredible, and I'm so proud to be with you.

Thank you to Steve Berry, too, for the advice and hospitality, and especially, the amazing novels!

Huge thanks, as always, to everyone at Evil Eye. Chelle Olson, I always look forward to your edits, and even more, I look forward to seeing you when we get the chance. Kim Guidroz, I can never thank you enough for all you do no matter how hard I try. I so wish we lived closer! And I have to throw out some major appreciation for Hang Le and Trinity Shain for bringing my covers to stunning life. The artwork is my favorite part of assembling a book, and I'm always awed when I get an Evil Eye cover.

Judie Bouldry, thank you for all the support and help and friendship over the years. I can't believe it's *been* years, lol!

Big shout-out to everyone in my Facebook Underworld group! I love having a place to talk about books and movies and pets, and I have to send tons of hugs and thanks to Cheryl Johnson and Kat Furgerson Daugherty for keeping the laughter going. You ladies are awesome!

Closer to home, I need to thank my family and friends for putting up with my writing schedules and giving me breaks to recharge. Michelle, I love our friend days (which we need to do more often), and Jennifer, I love our shared passion for pups. Filling in at Creekside Kennels and Shop never feels like a job when I'm surrounded by dog toys and treats!

And finally, thanks go out to Rose Graham for a fun contribution to this book. She'll know it when she sees it!

Oh, and Shanea? You waited a long time, but I've finally fulfilled my promise. <Insert maniacal laughter here>

Again, thank you all.

Let's get to it.

A Note from Larissa

So. It's been a long time, hasn't it?

Too long, you say? I get that. But these characters, the children of earlier heroes and heroines, weren't ready to come into the world until now.

The story had to percolate in my mind for a while. The children had to grow up, and the universe had to evolve. So much happened over the course of the Demonica and Four Horsemen books, and even more is going to happen in future books. This series needed extra time to come to life.

My good friend, editor, and publisher, Liz Berry, once asked of this series, "You love tortured, broken characters. How are you going to have that if the characters you're writing about were raised in loving, stable homes?"

Oh, let me show you the ways…

This book, and this entire series, is about consequences. That age-old notion that no good deed shall go unpunished and that the road to Hell is paved with good intentions.

And that children will suffer for the sins of their parents.

So…you know all the shit that went down in the Demonica and Four Horsemen series?

Yeah. That's gonna come back to bite 'em in the ass.

Which brings me to this:

Things might get kind of rough. Happily Ever After isn't Happily *Easily* After.

Especially when the past returns to haunt you.

We're going to be dealing with a lot as we work through the consequences of past actions and toward the ultimate conclusion. If you're new to my books, you can start here. The Demonica Birthright series is a spinoff, but it's its own thing. If you are familiar with the Demonica and Four Horsemen series but haven't caught up, I suggest you at least read the books Azagoth and Reaper (not *Reaver*, although you should read that too), otherwise this book will be super spoiler-y.

Okay, so let's do this. We are, after all, on borrowed time.

The Apocalypse is coming.

Glossary

Aegis, The - Society of human warriors dedicated to protecting the world from evil. See: Guardians, Regent, Sigil.

Agimortus - A trigger for the breaking of the Horsemen's Seals. An agimortus can be a symbol engraved or branded upon the host person or object, or it can be an event.

Camborian - The human offspring of a parent under the possession of a demon at the time of conception. Camborians may or may not possess supernatural powers that vary in type and strength, depending on the species of demon inhabiting the body of the parent at the time of conception.

Council - All demon species and breeds are governed by a Council that makes laws and metes out punishment for individual members of their species or breed.

Decipula - A marble-sized trap designed to capture and contain the souls of dead demons until Sheoul-gra can be rebuilt.

Daemonica - The demon bible and basis for dozens of demon religions. Should they come to pass, its prophecies regarding the Apocalypse will ensure that the Four Horsemen fight on the side of evil.

Dermoire - Located on every Seminus demon's right arm from his hand to his throat, a *dermoire* consists of glyphs that reveal the bearer's paternal history. Each individual's personal glyph is located at the top of the *dermoire*, on the throat.

Fallen Angel - Believed to be evil by most humans, fallen angels can be grouped into two categories: True Fallen and Unfallen. Unfallen angels have been cast from Heaven and are earthbound, living a life that is neither truly good nor truly evil. In this state, they can—rarely—earn their way back into Heaven. Or they can choose to enter Sheoul, the demon realm, to complete their fall and become True Fallens, taking their places as demons at Satan's side.

Guardians - Warriors for The Aegis, trained in combat techniques, weapons, and magic. Upon induction into The Aegis, all Guardians are inked with an enchanted Aegis shield tattoo. Each tattoo is tailored to its wearer, imparting gifts such as night vision or the ability to see through demon invisibility enchantments.

Harrowgate - Vertical portals, invisible to humans, which demons use to travel between locations on Earth and Sheoul. Very few beings own or can summon their own personal Harrowgates.

Marked Sentinel - Humans charmed by angels and tasked with protecting a vital artifact. Sentinels are immortal and immune to harm. Only angels (fallen included) can injure or kill a Sentinel. Their existence is a closely guarded secret.

Memitim - Earthbound angels fathered by the Grim Reaper and assigned to protect humans called Primori. Memitim remain earthbound until they complete their duties, at which point they Ascend, earning their wings and entry into Heaven.

Radiant - The most powerful class of Heavenly angel in existence, save Metatron. Unlike other angels, a Radiant can wield unlimited power in all realms and travel freely through Sheoul, with very few exceptions. The designation is awarded to only one angel at a time. Two can never exist simultaneously and cannot be destroyed except by God, Satan, or the Heavenly Council of Orders. The fallen angel equivalent is called a Shadow Angel. See: Shadow Angel.

Regent - Head of the local Aegis cell.

ReSpawned - Demons whose souls were returned to their former bodies and released from Sheoul-gra when Azagoth destroyed the realm. The freshly re-spawned demons were sent into Azagoth's war with the fallen angel, Moloch. Millions were killed, their souls free to wreak havoc, but those who didn't die became known as the ReSpawned.

S'genesis - Final maturation cycle for Seminus demons. Occurs at approximately one hundred years of age. A post-*s'genesis* male is capable of procreation and possesses the ability to shapeshift into the male of similar-sized demon species.

Shadow Angel - The most powerful class of fallen angel in existence, save Satan. Unlike other fallen angels, a Shadow Angel can wield unlimited power in all realms, and they possess the ability to gain entrance into Heaven. The designation is awarded to only one fallen angel at a time, and they cannot exist without their equivalent, a Radiant. A Shadow Angel cannot be destroyed except by God, Satan, or the Heavenly Council of Orders. The Heavenly angel equivalent is called a Radiant. See: Radiant.

Sheoul - Demon realm. Located deep in the bowels of the earth, accessible only by Harrowgates.

Sheoul-gra - Until its destruction, it was a holding tank for the souls of evil humans and demons. A purgatory that existed independently of Sheoul, it was overseen by Azagoth, also known as the Grim Reaper. It is currently under reconstruction.

Sheoulic - Universal demon language spoken by all, although many species also speak their own language.

Ter'taceo - Demons of any species who can pass as humans either because their species is naturally human in appearance or because they can shapeshift into a human form.

Ufelskala - A scoring system for demons based on their degree of evil. All supernatural creatures and evil humans can be categorized into five Tiers, with the Fifth Tier comprised of the worst of the wicked.

'Tis said that wrath is the last thing in a man to grow old.
~ Alcaeus

Prologue

"Mama? We go?"

Smiling, Regan looked down at her toddler son, the breeze ruffling his blond hair. "Yes, Logan. We're taking a walk and getting some fresh air." She rubbed her belly, swollen with a baby she already knew would be a girl. "Doctor's orders. And if your uncle Eidolon says to do something, we do it."

She almost laughed at that. Just three years ago, she'd hated all demons and hadn't believed that a single one of them could be anything other than pure evil. But Eidolon, the head doctor at Underworld General Hospital, had saved her life, delivered her son, and continued to prove himself a million times over. Now, Regan's life was filled with demons and angels, hellhounds and hell stallions.

And most unbelievable of all, her husband, Thanatos, was the Horseman of the Apocalypse known as Death.

Sometimes, she had to pinch herself to make sure she was awake.

"Miss Regan?" One of Thanatos's daywalker vampire servants, Eli, called out to her as she started out the gate.

"Yes?"

"You need a guard, ma'am."

Thanatos insisted she have someone with her at all times if she left the safety of the castle walls, but she wasn't planning to go far. Besides, multiple wards protected the perimeter from most demons within a hundred-yard radius. Beyond that, ancient runes scattered for miles around the Greenland countryside rendered the stone keep and outbuildings invisible to humans and most supernaturals, from demons to angels.

"I'll be fine," she assured Eli. "I promise not to go beyond shouting distance. But if it makes you feel better, assign someone to watch us from the battlements."

"Yes, ma'am." His tall, wiry body folded into a deep, formal bow. "I will keep an eye on you myself."

"Thank you, Eli."

Logan darted off, his favorite stuffed lion dangling from one little fist and a toy bow in the other. She hadn't been happy about her husband giving their son a bow and arrow set for his birthday, but Thanatos had pointed out that Logan had been practicing with real, miniaturized bows since he could walk.

Of course, Regan had known what she was getting into when she married the Horseman, but that didn't mean she didn't worry. She often struggled with the reality of life as the mate of a legend and what it meant for her children. It wasn't always easy to accept that they were fated to fight evil from birth until the Apocalypse. They might be destined to become holy warriors, but they would always be her babies.

Logan's little quiver of arrows bounced on his back as he ran, leaping over tufts of grass and rocks with remarkable agility for a child his age. Suddenly, he stopped, dropped his stuffed lion, and nocked an arrow.

"Remember," she called out, "we don't kill anything that's not evil or food."

"I know," he yelled back as he released the arrow. It sailed in a graceful arc and then plunged to the ground with a thunk. "Yes! I got it!" He darted toward his prize.

Puzzled, she strolled over to him as he crouched on the ground. He turned to her, a proud grin on his face. He looked so much like his father when he smiled. He'd gotten her hazel eyes, although they were flecked with the pale yellow of Thanatos's irises. Logan had his father's blond hair, but she'd passed down her darker skin, even if her son's was a couple of shades lighter. And he'd definitely inherited his dad's stubborn streak.

Thanatos would say their son got the stubbornness from her, but he was wrong.

"What is it, Logan?"

He held up an apple pierced at an angle by his arrow. "Daddy hid a whole bunch and told me to hunt them with my bow."

"Well, you know the rules." She reached out and tousled his hair. "You hunt it, you eat it."

"And you 'spect it." He sank his teeth into the crisp red fruit.

"Yes, you respect it and the life it gave up for you."

She smiled, remembering the bedtime story Thanatos had told Logan about growing up in an ancient Druidic society and how hunting had sustained them. He'd described rituals that thanked the animal for its sacrifice before releasing its spirit to be reborn...

"What about 'venge?" Logan asked.

"Revenge? You're asking if the spirits will want revenge?" Thanatos puffed Logan's Lion King *pillow. "Many do. But that's why you make clean kills and respect the life you took. Waste nothing. When that animal is born again, it could be friend or foe. Wouldn't you rather have a friend?"*

Logan nodded and snuggled into the covers, so young and innocent. But sometimes, he looked mature beyond his years, a glimpse into what he might become.

Like now, standing proud as Regan returned her attention to him, his face to the breeze as he cleaned and stored his arrow and devoured the literal fruits of his kill. He wasted nothing.

Then he became a kid again when he tossed the skeletal core to the ground, hugged his stuffed lion, and darted away.

She let him romp as she strolled within a stone's throw of the castle walls. Above, walking the battlements, Eli kept watch with a crossbow. She wished she could say that such tight security wasn't necessary, but the Four Horsemen had made a lot of enemies over the course of their thousands of years of history…enemies who had suddenly been brought back to life and now wanted revenge.

Thanatos had said the whole thing was practically Druidic.

Druidic, maybe, but karmic, definitely.

Still…it had been a long time since they'd been attacked at their home, and it was tempting to let things become a little more relaxed. Maybe after the baby was born, she'd talk to Thanatos about chilling out a bit when it came to security.

A gust of cold wind made her shiver and wish she'd brought a jacket. But she'd checked the weather and saw nothing but sun, warmth, and blue sky for the next two days.

"Miss Regan!" Eli gestured into the distance. "Looks like a storm is coming."

Frowning, she looked across the tundra to the rugged mountains in the distance. Sure enough, a wicked black cloud billowed and seethed, rolling toward them as if Satan himself drove it.

"Logan? Come on. We need to go back inside."

"Okay!" Logan stopped running and nocked another arrow. "I just gotta get this apple."

Lightning streaked across the sky, stretching impossibly far ahead of the roiling storm cloud that had now swallowed the northern hills. It throbbed angrily, seeming to double in size with each of her heartbeats. How had it gotten so close in a matter of seconds? A crack of thunder burst in her eardrums, and she clapped her hands over her ears as she ran toward Logan.

"Logan!" she screamed. "Come here! Run!"

He didn't move a muscle. He stood atop a mossy mound, legs spread, his bow positioned how Thanatos had taught him, relaxed but ready.

Oh, but he was his father's son.

And his mom was going to ground him for a week if he didn't listen to her.

"Logan! Come here!"

The storm lunged closer, covering half the distance in a split second. A howling gust hit her like a train, knocking her backward and nearly off her feet.

Still, Logan stood steady as if daring the storm to mess with him. Then, slowly, tauntingly, he raised his weapon and fired a little arrow into the dark depths of the boiling thunderhead.

Lightning seared the sky and burned the ground in sizzling zaps. The storm roared as a gaping maw formed in the clouds and sped toward her son.

"*Logan!*"

Suddenly, a hellhound phased in from out of nowhere, dodging electric spears as it raced the storm to get to the boy. Churning clouds spawned claws of lightning and explosions of thunder that rocked the earth. Regan stumbled, already off-balance from her pregnancy. Desperate and screaming, she ran harder—

The ground shook under the force of a violent thunderclap, and Regan went down in a heap.

"No," she gasped, half-crawling, half-scrabbling in a desperate attempt to find her footing.

Cujo dove on top of Logan, covering the child's little body with his bison-sized one. He snarled at the storm, spitting drool, his massive fangs flashing.

Panting and stumbling, Regan finally made it to her feet. She was only a few yards from her son now—

A bolt of electricity seared her from the inside out. Pain and sharp, scorching heat streaked through every cell in her body. Her skin shriveled, and her teeth rattled, but nothing was as bad as the cramp in her belly.

No, please, not again. Not my baby.

Almost as if it was alive, the storm growled, a resonant, chilling sound that pierced even the ringing in her ears. *Alive.*

"Oh, my God," she whispered. Even as the doubt tumbled through her mind, the reality was right there, breathing on her with foul gusts that reeked of brimstone and bowels. "The storm is a demon."

Half a dozen streams of lightning arched high before stabbing into the expanse of earth that separated her from Logan and Cujo. They raked the ground like claws, plowing deep furrows into the charred grass. Cujo spun toward the eye-searing bolts of light, and a split second later, he phased out of the storm's path, taking Logan with him.

Then, mingled with the hell-smoked howl of furious thunder, came the pounding of hooves.

Thanatos.

"Regan!" Death sat atop his pale stallion, Styx, as the massive beast charged toward her, his dinner-plate-sized hooves tearing up the ground and flipping chunks of earth into the air.

Fully armored, Thanatos leaped from the saddle of the galloping horse and landed in a combat roll. A violent downburst of wind and rain pelted them as he scooped her into his powerful arms and popped to his feet, all in one graceful motion.

Styx wheeled around, teeth bared, hooves kicking out in a futile attempt to engage the atmospheric foe. The air turned thick and still, and the acrid scent of brimstone and ozone hung heavily in the growing darkness. Styx reared up, snapping his deadly teeth, and as his front hooves slammed back down, a thick bolt of lightning lit him up. Screaming, he collapsed to the ground.

No! Regan couldn't breathe, couldn't even gasp for air as fear turned her lungs into useless, deflated sacks.

Styx lay motionless in the rain, his big body twitching.

"Styx!" Rare terror scoured Thanatos's voice and ramped up hers. Very little frightened her husband, but he'd been bonded to the beast for thousands of years. It was, literally, part of him. If he were to lose it… "Styx, to me!"

Come on, buddy…

For a heartbeat, nothing happened.

Another heartbeat.

Anoth—

Styx whinnied. His body collapsed in on itself and poofed into a wisp of smoke.

Yes. The horse's essence slid under Thanatos's right gauntlet and settled on his forearm like a tattoo. Now, Styx could heal, and Regan could finally take a breath.

"We're out of here," Than growled as he threw out his hand to open a portal.

Something struck his shoulder, cracking hard against his bone-plate armor. Swinging around, he angled his body to shield Regan from the storm and take the brunt of the baseball-sized hail pelting them like bombs.

A gale howled across the land and slammed into them with the force of a locomotive, knocking Thanatos backward. With an angry roar, he lowered his head and fought the wind for every step closer to the gate. He was as much a force of nature as the tempest, and as he finally leaped through the portal with Regan in his arms, she swore she heard the tortured, angry shrieks of countless souls enshrouded in the churning thundercloud.

Thanatos exploded out of the gate, his heart pounding so hard his armor thudded to the rhythm. Instantly, the staff of Underworld General Hospital ran toward him. Regan struggled to stand on her own, but he refused to let her out of his arms.

"Get Eidolon," he barked to the nearest person in scrubs. The guy scrambled away, his hooves clacking on the obsidian floor.

"Put me down." Regan struggled harder. She'd always been the stubborn one in the family. "I'm fine. The pain is gone, and I just felt the baby kick. You need to find Logan."

Reluctantly, Thanatos lowered Regan to the floor, but he kept a hand around her shoulders to hold her steady. "Logan is with Cujo."

"I know that." She braced her lower back with her hand and leaned into him with a heavy, exhausted breath. "But where?"

"Cujo is trained to take Logan to Greece in an emergency." Thanatos's sister-in-law, Cara, had used her hellhound-whispering skills to train the mutt to whisk Logan to the island she shared with his Horseman brother, Ares. "You know that. Are you sure you're okay?"

"Yes, of course." Looking up, she offered him a shaky smile. Her skin was way too pale, strain had put hollows under her eyes, and her miscarriage a year ago was much too fresh in his mind. Where the fuck was the doctor? "I'm just rattled."

So was Than, but he wouldn't admit that to Regan. She needed him to be strong right now, and he wouldn't fail her.

Eidolon burst into the Emergency Department from the direction of the hospital's office wing and gestured for them to follow him to an open exam room.

"What's going on?" The doctor, his dark hair molded to his head in the shape of a surgical cap, jerked the privacy curtain closed behind them.

Regan brushed aside Thanatos's helping hand and climbed onto the exam table on her own. So stubborn.

"I fell," she said as she reclined against the raised table back. "I think I might have been struck by lightning too. There was some pain in my belly, but it's better now, and I just felt the baby kick."

She was struck by lightning?

Eidolon snapped on some gloves. "You got caught in a storm?"

Than took Regan's hand in his. It was too cold. Or maybe he was just freaking out and being paranoid. "My family was attacked by a Tempestus demon."

"I knew it," Regan muttered.

Eidolon's gaze flicked up to Thanatos. "Tempestus demons are forbidden in the human realm."

"Not only forbidden," Than said, "they can't survive outside Sheoul for more than a few minutes."

"They're normally hellbound?" Regan frowned. "Then why was it here?"

Thanatos could only think of one reason, and it sent a chill down his spine. "Someone sent it. Someone so terrifying that it chose to risk its life in the human realm rather than refuse the order."

This was bad. Really fucking bad.

"Good luck narrowing down the list of potential senders." Eidolon placed his hand on Regan's belly. His right arm, covered in black glyphs from his fingers to his jawline, began to glow as the gift that gave him healing power flowed through the symbols and into Regan. "There are probably hundreds of high-level demons who want to hurt all of us."

"Hundreds?" Thanatos let out a bitter snort. "Try thousands."

They'd all made a lot of enemies, but the foes Thanatos and his siblings had made over the course of their thousands of years required a calculator to tally.

And the thing was, all those baddies shouldn't have been a problem. Their souls should have been contained in Sheoul-gra for all eternity— or at least until they were reincarnated as a completely different species of demon who wouldn't remember their pasts or their deaths at the hands of the Four Horsemen of the Apocalypse.

Unfortunately, Sheoul-gra's catastrophic destruction had released billions of demon souls, returning them to the bodies in which they'd died, memories intact. And bloody revenge took priority for many of the ReSpawned.

"I was being optimistic. It's a new thing I'm trying." The doctor stepped back from Regan with a satisfied nod. "Mother and baby are fine. I want to run a few tests, but I don't think there's anything to worry about."

Relief flooded Thanatos. But only for a moment. His family was safe, but something told him this was just the beginning…

Chapter One

The sins of the father are to be laid upon the children
—William Shakespeare, *The Merchant of Venice*

The club was on fire.

Literal fire.

Flames licked at a wall near Thirst's entrance, the remnants of an unruly *impignus* demon that had burst into flames and disappeared after being punched in the face by a bouncer. He'd regenerate in his family's eternal furnace, but if he was smart, he wouldn't show his face around here again. The club's owner, a vampire named Nate, didn't tolerate assholes who destroyed his stuff.

Logan led his buddy and fellow agent with the Demonic Activity Response Team, Mace, through a cloud of smoke and fire-suppressant vapors from the extinguisher in Nate's hands.

"Logan," Nate called out, his deep voice carrying over the din of music and rowdy patrons. "Haven't seen you in a couple of weeks. DART keeping you busy?"

"Always." Logan gestured to his friend. "Mace guilted me into an after-work drink."

"As if you've ever felt guilt in your life." Mace rolled his dark eyes and turned to Nate. "I bribed him. I'm buying. Also, I met a screaming hot Lilith who said she'll be here tonight." He tapped Logan on the shoulder. "And she said she wants to meet you."

Logan groaned. The word *Lilith* had become slang for *smoking hot chick* thanks to demon culture leaking into human language, and Logan couldn't wait for that fad to pass. But it wasn't Mace's jab at Logan's family history that annoyed him.

"Why were you talking about me? I don't need help getting a date." Mainly because he didn't *want* to date. He was thirty-three, a mere baby by immortal standards, and his dad kept telling him that the first five hundred years were for fucking around and *finding yourself*. Logan was fine with fucking around, but he didn't need Mace's help to do it. The guy had wild tastes in females.

But then, as an incubus who needed sex to keep from dying, Mace couldn't afford to have a lot of standards.

Mace shrugged. "She's the one who brought you up. We were talking about hellhounds, and she said she'd heard a rumor about some hot local who had one as a pet."

Shit. "You didn't tell her who I am, did you?"

"What, the son of the Horseman of the Apocalypse known as Death?" Mace snorted. "The hell with that. She would have lost all interest in *me*. All the females want to get you into bed."

"They want to get my *dad* into bed. I'm as close as they'll get."

"Yeah, well, you still get all the starfuckers."

"And you get all the females who want a twenty-minute orgasm." Which was most of them.

Mace's grin got cocky, and Logan just shook his head. Mace was…well, he was a Seminus demon, and his brain, body, and thoughts were wired for sex. If he wasn't fighting or playing video games, he was screwing. Human, demon, vampire, were-creature…he wasn't really picky.

His only stipulation was that his partner had to be female, which made sense since his species could only come with one, and Sems needed release several times a day. The poor guy couldn't even pleasure himself. Lucky for him, his uncle Eidolon, a renowned physician at Underworld General Hospital, had developed a drug that reduced a Sem's need.

Logan wasn't sure Mace was taking it, though. Dude was always on the lookout for a lay.

They left Nate to put out the last of the fire and moved deeper into the dark club, past the dance floor and the grinding, half-clothed bodies.

To the right was a hallway that led to rooms reserved for BDSM play, and to the left was a blood pit, where vampires and other blood-feeders could suck and fuck anyone who gave consent.

In some clubs, consent wasn't required, or if it was, accidents still happened. Not here. Not at any of Nate's six Thirst clubs. He employed on-site medical staff, and he would personally put down anyone who got carried away and killed their partner, whether it was in the blood pit, the BDSM rooms, or the main club.

As far as bars that catered to supernaturals went, this one in downtown Sydney, lurking like a squat mushroom in the shade of the massive StryTech building, was among the tamest and safest in the human realm despite the fact that Australia belonged to the demons now.

"I just got a message from Blade and Sabre," Mace said, looking down at his pride and joy, his wrist comm, the newest model with cloaking technology and a color holoprojector. "They'll be here any minute. Draven said he can stay for one beer, and then he's meeting Shanea for dinner…" His voice trailed off as his gaze, sparking with the gold flecks of arousal, locked on something behind Logan. "Oh, yeah, baby. It's *her.*"

Logan wheeled around, his combat boots squeaking on the stone floor. Bloody hell, Mace hadn't exaggerated about the female. She made a beeline for them, her skintight snakeskin dress showing off every curve and nearly every inch of creamy skin. Glossy black hair flowed over slender shoulders and full breasts. She was hypnotically gorgeous, transfixing every male in the room.

Which meant she was a damn succubus.

Logan cursed, unable to tear his gaze from the female's sinuous strut and the way her dress hitched up with every stride, teasing him with glimpses of inner thigh. And maybe more.

"You dumbshit," he muttered to Mace. "She's a fucking sex demon."

"Ouch. *I'm* a fucking sex demon, you know."

"Hard to forget." She was getting closer, parting the crowd with the force of her presence. She moved like a viper slithering after its prey. And she was…magnificent. "Number-one rule we all follow. Stay away from all succubi who don't live in a vase in our house and aren't named Masumi."

"Maybe her name *is* Masumi." The gold in Mace's eyes spread, swallowing the black as he hit peak excitement. "You don't know."

Yeah, Logan did know. Her name would be something long and beautiful, flowing over the tongue like a female's silky arousal. A faery name, like Aerilaya, or an angel name, like Celestia.

He casually reached down and adjusted his denim-pinched erection. The bastard.

"Besides," Mace continued, "not all succubi want to screw you to death or steal your seed or soul. Some just want what we Sems want. A couple dozen orgasms."

"Yeah, well, this one looks like she's after more than a good time." She looked like she wanted to screw her partner to a pulp and then devour the remains, Cujo-style. And her partner would beg for it.

"Hello," she purred as she slid up to them. "You must be Logan."

Logan started sweating. He never sweated. Mace was sweating a little too.

Anais, he thought. That fit her. *Or Isla.*

She reached out, resting one dainty hand on his forearm. Heat shot through him like fire in his veins, and a pulsing, carnal throb started in his groin. "I'm Beth."

Beth? No. In the heat of passion, he'd call her Elizabeth. He'd whisper her name against her tender flesh as he—

He shook his sex-addled head. What the fuck was he thinking? He had to get out of there. Succubi were *so* off-limits.

"Logan! Mace! Hey!"

Grateful for a distraction, he greeted Mace's Seminus cousins, Blade and Sabre. Draven came up behind them and gave Logan a fist bump.

"I hear you did an exorcism today…" Draven trailed off as he finally noticed Beth. "Holy…moly…" he breathed, and she graced him with a smile, the sharp tips of her fangs denting the glistening pillow of her bottom lip.

"So, Beth," Mace drawled, his voice thick with lust, "want to come back to our house to party?"

Oh, hell no. Mace was always inviting sketchy females to their compound, and they'd tried to rob them twice. Another time, the female had turned into a dire mantis and tried to eat him. Which was funny because when Mace told his dad, Lore, about it, Lore had confessed to being in the same situation back in his single days.

Logan never wanted to hear about his dad's sexcapades. Ever.

Beth's smile turned sultry. "I do love a Sem orgy," she said in a low voice that shouldn't have been audible in the noisy club. But Logan definitely heard her. Hell, he *felt* every word vibrate in an erotic cadence across his nerve endings. She squeezed his arm, and he damn near groaned. "What about you?"

Sem orgy? Oh, hell no. "I'm more of a one-on-one kinda guy."

"Ditto." Sabre's eyes, normally the color of dark coffee, had gone as gold as Mace's and Blade's, and his voice held a tortured note. As a sex demon, he was probably feeling some pain as his need intensified.

"Too bad the one you want is off-limits." Blade's gaze was zeroed in on Beth's deep cleavage.

"Aleka's not off-limits," Sabre said, tearing his gaze away to focus on the DJ.

Draven cocked an ebony eyebrow at Sabre. "You're not afraid of Ares?"

Sabre gave a nonchalant shrug, still clinging to the DJ like a life raft. "Ares loves me."

"Sure, he does." Mace popped a piece of gum into his mouth. "Until he finds out you're lusting after his baby girl." He looked over at Logan. "What do you think? Ares is your uncle. Will the second Horseman of the Apocalypse want his precious daughter banging a sex demon?"

Definitely not.

"Ooh." Beth rubbed up against Logan, her hip brushing his erection, and he had to clench his jaw to keep from moaning. This chick was throwing some serious sex magic, as powerful as any Logan had ever encountered. "Your uncle is War? Do you have a Horseman parent too?"

"His dad is Death," Mace interjected before Logan could lie and throw this female off track. "Thanatos."

"Mm." Her ruby lips parted on a soft, sensual gasp. "So, you're the one with the hellhound." She rubbed against him again, her pelvis rolling in a blatant invitation. "I want to stroke it."

Logan backed up a step, but she moved with him, not missing a beat. "Ah, yeah...Cujo isn't that friendly. He's pretty reactive around strangers..."

She hooked his T-shirt with her nails and leaned in, her body scorching hot against his. "I wasn't talking about stroking the hellhound." She cupped his cock through his jeans, and he let out a strangled, extremely humiliating noise. Holy hell, he was on fire. Where was Nate and his damn fire extinguisher now? "I need to fuck you," she breathed against his throat. "Right now."

Suddenly, the crowd parted, and an ominous breeze blasted through the channel of bodies. Logan's gut clenched.

He knew that breeze.

That angry, scorching breeze.

Thanatos, the Horseman known as Death, stormed toward Logan, his massive boots striking the floor like thunderclaps, his long leather coat flapping against them with every step. His pale-yellow eyes flashed like blades.

"Dad! What the——?"

"Move away from her, Logan." Thanatos knocked people out of the way like a hell stallion charging through a flock of sheep. "Move away from her *now*."

What kind of bullshit was this? And not embarrassing at all. Pissed and humiliated, Logan squared his stance and stood his ground. He and his dad hadn't gotten into it for decades, not since Logan was a rebellious asshat of a teen.

Actually, this felt more like he was back at the school for supernatural kids, and his hyper-paranoid dad was bursting into his classroom because some Big Bad wanted revenge, and Logan needed *protection*.

Fuck that. He was an adult now, with deadly skills and a hellhound. He didn't need Daddy running to the rescue.

"What the hell, Dad?" Logan grabbed Beth's hand out of sheer stubborn defiance. "I'm not Amber. You don't have to protect me from anything——"

"Dammit, Logan!" Thanatos roared as he swiped his finger across the crescent-shaped scar on his neck. Bone-plate armor clacked into place, a sheathed knife appeared at one hip, and a sword at his other. "She's not who you think she is."

The air went still. Everyone went still. If a Horseman armored up, shit was real. And if the souls trapped inside Thanatos's armor started swirling around his feet, it was time to run.

Out of the corner of his eye, Logan saw all his friends lock and load. They'd been around the Horsemen all their lives and knew the deal. Mace and Blade, more in sync as cousins than any brothers, dropped their hands to the knives they kept at their hips. Sabre casually reached for an empty beer bottle on a nearby table, but his right arm, with its glyphs from finger to throat, was a weapon in itself.

"Oh, for Satan's sake," Beth huffed. She released Logan's hand and plumped her breasts so her nipples were one deep breath away from popping out of her dress. "You were always so fucking wound up, Thanny."

Thanny?

Logan looked between her and his father with growing horror. "Oh, shit," he croaked, taking a step back from her. "Did you and my dad fu—?"

"Dude," Mace interrupted. "You know the story. Your dad was a virgin until your mom came along." He eyed Beth speculatively and gave a satisfied nod. "He could have cheated on your mom, though, I guess."

There was the sharp, quick hiss of a blade clearing its sheath, a blur of motion, and then Mace was flying backward. He slammed into the wall with a clack of teeth and a grunt, his arm pinned to the plaster with a knife through the sleeve of his leather jacket.

"We will have words later, Mace," Thanatos growled as he came to a halt a foot away from Beth. He towered over her, a mountain of menace made even more frightening by the wispy souls wriggling at his feet, anxious to be released. Anxious to kill.

Logan leveled an apologetic look at Mace before rounding on his father. "Are you going to explain what the hell is going on? Why are you cockblocking me and stabbing my friends? How do you even know Beth?"

"Yes, Thanny," she said coyly, one finger slipping inside her dress to stroke a nipple. "Do tell this tasty boy how you know me."

With a growl a hellhound would envy, Thanatos grabbed Beth by the throat and backed her into a support beam. A drop of blood welled at the tip of his sword, where it pressed into her breastbone.

Logan started forward, prepared to intervene…although he wasn't sure who would need the help. "Dad—"

"Her name isn't Beth, Logan. It's Lilith."

Logan stood there like a dope for a second, unable to comprehend what his father was saying.

"Not *a* Lilith. *The* Lilith," Thanatos prompted. "My mother." He stabbed Logan with his finger. "Your *grandmother*. Your *dead* grandmother."

Shock stole Logan's breath. She was his grandmother? The one who had committed countless atrocities? The one who had worked with Satan in a failed bid to start the Apocalypse? The one his uncle Reseph had slaughtered over three decades ago?

And she'd tried to get into Logan's bed?

"I—she—*what?*"

Lilith smiled at him, running her tongue suggestively along her lips as if she wasn't being held by the throat and at sword point by one of the Four Horsemen of the Apocalypse. One of her *sons*.

Thanatos's lips peeled back from massive fangs he rarely let anyone see. "Please, tell me you two didn't…"

"No!" Logan did a full body cringe and threw in a shudder for good measure. "Hell, no. Holy shit!" He wanted to puke just thinking about it.

"Oh, this is fucking hilarious." Mace yanked the knife free and unpinned himself from the wall. "Logan got granny humped."

Thanatos didn't need to pin Mace to the wall with a dagger again. He did it with an ominous glare. "Open your mouth one more time, and we will have more than words. I will be so far up your ass that we'll both be chewing your gum."

Mace, not being *completely* stupid, spit out his gum and inclined his head in a deep and respectful nod. "Yes, sir."

Technically, he'd opened his mouth, but Thanatos let it go and turned his full attention back to Lilith.

Logan's *grandma*.

And there came the nausea again. Logan had heard stories of the infamous and powerful succubus, Lilith, his entire life. She'd been evil on a level most demons didn't even achieve, and she'd deserved to die long before her son killed her. But after Azagoth destroyed Sheoul-gra and sent every soul back into a physical body, the entire family had hoped she'd been among the staggering number of casualties suffering in the battle Azagoth had sent his newly re-embodied army into.

Obviously, she'd survived.

Logan tore his gaze away from her, which was easier now that she wasn't putting out succubus pheromones, and he wasn't boiling over with lust for her.

Gross. So. Fucking. Gross. He needed a shower.

Swallowing sickly, he glanced at his dad. "How did you know—?"

"Nate called me." Thanatos nodded in thanks at the club's owner, who monitored the situation from near the bar. "Seems he met Lilith back before she died, so he knows who she is." He gnashed his teeth at her, his fangs flashing like tiny daggers. "We're going to leave now. I don't want to kill you inside Nate's shiny club."

Nate acknowledged with a nod and a gesture toward the back of the building. "Appreciate that. Take the rear exit. Through those doors."

Logan and his buddies were on Thanatos's heels as he shoved Lilith through the club and out the back doors into an empty parking lot. Logan doubted there were ever any cars in the lot. Most demons, even the locals, arrived via the Harrowgate in StryTech Square.

As the heavy metal door slammed closed behind them, the sound of hooves vibrated the air.

Hell, yeah. Logan would know the cadence of those two sets of hoofbeats anywhere.

The cavalry was coming.

Seconds later, Aunt Limos and Uncle Ares, astride their massive mounts, galloped into the lot. They drew the reins, and both beasts reared up in protest. Limos's carnivorous hell stallion, as black as Cujo, almost twice as large, and always ready for a fight, snapped at Ares' blood bay warhorse with its serrated teeth, but Battle danced away from its slashing jaws.

"It's you." Limos, garbed in ornate Samurai armor, stared at Lilith with stunned violet eyes. In her fist, her katana trembled. "It's really you."

Lilith smiled as Thanatos shoved the succubus roughly to her knees. "Daughter," she said silkily. "Dear, dear daughter. You're going to be the first to feel the pain of my vengeance."

Lilith's eyes became red-hot pools, literally steaming as they overfilled with glowing lava that flowed from the sockets like tears. Thanatos raised his sword, the silver glint of his killing blade reflecting another set of glowing eyes.

A million sets. Oh, shit…

"It's a trap!" Logan shouted.

A bone-chilling shriek pierced the night, a split-second warning that came too late. Human-sized creatures dropped from above, eyeless, winged nightmares with gaping mouths full of rows of needlelike teeth. Logan barely had time to summon a sword and shove it down one of the demon's throats before it took his head off. He chopped at another and another and then ran one through before it ripped off Sabre's arm.

Cujo!

Instantly, a massive, inky blur shot through the square, chewing up demons like a chainsaw with fur.

"Good boy!" Logan shouted to the hound, but damn, there were so many demons. Too many. That anyone would dare attack his family filled him with rage…and memories.

He'd been through this before, overwhelmed by demons attacking friends and family. This battle felt like that. It wasn't the kind of exhilarating brawl that followed the discovery of the demons' hotbed or a vampire nest you'd been hunting.

No, this was personal. It was pain. It was hate. It wasn't exhilarating in the least.

The sounds of battle, of breaking bones, clanking weapons, and agonized screeches rent the air as Logan and Draven backed up to their friends. They were all skilled warriors, trained from the cradle, but Sabre had only a broken beer bottle as a weapon, and Mace and Blade only had knives. Granted, they were lethal as fuck with their natural Seminus gifts that could kill, but those only worked if they could come into contact with their opponents. By then, it could be too late.

Inky wisps exploded from the bodies of dead demons and swirled among the living, noticeable only by those like Logan, who could see souls. He slashed upward with his sword hand, catching a demon's wing. With is other hand, he plucked his last crystal *decipula*, a marble-sized containment vessel made for demonic spirits, and tossed it at one of the smoky wisps.

Ares' curse rang out. "They took Lilith!"

Logan looked away from the trap in time to see the succubus in the claws of one of the demons, smiling victoriously down at them before disappearing into a cloud. The remaining demons took off after them, but one drew Logan's attention. He squinted up at it, trying to discern what that big, dripping thing was in its claws—

A heart-wrenching scream shattered the night.

Limos.

His aunt Limos, her face drained of color, scrambled over the bodies of dead demons. Her sword clattered to the ground as she fell to her knees in the river of blood pumping from the shredded remains of her headless mount's throat.

Oh, no. Logan's gut plummeted to his feet. Limos claimed to despise the beast, but he'd been her companion for thousands of years. Like her, like all the Horsemen and their mounts, he was immortal.

But decapitation had a way of killing everything, including hell stallions.

Again, the memories of that day so many years ago slammed into Logan, and he spun away from the horror and grief, his chest clenching so hard he could barely breathe. Sabre and Blade watched with haunted eyes. They'd been there too. And they had been far closer to the tragedy than Logan.

Despite the river of blood flowing from multiple head and face wounds, Ares, always the warrior, strode into the center of the lot, his heavy boots squashing through the gore as he barked out a command.

"Dispatch any demon that's not dead. Save one for interrogation. And everyone, check your injuries. Healers, get healing."

They'd all taken damage, but Blade, Mace, and Sabre had badass healing abilities, and within minutes, cuts were sealed, and bones were knitted back together.

Only Bones was beyond help. Still on her knees, Limos whispered some words to her fallen mount and then, in a ragged voice, croaked, "To me."

The stallion's body dissolved into a wisp of smoke that streaked to Limos's arm, but instead of forming a living horse glyph on her skin, it wound around her wrist a few times as if saying goodbye. A moment later, the smoke turned to ash and floated to the ground.

Cujo whimpered as Logan's sorrow for Limos and fear that something like that could happen to his pup flowed through their bond.

Logan gently reached out and pulled the beast's massive forehead against his, inhaling his comforting, smoky scent. When he was a kid, huddled in the dark under his covers, the smell of brimstone and smoke had always comforted him because it meant Cujo was there, guarding him from the night and the imaginary monsters under the bed.

"It's okay, buddy," he murmured. "Nothing will happen to us. I got your back."

An affectionate rumble rose from deep in Cujo's chest, along with a mental image that translated to, *And I've got yours*, and then he phased out of there to go do the horrible things hellhounds did in their spare time. Thankfully, Cujo kept that shit to himself and out of Logan's head.

While the others finished killing the few demons that were still alive, Logan went to his aunt and kneeled with her.

"I'm sorry," he said. "Is there anything I can do? Want me to call Arik? Or Leilani?"

Limos shook her head and dabbed at her tears. "No." She stood, sniffling and putting on a brave face. "I'm fine. I'll be fine. I hated that fiend anyway."

She was lying, and everyone knew it. But clearly, she wasn't ready to deal, so they spent a few minutes gathering their weapons and wits, and then they did what one does after getting their ass kicked by an evil relative and her minions.

They got shitfaced.

Chapter Two

Shit, shit, shit.

Eva was running late, and she was *never* late. Granted, it wasn't her fault. The summons to a meeting with the Aegis bigwigs had come last minute. *And* while she was on a conference call with the head of public relations for The Aegis's Chinese division. But she doubted her bosses would care whose fault her tardiness was. The urgent message from the Elders had been clear: Don't be late.

And why was she being summoned, anyway? Was she in trouble? Had something major happened? Her heart gave a big, hopeful squeeze at another possibility.

Maybe she'd gotten that promotion. Oh, please let it be the promotion!

Her crimson Jimmy Choos thudded softly on the carpet as she jogged toward the conference room, careful not to spill a drop of her coffee. She'd paid fifteen bucks for the double-shot mocha latte, and she was going to drink it, dammit.

She rounded the last corner and slammed into her parents. The coffee sloshed over her hand and splashed onto her freshly cleaned cream silk shirt and black slacks.

"Son of a—"

"Eva. There you are." Her mother, Tessandra, thrust a tissue into her empty hand and steered her toward the conference room doors. "You're late."

"I know." Eva dabbed at the coffee stains. "But how do *you* know?"

Her father, Charles, made a sound of disapproval at her futile efforts to clean herself up with the tissue. "The Aegis's legal firm, Tennant, Tennant, and Chesterleigh, was asked to sit in on this."

Eva let out a frustrated sigh and stopped walking long enough to toss the tissue into a garbage can. "What *is* this?"

Her mother grabbed her elbow and started dragging her down the hall that wound deep beneath The Aegis's official headquarters in Washington, DC. Sprawling tapestries, depictions of ancient battles waged by the Templars, angels, and The Aegis against demons, stirred in the breeze of their hurried passage.

"The Elders have made their decision about who will be part of the first DART and Aegis exchange assignment."

Eva shrugged out of her mother's grip, readjusted the tablet and notepad in her arms, and picked up her pace, more to outrun her parents than to get to the meeting.

"I can walk on my own, Tessandra." Her parents had demanded she call them by their first names since she was ten, especially in public. "And what does any of that have to do with me?"

"We were given a heads-up that you've been chosen as spokesperson for the mission. And you know that Jennifer is retiring. Word is that you and Stefani Hughes are the two running favorites for her job. A promotion to Chief Spokesperson would be quite the coup, and this assignment could be the deciding factor."

Eva jerked to an abrupt halt as she reached for the door handle. "I've been chosen to spend two weeks at DART's international headquarters?"

Wow. The Aegis had put out a call for volunteers, but she hadn't applied. She'd certainly thought about it; her roots as an investigative journalist had her itching to get a look at the DART's inner workings. But she hadn't wanted to be away from work that long, not with that weasel Stefani hot on her heels and vying for the job Eva wanted.

On the other hand, this could be a great opportunity.

"I don't need to tell you that this is a big deal," Charles said in his stern lawyer voice. "It's the first collaboration between the world's two largest and most respected demon control agencies. The entire planet needs this to work, and they'll be watching. I know you'll make us and The Aegis proud." He opened the door and ushered her into the featureless, windowless room meant to minimize distractions.

It didn't work. Eva was always distracted by the utter *lack* of character. Would it kill them to put a soothing painting of mountains or a vibrant Parisian print on the wall?

"Ah, good. You're finally here." Willa Peters, The Aegis's Director of Public Affairs, gestured to an empty seat at the main table while Eva's parents made their way to the row of half-filled chairs lining the east wall.

"I'm not going to drag this out," Willa said in her clipped English accent as she slid a stack of papers across the table. "We have a lot to do and little time to do it in. Everyone take a packet." She put her fists on her slender hips and waited until all stapled stacks of paper had been distributed. "Now then, you're here because you were selected, out of nearly a thousand applicants, to spend fourteen days at DART headquarters in Brussels as part of a global desire for our agencies to cooperate more." She cleared her throat. "Yes, Mr. Olsen."

Eva looked across the table at Sigfred, who put down his hand and leaned back in his chair. "I didn't apply."

Willa's tolerant smile didn't reach her sharp green eyes. Sig was the son of an Aegis Elder, and he played the nepotism card whenever he could. The few who got along with him were just like him—birds of a feather and all that—and everyone else merely tolerated him because they had to.

"Several of you didn't apply. Most of the applicants were street-level fighters or cell leaders. We really wanted top people on this first cooperative mission." Willa looked out at each of them in turn, her sleek ginger hair pulled back in a bun as severe as her expression. "You are all here for a specific reason. Keeley, as Assistant Personnel Manager, you have recruitment and mental health assessment experience. You will analyze DART employees and poach them where you can."

Willa turned to the man sitting next to Keeley, Carlos Martinez, a former Navy SEAL whose sense of humor was as dark as his skin. He and Keeley had dated for a few months. It hadn't worked out, but they were still friends. He was smart, confident, and, according to Keeley, amazing in bed. But he was also surrounded by an emotional wall a mile thick, and after four months, Keeley had barely even put a dent in the barrier. Eva didn't blame Keeley for breaking up with him. He sounded like a lot of work.

"Mr. Martinez. We want you to assess their weapons, battle strategies, and training programs. This will be an exchange in every sense of the word, so you'll need to share some of your unique knowledge and weapons with them, as well."

"Excuse me." Mason Devino, the Deputy Director of The Aegis's School of Magic, sat forward in his chair. "Should we really be sharing intel and weapons with traitors and hellspawn?"

"First," Willa said, glancing pointedly at Sig, "do not call them hellspawn while you're at DART headquarters. The supernaturals say it's"—she did the air quotes thing—"derogatory. Don't call them hell bringers, hellspawn, or children of Satan. Apparently, the proper broad term for anyone non-human is *supernatural*. Maybe underworlder. If you know for sure what kind of supernatural being they are, the acceptable terms are demons, vampires, were-creatures, and shifters." She let out an annoyed huff. "So ridiculous. Hellspawn is hellspawn. Anyway, back to Mason's question. Eva?"

Eva nodded. "Ma'am?"

"You will be the team's spokesperson. How would you answer Mason's question if it came from a reporter?"

Yes. Eva loved being put on the spot and forced to think fast. It was what made her good at her job. She lived for the rush of adrenaline spiked by the split second of fear that she'd look like an idiot. Thankfully, looking like an idiot rarely happened.

"I would say that our past histories as rivals are exactly that, in the past." She looked around the room at everyone, projecting confidence and daring anyone to challenge her. "We're working toward the same goals, even if we take different paths to get there. We all want peace in the human realm."

Sigfred snorted. "That bullshit might fly with a reporter, but it doesn't fool anyone in the real world. DART was founded by traitors who turned on their colleagues. They chose the side of evil when they collaborated with the Four Horsemen of the Apocalypse and their demon brethren. Fuck DART. We shouldn't share jack shit with them."

"I hate to say it, but I agree with Sig," Carlos said.

"Ditto. DART works with hellspawn, ah, I mean, *supernaturals*," Keeley added with an eye roll. "Some have *married* them. A few of their members *are* supes, demons, even. And they stole artifacts like Heofon and Deliverance that rightfully belong to us. We can't trust them."

"We *don't* trust them," Willa said. "But that doesn't mean there can't be interagency cooperation at times. What Eva said was right. We do have common goals, even if we have very different philosophies. DART wrongly believes some demons are good, and they want a world in which demons and humans coexist. The Aegis knows the only good demon is a dead demon, and we want a demon-free world. But we both want humanity to survive Armageddon. And given that humanity is a shit show right now, world leaders feel it would benefit everyone if The Aegis and DART could put on a show of unity."

Eva didn't miss how she'd said, "a show of unity," emphasis on *show*. Looked like maybe The Aegis's top leaders weren't on board with a genuine cooperative effort. They'd paste on smiles, make token gestures of friendship, and maybe share select intel now and then, but this wouldn't be an enthusiastic embrace of long-estranged relatives.

After everything DART had done, Eva didn't blame anyone in The Aegis for their attitude. She couldn't believe they'd agreed to work together on anything. Heck, The Aegis had only recently dropped its standing *capture* order for several traitors, including DART's Director, Kynan Morgan.

Willa looked at her wrist comms device and turned her attention back to those in the room. "Any questions? You'll each meet with two Elders in five minutes. You have until then to ask me anything."

"Can we take weapons?" Carlos asked.

Willa nodded. "DART will allow each of you to carry a stang. They understand that it is our signature weapon, and that no Guardian is ever without one."

Sig swiveled in his seat like a bored child. "I'd feel a hell of a lot more comfortable with the new demon-shredder pistol."

"Absolutely not. DART doesn't even know we possess a firearm that kills demons, and we don't want them to learn of it."

Eva understood, even though she'd feel safer armed with one of the new pistols, aptly named Smiter, as well. Most demons were unaffected by bullets, but StryTech recently developed a weapon for The Aegis using advanced technology and bullets that turned demons into confetti. A gruesome demonstration using live, captured demons last month had confirmed its potential, and the memories still turned Eva's stomach.

Willa looked out over everyone. "Any other questions?"

"When do we leave?" The Aegis's head of Research and Development, Benjiro Shimosaka, tapped idly on his digital notepad. Whatever he was doing made tiny, inch-tall demon holograms dance on the face of his wrist comms device. In Eva's nine months at the DC headquarters, she'd never seen the guy sitting still. "My team is close to releasing a new update to our Guardian tats, and I don't want to delay it."

"Cool." Sig kicked his foot up on the empty chair next to him. "What's the update, Ben?"

"It's Benji or Benjiro," Benji said in a voice that made clear how tired he was of being called *Ben*. Eva got that. Her name was pronounced EH-vuh, but some people insisted on using a long *A*. "The update will improve upon our already enhanced night vision and make Harrowgates visible to anyone with astigmatism."

"That's the dumbest update I've ever heard of," Sig said, and Eva had to admit that it kind of sucked if you didn't have astigmatism. But wow, the ability to detect Harrowgates was *huge*. Right now, Guardians needed migraine and nausea-inducing glasses to view the invisible portals supernaturals used to travel vast distances and between their hell realm, Sheoul, and the human realm.

"Fuck off," Benji shot back.

"Sig, behave," Willa snapped. She didn't put up with crap from anyone. "Benji, your update will have to wait until you return. You all fly out this afternoon to DART's headquarters in Brussels."

A chorus of groans and curses echoed around the room. Personally, Eva thought this was an awesome opportunity to see how their rivals operated, but the extremely short notice would be an issue. She was still dealing with a PR disaster in China, where an Aegis Guardian had been accused of raping a woman, and in Missouri, where two Aegis Guardians had gone missing following a raid on a vampire nest.

Willa rechecked her comms. "Eva, you're first."

Eva's gut flipped over as she came to her feet. She'd always interviewed well and was comfortable in front of a camera and powerful people. Her self-confidence made men either appreciate or fear her, and women either love or hate her. But right now, her nerves were in knots. She'd met each of the twelve Elders at some point since her promotion and transfer from the LA Aegis division to the DC Headquarters nine months ago, but she'd never had a formal meeting with them.

Willa escorted her down the narrow corridors to a room on the south side of the building.

"Did you apply to go on this assignment?" Eva asked, mostly to break the awkward silence.

"Absolutely not." Willa waved at someone in the accounting office as they passed. "I don't trust myself to be around those people for that long. I'd probably end up killing someone and triggering an international incident." She stopped at the door to the Elder Suite and smiled. "But I would love to see behind the DART curtain. I can't imagine what it's like to work with demons. I'll bet they have some spectacular weaponry."

Eva would put money on that. Sure, The Aegis had an impressive arsenal of weapons, some demon-made, some of Heavenly origin, and a handful of invaluable high-tech pieces like the Smiter from the Sydney-based company run by a demon who apparently hated other demons. But The Aegis had fewer arms than they once had because the traitorous defectors who founded DART had stolen weapons, artifacts, and rare tomes when they left. Plus, DART employed supernatural beings, and they, themselves, were weapons.

"Are you ready?" Willa asked.

Sure. Why not? This was an opportunity to shine. Eva braced herself with a brisk breath and straightened her shoulders. "I am."

Smiling, Willa opened the door. "Congratulations. And good luck."

Eva entered the brightly lit third-floor corner office for only the second time since she'd started work with The Aegis. Two entire walls were comprised of massive floor-to-ceiling windows, and shelves of books and demonic artifacts lined the other two. In the center, seated at a six-person table, were two Elders Eva had briefed just yesterday about the Chinese rape case.

"Hi, Eva." Maja Weso gestured to one of the chairs across from her. "Please, have a seat."

The other Elder, a sixty-something, round-faced Russian, eyed Eva coolly as she sat. "Thank you for coming."

As if she'd had a choice. "Thank you for naming me for this project."

"Obviously, this is a very important and public undertaking," he said. "We are placing a good deal of faith in you."

In other words, don't fuck up.

"I understand."

Dmitri looked skeptical, but Maja smiled warmly. Maja, at thirty-two, was four years older than Eva, two inches shorter, and drop-dead gorgeous. She'd been a warrior for The Aegis for a few years but had chewed through the ranks to become one of the youngest Elders in history. Most acknowledged that it was due to her intelligence, historical knowledge, and extraordinary successes at rooting out demon nests. Others said it had been thanks to her extraordinary sexual favors.

What bullshit. Sig's dad, Lukas, had shot to the top even more quickly than Maja had, but no one ever suggested *he* hadn't earned his place on his own merits. Even though, as far as Eva could tell, he'd lucked into it. Or maybe bought into it. He certainly hadn't earned it. He'd never fought even a single demon. As the only son of the wealthiest demon antiquities trader in the world, he'd joined as a consultant. Arrogant, rude, and entitled, he drove everyone as nuts as Sig did.

Maja braced her elbows on the desk. "We'll make this quick. I assume Willa told you about the flight this afternoon." At Eva's nod, the other woman continued. "You'll need to brief Stefani on your current business, as she'll be taking over. Your entire focus needs to be on this operation, and we need you to keep your fighting skills under wraps."

The Stefani part made sense, even if Eva didn't like it. But the rest was entirely unexpected. "What do you mean? Why would we not go into this from a position of strength?"

Dmitri answered. "We need them to underestimate all of you. You're going to be the helpless ditz."

Eva blinked, unsure she'd heard that correctly. "A…what now?"

Maja shot her colleague an annoyed glance but didn't dispute his words. "Their eyes are going to be on Sig, Carlos, Mason, and Benji. So, they won't see petite Keeley or media darling Eva as threats."

She went taut in her seat, her spine pressing into the hard wood behind her. "Why? Because we're women?"

"No," Maja said irritably, but Eva got the feeling the other woman was aiming her sharp tone at Dmitri. "It's because Keeley limps and works at a desk. They have no idea she was one of our fiercest demon slayers before the accident. And you? Last year, when you tripped on stage during that awards ceremony, it went viral. I know it sucks, but we need you to foster that klutzy image. We realize you're smart and good with a stang, but we don't want DART to know that."

This was bullshit. Unfortunately, the part about being good with the stang was crap too. Eva really wasn't that proficient with the Aegis's proprietary double-bladed, S-shaped weapon. And frankly, she wasn't that great of a fighter. She trained weekly and had for years, and thanks to a gymnastics background, she did have one signature move that always put her opponents on their backs. But she really didn't enjoy being hit, thrown down, or kicked. And a black eye or split lip in her profession meant someone else got to do her job while she healed, and that someone was Stefani.

No way in hell would Eva ever give that cow a leg up. Hell, nine months ago, Eva had broken her ankle minutes before delivering a televised Q&A following an Aegis sweep of the largest vampire nest ever, and she'd refused to let Stefani take her place. She'd done the half-hour-long interview and then went straight to the hospital.

"I seriously don't feel like I need to play dumb damsel here."

Maja nodded. "I agree. You don't have to. You're smart enough to play it your way and not show your hand. You all are." She lowered her voice to a conspiratorial grumble. "Except maybe Sig."

Dmitri chuckled, but a heartbeat later, he was all resting jerkface again. "Fine. But, Eva, we're counting on you. The others don't always play nice, and we need you to keep things on track. Sig's an arrogant hothead, Keeley has no filter, Carlos can be intense, and both Benji and Mason think they're smarter than everyone in the room. You must be the voice of reason."

Great. What should have been a career opportunity had just turned into a nanny position.

Maja reached for the bottle of water on the table next to her. "I will be your sole point of contact. You won't report to Jennifer while you're in Brussels."

Eva didn't like the sound of that. The fact that she'd essentially be cut off from her job was only the beginning of her concerns.

"How am I supposed to handle media blitzes and Aegis news if I'm not in contact with my office?"

"Stefani will manage all of that," Maja said. "You are to concentrate solely on this assignment. When and if you speak to the media about this joint venture, it will be arranged through the Elders, not the Media Affairs office."

Dmitri cleared his throat. "This doesn't reflect a lack of faith in our people. It's just that this venture with DART is delicate and of utmost importance. We will be overseeing it directly."

Wow. The Elders seemed to keep their fingers out of most things, especially as a group. Each was already high-ranking in their respective departments, so they managed the biggest challenges. But she'd never heard of them taking over all aspects of an operation. Definitely not as a united force.

"Now," Maja said, "if there are no questions, you'd best get ready for the trip."

Dmitri stood, clearly done with the meeting and not waiting for any of her questions. "Thank you for your service. This is a major undertaking, and we know you'll help make it a success."

"Of course." Eva pushed to her feet and shook their proffered hands.

Excitement coursed through her at the realization that she'd be participating in a historical event, an exchange of personnel, ideas, and knowledge.

And yet, as she exited the room, the gravity of the situation cast a pall over her enthusiasm. Because one wrong move could not only destroy her career…it could also destroy the hopes of humanity winning the war against demons.

And the world was watching.

Chapter Three

The Demonic Activity Response Team's headquarters, a nondescript, unremarkable building near Brussels' historic center, always smelled like coffee. This morning, there wasn't enough caffeinated brew in the world to cure Logan's hangover.

Not the alcohol one—his immortal metabolism prevented the worst effects of too much liquor. The hangover he was dealing with had *Lilith* written all over it.

His sleep had been so laden with bad dreams that he wondered if the succubus had hired a nightmare fiend to torture him. She'd made it clear that she was out for revenge, and anyone the Four Horsemen loved was a target.

Holy hell, he'd dodged a bullet. If his father hadn't shown up…he shuddered. Had to remind himself that nothing sexual had happened.

But it could have.

Yeah, and no one, especially not Mace, would let him forget it.

As Logan made his way toward the first-floor cafeteria for his second triple-shot cappuccino, Director Morgan called his name.

Logan swung around to Kynan as the tall, dark-haired former soldier caught up with him. "Hey, boss."

"Hey." Ky's deep, gravelly voice, the result of damage from a demon battle decades ago, rolled like thunder between them. "I heard you had a hell of a night."

Heat flamed in Logan's cheeks. Of course, Kynan had heard. Mace had probably put *Logan Got Felt Up By His Granny* all over social media by now. But Kynan wasn't the type to rub salt into wounds, so while he probably knew about Lilith's attempt to seduce Logan, he was likely talking about the shit that went down afterward.

"It was pretty bad," Logan said. "We got ambushed, and I only had one soul trap on me, so most of the spirits got away. I dropped the one I got into the vault." He scrubbed his hand over his face, as if he could scour away everything that happened last night. "And poor Limos. She had that hell stallion for a long time."

Kynan's expression was grim as he gestured for Logan to walk with him to the cafeteria. "How's she doing?"

"Better than I'd be doing if I lost Cujo." Logan couldn't imagine being without the hellhound companion he'd been bonded to since they were both newborns. The beast was part of him, a comforting tingle in the back of his mind.

"Let me know if you need our resources to hunt Lilith," Kynan said. "I've already talked to Ares, and you know DART's here for you, no matter what."

"I know."

Kynan clapped him on the shoulder in a fond, fatherly gesture. "Have you heard from Roman?"

"Nothing new." Scott Roman had a hell of a demonic case on his hands at DART's Pacific Northwest headquarters in Seattle. His office believed that a Soulshredder had formed a rare partnership with a Neethul to terrorize a religious community near Pendleton, Oregon, and they'd just lost a DART agent to the demon's deadly claws and teeth. "They haven't even seen the Neethul, and every time they get close to the Soulshredder, it poofs away." Soulshredders, rated as Tier-Five demons on the Ufelskala scale of evil, making them the worst of the worst, were also some of the most difficult demons to kill. Their ability to phase instantly between Sheoul and the human realm made it easy for them to escape or disappear and then reappear suddenly behind their victims. Long, razor-sharp claws and fangs were the least of their weapons.

And Kynan, being married to a human who was half-Soulshredder, knew that firsthand.

"Tayla's going to send in Mace, Blade, and Scotty, but if they need more muscle, think you and Cujo could give them a hand?"

"No problem." Logan didn't mind temporary assignments to other departments. Good thing too, because he got tapped for many cases that had nothing to do with his Spirit Management division. He liked to think it was because of his fighting skills and ability to see demonic spirits, but really, his hellhound was the weapon everyone wanted. "Give me half an hour to arm up and summon Cujo."

Kynan acknowledged one of the passing magi-techs with a wave, making the pendant around his scarred neck bounce. The gleaming round crystal gave Ky special protection, and it would never *not* leave Logan in awe. A literal piece of Heaven. So damn cool.

"Not yet," Ky said. "I need you here this morning."

"What's up?"

"The personnel exchange with The Aegis started today." He gestured down the hall to the smallest of three briefing rooms, a twenty-four-seater auditorium-style setup. "They sent half a dozen jet-lagged Guardians, all waiting to hear Aaron brief them on DART's history and its origins in The Aegis."

Sensing a trap, Logan shifted uncomfortably. "Uh-huh…"

"Aaron called in sick. I need you to go in there and keep them busy until Shanea gets here to take them on as their handler today."

Logan suppressed a groan. The last thing he wanted to do was babysit a bunch of Aegis assholes. "Can't Mace do it? He just posted a pic of himself kicking his feet up in the break room, looking all bored and shit—"

"Mace?" Kynan stared. "*Mace?* Alone with a bunch of Aegi? Seriously?"

Okay, yeah, Logan hadn't thought that one through. Mace was the guy you wanted at your back during a fight with, say, a Soulshredder. Mace was the guy who got you out of sticky situations. But Mace was probably the one who got you *into* the mess in the first place, as evidenced by the groping granny fiasco. He was definitely not the guy you wanted to represent your professional agency to a bunch of adversaries.

"You do know that The Aegis tried to kill me as a baby, right?"

"They've tried to kill almost everyone I know. Me included," Ky pointed out. "Get another excuse. Look at it as your chance to get back at them."

Logan perked up. "I get to kill them?"

"No, but you'll get to make their lives miserable for a little while. Take the win, kid."

Kid. It was funny to hear Kynan call him that, given that Ky looked the same age as Logan, even though he was in his sixties.

Being immortal was awesome.

"Okay, okay." Logan glanced at his watch. It was nine-eighteen. "I'm guessing the Aegi have been waiting almost twenty minutes, and you need me in there immediately."

"Good guess." Kynan didn't wait for Logan to say yes because, of course, he would. "Thanks. Shanea will be there to take them off your hands in half an hour or so." Ky clapped him on the shoulder again. "And keep me posted on the Seattle situation. I have the White House breathing down my neck. A demon attacking Christians is not helping our argument that not all demons are the same. They're talking about bringing in The Aegis."

"What, they think we'll go soft on demons torturing and killing humans? Jackasses. I'll get out there as soon as I'm done with the other jackasses."

"Take it easy on those jackasses," Ky warned. "We're trying to build bridges, not burn them." Kynan's denim-blue eyes darkened with annoyance. "I think trying to build bridges with The Aegis is pointless, but the people who fund us want to see cooperation between our agencies."

"I'll behave," Logan muttered. "But it's bullshit. We shouldn't have to suck up to them. We're giving way more to this trial alliance than they are."

"Agreed." Kynan's wrist comms device beeped, and he cast it a quick glance before giving Logan a see-ya nod. "Thanks again."

He took off in the direction of his office, speaking to whoever was on the other end of the comms. The guy never stopped working. Even at the big family get-togethers, Kynan was rarely able to go more than an hour without having to address some sort of crisis.

And speaking of crises, Logan was now stuck keeping an eye on members of a rival agency that operated under the belief that the only good supernatural was a dead supernatural. And given that DART employed supes, they tended to clash.

No doubt one of the first questions the Aegis people would ask would be if he was human. He'd say yes, as usual, and it wasn't technically a lie. His mother was human. That his father was half-angel, half-demon, and one of the Four Horsemen of the Apocalypse didn't matter. Today, he would identify as *human* instead of *other*.

He had to wonder what they'd do if he told them the truth, though.

Whatever. He had more to worry about than the reactions of a bunch of sanctimonious dickheads. Like the new picture Mace had just posted on SuperSocial of Logan's face pasted onto a flabby naked grandpa doing unspeakable things with a bunch of flabby naked grandmas.

He would never be able to unsee that.

"Not funny, Mace," he muttered as he flicked the pic off the screen of his comms unit and sent Mace a message promising an ass-kicking.

Yup, today was turning out to be one giant hangover.

Eva wasn't sure what she'd expected the inside of DART's main office building to look like, but a modern, brightly lit headquarters with a jungle-themed fountain in the lobby wasn't it. Although the demon and angel statues eyeing each other with suspicion in the center of the spray weren't all that unexpected.

Keeley had thrown a coin into the crystal pool out of some sort of superstition as they walked toward the auditorium where they now sat, waiting impatiently for someone to show up and give them the scheduled orientation.

"Of course, they're late," Carlos growled. "Go figure that a bunch of Aegis traitors can't be trusted to handle shit efficiently."

"Idiots," Sig said, kicking the stage in front of him, leaving a dusty boot print.

Eva wasn't so sure they were idiots, but this was definitely not a professional start to the cooperative mission.

The door near the back of the stage whispered open, and everyone went silent as a figure emerged from the shadows.

"Holy shit." Keeley sounded a little breathless as she jabbed Eva in the ribs. "No way that guy is a demon. Angel for sure."

Keeley wasn't serious…probably…but Eva understood where she'd gotten the angel thing. The man who'd just entered the chamber was stunning. *Really* stunning. His wavy blond hair gleamed like a halo under the harsh stage lights, and ropy, thick muscles in his forearms flexed under tan skin as he strode across the stage. The strike of his combat boots echoed through the chamber, making her heart pound with every step. His black DART T-shirt was tucked into midnight tactical pants that cut a shadowy figure against the dark curtain behind him.

He gave them all a bored glance as he walked toward the mic. Seriously, he was going to use the mic to talk to a whopping six people?

She felt a little foolish when he strolled past the mic and plopped down on the edge of the stage, his long legs dangling over the side.

"My name is Logan," he said in a deep, rumbling voice that made heat curl in her belly. "Apparently, I drew the short stick, and now I have to give you the DART 101 lecture. You probably don't want to be here any more than I do, so here are the basics. DART stands for Demonic Activity Response Team. We formed thirty-five years ago when we broke off from The Aegis because, I dunno, let's go with *philosophical differences*. Now, we're doing this prisoner exchange thing, where people from DART hang out at Aegis headquarters, and you guys hang out here—"

"Excuse me." Sig, being rude as ever, raised his hand as he interrupted. "Are you human?"

Logan's hazel eyes turned frosty as he narrowed them on Sig. "Yes." He raked the rest of the room with his gaze, and Eva shivered when he paused for a split second on her. "Anyone else got an irrelevant, offensive, or asinine question?"

Eva hid a smile behind her hand. The question wasn't irrelevant, but Sig *was* an arrogant ass, and she loved seeing him put in his place. Hell, he should be feeling frostbitten after that exchange.

It was also good to know that Logan was human. Keeley waggled her brow, clearly as pleased with the information as Eva, but likely for different reasons. No doubt Keeley was mentally undressing him. Eva was just glad she wasn't sitting in a room with a demon.

Although she'd bet he was beautiful without clothes…

The auditorium door opened again, and an ebony-haired man in faded jeans and a partially tucked black button-down strode inside, his white sneakers not making a sound as he crossed the stage.

Not a single squeak or thud.

Logan gestured to the newcomer. "This is Draven. He's on the team that oversees security for the building and personnel."

Draven looked over at Eva and her colleagues and gave a lazy nod of greeting. A *deceptively* lazy nod. His body was loose, his gait an easy swagger, but his cold, black eyes held a sharp, dangerous light. He'd only looked at them for a second, but she had no doubt he'd committed her and her teammates to memory, right down to the size of the topaz on her right pinky.

Demon. I'll bet he's a demon.

The thought made her mouth go as dry as the inside of her tote bag. She adjusted it in her lap, taking comfort in the weight of the weapon inside it. Everyone else here could handle a stang better than she could, but that didn't mean she couldn't—or wouldn't—use it if needed.

She glanced at her colleagues, glad to see they'd all shifted their hands nearer to their stangs, and that she wasn't the only one who had grown uneasy at the newcomer's presence. There was nothing overtly demonic about him…it wasn't as if he had horns on his head or hooves for feet. In fact, if she'd seen him in a crowd, she'd have been drawn to his drop-dead good looks. But here, in a place that proudly employed werewolves, witches, and even demons, her instincts were in overdrive.

"Shanea's right behind me," he said to Logan. "I just wanted to ask these guys a question."

Logan gestured at them. "Go for it."

Draven swung around, his demeanor affable, a smile turning up the corners of his mouth. But those eyes…she shivered. "Is it true that The Aegis doesn't have a single Guardian who isn't human?"

Everyone turned to Eva. It was for precisely this reason that she'd been sent on this mission. Placing her tote on the floor, she stood and addressed Draven's question. "The Aegis embraced a human-only policy after the Richmond massacre twenty-five years ago."

He hooked his thumbs in his pockets and appeared to consider that. "So, *one* werewolf employee committed workplace violence—while in human form, mind you—and you assume no super can be trusted?"

"There were other incidents," she said, using her steady, calm tone as a check against his antagonism. "That was the final straw. We've found that our members are far more productive and less distracted when they don't have to wonder if there's a demon in their midst." She smiled, doing her best to appear friendly and non-confrontational. This was her wheelhouse, her comfort zone, and she loved controlling the direction and tenor of the conversation. "No offense, of course."

The black in Draven's eyes expanded into inky pools of warning, the whites receding as if in fear. Shit. She'd stepped into a confrontation, the exact thing she'd been sent to avoid.

"Why would I be offended?"

She continued to smile politely, but the suspicion that this guy was a demon made her lips quiver.

"DART is known for employing demons." She spoke in a low,

soothing tone, attempting to steer herself back into her zone of confidence. "You might be a demon. If so, I meant no offense."

"Really."

"Be nice," Logan murmured, but Draven stepped closer.

"So, you won't take offense if I say that I think The Aegis would be more productive and less distracted if they didn't have any females in their midst?"

She blinked. *Had…had he really just said that?* Keeley's soft gasp pretty much answered the question.

"It's hardly the same thing—"

Logan leaped to his feet in a graceful surge. "Hey, let's keep the interagency peace and avoid debating shit our governments can't even figure out."

Pretty much every country in the world was having trouble deciding how to handle the underworlders in their midst. Just last month, Bulgaria passed a law allowing supernatural beings to live there as residents, but only if they made themselves obvious, which meant a reverse pentagram tattooed on the backs of their hands. Any resident underworlder found without a mark was subject to severe penalties ranging from a crippling fine and jail time to execution. Other countries had made it a crime for demons to not only live there but to even visit. Most made slightly more allowances for were-creatures and vampires, and some—*very* few—tolerated everyone as long as they behaved.

It was a volatile topic everywhere.

"Draven was just trying—and failing—to make a point," Logan continued, shooting his buddy a scorching look.

"By being a misogynistic ass?" Keeley snapped.

"See?" Draven gestured at Keeley. "I didn't fail to make my point."

"Okay." Eva cleared her throat, allowing everyone a moment to take a calming breath. "We all knew coming into this that our agencies have their differences. Let's follow Logan's advice and not debate subjects best left to global leaders."

Logan shot her a grateful nod and steered Draven toward the door. "Glad you stopped by. Let's not do this again."

Draven laughed, and Eva got the feeling the two were good friends. "It's a mystery why Kynan never asks me to do social stuff."

"Yeah," Logan muttered, "total mystery."

Just as Draven reached the door, it swung open. A curvy, attractive woman stepped inside, her yellow-and-turquoise sleeveless dress draped over ample curves and glowing dark skin. The brief sultry look she gave

Draven was tellingly intimate.

"Am I interrupting?"

"Shanea." Logan didn't hide his relief at seeing her. "You're definitely not interrupting, and your timing is perfect." He gestured to the group. "They're all yours."

"Actually…" Shanea hesitated, her tone apologetic. "I've got a situation I need to handle. Shouldn't take long. Would you mind walking the group to the training center? I'll meet you there."

Logan looked like he'd rather be roasted over hot coals, but he nodded. "You owe me."

She smiled and mouthed, *thank you*, before hooking Draven's pinky with hers and taking him with her. Interesting. Did Shanea know Draven was probably a demon? But maybe Shanea was too.

Eva rubbed her bare arms, even though she wasn't cold. She was just…off-balance. She hadn't anticipated the anxiety of being so out of her element in a place where she was constantly wondering whether or not each individual she met was a demon.

"Come on." Logan gestured to Eva and her colleagues. "You heard her." He eyed them all in turn, his gaze measuring, then amused, and then, finally, insultingly dismissive. "We'll see just how good you guys are."

Carlos, Keeley, and Sig grinned. Of course, they'd be thrilled about showing off their fighting skills. Benji and Mason seemed less excited to spar with DART agents, but she doubted they felt like she did. Like she was a gangly kid back in grade school, counting down the minutes until gym class and praying she wouldn't get chosen last for any of the teams.

As they filed out the door, Keeley nudged Eva in the ribs. "This is gonna be fun."

Eva plucked a packet of papers out of her tote. "It's not on the schedule."

"So?"

"We don't have any gym clothes."

"No, but we're all wearing Aegis-altered or designed clothing meant for fighting. It'll be fine."

No, it wouldn't. She didn't care that her skirt sported hidden shorts and was split to allow for extreme movement or that her Emmy Londons had been altered to hide a blade, a vial of holy water, and an ancient symbol of protection from spirits. She was going to look like a fool.

Maybe she could get out of it. Logan seemed reasonable.

He turned to look back at them, and she revised that thought. He looked like a predator deciding which prey to separate from the herd.

Keeley leaned close and whispered, "Do you think he's really human?"

"He said he is."

"Demons aren't known for telling the truth, Eva. And he could be a werewolf. They identify as human. So do vampires."

"Does it really matter? He's going to destroy us on the mat."

"Would you rather be destroyed by a demon or a human?"

Again, it didn't really matter. Either way, she'd look like an idiot.

"Neither. Excuse me." She squared her shoulders, put on her brave face, and picked up her pace.

It was her turn to be the predator.

Chapter Four

"Excuse me."

Logan didn't slow down, just kept walking through the long corridor as one of the Aegi females jogged to catch up. The slight click her shoes made on the floor said she was wearing heels. He wondered if she could fight in them. Scratch that. He wondered how *well* she could fight in them. She was an Aegi, which meant the shoes themselves were weapons.

"Excuse me, Mr…Logan?" The female human sidled up next to him. It was the busty one with the wavy dark hair and shrewd coffee eyes. Eva Tennant. He'd always thought she'd be taller in person than she was on camera, and sure enough, she was probably five-ten without the two-inch heels. He liked tall women. Made things easier, whether he was fighting them or fucking them.

"Just Logan."

"Of course." She offered a slender hand adorned by two silver diamond rings, a topaz pinky ring, and three silver and gold bracelets, one of which sported anti-evil and protection charms. "I'm Eva Tennant."

"Yep." He had no idea who any of the other Guardians were, but he'd seen Eva in the news. As Deputy Spokesperson for The Aegis, she got quoted a lot, and clips of her press conferences were often featured in various media outlets.

But aside from that, he knew little about her except that she appeared to be poised, well-spoken, and smart. Her designer jewelry and clothes, from the knee-length black skirt that made artwork out of her ass, to her sassy, multicolor pumps, said she had money and taste. Even her wrist comms was the latest model, the silver band encrusted with what he assumed were diamonds. No doubt if the implant behind her ear connecting her to the comms could be made from gems, it would be super-blinged out too. But was her wealth from old family money like Logan's? Or had she made it herself as she'd risen in the journalistic and political ranks?

His gut said both.

"We're not supposed to shake hands, remember?" He gestured to the packet of papers in her other hand. "It was in that ridiculous list of demands from The Aegis."

"Ah, yes." Irritation flashed in her eyes as she held up the packet. "It's right here, and I completely spaced it." She flipped a page and thrust it in front of him. "I just wanted to address today's itinerary."

"Today's itinerary for me is to hunt demons and demonic spirits. Might even squeeze in an exorcism. I don't know what's in your plan for the day. I'm just a temp, unlucky enough to be in the wrong place at the wrong time. Take it up with Shanea."

She let out a frustrated huff and glanced back at her colleagues, who were too busy gawking at the demon artifacts lining the walls to pay them any attention. With no support to be found, she turned back to Logan.

Man, she was gorgeous. Intense and elegant like a hawk, with a slight tilt to her almond-shaped eyes and a delicate aquiline curve along the bridge of her nose. Made him want to boop it.

He doubted she'd appreciate that.

"It's just that sparring isn't on the schedule." She jabbed the paper with her red-lacquered finger. "See? Right here, it says we'd have orientation and a tour of the facility, but sparring and tactical weapons demonstrations isn't until tomorrow—"

"What's the matter?" He spent a pointedly long time sizing her up, wondering how fast those slender legs could sweep an enemy off their feet, and how quickly those delicate fingers could flip a blade into an opponent's eye. Then he smiled at how easy it would be to put her on the mat, no matter how good she was. The only one of the lot who looked like he could give Logan a run for his money was the big guy who practically screamed special forces. Although the other female looked like a scrapper who could get in some lucky strikes. He had a feeling her scars and limp could tell a lot of tales. "Afraid to take me on?"

He got a kick out of the way her mouth worked soundlessly for a second before she found her voice. "*Words* are my weapons, Mr., ah, Logan."

"The pen is mightier than the sword, eh?" He opened the door to the training facility. "Personally, I think actions speak louder than words."

Her smile was downright condescending. "I'm sure you do."

Laughing, he ushered her and the other Aegi inside.

The special forces guy who nearly matched Logan's six-four height and looked like he spent most of his time in the gym, gaped through the armory door at the rows of weapons inside. "Holy...wow."

"Carlos is our Chief Weapons Master," Eva explained, not that Logan gave a crap.

"I can't believe this," Carlos breathed. He was practically drooling. "Is that a Djevith bone breaker? How many do you have? Can I see it?"

Logan didn't see any reason to refuse. All the weapons here were for training purposes only, their edges dulled, and their magical properties, if any, either disabled or diminished.

"Have at it. All of you. When you're done, meet me on the mat. If you have questions about any of the weapons, I'll show you how they work."

Carlos disappeared inside, followed by everyone except Eva. She walked with Logan to the other side of the room while the others swarmed the armory like a succubus in a sex toy store.

Which made him picture Lilith in a sex toy store.

Which caused some mental trauma.

Son of a bitch. He would never be able to hear the word *succubus* again without thinking of that psychopath and what she'd done to his family. What she wanted to do to him.

Needing a distraction, he swung around to Eva. EH-vuh. He liked the softness in the pronunciation, the way it was spoken on a breath, crossing the lips like a caress.

"You aren't interested in the weapons?"

She dropped her tote next to the wall. "Not especially."

He gestured to her bright blue bag. "Got a stang in there?"

Surprise flickered in her eyes, quickly snuffed. "What makes you say that?"

"It says in that stack of papers that you were all allowed to bring one. Did you?"

"I did."

"So, get it out. Let's see what you can do with it."

"I'm not exactly dressed for combat, Logan. That's what I was trying to tell you."

"Bullshit." He emptied his pockets of his various knives and throwing stars and tossed them to the corner of the mat. "Every Aegi I've ever known could slaughter an Oni while wearing an evening gown or in the nude. You require every member to be battle-trained to their highest ability, and you mandate refresher courses to maintain proficiency. The Aegis wants its people to be able to handle themselves in any situation, same as DART. The Aegis isn't a job. It's a lifestyle." He'd wanted to say that it was a cult, but maybe he shouldn't antagonize them too much on the very first day. "Are exceptions made for certain jobs like yours? Or are you not considered a Guardian?"

Her narrow nose came up so she could stare down it at him. "Every Aegi is considered a Guardian. I have the tattoo, and I carry a stang like everyone else. And believe it or not, I can hold my own with a variety of weapons."

He couldn't decide if he believed her or not. Time to find out.

Without warning, he spun, kicked, and took her to the mat with a sweep to the back of her legs.

"Disappointing," he said as he looked down at her. "I expected better of an Aegi. If I had been an enemy, you'd be dead."

Fire sparked in her cool espresso gaze. Glaring, she kicked off her heels and shoved to her feet in an angry surge. "You cheated," she snapped. "I wasn't expecting that."

"Most people don't expect demons to pop out of manholes, but it happens."

"Are you saying I should be on guard here?" She made a wide, encompassing gesture around the room. "In DART headquarters, which should be the safest place on the planet outside of an Aegis building?"

"I'm saying you should always expect—"

And then *he* was on his back, and that magnificent woman who smelled like flowers floating on the ocean was straddling his chest, the silver end of the stang at his throat.

It was hot. As. Fuck.

Damn, he might have just found his soulmate.

Eva didn't usually allow herself to feel smug. But as she squeezed her thighs into Logan's ribs and looked down into his surprised eyes, she reveled in the smugness.

Reveled.

He'd needed to be taken down a peg. By her estimation, she'd taken him down several.

"When did you get your stang from your tote bag?"

She basked in more self-satisfaction. She'd slipped the weapon from the bag before putting it down, and while he disarmed, she'd slid the blade into the sheath sewn into the fabric at the hip of her skirt.

"Does it matter?"

"I guess not," he said, his gaze raking her body, assessing it, making her sweat. That wasn't the look of someone who'd just gotten their ass handed to them. That was the look of a man with a woman straddling him...on a mattress. In a bedroom.

Not on a mat. In a gymnasium.

"Now," he continued, his voice like warm caramel, "what is your next move?"

She deftly twirled the stang between her fingers and pressed the gold blade deeper into his skin, careful not to break it. Would be a shame to mar that perfectly tan canvas made for the kiss of a woman's lips.

"If you were a demon, I'd slit your throat."

"Would you?" Suddenly, his hand clamped around her wrist and wrenched the blade away from his neck. Pain shot up her arm as he flipped her and sent the stang clattering across the mat. In a heartbeat, she was flat on her back, and he was holding her down with the strength of his powerful legs and his considerable weight.

"Oh, come on," she snapped up at him, humiliated by his effortless takedown. "If you were an enemy, you'd be dead, and you wouldn't have had the chance to pin me like this."

His face was inches from hers, heat rolling off him in waves that scorched her. If she lifted her head just a little, their lips would touch. She had a feeling he was a *great* kisser.

And she really, really shouldn't be having thoughts like this.

"Maybe." He rolled off her and sat on the mat, one arm casually laid across his bent knee. He wasn't even breathing hard. Meanwhile, she was panting like she'd run a marathon. "But I'll admit, that move was impressive."

Of course, it was. She had a background in gymnastics and was freakishly flexible. Sitting up, she tugged her clothing back into place. "Thank y—"

"But it's flawed."

She blinked. "Excuse me?"

"If you fail to kill your target, you can't use that move again."

"Of course, I can use it again." Heat seared her cheeks at the realization that Keeley and Benji had apparently grown bored of the weapons and were watching from the edge of the mat. Hopefully, they'd seen her epic takedown and not just the humiliating aftermath.

Logan popped to his feet. "No, you can't. I'll show you."

"It's okay, really. This can wait until the sparring class tomorrow when I'm in sweats and a T-shirt."

"I won't be your instructor tomorrow, and what you're wearing is fine. Like I said, you need to be ready to fight in an evening gown." He waggled his brow. "Or naked."

He was way too charming for his own good. "Yeah, well, you're wearing tactical pants and a T-shirt, and you still got taken to the mat by a girl in heels."

"Touché." He offered his hand to her. She could have popped to her feet just as easily as he had and thrown in a backflip for good measure, but she couldn't reveal all her secrets all at once. The Elders would be apoplectic enough at what she'd already revealed.

Dumb klutz? I don't think so.

But it couldn't hurt to be polite. Reluctantly, she took his hand and let him tug her to her feet.

"Let's go again," he said. "We know what to expect from each other. Show me what you got."

"Yeah, do it," Sig called out as he joined the others. "I've never seen her spar with anyone except reporters."

God, she couldn't stand that guy. "Perhaps," she replied calmly and through gritted teeth, "you'd prefer to take on Logan?"

Sig's blue eyes flared slightly, but the shit-eating grin came back a heartbeat later, probably after his weasel brain came up with a way out of having to go up against a guy who was bigger and in better shape than all of them.

"I'm not the one he wants on the mat."

"Come on, Eva." Carlos said as he tested the edge of a wicked-looking blade he'd taken off a rack. "You haven't been to one of my classes in weeks. Let's see how you're doing."

She would kill him later. Maybe with that demon blade he was fondling.

There was no way out of this without looking like a fool, so she gave a resigned shrug and turned back to Logan. "Fine. But faces are off-limits." She paused. "And breasts." Getting boob-punched was not fun.

Logan's smirk was shockingly sexy. "Sure thing."

She sank into a defensive stance, fists up and ready for whatever he did.

Except it turned out she wasn't ready for the way he strolled in a circle around her, his gait loose, shoulders relaxed, hands at his sides. He was either very sure of himself, or he doubted her skill.

Probably both.

She was going to look like an idiot, wasn't she?

No. Now wasn't the time for the doubt demons. The figurative kind, not the evil, in-the-flesh devils. Still, she'd banish them with a mental mantra she'd relied on since she was six years old, and a demon had haunted her dreams. She took comfort in words she'd been taught to repel it before she got a ward tattooed around her navel in a more permanent solution.

I exorcise you, spiritus diabolica!

Doubt demons banished for the moment, she returned Logan's cocky smile. "If you're waiting for me to throw the first punch, you'll be waiting a long time. I'm not going to give you what you're expecting—"

She didn't even see him move. One moment, she was standing there, fists up, feet in a right-foot-forward combat stance. The next, her spine was getting intimate with the mat, and she was gasping for air. Again.

"Not. Fair," she croaked.

Laughing, Logan offered her his hand once more. This time, she refused it. If he was going to play dirty, she could too.

Taking a deep breath, she bounced to her feet, and in a single, fluid motion, cartwheeled, catching Logan in the jaw with her foot. Oops. She'd meant to hit his shoulder, but she didn't feel too bad, not when he recovered with a sweep of his arm that knocked her backward several feet. He lunged, and she spun, but he avoided her kick this time. In a short, ruthless jab upward, he caught her shin as she rotated, and she landed awkwardly.

Her knee screamed in pain, but it only made her more determined. She didn't enjoy hand-to-hand combat, but once she was in it, she was in it to win, dammit. Her competitive streak ran deep, encouraged by her parents to the point of ruthlessness, especially when it came to her job. They'd raised her to be a shark in an ocean full of other sharks— and worse.

Her colleagues cheered for her, boosting her confidence. As Logan came at her again, she dodged and jabbed at his midsection. He wheeled away, diluting her blow into just a whisper of her knuckles against his rib cage.

His sexy little grin said he was toying with her. On some level, she'd known that, but he didn't need to make it so obvious. It was time to employ her super move.

Casually, she moved closer to her stang, keeping her back to the wall and her front to Logan, who tracked her like a predator, his gaze locked on hers, his every step silent and lithe. He reminded her of a wolf, chin down, eyes up, a low growl coming from deep inside his chest. Or maybe she was just imagining the growl because it seemed like something natural. Like, *of course* this guy would growl. It would be deep and resonant as he prowled up his partner's body…

Shit. She stepped back and shook her head. Looked like doubt demons were the least of her worries with this guy. The lust demons were way worse.

He moved in like a lightning strike, one arm hooking her so she slammed into him, her spine hitting the hard wall of his chest. His fingers encircled one wrist and held it like a steel band at her side. She smiled. Carlos winked at her. He'd taught her how to get out of this hold.

As hard as she could, she jammed her elbow backward, and her head upward. Jarring pain vibrated through her as her skull cracked into Logan's chin and her elbow met the substantial resistance of his abs. Still, he grunted and loosened his grip. She took advantage, letting her legs go noodle and using her dead weight to wrench free. She dove for the stang and popped to her feet at the end of a roll.

Then, she went for it.

She met him at the center of the mat. He swung, and she swept low with one arm as she slapped down on the mat with the other. A twist of her legs and—

Shit!

He should have gone down like he had before. But he caught her calf, spun her, and suddenly she was in his arms again, her stang in his hand. He made a dramatic sweep across her abdomen, slicing through her blouse, and then he tossed her and the stang aside.

"I told you that trick will only work once. You try that move with someone who knows it, and instead of a ruined shirt, you'll be cleaning your bowels off the floor." He gave her an amused smile and a slight nod. "Don't take it to heart, though. You did manage to surprise me. Nice. Sorry about the shirt."

His gaze flicked to the gaping hole in the material. Instinctively, she closed the gap, hiding the glyph that protected her against the nightmare demon and was the reason she didn't wear bikini swimsuits. He jerked his gaze away and looked at her colleagues as she made an effort to pick her pride off the mat.

"Who's next?"

Clutching her ruined shirt and nursing her bruised ego, she plopped down at the edge of the mat and watched as Logan tore through her colleagues like claws through wet tissue paper. Carlos appeared to give him a run for his money, but she had a feeling Logan hadn't given a hundred percent. Or even fifty percent.

By the time Shanea showed up to take over the tour, Eva's coworkers had gained a new respect for DART. Or, at least, for Logan.

Shanea came toward them, her black flats clicking softly on the floor. "Logan, Kynan said you're needed on an assignment. He wants to see you ASAP."

Logan, who hadn't broken a sweat after fighting every one of them, gave them all a see-ya wave. But she swore his gaze lingered on her longer than any of the others. Suddenly, she was breathless again. She gave him a flustered wave and watched as he met Shanea halfway across the room and high-fived her.

"He's a demon," Sig declared as the door shut behind Logan. "For sure, he's a demon."

"Yeah," Keeley breathed, her hungry gaze still locked on the doorway Logan had disappeared through. "A sex demon. A go-all-night demon between the sheets."

Eva wasn't sure about that, but there was one thing she *was* sure of.

Logan was dangerous.

Dangerous in ways that made every female instinct scream to run away.

Or let herself be caught.

Chapter Five

The stench of blood, bowels, and death hung thick in the old building's dank basement. Several floors above, business people toiled away in the ten-story Boston office building, oblivious to the fact that two demonic spirits were on the loose.

Maybe a human one, as well, but Logan couldn't say for sure. His ability to sense the presence of an entity's soul was limited to demons.

"Mace?" Logan stepped over the greasy stain that was all that remained of one of the two demons an Aegis Guardian had killed before he bled to death. The guy's body was propped against the wall near the stairs—most of it, anyway. Logan had found his left arm twenty feet away. "Man, are you sensing them?"

"Of course, I'm fucking sensing them." Mace eased from around a fat support column, a salt-encrusted blade meant to dissipate a spirit or decapitate a corporeal form in one gloved hand and a salt shotgun in the other. "But I can't tell you where they are or what species. Why are you even asking me that? You can actually *see* spirits."

Logan rolled a *decipula* between his fingers as he peered through a doorway into a corner office. Inside, a dusty monstrosity of a desk dominated the room under the flickering light from a single dying bulb. "I can't see them if they're hiding."

"Then draw them out."

"No shit. You think I didn't think of that? These bastards are resisting my pull."

Mace swore under his breath. "I don't work in Spirit Management. I fucking hate this evil soul shit. I should be out with Blade and Scotty, hunting a Soulshredder and turning it into a spirit for *you* to catch. Why the hell did DART put me on this job?"

"Because you were already here in Boston screwing one of Dawn's roommates. And you can sense spirits."

"Which, again, does no good if I can't see them." Mace came up from behind Logan, his head swinging from side to side as he scanned the area for their targets. "I have the most useless superpower ever. You're an immortal badass, and I'm your lame-ass sidekick."

"Quit whining. You're a sex demon. Your magic dick is your superpower."

Mace barked out a laugh. Logan was screwing with him, but the truth was that despite the fact that their primary talents were meant for sex, Seminus demons were deadly motherfuckers with gifts that could heal…or kill.

An icy puff of air chilled the skin on the back of Logan's neck. He spun around and came face to fucking face with a gaping maw full of fangs.

Fangs that were too solid, pulsing between near-transparency and partial-opacity.

Shedim demon. *Shit.*

"It's regenerating!" he shouted to Mace as he dove to the floor. The Shedim snapped its jaws together where Logan's head had been.

Son of a bitch, he hated these things. Shedims could grow new bodies three times in their thousand-year lifespans, becoming nine-foot-tall nightmares that could bite a man in half. Logan might be immortal, but like Limos's hell stallion, he wasn't immune to injury, pain, or having his head bitten off.

Suddenly, a snarl rumbled through the darkness, and the foul stench of hellhound breath filled the air. A streak of fur so black it absorbed what little light surrounded it slammed into the half-formed spirit and scattered it into a million pieces.

"Good boy, Cujo!" Logan shouted as the massive canine skidded to a halt short of colliding with the wall, his serrated claws ripping deep, steaming gouges in the floor tiles.

The demonic spirit reformed with a slurping, gurgling sound. It streaked toward Mace with a skull-shattering shriek. Logan hurled the *decipula* at the spirit, but the crystal sphere merely bounced off the bastard and rolled across the floor.

"It's too fully formed for the soul trap!"

"No shit!" Mace launched sideways and kicked off a support beam into a mid-air flip. He came down in a powerful arc, slicing at the demon with his blade. The Shedim glided under the sword in an impossibly fast blur. Mace leaped backward. Too late. The creature's claws raked his chest, shredding his leather bomber jacket. "Motherfu—"

Mace dodged another strike, this one aimed at his throat. Unlike Logan, Mace wasn't immortal. Super strong, quick-healing, and long-lived, with a five-hundred-year lifespan, sure, but he'd bleed out almost as easily as a human if he caught a claw to the carotid.

Calling Cujo to his side, Logan charged up his soul gift and hurled himself across the space. Leaping into the air, he came down hard with a hammer-fist to the back of the demon's thick neck. A surge of power punched down his arm, knocking the demon's soul from its physical body. A furious scream exploded from the creature's throat, fading away as its wet flesh and soft bones dropped to the floor in a quivering blob that Cujo snatched up between his powerful jaws.

The Shedim, now a wispy, inky abomination with crimson eyes, spun into a whirlwind of hate so palpable Logan felt it like a million lashes on his skin. The funnel's tail whipped out, catching Mace in the jaw and sending him tumbling into an old desk. The funnel came at Logan, shrieking and growling, a million mouths with rows of teeth snapping at him.

A split second before the specter reached him, Logan hurled a *decipula* into the core of the demonic tornado.

A burst of light exploded from the marble, and in a torturous slow-motion sequence, the shadowy spirit got sucked into the tiny ball. Screeching, it fought the vacuum, its claws dragging across the walls and floor. Finally, with the bulk of its form inside the trap, its claws wrapped around the sphere as it hung in the air until, with a click, the light shut off, and the marble, now swirling with black clouds, plinked to the tile.

"One down," Logan said as Mace flopped back against the wall, one hand splayed across his bleeding chest.

"Great," Mace breathed. "Where's the other one?"

As if Mace's question had summoned it, the remaining spirit shrieked from above and shot toward Logan. He wheeled hard and chucked another soul trap into the center of the wispy creature. It went the way of the first Shedim, fighting its fate until the end.

While Mace struggled to his feet, Logan retrieved the *decipulas* and tucked them into his pocket to drop off at DART HQ.

"Come on," Mace said through clenched teeth, one arm still holding his ribs. "I need a beer, and it's succubus night at Thirst. Maybe your granny will hit on you again." He shrugged at Logan's fuck-you look. "What, too soon?"

"Maybe ask Limos that."

Shame put a shadow across Mace's face, but only for a second—a fraction of a second. The guy possessed all the empathy of a deer tick.

"Anyway," Logan continued, not bothering to hide his irritation, "I can't. I have to stop by the hospital to pick up some meds for my mom."

Mace rolled his good shoulder in a shrug and limped toward the exit. "Come after. And for demon's sake, get your dog some proper food."

Logan glanced over at Cujo. The hellhound was slurping up the last remains of the demon, his tail wagging like it was the best meal he'd ever had.

Hellhounds were disgusting. Great protectors, but disgusting.

"Maybe he'll eat the Guardian." Logan wasn't serious about that, though. Cujo *would* eat the guy if Logan let him, but that would probably end Aegis/DART relations.

Mace snickered. "I hear there's a Guardian *you* want to eat."

Logan started. "What?"

"That Aegis chick you rolled around with on the gym mat."

They'd rolled. Tangled. Exchanged a lot of heat. But Mace was the last person who needed to know that. "Who told you?"

"Draven. He saw you decimate those assholes. Said you were careful with one particular female, though."

Whatever. Draven was a dead man.

"Draven's full of shit," Logan said, but his cheeks heated at the memory of having Eva's curvy body beneath him. He was so done with this conversation. He popped Mace on the shoulder. The injured one. "Tell you what. I'll meet you at Thirst after I drop the soul traps off in the vault and grab my mom's meds. But only if you shut up about the Guardians, and you file the Shedim incident report with DART."

"What?" Mace swore. "I hate paperwork." He glanced at the Aegis Guardian's wrecked body. "On the upside, I don't mind reporting dead Aegi."

Logan didn't bother with any pro-Aegis arguments. He didn't care that, like DART, they were dedicated to destroying evil demons. The Aegis had tried to kill him before he'd taken his first breath, and he held a grudge. They made no distinction between evil demons and good ones, and they'd kill Mace, Draven, or any of Logan's friends if they got the chance. So, no, he wouldn't defend them.

But as they passed the dead Guardian, Logan said a silent prayer for his soul.

The guy and his partner, who was currently puking in the grass outside, had managed to take down two badass demons before the one Aegi died, and that deserved at least a modicum of respect. That kind of skill was hard to find in the human population. The human had died protecting people, and Logan couldn't fault that.

"Sorry, man," he murmured. "You did good. Rest in peace."

"That was the most fucked-up day ever." Sig plopped down at the table Eva had reserved at a posh Brussels restaurant featuring a private room for large parties and meetings.

Benji shot him a snarky look as he took the seat opposite. "You still mad about Logan putting you face down on the mat?"

"Pfft. No." Sig reached up and rubbed his nose. "But that guy is a dick."

Keeley took a sip from the glass of water the waiter had just brought. "I think he's fucking hot."

"I like anyone who can make Sig eat dirt," Benji said.

Mason laughed, and Carlos let out a deep chuckle. Sig sneered.

"Logan might be a dick," Carlos said as he reached for his sparkling water, "but he knows his shit. I wouldn't mess with that one."

"You?" Sig grabbed a slice of bread from the basket at the center of the table. "Big bad SEAL dude wouldn't mess with a DART douche?"

Carlos leaned back in his seat, his long body taking up a lot of real estate. And he took it up like he owned it. "You need to learn to check your ego, kid. Recognize when someone is as good—or better—than you are. I think I could hold my own with the guy, at least for a little while, but I'm not sure I want to test my theory in a life-or-death situation. Respect your opponent. You get cocky, you get dead."

Sig snorted. "Whatever."

They stopped the shop talk as the server approached to take their orders. As soon as he was gone, Keeley settled her elbows on the table and kept her voice low. "Is anyone else supposed to contact their Elder handler when we get to our rooms?"

Everyone nodded. Sig popped a bite of bread into his mouth and spoke while chewing. "I'm reporting to Anthony. What about you guys?"

Everyone looked at each other, unsure if they were supposed to reveal the names of their handlers. Finally, Mason shrugged. "No one told me I couldn't tell. Miguel is my handler."

Everyone rattled off a different name, and it was kind of nice knowing that Eva wasn't sharing Maja with anyone else. Not that it would be a big deal, but having Maja to herself made it less likely that any information Eva shared in confidence would get back to her colleagues.

"So," Eva said, "did anyone see, hear, or learn anything interesting today?"

Excitement sparked in Carlos's cocoa eyes. "Those weapons. Man, they have some crazy shit. We don't have half of what they've got in their Brussels office alone. And we only have one Sobek hook in the entire Aegis. They have three just for *training*. Draven showed me how to use it. I could never get the damn thing to work before."

"What would you even use one for?" Benji asked.

Carlos rubbed his chin thoughtfully. "It's not that practical for humans because of its size and weight, but giant Sobeks can knock something twice their size backward several yards with the right swing. And the Sobek hook is one of the few weapons that can neutralize a Nebulous demon."

"Hmm." Benji stared into the butter dish. "What if we could miniaturize them but still keep the same magical properties...?" He trailed off and then started tapping notes into his wrist comm, losing himself in his work as if he was back in his sterile DC lab and not sitting at a table in a fine European restaurant.

The server brought their drinks, and Eva thought she'd never been so happy to see a glass of wine. It had been a long day, and their schedule indicated that the days were going to get even longer and busier now that they'd finished their orientation.

"What's on the agenda for you all tomorrow?" Mason asked. "I think I'm meeting with one of their spellcasters in the afternoon. Are you guys meeting with people in your respective departments?"

Eva dug her schedule from her tote and gave it a quick scan, even though she knew it by heart. "It looks like the time after lunch is entirely blocked off for us to meet with our DART counterparts." She would be spending the afternoon with a woman named Runa, which should be interesting since she was openly a werewolf. And married to a demon. "The morning is reserved for combat training and tactical weapons demonstrations."

"I can't wait," Carlos said. "After seeing their weapons and facility today, I'm stoked."

"Me too," Sig said, taking a big swig of his Duvel, chosen, he said, because the name meant "devil" in certain Dutch dialects, and he was going to "slay some "duvels."

Eva had a feeling the beer was going to slay him.

"Ditto," Keeley said to Carlos. "I can't wait to see how good these people really are. I guarantee we're better trained than they are." She paused. "Logan excepted, of course."

"What did I just say, Kee?" Carlos shook his head. "Don't get cocky. Cocky gets you killed."

"They're not going to kill us." Keeley slathered butter on a slice of bread. "Besides, I have to pretend I suck so they'll underestimate me."

"Same." Benji sighed. "I'm supposed to act like I'm of *average* intelligence. How do I do that? If I was average, I wouldn't be in charge of The Aegis's entire R&D department, and I definitely wouldn't have a doctorate in physics from Stanford University."

Benji always found a way to work Stanford into a conversation. He'd become a drinking game at parties.

Benji said Stanford again! Take a drink!

"They don't want you to play dumb," Eva said calmly, taking a piece of warm bread for herself before her stomach started growling. "They just want you to not make others feel dumb."

"I don't do that," he said, all offended. But his cheeks flared pink because he knew damn well he did.

"I'm supposed to act like I don't know much about magic." Mason looked over at Sig. "What did the Elders tell you to do while you're here?"

"Nothing." Sig grinned. "I'm perfect."

Eva rolled her eyes as the server interrupted with their food. Flemish stew and mashed potatoes for her. Her fork tinked on the plate as she scooped up a bite-sized portion of beef and gravy. The savory aroma of onions and Belgian beer reminded her of the European trip her parents had gifted her for high school graduation.

But as she opened her mouth, her wrist comms beeped, joining a sudden chorus from every comms device in the room.

"It's an Aegis alert." She put down her fork. "Press conference from the home office." What the hell? She should have been consulted, or at the very least notified, about anything media-related. Like a damn press conference. "Does anyone know what this is about?"

"Us? You're the one who should know," Keeley pointed out, less than helpfully.

"I know, but—"

Dammit. She started to dial Jennifer but remembered halfway through that she was only supposed to be in contact with Maja. Surely it would be okay to contact Jenn about her own office's work, right? Maybe she should call Maja. No, she definitely didn't want to do that. One didn't bother an Elder just to ask what a press conference was about and why she hadn't been notified.

"Hey." Keeley tapped Eva on the arm. "It's starting." She flicked her device, throwing a grainy, two-foot-tall lighted hologram of a podium into the middle of the table. A heartbeat later, Stefani walked up to it, all spiked heels, tight skirt, and just enough cleavage to draw eyes but not criticism.

Eva practically snarled.

"Good evening."

Stefani removed the fake glasses she claimed made her look smart and placed them on the podium with a calculated amount of drama. It was her signature move. The longer it took her to take them off, the worse the news. Or, at least, the worse she wanted the audience to *think* it was.

"As you know, The Aegis and the Demonic Activity Response Team is currently working together to share ideas, technology, and resources." She paused to glance down at her notes before once again addressing the camera. "Tonight, our agencies worked on its first joint operation to neutralize dangerous demons. At approximately ten-thirty a.m. local time in Boston, Massachusetts, United States, two Aegis Guardians and two DART agents engaged more than one Ufelskala Tier-Four Shedim demon. The demons were neutralized, and their spirits captured, but we regret to report that one Guardian was killed. We will bring you more information as we receive it."

The hologram faded away, and for a moment, they all sat silently, stunned.

"Wow," Carlos finally breathed. "Must have *just* happened, or I'd have heard about it by now."

"Wonder who it was," Sig said, taking a break from shoveling his food into his mouth. "I know people in a couple of the Boston cells."

"Same," Carlos said, but he was probably telling the truth. "I'll see what I can find out. My buddy, Craig Shaeffer, is the Regional Director." He tapped away at his comms device as Eva stared into the empty space where the hologram had been.

"Stefani looked great," Sig said. "Don't you think so, Eva?"

Keeley threw a chunk of bread at Sig. "Don't be a dick."

"No, it's okay," Eva said, although Keeley wasn't wrong. Sig was definitely a dick. "Sig's right. She did look great."

Which pissed Eva the hell off. Stefani hadn't stumbled once, and she'd even managed to look like she gave a shit about some nameless Guardian she'd never met.

"So," Carlos began, "the dead Guardian is a twenty-four-year-old named Robert Lynch from the South Shore cell." He cursed softly. "Damn, man. He has a toddler son with another Guardian. Craig says…oh, shit. The Guardians went to investigate a disturbance in the basement of an office building. When they got there, they were attacked by Shedims. They called for backup, but headquarters wanted DART in on it instead."

"What?" Sig slammed his beer down. "So we didn't send our people? Those guys had to wait on DART assholes, who probably can't find their own dicks?" He spat a raw curse. "That Guardian is dead because of DART."

"We don't know that," Eva said. "We don't know anything."

"We know one of our people is dead," Sig snapped. "I'll bet the DART guys didn't do jack shit and are taking all the glory."

Eva was about to tell Sig to shut up with his insanity when her comms beeped.

Stefani.

The holo-message popped up in a bright pink, loopy font that screamed spoiled ditz.

Did you see the presser? Jenn said I did great. Miss you!

And there were five—five!—kissy and heart emojis.

"Miss you," Eva mocked. That bitch.

"Don't worry about her," Keeley said. "Everyone knows you're the frontrunner for Jennifer's job. No one can stand Stefani."

"I like her." Sig wiped his mouth with a napkin. "I think she wants me. And she just broke up with that producer she was dating."

"You don't have a shot with her." Carlos popped a mussel out of its shell. "She's got a type, and you ain't it."

Yeah, Stefani's type was rich, handsome, and in a position to raise her social status.

Bitter much?

Okay, sure, Eva was a little bitter. But Stefani had undermined and sabotaged Eva half a dozen times in the last four months alone, from stealing assignments by lying about Eva being busy, to deleting a speech Eva had spent hours writing. No, she couldn't prove Stefani had wiped the file, but she was one of the few people with access to the system, and the only one who would benefit from Eva making a fool of herself.

Taking a long, deep drink of her wine, she listened to her colleagues banter. Sig was right. This was the most fucked-up day ever.

And it wasn't even over yet.

Chapter Six

As usual, Underworld General Hospital was knee-deep in patients and noise. In the thirty-three years Logan had been alive, he'd rarely seen the demon-run hospital in any other state than organized insanity. The five demon siblings who ran it somehow managed to keep the main facility and its globally situated clinics functioning in an almost military-like operation. But given that most of its patients and staff were underworlders, many things could—and did—go wrong.

Many.

He stopped at the front desk and spoke to a ginger-haired nurse who could have passed for human except for her orange eyes and rust-streaked ivory tusks that curled to nearly her nose.

"I'm here to see Eidolon."

She sighed. "You and everyone else. Name?"

"Logan."

She sighed again, this time with attitude. "Last name?"

"You got a lot of Logans asking for Eidolon?"

"You got a last name?" she repeated, getting grumpier by the second, and he decided to stop messing with her.

He'd taken his mother's last name, Matthews, for human interactions, but he'd found that using his father's name when dealing with demons was often more impactful. "It's Logan Thanatos."

Her head snapped up, and her eyes went wide. "Thanatos? As in the Four Horsemen of the Apocalypse, Thanatos? *You're* his son?"

"Yup." He leaned in and winked. "And Eidolon's my *daemo-da*." Roughly translated, the Sheoulic word meant godfather.

She no longer looked bored or annoyed. Thanatos's name usually did that to people.

"Sorry, I've only been working the front desk for a few months. I've never been here when you came in. You are definitely on the list of people to let through." Her fingers flew to a switchboard, and she mashed a button with her finger. "Hello, sir. There's a Logan Thanatos to see you." She nodded at whatever response she got in her ear and glanced up at him. "Eidolon will see you in his office now. It's down the hallway on your left, and then—"

"Thanks. I know where it is." He'd practically grown up here. Well, he'd grown up mainly in Greenland at his parents' castle, but he'd spent a lot of time at his aunt Limos's and Uncle Ares' places, as well. And because the people who ran Underworld General were good friends of the Horsemen, Logan had spent countless hours running up and down the hospital halls with the Seminus kids.

They'd been tight back then. Still were, mostly. He counted Talon and Sabre among his closest friends. And he was cool with the rest of them, although Mace and Rade could get on his nerves. But Stryke…Logan hadn't seen him in years. He wasn't sure anyone had, except Stryke's mother, Runa. His estrangement had rocked the family extra hard, coming on the heels of the tragedy that had cracked their foundations and left them on shaky ground.

He smiled fondly as he passed a serpent statue that sensed murderous thoughts. Anyone with bad intentions got a painful bite that required immediate medical attention. The hospital was already protected by a Haven spell that prevented violence by causing disabling pain, but spells could be broken or bypassed, and Eidolon had installed several backups over the years. Usually, after some painful lessons.

The serpent had been the most fun to fuck with, though. Logan, his Horsemen cousins, and the Sem kids had made a game of thinking murderous thoughts to see if they could trigger the statue. They'd walk past the scaly black snake over and over, imagining themselves slaying evil demons.

None of them had been bitten. Not back then. Eidolon said it was because the serpent sensed intent, not thoughts. So, Logan had always wondered why, several years later, Stryke had been bitten. Who had he intended to kill?

"Logan."

Jostled out of his thoughts, Logan spun around to the sound of Eidolon's voice behind him.

"Oh, hey." He frowned as he tried to orient himself in the hallway intersection. He'd been so wrapped up in the past that he hadn't paid attention to where he was going. "Did I go past your office?"

"No, I was just coming back from the coffee machine and saw you ahead of me." Eidolon gestured with his steaming cup. "Just ahead on the right."

Feeling like a dolt, Logan entered the spacious room, its shelves laden with antique medical equipment and demon skulls.

"Good to see you." Eidolon closed the door behind him. "Been a few months."

"You've missed a couple of get-togethers. Sabre says you've been super busy." Eidolon and Tayla's son worked at the hospital, but he ran his own forensics lab and, to his father's great disappointment, wasn't a physician.

Eidolon grunted as he sank into his chair. "We're overwhelmed. I can't get the new hospital in Australia built fast enough. And when it *is* finished, I don't know if I'll have enough personnel to staff it. It takes forever to get people through any kind of medical training, let alone a doctoral program. My medical school isn't pumping out healers fast enough." He put down his coffee with a thunk and gestured for Logan to take the seat across from him. "But that's my problem, not yours." He steepled his fingers together on the desk and shifted the topic. "We'll try harder to make it to the next party."

"Good, because there's a bash at Limos's place this weekend. You gonna make it?"

Eidolon's dark eyes grew troubled. "I'd have thought she'd cancel after what happened."

"You know Limos. She needs to keep busy when shit hits the fan. She's never been good at sorting through her emotions."

None of the Horsemen were. But Logan supposed thousands of years of life caused a lot of scar tissue that was difficult for anything, even strong emotion, to get through.

Eidolon gave a shallow nod as he unwrapped his stethoscope from around his neck. "Tayla informed me we *will* make it, come hell, high water, or Satan escaping his cage and starting the Apocalypse."

Which wasn't likely. Logan's angel grandfather, Reaver, and his uncle Revenant, who was the current king of Hell, had locked Satan away for a thousand years, and there were still about nine-hundred and sixty-five left before they'd have to deal with the end of the world as they knew it.

"So," Eidolon said, tossing the stethoscope onto the desk, "what brings you here? You finally going to quit DART and come work for me?"

Logan laughed. The doctor had been trying to lure Logan into the medical field since he was a toddler. But Logan had learned early on that he needed to be out in the world, putting his immortality to the test. Also, he had Cujo to think about. The hellhound needed to run, hunt, and be challenged, and if Logan was cooped up in a hospital, the beast would become destruction in the flesh.

"I'm here to pick up my mom's meds."

Eidolon reached into a drawer and pulled out a plastic bag. "I thought your dad was going to stop by for them."

"He was, but he asked me to do it on the way home from work. He's investigating a lead on Lilith, and he doesn't want Mom leaving the house while he's gone."

"Given Regan's difficult pregnancies, I don't blame him. Your sister will be there while he's gone, right?"

"Seriously?" Logan stared at Eidolon.

Eidolon's *dermoire* writhed on his arm as he pushed the bag at Logan. "Yeah, I know. She doesn't leave the castle. I just keep hoping that someday she'll surprise us all."

Logan hoped so too. Amber was making progress, though. She was comfortable traveling alone to Uncle Ares' and Aunt Limos's islands, and last week she'd even gone with Logan to Uncle Reseph's new island home in the Malay Archipelago. She'd had an anxiety attack within half an hour, but it was a start. Every time she went back, she'd be able to stay longer, until she could come and go freely by herself and eventually spend the night.

Eidolon's wrist comms lit up with strobing red and white lights, and he looked down at the device with a curse. "We have a soul on the loose. Nightlash." He looked across the desk at Logan. "Good thing you stopped by. You want to handle this?"

Logan always had at least one *decipula* on him, but Underworld General should have its own supply. Demons died here every day, so there would be a lot of souls roaming around if UG's staff couldn't catch them. "Don't you have soul traps?"

"We do, but unless there's someone on duty who can see souls when a patient dies, they're useless. We usually call in trappers."

"Where is the Nightlash's body?" Logan asked. "Spirits usually hang out near their physical form until they gain their bearings."

Eidolon gave Logan a follow-me gesture and led him toward the operating theater.

Cool. The day had been one nonstop battle, from his time in the gym with the Aegi, to the Boston Shedim scrap, and now he was ending it with some ghostbusting.

I'd rather end it with the Aegi.

One particular Aegi.

For some reason, he couldn't get Eva out of his head. He'd hugely outmatched her, but she'd fought like a cornered hellrat. She had spirit, a flexible body, and a hard head, all of which she'd put to good use. Then there was the tattoo that peeked through the slice in her blouse. Maybe after he bought her a new shirt, he'd ask about it. He'd only caught a glimpse, but he'd seen enough to know the tat wasn't the shield glyph sported by all Aegi to give them special protection and powers. No, the tat on Eva's hard abs hadn't been inked in any human or angelic script.

Her tattoo had been written in Sheoulic, the language of demons.

Curious.

He smiled. None of this would help him capture a Nightlash's soul. But it did give him one more reason to look forward to work tomorrow.

Chapter Seven

"Hey, Logan, one of the exchange Guardians left a tablet behind today. If you're not busy, do you mind dropping it off at her hotel?"

Logan cursed Kynan's name as he strode through the boutique hotel's lobby, his mission cut and dried: hand off the electronic notepad and get the hell out of there.

He'd gone back to DART HQ for two seconds to drop off the trap containing UG's renegade Nightlash soul, and Ky had ambushed him. Again.

He really needed to learn to avoid the guy.

That said, when Kynan told him the tablet belonged to Eva, the mission didn't seem so bad. His blood had even pumped a little faster and hotter at the idea of seeing her.

He spotted her in a private corner near the window, her laptop on the table in front of her, a glass of red wine near her right hand. She'd changed into a green and black silk top that matched her skirt and emphasized her full breasts. Her long hair fell across her face, hiding her eyes, but he found himself hypnotized by the feminine silhouette of her nose and full lips backlit by flickering candle sconces on the wall.

She looked up as he approached, her sable lashes lifting in surprise. "Logan. Hi."

"Hey." He held out her tablet. "Kynan sent me to drop this off. You left it." *You left it.* Could he sound any lamer?

Frowning, she took it. "Wow, I can't believe I did that. My brain must have gotten rattled during your beatdown in the gym."

He forced an expression of contrition. "Sorry about that."

"He said, not sounding sorry at all." She narrowed her eyes at him, but her smile was teasing. "It's okay. I had to run back to the hotel for a new shirt, and it was only total humiliation in front of my colleagues. Nothing I can't ever live down or anything."

"Nah, I humiliated them too."

Laughing, she gestured to the seat across from her. "If you want to make it up to me, I wear a size ten in blouses and drink merlot. *Good* merlot."

He gestured to a nearby server. "I'd like a bottle of whatever she's got in the glass." He'd get his cousin Leilani to buy a new shirt. Limos's daughter lived for shopping and keeping up on fashion trends.

"Yes, sir," the guy said, scurrying off.

Logan sank into the plush black-and-gold chair as Eva held up her glass. "You should know that this is four hundred dollars a bottle."

"Then I'm definitely staying to drink it with you."

One shapely eyebrow arched. "You weren't before?"

"I didn't want to intrude. But I'm intrigued by the wine now." Though not as much as he was by her. "And I'm curious about how your day went."

"It was interesting." She closed her laptop and sat back in her seat with her glass of wine. Her long, shapely legs crossed at the ankles, she settled in for a chat. "Not what I expected. Runa *definitely* isn't what I expected."

"What did you expect? Fangs and a taste for raw flesh? She's more human than she is werewolf."

"I don't know." Eva toyed with the rim of her glass, one slender finger doing lazy laps. "I didn't expect her to be so down to earth and nice. And so in love with her husband. Oh, sorry. *Mate.*"

"Why would she not be in love with her mate?"

She crossed her toned legs at her thighs now, and her skirt hiked up, revealing enough creamy skin to intrigue him even more. "He's a demon."

Disappointment filtered through him. Her response wasn't unusual for a human, but he'd hoped for something different from her, despite her allegiance to The Aegis. Which made him a fool because he knew firsthand that human females could rip out a heart as efficiently as any demon when they learned he wasn't one hundred percent purebred Homo sapiens.

"And?"

There were a couple of heartbeats of hesitation, and he wondered if she was choosing her words carefully. "I guess I didn't think they were capable of love. Not like we are, anyway."

He was so sick of this shit. Sure, demons were mostly depraved fiends. But even the worst of them loved *something*, even if it was only themselves.

"Why would you assume they couldn't love? Humans and animals feel love and pain and sorrow and joy. Why not demons? What about people who are half-human? Do you think they can't feel love?"

She sipped her wine, her expression contemplative. "I suppose I never really thought about it. But from what Runa said, her demon mate treats her like a queen."

"As Shade should," he said, mildly surprised by her response. At this point, humans usually started arguing that underworlders had no redeeming qualities. "Runa is awesome. She's always bringing cupcakes to work. You might have seen her sons around. Blade works on the Special Forces team, and Rade is an interrogator. You can't miss them. They're Seminus demons, so all females notice."

"Incubi." She shook her head as if unable to comprehend the existence of demons that needed sex as much as they needed air. "I've never seen one in person. I'll keep an eye out for Runa's sons tomorrow. The time I spent with her this afternoon was eye-opening." Her gaze turned inward, maybe a little troubled as she looked into her wineglass. Did it bother her to discover that not all supernaturals were monsters? "So, I'm guessing you heard about the Boston incident."

"I'm familiar with it," he said vaguely, unsure what, exactly, she'd heard.

The server appeared with the bottle and another glass, so they tabled the conversation until he'd presented the wine, poured it, and left.

"Sounds like it was a bit of a cluster." Eva swirled the wine in her glass, studying him, probably taking note of every blink, breath, and sentence.

She'd been an award-winning journalist before The Aegis hired her, and now he had an idea how her interview subjects must have felt. Like being analyzed under a microscope. Not that Logan felt that way. He'd faced far more dangerous opponents than Eva Tennant.

"You could say that."

Laughter from a nearby table rang out, and instead of raising her voice to be heard, Eva scooted closer, bringing her seawater and orchid scent with her. It made him think of jungle beaches and warm ocean waves, which made him think of her in a bikini, and then things got raunchy in his head, and he had to stop thinking.

"Our agencies are doing a good job of making it *sound* like it went off without a hitch."

Now, he was confused. "It did go off without a hitch for DART. We cleaned up *your* mess. The clusterfuck is all on The Aegis."

"Excuse me?" Both of those manicured brows shot up. "I think you're quite mistaken."

"I guarantee I'm not."

She looked so taken aback that he took a victory drink. *Always keep people off-balance, friend or foe.*

Uncle Ares kind of took his warrior lifestyle to the extreme, but he usually had sound advice.

The wine was, unsurprisingly, good. Smooth and rich. Eva might work for an extremist organization that could never be trusted, but she had good taste in merlot.

"And why are you so certain you're right?" she asked, still leaning close enough for him to feel the heat radiating off her bare arms.

He considered lying because the truth would invite questions he wasn't ready to answer. Hell, he'd never be ready to confide in a human again. But then, he supposed he didn't have to.

"I was there," he said, watching her carefully for her reaction. "In Boston. Kynan sent Mace and me the second he got the call from The Aegis. We were on scene within five minutes. One of your people was already dead, and the other was outside, heaving his guts up."

She blinked, and he could practically see the wheels turning in her head. "You? You were there? How? Boston is an eight-hour flight from here."

"Come on. You don't expect me to give away all of DART's secrets, do you?"

She muttered something about demon magic and gave a little huff before downing what was left in her glass. "Lucky for you, I'm a little too tipsy to care much."

A boisterous group came in and settled in the lounge. Suddenly, it got way too loud and annoying in the little bar area.

"Ugh." She shot the group a glare. "It was so nice in here until now."

He scanned the crowd, instinctively sizing up the newcomers and making threat assessments. They looked human. Mostly men in their twenties and thirties. None appeared to be demons, but *ter'taceo* never did. And Logan's internal demon detector only worked when he sensed a threat, so he wouldn't know if a demon in a human suit was present anyway.

But one of the males had the look of a shapeshifter, with serious, vulturous eyes that didn't match his affable manner. He was probably just trying to fit in with his human friends, but Logan made a mental note to keep an eye on that guy.

And, yeah, he knew he was being paranoid, but he didn't care. He didn't like crowds. His aversion to large groups of people was yet another carryover from the tragedy at the theme park that had killed a child and torn apart a family.

As he turned back to Eva, a warning tingle skated over the back of his neck. Instantly, he froze, moving only his eyes as he searched for the reason his demon detector had activated.

And then he saw it.

Saw *her*.

Son of a bitch.

Lilith.

Casually, and keeping his voice low, he stood. "Let's go someplace quieter." He tossed five hundred euros onto the table and swiped up the bottle of wine and his glass.

Eva gathered her things and hurried after him. "What's going on?"

"Nothing." He forced himself to walk slowly, more to blend with the crowd than to let Eva catch up. "Just tired of the noise. The band's terrible. How about your room?"

"There's no band. And that's a little forward, don't you think?"

"Don't worry," he said as he made his way to the elevator. "I don't do Guardians."

"Well, we're even then, because I don't do DART agents."

"Good. We're in agreement. No one gets done."

He looked back at Lilith, who stood in the bar, hands on her curvy hips, her dark gaze prowling the throng of customers. Nearly every male in the room had noticed her, and those who hadn't were getting elbowed by their gawking buddies. She was a stunning, dangerous, perfect carnivore, and half of those guys would sell their souls to die between her legs.

"Hurry." He guided her toward the ding of an elevator. "We can catch that one."

Eva grasped his hand as they wove through the crowd of people who stepped out of the way, and as they ducked into the empty elevator, she peeked back at Lilith. "Oh, wow. She's gorgeous. An ex?"

The thought made him want to puke. "I told you, I'm tired of the noise."

"You're full of shit," she said as the doors closed. "*Is* she your ex?"

"I don't want to talk about it." He released her hand and stepped over to the elevator buttons. *Buttons.* How rare and retro. Most elevators either had a touchpad or they asked where you wanted to go. In general, advancement in human technology had stalled since the existence of the otherworld became known. Most companies shifted their focus toward anti-demon and security tech. But a few sectors, like communications, gaming, and elevators, had made impressive leaps forward. "What floor?"

"I'm not going to tell you until you admit she's your ex."

"Don't make me push every one of these." He hovered his finger over the first-floor button. "Because I'll do it like a toddler hopped up on candy."

She laughed. "I believe you. Six."

He smashed the button, and the elevator jerked upward. Closing his eyes, he sagged against the wall. That had been close. Too close. He could only imagine the scene Lilith would have caused if she'd found him. According to his uncle Ares, she got off on using her succubus powers to inflame the lusts of large groups of humans, inciting orgies that churned for days without rest. But as exhaustion and hunger took hold, the sexfests grew increasingly frenzied and bloodied, until all participants, save Lilith, were dead, and she'd gained even more power.

Logan doubted she was here for that, but she was definitely on the hunt, and he was the prey.

When he looked at her again, Eva was watching him with eyes that were sharp even through the alcohol glaze. He wanted to be annoyed that she'd called him on his bullshit, but he liked it. He usually went for harder types—fellow warriors with athletic builds and physical hobbies like archery and mountain climbing. Females who could crack a male's hipbones with her thighs inside their tent at the top of the mountain and revel in it.

Eva was not one of those females.

According to the bio he'd found during his casual research on her—which was probably more in-depth than it needed to be—her hobbies included reading, writing, and piloting torpedo racers in mixed and advanced reality game rooms. Reading was cool—he was a reader too. Writing? Besides old articles about demons, he hadn't found any information on what she liked to write for fun. And he'd searched long enough that Draven had called him a stalker. Whatever.

The thing that really threw him was the virtual piloting thing. Apparently, she'd won some championships in college, enough to get sponsors and earn notoriety in the field. Eventually, the Advanced Reality Sports League had hired her as its first spokesperson.

She also had an active childhood full of gymnastics and beauty pageants, and he sensed a competitive fierceness beneath that personable, playful exterior. She was sleek and polished as a thoroughbred, but he wouldn't be surprised if she suddenly morphed into a hell mare.

"Tell me," he said as he shoved away from the elevator wall, "why do you work for The Aegis?"

The door dinged and opened on the sixth floor, and she spoke as they stepped out. "They offered me a job." She gestured to a door ahead with her key card. "My room."

He followed her inside, took one last peek out into the hallway for Lilith, and locked the door. By the time he turned around, Eva had kicked off her heels and melted into the overstuffed leather chair next to the sliding balcony door. Beyond her, the Brussels city lights sprawled across the landscape and into the night sky.

He put the wine and his glass on the dresser. "So, why did you take it?"

"Take what?" She gazed out the window, her hand draped over the armrest, the glass of wine dangling from her fingers.

"The job."

"Oh, that." She swung the chair around and kicked her feet up on the bed, flexing her slender calves. "It was a natural progression, career-wise. I started by earning a spokesperson position for a sports organization, then I got various jobs as an investigative or broadcast journalist. The networks where I worked tended to have a pro-human, anti-supernatural agenda, and somehow, I ended up being the person who always reported on Aegis and demon activity. So, when a press job opened up at The Aegis, they came to me with a great offer."

He sat in the remaining chair and did his best to avoid staring at her legs and imagining them wrapped around his waist. "Did you like it?"

"What? Being a journalist?" She snorted softly and buried her face in her glass. "It's too much work, not enough pay, and there are too many assholes."

"You're saying you joined The Aegis to get away from assholes? Seems like a lateral move, but whatever."

She laughed as she stretched to snag the wine bottle from the dresser. "You really don't like The Aegis, do you? We're all just a bunch of assholes to you, aren't we?"

"It's no secret that I'm not The Aegis's biggest fan. But, yeah. Assholes. Mostly. You're different. So, what's your deal?"

The wine *glugged* cheerily from the bottle into her glass. It seemed as amused as she did by his question. "You're asking why I want to work with a bunch of assholes if I'm not an asshole?"

That was the gist. "The Aegis is an extremist organization that espouses the eradication of all supernatural life except angels. They have their fingers in everything from politics to children's toys. You don't join them unless your views align with theirs. I've never met an Aegi who wasn't a True Believer."

"Kynan was once a True Believer," she said, wiping a drip of wine off the neck of the bottle with her thumb.

Do not lick that. Do not—

He nearly groaned when she sucked the wine off her thumb.

"He was until he escaped the cult."

Eva corked the bottle and plopped it onto the floor next to her chair. "Well, it's no secret that I'm not a fan of demons," she said, echoing his comment about The Aegis.

The chair creaked as she sank back into it, almost sloshing wine onto her blouse. Oblivious to the near catastrophe, she shifted to get comfy, and the blouse gaped open, revealing a swell of plump flesh cupped by a black satin bra. Logan freaking loved satin.

"But you're right," she said absently, with just enough of a shrug to make the blouse gape even wider. "I don't really fit in. Most Aegi are driven by their ideology, faith, or trauma. I believe in God, but I'm not religious. I've had more bad encounters with humans than I have with demons, so if they stay out of my way, I'll stay out of theirs." She paused, her right hand brushing casually over her abs, where he'd seen the glimpse of the Sheoulic ward. "Mostly. Do I agree with The Aegis all the time? No. Do I support their overall efforts to keep humans safe from the underworld scourge? Yes."

"Underworld scourge." He could have let the insult go since he was pretty sure he was considered part of the *scourge*, but he was in the mood to poke around a little and see what made this female tick.

"You disagree, of course." She gestured at him with her glass. "You people love your demons."

You people. So casually derogatory. Now, she was poking *him*. "You have no idea what you're talking about."

"I know you employ demons." Her espresso eyes locked with his, daring him to deny it. "I know many of your agents are married to them."

"That's because not all demons are bad."

"Seriously? That's all you got?" Her tone was taunting but not malicious. She was enjoying this as much as he was. He detested everything about The Aegis, but he loved a good debate, and even more, he loved debating a beautiful female who was willing to go toe-to-toe with him, physically *or* verbally. "Okay, then. Let's say I accept your premise." She scooted forward in her chair and leaned closer. "Runa seemed really cool for a werewolf, and clearly, her demon husband hasn't slaughtered everyone around them or eaten their children. But I would say that's the exception rather than the rule."

"You'll get no argument from DART. Or me. Most demons are scum and belong in Sheoul, not the human realm."

She didn't bother to mask her skepticism as she stood and gazed out the window. "Can I ask you a question?" She was still facing the Brussels' city lights, her profile both highlighted and shadowed, severe and delicate. It made him want to explore all her contradictions. All her hard angles and soft curves.

"You can ask." He watched an ambulance weave through traffic on the street below and wondered if it was heading to a demon-related injury. "I can't guarantee I'll answer it."

"Fair." She knocked back half her wine as if needing some liquid courage. "Have you ever fucked a demon?"

Huh. That wasn't the question he'd expected. This female kept him on his toes, always wondering about her motives. He liked that.

His chair groaned as he pushed to his feet and eased up next to her. Below, the ambulance had disappeared around a corner, and folks had resumed strolling between restaurants and pubs.

"Yes," he said bluntly. "Now, what will you do with that information?"

Her surprised gaze flickered up at him, and a spark ignited somewhere deep inside her eyes. Anger? Disgust? Her jaw tightened, and she went taut, clenching her fists.

And then, just as he thought she was going to nail him with a right hook…

She kissed him.

If Eva suddenly sprouted horns and claws, she wouldn't be more surprised than she was right this very second.

She couldn't believe what she'd just done. And from the rigid set of Logan's lean frame, he couldn't believe it either. But even as humiliation cooled her wine-fired blood, his lips softened, and his tongue swept across the seam of her lips as that muscular body leaned into hers.

Have you fucked a demon?

Yes.

A rush of heat flooded her from her breasts to her pelvis. Good God, why had his answer turned her on? Why had she even asked the question in the first place? It didn't matter. It wasn't as if this…whatever it was…between them could go anywhere. She wasn't looking to date, and even if she was, he wasn't her type.

Her type didn't work for DART, and they certainly didn't screw demons.

Logan's tongue breached the barrier of her lips, and she forgot everything she'd just thought about and opened to him as if she was a traitorous gatekeeper, and he an attacking marauder. She practically tossed her glass onto the dresser, spilling that luxuriously expensive merlot and not caring.

Logan pressed against her, backing her into the wall and holding her captive. She moaned, loving how he took control and made her his prisoner. Was this how he'd been with the demon? Had he been the one to dominate the lovemaking?

Could it even be called lovemaking when it was with a demon? Or was it fucking, like she'd said? What kind of demon had he slept with?

And why the hell was she so obsessed with it?

She shot a glare at her wineglass. Damn, that merlot was dangerous.

But maybe not as dangerous as the man currently kissing her

senseless.

One of his hands rose to cup the back of her head as the other gripped her waist, his strong fingers digging into her hypersensitive skin. His lips were punishing, his tongue seeking, and she had a feeling he would be a demanding lover in bed.

She'd always liked being the aggressor when it came to physical relationships, had always liked to be in control, and she sensed the same in him.

If this went any further, they'd be engaging in a battle of wills.

But just as she began wondering how far she should allow things to go, he murmured, "What is this?" against her lips.

"I don't know," she breathed. "Too much wine?"

He pulled back, his pale-hazel eyes drilling into her, and she suddenly felt laid bare. Like Logan knew too much about her, and she didn't know nearly enough about him.

"I think I should go," he said, and her heart sank despite him being right.

They had no business getting involved, not when they were playing on opposite teams and knew nothing about each other. Not when she had so much wine flowing through her veins and running the show.

But that didn't stop her from digging her nails into his biceps and murmuring, "You don't have to."

Closing those piercing eyes, he shook his head. "I do. There's so much shit…too many complications. I gotta split."

"Yes, of course." She shook herself out of it, digging deep for Sober Eva. But the weird thing was that she wasn't that drunk. A little tipsy, but it wasn't the wine giving her that buzzed feeling.

It was Logan. And it was something she hadn't felt in a very long time.

He took her hand in his and gave it a gentle squeeze that made her heart do a little flip. "I'll see you tomorrow."

"We're spending time in your library and historical archives tomorrow. So, unless you hang out there much…"

"I don't." He smiled, and she felt it all the way to her core. The man definitely knew how to wield a panty-melting grin. "But I'm guessing you're going to be in your element."

"I *am* very curious."

"I picked up on that." He kept her hand in his as he walked toward the door. "Maybe we'll run into each other somewhere."

"Maybe."

It was weird how she was both disappointed and relieved that he wasn't suggesting they see each other again beyond *running into each other*.

Kissing Logan had been a mistake. No, she definitely wasn't in the market for a relationship, whether long-term or a fling. Her career was on an upward trajectory, and that was where her entire focus had to stay. She couldn't afford to waste even one drop of energy on a man.

No matter how hot he was.

And yet…something told her he was unique.

Cursing her vacillating feelings, she reached around him and opened the door. "Thank you again for the wine and the tablet."

He inclined his head and stepped into the hall. There was a brief moment of awkwardness, like, were they supposed to kiss again? And then, way down at the end of the hall, a woman appeared.

The one from downstairs.

Logan's ex.

The wine in Eva's belly soured.

Logan's head cranked around, and Eva swore she heard him growl as a dark cloud fell across his expression.

The woman smiled as if she'd hit the lust jackpot.

That bitch.

Eva had no idea what came over her next. Maybe it was the sight of that absurdly stunning woman coming toward them like a cat stalking a mouse. Maybe it was the idea that Logan probably knew every inch of her curvy body. Or maybe it was the alcohol. Whatever it was, it demanded action.

Plus, she'd always had a competitive streak.

Reaching up, she hooked Logan's chin, tipped his face around to her, and went on her tiptoes. Her lips met his in a fierce, possessive kiss that made him groan. Then, as if he'd been goosed, he jerked his head back.

"Dammit, Eva," he snarled under his breath. "She can't know."

She? The other woman? She couldn't know what?

Logan shoved her roughly inside her room. "Lock your door and go to bed. Now."

He pulled the door shut, and she stood there, stunned and staring at the no-nonsense evacuation instructions hanging on the back of it. What the hell had just happened?

And how dare he just shove her away and tell her to go to bed like some child?

Angrily, she cranked the door handle, and the door flew open again.

Startled, she leaped backward, grabbed the wine bottle, and prepared to crack some skulls. When Logan's head popped inside, she was actually tempted to go ahead with the cracking.

"*Lock it!* All the locks." His gaze darted to the bottle in her hand. "Were you seriously going to use that as a weapon when there's a stang mounted on your inner thigh?"

"Of course, not," she snapped. And how did he know about the stang?

"Bullshit. We need to schedule some gym time. You wouldn't have gotten that bottle within two feet of my head." He slammed the door closed.

Heavy footsteps pounded on the carpet outside, and as much as she wanted to defy Logan out of sheer stubbornness and irritation, she darted to the door and engaged the deadbolt and metal doorstop. She might be annoyed, but he also sounded like he knew what he was talking about.

Voices rang out—Logan's coming across pissed, and the woman's sounding amused. There were some curses. Some laughter. Some thumps.

Curiosity overrode caution, and very slowly, Eva turned the deadbolt mechanism, but she left the doorstop in place. She eased the door open as silently as she could and peeked out.

Logan towered over the woman, his face mere inches from hers, his hands clenched in fists at his sides. The woman murmured something, and with a snarl, he caught her slender throat in his powerful grip. The woman didn't even flinch as he lifted her off the ground and slammed her into the wall so hard the light fixtures shook.

Eva clapped her hand over her mouth to muffle her gasp. Logan shouldn't have been able to hear it. No way. And yet, his head swung toward her, his eyes pegging her like lasers.

Shit!

She jerked back behind the door, closing it with her body as she fumbled for the deadbolt.

Had Logan…had he just committed assault?

Legs shaking, her heart pounding in her ears, she forced herself to calm down and listen to what was going on outside. Tentatively, she put her ear to the door.

She listened between deep breaths, but there was nothing but silence now. For a full two minutes, nothing. Then the ding of the elevator had her nearly jumping out of her skin.

Quietly, her fingers trembling, she opened the door and peeked out again.

The hall was empty. On the far end, the elevator doors opened, and a man stepped out, eyed the room number signs, and headed away from Eva.

The dizzying intensity of a sudden adrenaline crash made Eva's knees weak as she ducked back inside the room and double-checked the locks.

"Holy shit," she murmured, falling back against the door and letting it hold her up. "Holy fucking shit."

Either Logan was an abusive, violent asshole, or that woman was somehow dangerous. A demon, even. A jealous demon who might not want to see her ex with another woman.

No matter what, this was a lose-lose situation.

She eyed the bottle of sleeping pills next to the bed, the ones that helped her sleep through any attempts by a nightmare demon to get past the ward tattoo. Then she eyed the wine bottle. If she drank the rest instead of taking a pill, she'd definitely have a hangover tomorrow.

But hey, maybe by the time she finished it, she'd have convinced herself that this was all worth getting her dream job with The Aegis.

And she had a brand-new bottle of aspirin in her bag.

Hangover, here I come.

Chapter Eight

Lilith could teleport.

Would have been fucking great information to know before Logan let her grab hold of him and flash them both out of the hotel and into a scorching-hot magma chamber.

She shoved him backward, and his feet skidded across a stone slab as he narrowly avoided stepping into a stream of lava that would have melted his foot right off his body.

Steam rose all around them as she moved like a viper toward a pedestal on the far wall. The chamber, probably a natural feature of an active volcano, was steeped in evil, but he sensed they were in the human realm, not Sheoul.

Erotic carvings and statues rose out of the glossy black columns of hardened magma, and a well and a slab he was pretty sure was a sacrificial altar sat atop a flat mound of rock.

He exhaled on a stunned curse. This was a temple. A temple dedicated to Lilith.

"Finally, my boy, I have you to myself," she said.

Hopefully, not for long. While her back was to him, he tapped his comms to send an SOS…but there was no signal. He hadn't expected a good Verizon hit or anything, but demons had their own networks, and they were accessible from almost anywhere.

"Don't bother trying to get a message out," she said, turning to him. "I don't allow outside distractions in my temples. Sorry, no fancy communication services down here."

Dammit.

He dropped his wrist but let a stream of energy open inside him, the type that could either create a weapon or blow a soul out of its physical body. Time would tell which he'd need.

"What do you want with me?"

She affected an innocent expression, her eyes going wide and liquid. "I simply wish to get to know my grandchildren. Lucky you, you get to be first."

"Because I'm the oldest?"

"No, because you're male." She trailed a long, sharp fingernail along her cleavage. "I have a preference for males. My...influence on them is greater."

Erotic energy rolled through him in a gentle wave as if he was being lapped at with quick, hot licks.

Disgusting.

He forced his thoughts from the evil succubus and onto Eva, his mind clinging to her kiss. She'd been so soft against him, her skin so smooth that even now, he could practically feel his fingers sliding over the silky flesh of her inner thigh.

"Yes," Lilith whispered. "I can feel your arousal."

"Fuck off. It's not for you."

A sexual wave hit him again, but this one was bigger, crashing down on him so hard he clenched his teeth. His cock throbbed in his pants, and his balls felt heavy and full. Once again, he thought of Eva. She was in the hotel room. Naked and splayed on the bed, waiting as he knelt between her legs.

And then Lilith was there in Eva's place, her nude body writhing as she caressed her breasts with clawed hands.

Logan roared at the intrusion. Panting, he dug his fingers into his thighs to the point of mind-numbing pain and glared across the steamy space at Lilith.

"You're vile," he ground out.

"Oh, I haven't even started being vile. That was just the tip of the clit." She traced her fingers over a remarkably detailed wall carving of female genitals. "I can do so much more to you. And I will. I just haven't figured out how I'm going to approach your cousins. They're all so boring. Aleka works in a dusty museum, and Leilani is self-centered and always busy doing whatever she does at that demon's tech company. Now, Scotty...she's got potential. She's bold, crude...totally worthy of being my granddaughter. What a spitfire. She reminds me of my darling Limos, back before she betrayed me." She smiled with what Logan assumed was fondness. "And then there's your sister, Amber. Poor child. So frail and helpless. Your father should have drowned that little cum-stain at birth. Your whore mother has made him weak."

Anger seared his veins, but he forced himself to remain calm. No doubt Lilith was testing him. She was on a recon mission, and he wouldn't give her any information she could use against him or anyone else.

Lilith twined a long lock of black-as-midnight hair around her finger and played coy. "Who was that woman at the hotel?"

"You'd hate her," he said casually. "She's part of a visiting Aegis team. I'm sure any of them would love a shot at carving out your heart."

Her deep laugh was as smoky as the air around them. "As if I fear a puny human, demon slayer or not. Are you fucking her?"

Logan didn't know much about his grandmother, but he knew she wasn't stupid. She wouldn't believe his denial. She'd seen him kiss Eva, and even if she hadn't, Lilith would have sensed the sexual energy that pulsed between them. Hell, everyone on the sixth floor probably had. When they'd been wrapped around each other, tongues tangling, lips tasting, the fire between them had felt as hot as the magma chamber.

He'd wanted to flip Eva around, take her down to the bed, and spend a few hours exploring that svelte, firm body. Backing off hadn't been easy. But it had been necessary, as this situation proved.

"I was hoping to get lucky with her," he said, running with something she'd believe. "But you went and ruined that. It was my last chance before the team heads back to the States. So, thanks for the cockblock, Granny."

"I'm sure you have plenty of other willing females to choose from." She gave an imperious wave of her hand, the topic of Eva apparently dismissed. Logan let out a silent sigh of relief. "Now, would you like to get to know me? Ask me a question. Any question."

What was her game? He studied her for a moment, measuring her against the backdrop of the obscene artwork that filled the temple with both erotic and gruesome images. All manner of beings, from animals and humans, to demons and angels, were represented in the wall carvings and statues, all in excruciating, tormented detail.

Damn, his grandma was a monster. Inside that perfect, curvy body covered in smooth, creamy skin was a demented sex fiend with some twisted kinks and a taste for torture.

"Okay, I'll play." He glanced around the temple as if fascinated, taking note of potential escape routes, weapons, and hazards, a survival tactic that had been drilled into him since birth. And not just by his warlord uncle, Ares. Nope, as the children of Horsemen and the grandchildren of an angel, he and his cousins were fated to fight in the Final Battle, which meant training twice per week with a contingent of battle angels.

The Apocalypse is coming, you know.

How many angels had said that to him over the years? Way too many. They were holovids stuck on replay with giant sticks shoved up their asses.

Which, according to one of the wall paintings, was something Lilith enjoyed doing to others. Big, pointy sticks, and clearly unwilling victims.

"Why now?" he asked her. "You were released from Sheoul-gra thirty years ago. Why wait this long—?"

"To fuck with you." A hot gust of volcano gasses blew through the space, searing his exposed flesh. Instant blisters erupted on his skin, and his nose and throat burned like they were on fire. Lilith didn't seem affected at all. "I stewed over the loss of Sheoul-gra for a while. For powerful entities like me, it was demon heaven. So much pain, suffering, and torment." She shuddered in what he could only call excitement. At least, it looked like a shudder through his dry-roasted eyes. "After Azagoth was through torturing me, he threw my broken body into the fifth ring to rot. But my reputation and my strength propelled me quickly through the political hierarchy. The fifth ring was filled with the worst of the worst, and I practically ruled it. I had Hades eating out of my hand, and I think I could have had him eating *me* out soon."

Logan doubted that. By all accounts, Hades was fiercely loyal to his fallen angel mate, and she wouldn't take too kindly to Lilith making a move on her male.

Lilith slid her hand down her chest and over her abs, then lower, as she fantasized about sex with the fallen angel. Logan averted his gaze when her fingers slid under the hem of her minidress.

"And then Azagoth had a fucking temper tantrum and destroyed it all." She yanked her hand from between her thighs. "I didn't want to come back to a Sheoul where Revenant rules instead of Satan. I lost most of my worshippers when Reseph killed me, so I had nothing in this realm. Nothing." Her expression twisted in rage, her lips peeling back from teeth that hadn't been sharp just seconds earlier. "Reseph. The most worthless of my children. If only *he* had children. I'd rip them apart in front of him. I'd make him watch as I tortured them over and over for months on end. Maybe he'd turn back into Pestilence and make me proud."

Disgust and loathing filled Logan, along with a healthy dose of shame. He'd heard the stories of his lunatic grandmother, of course, but deep down, no one wanted to believe their relative could be so evil. He'd even once wondered if Uncle Reseph had really needed to kill her.

He got it now. He *so* got it.

"Right. Okay, so that doesn't answer my question."

The cascading magma walls reflected in her eyes, intensified by the anger in them. "You're as insolent as your father, you little wretch. Waiting thirty years is nothing. It's the blink of an eye when you're thousands of years old, child. But don't worry, I did spend some of those years getting ready."

"Getting ready for what?"

She looked at him with pity. "So, you're handsome but stupid. How sad. What do you *think* I was getting ready for? Revenge, you idiot. Was I not clear the other night? But it won't come all at once. I'm going to drag this out. I'm going to make all of you as miserable as I am. And when Satan is finally freed from his prison, I will take my place as queen at his side. Those of you still alive will suffer the greatest torments anyone has ever known."

Man, Logan liked his grandpa a lot better than his grandma. One was an angel who had fought Heaven and Hell to save humanity. The other was a psychopath.

Time to get the fuck out of here.

Cujo! To me!

"Nice hanging with you, G-ma," he said, using Scotty's name for Harvester. "But it's late, and I have to report all of this to a lot of people before I go to bed—"

"If you put out a call to your hellhound, you wasted your time. No one but I can materialize directly into this shrine. Everyone else has to use the physical doorway and nearby Harrowgate." She gestured behind her. "It's right there. Go ahead and leave."

Aaaand that would be a trap.

"What the fuck is your game, Granny? Did you bring me here to kill me?"

"Kill you? No, those bowels have already been spilled. I've moved on. There are far more satisfying things to do with someone than kill them." She smiled. "I *will* see a grandchild die, but I think for you...there are better ways to ruin you than taking your life."

As if on cue, black, oily stuff began flowing from the sex organs of the eight-foot-tall male demon statues. Logan leaped back as some of the substance splashed close to his boot.

"What the—?"

He snapped his head back up to stare at Lilith, who, in the three seconds he'd had his eyes off her, had lost every stitch of her clothing. Except her stilettos. The pointed heels fit perfectly in two depressions in the ground, divots in the center of a glowing symbol in the stone, where she stood, long legs spread obscenely wide.

The black stuff from the statue closest to her streamed through a maze of channels on a path toward her. The oily substance spewing from the others began solidifying into crude humanoid shapes.

"You will be mine, Logan," she called out. "Or you will kill someone you love. Your choice."

His fingers tingled as he punched his power through them to summon a sword. "Neither of those will ever happen."

She cast a bored glance at the blade. "Showing off the abilities you inherited from your father, I see. But a magic weapon won't save you, my boy."

Her laughter rang out as the oil spiraled up her leg. Logan watched in disgust and horror as it slithered like a serpent between her thighs and penetrated her. Throwing back her head, she cried out in ecstasy.

All around Logan, the other five blobs morphed into shiny black demons that towered over him, twice his height and sporting dicks made of blades as long as his arm.

Granny was seriously tweaked in the head.

"Take him," she shouted at them. "Rail him until he's bleeding from his eyes and begs for mercy!"

One of the dickblade demons wrapped his clawed hand around his penis-sword and gave an obscene pump of his fist, his eyeless face somehow managing to leer at Logan.

Oh, hell no.

Leaping into the air, Logan spun, kicking out at the bastard even as he landed a blow with his blade on another.

Both his boot and sword slipped through the things as if they were made of gelatin, and his heart sank. This was not going well. Determined not to end his day with bleeding eyeballs or impaled on a dicksword, he hit the ground at a run, dodging statues and vaulting across streams of lava as he made a desperate scramble for the exit.

Lilith screamed in pleasure, her body contorting grotesquely as the black stuff disappeared all the way inside her. Black veins pulsed atop her pale skin, and her eyes, black as night, tracked him as she moved to block him. He swung his sword but, like the Jell-O cockblade demons, his weapon slid harmlessly through her.

The demons closed in, surrounding him, their meaty fists closed around their phallic swords.

Logan rarely felt real terror. But right now, he felt the first stirrings of panic at the increasing risk of being skewered by those things while Lilith got off on it. Hastily, he reached for his most devastating weapon, the one he called a soul bomb. The one he hadn't used in decades.

Power filled his veins with fire and ice, setting his skin aflame even as a spear of burning cold shot down his spine.

The energy flowing through him, drawn from both Heaven and Sheoul, was divine and evil, pleasure and pain, and he shouted in exquisite agony as he filled to bursting.

A heartbeat before he burned himself to ash, he released the bomb.

A superheated wave of interdimensional energy blasted from him in every direction, targeting all souls inside any physical body within a fifteen-foot radius. Unlike his targeted soul-punches, this one didn't discern between friend and foe.

He'd learned that the hard way.

The wave struck the demons…and passed harmlessly through them.

Which meant they were soulless, and he was still in a fuckton of trouble.

But Lilith…*yes!*

She screeched as her soul, an inky wisp, exploded from her body. He fumbled in his pocket for a *decipula*, but he froze in disbelief as the black stuff that had filled her snapped out like a million wormy tentacles and snatched her soul before sucking it back into her body.

"Ouch," she snarled. "That stings, you asshole." She rolled her head on her shoulders as if working out kinks. "You think I didn't do my research? You think I don't know all about your powers? I told you. I've been preparing for this."

This was bad. So, so bad.

Wheeling toward the exit, he dodged and wove between cockblade demons. One swiped at him, slicing deep into his thigh. Pain stabbed him all the way to his skull as his leg crumpled, and he hit the scorching ground in a bloody sprawl. A demon dove at him. Clenching his teeth in agony, he rolled just in time to avoid being impaled through the gut by a dickblade.

Somehow, he managed to shove to his feet and avoid another impalement, but he was outnumbered and outgunned, and he was in some deep shit.

Let your instincts guide you. You have fast reflexes and excellent timing. Use them.

Jarvus's words echoed through his head. One of several battle angel trainers he'd been working with since he was a toddler, Jarvus liked to distill the essences of his students down into their strengths and weaknesses. Logan had fast reflexes, excellent timing, and, as Jarvus put it, an "unreasonable fear of killing bystanders."

In the battle between good and evil, there will be a lot of collateral damage. Remember that, because when the time comes, you cannot hesitate.

The angel was full of fun advice.

But he was dead on about Logan using his strengths. He had fucking amazing reflexes and precision timing when it came to springing traps.

Limping, panting, his vision starting to blur from blood loss and searing heat, he plucked a *decipula* from his pocket and summoned the last dregs of his power. The soles of his boots, enchanted by sorcerers to resist even the hottest fires of Hell, sizzled as he wheeled on his heel and hurled a targeted soul-blast at Lilith. The concentrated stream of energy struck her full force, knocking her body into a wall. It spasmed wildly as her soul was ejected like a pilot from a jet. With a practiced flick of the wrist, Logan lobbed the soul trap.

The black tentacles reached for her hazy spirit as the little sphere closed in.

Logan held his breath and then yelped in victory and relief as the *decipula* pierced her smoky soul and began sucking it inside.

Yes!

The demons shrieked in fury and agony, freezing where they stood before melting into tarry puddles. Even the demonic fluid that had been inside Lilith's body splashed out from between her legs. Her body crumpled to the ground, one of her arms landing in a stream of magma.

Her flesh cooked and melted away as he scrambled to seize the trap and get the hell out.

Got it. He whirled toward the exit.

Suddenly, his hand was on fire. Agony nearly swallowed his consciousness as black flecks killed his vision.

What the—?

He stared down in disbelief. His hand was shredded, his palm and fingers pierced by shrapnel from the exploded *decipula*. He stumbled, dizzy with pain, as Lilith's inky soul shot back into her body.

No soul had ever escaped a *decipula*. Now he was out of power, options, and, nearly, blood. He had to get out of there before Lilith recovered.

Stunned by his massive defeat and the soul trap's failure to contain Lilith, he hobbled to the shadowy tunnel. Lit by torches made of bone embedded in the smooth walls, the path extended as far as he could see. Squinting in the darkness, he gritted his teeth against the pain and made his way around a couple of bends. By the time he saw the Harrowgate ahead, its glittery curtain a beacon of hope, he was dragging one leg and struggling to stay upright.

With a pained shout, he threw himself inside the gate. He wrenched around, and the last thing he saw before the curtain solidified into a black wall, was Lilith. She stood in the shadows, cradling the shard of bone and burned flesh that used to be her arm. And she was smiling like she'd won the lottery.

The insane lottery.

Logan fought to keep down a shudder as the dark space lit up with three glowing symbols, one for each of the human and demon realms, which, if pressed, would expand into maps. The other, the Underworld General caduceus, would expand into choices to go directly to the main hospital, any of its three clinics, or its school.

Logan didn't need any of those. Well, the hospital might be a good idea, but he didn't have time for that.

To the right of the symbols, a keypad panel glowed with Sheoulic letters and numerals. Using his good hand, he entered the code for his uncle Ares' private Harrowgate on his Greek island.

Instantly, the gate opened onto warm, white sand in a roped-off area near Ares' towering manor. Logan stepped out, and went down in a heap when his leg buckled.

He heard a shout from the direction of the training facility, and then his uncle Ares and one of the Memitim angels who lived on the island were jogging over, barefoot and carrying swords.

"Logan." Ares hauled him out of the bloody sand as if he weighed nothing and braced him against his tank of a shoulder. "Why did you not go to Underworld General?"

Logan hissed in pain with every step they took toward the house.

"Blade can heal me."

"Blade isn't here."

"We need to get him here." Logan's mangled hand dripped blood onto the steps with loud little splats, and he had to fight a wave of nausea. "We need to get everyone here. We have a situation."

Ares went taut. "Lilith again?"

He nodded as Cujo phased onto the stony ground a few yards away, clearly sensing Logan's pain. The hellhound nosed him, assessing his injuries, which were already healing, thanks to their bond.

"It's okay, buddy," Logan gritted through a fresh wave of agony. "Go play with your friends."

The beast licked his face and then bounded away to join the rest of the hellhounds that called the island home and Ares' mate their queen.

Ares gestured to Logan's leg. "Did she do this?"

"You could say that," he muttered through a panting breath. "I'll call Draven, Mace, Blade, and Scotty if you'll get everyone else."

"We don't need anyone but Scotland." Ares barked at one of his Ramreel demon servants to hold the door open for them. "Lilith is after our family, not your friends."

Ares, a warrior to his soul, was doing what he did best in an emergency: circling the wagons and preparing for battle. In any other instance, Logan would have deferred to his uncle's wisdom. But DART needed to be involved. The more help, the better.

"I need Blade to heal me," Logan pointed out. "And Mace will find out through Scotty anyway." He shifted so he could look Ares directly in the eye. "I want my people in on this."

Ares paused at the threshold, his expression stony, his gaze calculating. No one questioned his authority or decisions except his mate.

Finally, Ares inclined his head. "They can be here on one condition. Keep Mace muzzled." His lip twitched in what amounted to amusement in a guy whose face was stone, and Logan grinned. Well, it was more of a grimace.

"I'll do my best."

"Do. We don't have much of a sense of humor when it comes to Lilith."

Logan was beginning to understand why. "Have you told Reseph about her?"

"Not yet." Ares guided Logan inside the opulent manor. "We were planning to meet tonight to discuss how to tell him the news."

A wave of pain took away Logan's breath, and he had to recover for a moment before asking the question he dreaded. Or maybe he was just stalling because he wasn't sure he wanted to know the answer.

"Are you worried Pestilence will return?"

"No," Ares said quickly—too quickly.

His voice was strong and dripping with confidence.

But his eyes were shrouded in dread.

Fifteen minutes later, everyone had gathered, and Logan was no longer bleeding or in pain, thanks to Blade's ability to heal wounds almost as well as his uncle Eidolon. Now, everyone was gathered on the patio his aunt Cara had built to accommodate their frequent large get-togethers. Ares stood next to her near the outdoor kitchen island, his intense gaze focused on Logan.

"Do you think the temple made Lilith powerful enough to escape the soul trap, or do you think she's that powerful on her own?"

"I wish I could answer that," Logan admitted. "But I got the sense that the oily sword-dicked demons were bound to the shrine."

Ares seemed to think on that. "And one of them entered Lilith while the rest penetrated you in some way or another?"

"They didn't penetrate—" He shook his head, figuring it didn't matter. Besides, his dad already looked like he was ready to blow his stack, especially given that his lead on Lilith had turned out to be a dead end.

Mace laughed. "Dude, your luck lately has been hilarious. Your granny humped you, and you got impaled by a demon dick."

Logan shot Mace the bird.

Thanatos's head swiveled around to Mace. "Do we need to have another talk?"

Mace went about as pale as Logan had ever seen him. "No, sir."

As soon as Thanatos turned away, Mace returned the bird to Logan.

"I saw that," Thanatos growled. He'd always had eyes in the back of his head. Logan hadn't gotten away with jack shit as a kid.

Mace's hand snapped down to his side, and he even managed to look a little contrite. Wouldn't last long. Mace didn't feel shame like normal people.

"Have you ever encountered a demon that could break a *decipula*?" Limos asked from where she mixed drinks behind the bar. As the self-appointed bartender, she basically lived back there during gatherings, but today, she was mixing extra strong, and she looked like she'd been crying.

Bones' death had hit her hard.

"Never," Logan said to his aunt. "She's as powerful as a fallen angel." Not that Logan had ever fought in a real battle with a fallen angel. But he'd sparred with plenty on this very island during his life of hardcore training sessions.

Thanatos turned to one of the other people who wasn't related by blood but was as close to the family as the Sem boys. "Raika, did you know Lilith was alive before this?"

Raika stopped pacing around the fire and stood with her arms folded across her chest, her black tank top tucked neatly into tactical pants loaded with weapons. Even though there was no breeze, her blue-black hair billowed around her bare shoulders. The only child of an angel named Lilliana and the Grim Reaper, she was a hardcore warrior tasked with capturing the worst of the demons he'd released when he destroyed Sheoul-gra.

"No." Her emerald gaze was as hard and penetrating as her father's, as if she dared Thanatos to call her a liar. "My father believed she was killed during the war with Moloch. I'll add her to the Gra's Fugitive Database and see what he knows. There have been a few sketchy reports that some of the ReSpawned are more powerful than they were before they died. Right now, it's just a rumor, so I haven't asked my dad about it, but I'll do it now. Don't worry, we'll get her." She winked out silently.

"Get who?" Reseph's deep voice silenced everyone and everything. Not even the birds wanted to be around for the answer.

"Reseph." Cara glided forward with a smile, her long, teal sundress swinging around her sandaled feet. "Jillian. You're just in time for hors d'oeuvres. They'll be out in a minute."

Jillian glanced around, her dark hair swinging loosely around her shoulders. "And here I thought we would be early."

Logan winced. This was beyond awkward.

"Reseph. Hey, bro." Limos came from behind the bar and thrust a frothy pink concoction into his hand. Logan would lay bets on it being strong enough to kill a human—and maybe laced with sedatives. "Glad you could make it."

The blue in Reseph's eyes became murky with suspicion. "The message we got was to get here in an hour. We're half an hour early. How long have you all been here?" His gaze zeroed in on Logan. "And why is he injured and burned? What the hell is going on?"

"Nothing." A gazillion bracelets on Limos's wrist clinked as she gestured to the drink. "Try it."

"Tell me."

"After you try it."

Reseph set the glass down on the nearest table and tucked his hands in the pockets of his jeans, settling in for a battle of wills and glares.

Limos folded first with a sigh. "Fine. It's Mommy Dearest."

For a heartbeat, maybe two, Reseph looked puzzled. Then his eyes shot wide. "No."

No one said anything, giving him time to process. Logan kept an eye on Mace, ready to intervene if the guy's mouth so much as twitched.

"She showed up two days ago," Thanatos said quietly. "She—"

"Two days ago?" Reseph's voice was eerily calm. Like how everything went still before a swarm of ghastbats tore apart an entire town. He looked between his brothers and sister. "You've *all* known for two days, and you kept it from me? Did you think I couldn't handle the news?"

"No." Limos said at the same time as Ares said, "Yes."

Thanatos shot his siblings a look of frustration before turning back to Reseph. "You're here now, and that's all that matters. The short of it is that she's back, and she wants revenge. You and Jillian need to watch your backs. She's dangerous and powerful, maybe even more so than before."

Reseph's jaw tightened, and his fists clenched. He looked like a bomb about to go off. Abruptly, he turned on his heel and walked away. His mate, Jillian, matched that incendiary look, her eyes burning like lit fuses as she glared at each of them.

"Shame on all of you!" she snapped. "What were you thinking, keeping this from him? He's spent over thirty years proving himself, and you still don't trust him? How much longer are you going to punish him for what Pestilence did? Do you not think he punishes himself enough for all of you every single day? What is wrong with you?"

Logan glanced at Reseph's back as he neared the corner of the manor. His uncle might be ready to blow, but his aunt already had. Logan was going to take his chances with shrapnel from Reseph. Maybe he could even defuse the guy. Jillian looked like she was ready to start knocking heads.

"Uncle Reseph?" Logan called out. "Can I talk to you?"

Both Ares and Thanatos gave him grateful nods before withering under Jillian's glare. Limos just looked down at the sand and gnawed on her orange-painted nails.

For as long as Logan could remember, his family had walked on eggshells around Reseph. Even when he wasn't around, certain topics could spark tension. Sometimes, if the mood was wrong, and the alcohol was strong, the tension turned into arguments. How could it not? When Reseph's Seal broke and he became the demon known to the world as Pestilence, First Horseman of the Apocalypse, he'd caused a lot of damage, emotional and physical.

Logan had as much, if not more, reason than any of them to hold a grudge, given that Pestilence had attempted to murder him as a baby after The Aegis failed, but he didn't remember any of that. The only Reseph Logan knew was the one who had carried him on his shoulders when he was a toddler and given him the best Christmas gifts. The one who took him skiing and mountain climbing. Limos was the chill aunt, Ares was the wise uncle, and Reseph was the fun one.

And yet, Logan had caught Reseph's gaze drifting somewhere Logan couldn't go at times. Somewhere dark and troubled—and very, very sad.

He stood, his injured leg groaning. Blade's healing had gotten it to ninety percent, and being immortal would get him back to one hundred in a couple of hours, but he still felt like he'd been hit by a truck. He tried not to make his limp too obvious as he hurried toward his uncle. Reseph had always had a soft spot for his nieces and Logan, but secretly, he thought Reseph favored him.

Of course, the I-tried-to-kill-my-nephew guilt might be responsible for that.

Reseph stopped on the path and waited for Logan. When he finally caught up, Reseph started walking again, hanging a right toward the beach.

"You're injured," Reseph said in a taut, tightly controlled voice, his gaze focused somewhere out across the crystal sea.

"Not badly," Logan said.

"Was it Lilith?"

"Sort of."

The sea breeze ruffled Logan's hair, but Reseph's short platinum spikes barely moved, as if the air itself didn't want to mess with this male. Logan had seen pictures of Reseph from before Logan was born, back when his hair had been longer than Limos's. But Logan had never known Reseph to have anything but short hair. He'd overheard Jillian telling his mother that he'd cut it as if trying to cut out anything that reminded him of his days as Pestilence.

"I'm sorry."

"It's not your fault. There's nothing you could have done."

"No, there's not," he growled, his hands forming fists at his sides. "Because no one told me she was alive." He cursed. "She was depraved *before* I became Pestilence, but Pestilence took her depravity to a new level. I should have demanded that Azagoth destroy her soul. I should have let Thanatos kill her and keep her soul forever in his armor. But I couldn't wait. I was rash, and now she's back."

Logan shook his head as they stepped onto the warm sand. "You can't blame yourself for this."

"That's what everyone always tells me when Pestilence comes back to haunt us. But they're wrong."

Logan grabbed Reseph's arm and forced him to stop. "Uncle, I know...I know how you feel."

Surprise cooled the heat in Reseph's blue eyes a little. One pale eyebrow even arched in amusement. "Do you?"

"No, I mean, not exactly," he said hastily. "No one can understand what it's like to be you." Reaching up, he rubbed the back of his neck and let his eyes take in the island's white shoreline and the birds wading in the shallow waves. "But...I think maybe we can help each other." Man, he didn't want to talk about this. He wanted to forget it. But if there was ever someone he *could* talk to, it was Reseph, and he'd already gone too far to back down now. "Something haunts me too."

Every drop of tension inside Reseph seemed to melt away. Even his voice lowered, barely carrying over the calls of the seabirds. "It's Chaos, isn't it?"

All these years later, it still stung to hear that name. "Yeah. I hate talking about it, but everyone says I should. Like it'll help me get past it. Rade offered to help, but I don't know if I want him messing with my head." He shrugged. "Plus, it feels like it would be cheating. Dad told me he cheated to keep from facing the things he'd done, and I don't want to do that too."

"You didn't do anything," Reseph said, and yeah, that was the problem. He'd failed to save Chaos. Everyone had failed that day.

But Logan didn't want to debate what was and wasn't his fault. He'd already settled that argument in his head.

"Do you talk about what you went through?" he asked his uncle.

Reseph shrugged one big shoulder. "Sometimes."

"With Jillian?"

"Yeah. But even with her, I can't share all of it."

No, Logan supposed he couldn't. The guy had become a literal plague upon the Earth and killed millions of innocent people in the worst ways imaginable. The burden Reseph lived with couldn't be shouldered as well by anyone in all the realms, and Logan had a lot of respect for the guy.

"You can talk to me," Logan said.

Reseph looked startled, and then his expression turned bemused. "No, nephew, I can't. The only one who can understand this shit inside my head is Lilith. And she has to die."

His fists clenched again, and just as Logan began to wonder how he could change the subject, Jillian joined them.

"Hey," she called out, her warm smile bringing a grin to his uncle's face. "Why don't we go grab some dinner? I read some awesome reviews about that new fusion restaurant in Honolulu. They use human-realm vegetables grown in Sheoul soil. It's supposed to make them taste completely different. I might actually like bell peppers for once."

Reseph gestured back toward the house. "I need to talk to everyone first."

"No, you don't. We all agreed to discuss Lilith and what we're going to do about her on Saturday at Limos's place. Ares is going to try to contact Reaver and see what he knows and if he can help."

"We haven't heard from my father in months. I don't know if he's even getting our summonses."

Logan's grandfather, Reaver, one of the most powerful angels to have ever existed, had been MIA for a long time, along with his mate, Harvester. Time ran differently in Heaven, and Logan was used to them disappearing for weeks, and sometimes months at a time. But when summoned, they usually came. Logan was beginning to worry.

"Well, they're going to try." She patted Logan on the shoulder. "Blade and Mace are headed home if you want to hitch a ride in the Harrowgate with them.

"I'll do that." He inclined his head at his uncle. "Thanks for the talk."

"You know where to find me if you need me." He reached out and mussed Logan's hair like he used to do when Logan was a kid. "And don't let Rade near your head. I don't trust any of that Sem mind-scrambling shit."

"I won't."

Jillian gave him a hug, and then Reseph threw open a private Harrowgate that led to their home. They stepped inside and flashed away, leaving Logan alone on the beach.

He looked up at the sky and sighed. "Gramps, if you can hear me, we could use your help."

A puffy cloud mocked him, hovering silently over his head like a jerk. He'd take it as a sign that Reaver either wasn't listening or couldn't hear. Either way, it looked like they were on their own.

Chapter Nine

Harvester loved Heaven. It was like the very best, most beautiful places on Earth times a million, minus the bugs and bad weather. She'd been back for three decades, and she still wasn't over how awesome it was. She'd forgotten after thousands of years spent in Hell as a fallen angel, and now she tried to spend as much time as she could exploring all the endless nooks and crannies.

But sometimes, like today, she liked to hang out in a favorite spot and allow the positive, loving energy to flow like a sensual current on a raft of happiness.

The old Harvester would have gagged at such flowery joy, but that was hard to do when all you felt was endless pleasure. And it wasn't just the energy that flowed into her from the extensive verdant fields in the Meadow of Azna. It was the beauty, the vibrant pinks, purples, and blues of the flowers dotting the hills, the herd of glittering unicorns frolicking in the dale, and the magnificent blond angel striding toward her.

"You finally made it, my lover."

Reaver swept her into his arms and planted a hot, lingering kiss on her mouth. "I would never turn down an invitation to meet you for a picnic." He glanced around, taking in the fields of singing irises and the Covenant Mountains, above which the ancient Gaiaportal hung.

Once a gateway between Heaven and Earth before angels were given the power to flash in and out at will, the gold-flecked-white ring had been deactivated and now served as a crown over the vast, violet mountains. The necklace Harvester wore right now, was in fact a replica of the portal, given to her by Thanatos's daughter, Amber, nearly a decade ago.

I saw this in a vision, she'd said. *I saw you too. And my brother, wrapped in your Grace. I don't know what it means, but I had this made for you anyway.*

Harvester adored the girl, and when Amber had a vision, it was best to apply importance to it, because eventually, somehow or someway, it would become relevant.

"But why here?" Reaver asked. "You're usually all about cheese and wine while perched precariously from a cliff on an active volcano."

He said it as if he didn't enjoy an element of danger and discomfort.

Oh, right, that was her. She'd rather ride a hell stallion than a unicorn any day.

Unicorn glitter got all over everything.

"Because I know it's special to you." His mother had walked here when she was pregnant with Reaver and his twin, one of the few stories he knew about her.

He smiled sadly. "It's the only place I can feel my brother now." He looked at the hundred blackened pockmarks that scarred the otherwise pristine meadow. "But for how much longer? Soon, the damage from his visit will be healed, and then what?"

As an angel raised in Hell—and currently running it—Revenant's presence in Heaven destroyed anything he touched, and because of that, he'd been forbidden to enter. The Council of Orders feared him so much they'd constructed a temporary barrier that kept him from leaving Sheoul until the Investigative Council made a determination regarding his threat level.

"That's kind of why I brought you here. The thirty-year deadline is almost up. Surely, the Investigative Council will finally allow Revenant to at least enter the human realm."

Reaver snorted. "The Thrones and Powers will never allow that to happen."

A terrible thought popped into her head. "You don't think they'll go back on their agreement with *us*, do you? We agreed to stay here in Heaven and break off all communication with everyone in the human realm for six months while the IC wrapped shit up. We kept our part of the bargain."

And it hadn't been easy. But the IC was in its final stage of a three-decades-long investigation into angelic involvement in the destruction of

Sheoul-gra, and Reaver hadn't wanted to antagonize the investigators—not when so many involved were friends and family.

A muscle in Reaver's jaw twitched angrily. "We made a huge mistake agreeing to that. I've missed my grandchildren." He sank onto the grass next to the basket of food and wine she'd brought. "And they had better give Revenant his freedom. Word is he's furious."

She'd heard that through the grapevine too. The Archangels were terrified of him, and pretty much everyone had wanted him punished for the damage he'd done during his last visit to Heaven, and they didn't want to rely on Reaver to keep his brother under control. Especially because they didn't like Reaver either. His status as the only Radiant angel in existence made him a target for bitter, envious angels of every Order. His twin brother, his evil counterpart, a Shadow Angel, terrified them even more, and they were looking for any justification to keep him shut down in Sheoul until the Final Battle when, hopefully, he'd fight on the side of Heaven instead of Satan.

And the fools were too arrogant to see that their treatment wasn't endearing them to him. They might as well be pushing him to ally with Satan.

"I get the feeling that no matter what the bastards in charge of the investigation find, there will be pressure to keep Revenant in Sheoul indefinitely."

"What?" Harvester swore. "That's a load of crap. The Archangels know how important he is. Why are they caving to the other Orders? I understand that no one wants to trust Revenant. He is the king of Hell while Satan is imprisoned. And he's a giant douchebag. But he's also an angel. And your brother. Don't you have any say in it? Or Metatron? You're the two most powerful angels in existence. Surely, the Archangels will listen to you."

The herd of unicorns moved closer, their pearly hooves stepping lightly. Near the rear, a mare leaped into the air, her massive white wings lifting her into the sky. She swooped in expansive circles, watching over her herd. The rare product of a union between a unicorn and a pegasus, winged unicorns were always female, never sparkled, and always took over the herd.

They were pretty badass. Harvester would ride one of those.

"Those fools don't listen to anyone," Reaver growled. "Not even Metatron." Reaver pulled her down next to him. "The Council of Orders Summit is only days away. I can't shake the bad feeling I have about it."

She waggled her brows at him. "Then let me distract you with good feelings."

She stripped him with her mind, but she put herself in a black satin corset, crotchless panties, and thigh-high boots. And quickly, before anyone saw them—the vastness of Heaven made the chances of being accidentally found incalculably low, but there was a pretty good chance they might be spied upon intentionally—she constructed a privacy dome that made them invisible and unable to be heard.

Reaver's sapphire eyes darkened, but it wasn't with lust. No, the fire fueling him today was determination and more than a little fury.

A deliciously hot shiver skittered over her skin. She loved this side of her mate. The wrathful, dangerously intense side of an angel who embodied *fuck around and find out*. Sure, he could be fair and merciful and goofy. But those who fucked around…found out.

It was so hot.

Made her think of all the times they'd fought each other as enemies, back when she'd been a fallen angel full of bitterness, cruelty, and darkness. She'd absolutely wrecked him. Physically. Sexually. In every way she could twist him into knots.

But right now, he needed to be brought down a notch. And she'd keep at it for as long as it took. Days, even. He couldn't go into one of the most consequential Council of Orders Summits in centuries worked into a frenzy. She was going to take that frenzy out of him right now.

But first she had to work him into a different one.

She materialized a length of soft, white rope and a whip, and then she popped her wings and plucked a feather. The fury in his eyes abruptly became fire.

Now, she was going to fuck around. And definitely find out.

Chapter Ten

Logan had only been waiting in Kynan's office for a few seconds when the guy entered through the hidden rear entrance.

"Hey, Logan. Sorry I'm late." He sank into his desk chair and threw his head back as he took a deep breath. He blew it out and sat up to face Logan. "I have about a million fires to put out. The world is going crazy."

"It's about to get crazier."

"I heard. Lilith grabbed you last night." He gave Logan a concerned look, his dark brows framing serious eyes. "You okay?"

"I'm disgusted that I'm related to that monster, but otherwise, I'm fine." He rolled a *decipula* across Kynan's desk. "And we need to upgrade our weapons."

Kynan caught the little marble before it fell to the floor. "What do you mean?"

"I mean that the soul traps failed. She's too powerful for them. Didn't you say StryTech was working on stronger ones?"

"Stryke said they should be able to increase the strength of the existing ones by about ten percent next year."

Ten percent? Ten percent of shit was still shit. "That's not good enough. We've been waiting for containers that'll work against beings as strong as fallen angels for a decade." He became aware that he was pacing and making a lie out of being fine. He was a giant ball of stress, and it occurred to him that the only time he wasn't stressed about Lilith was when he was with Eva.

Who he couldn't be with because of Lilith.

"Fuck me," he muttered as he sank into a chair across from his boss. "Raika has traps strong enough to hold any demon or fallen angel, so they obviously exist."

"Raika operates under Heaven's mandate, not ours, The Aegis's, or any human government or organization. The traps she uses are Divine," Kynan pointed out. "Made in Heaven. We lowly humans don't have access to them, and Stryke hasn't figured out how to reverse engineer them. If *he* can't do it, it can't be done."

Ah, the great and mighty Stryke, trillionaire recluse, tech genius, asshole extraordinaire.

"But I promise, we're going to direct every available resource at finding Lilith and putting an end to her before she causes any more trouble. We'll be working closely with your family. Have they told Reaver about these new developments?"

"I don't know. I think my dad put out a summons, but Reaver hasn't answered. Dad was even desperate enough to call for Harvester."

Ky leaned back in his seat. "Wow. That *is* desperate."

Harvester had been the Horsemen's evil Watcher back when they'd had Watchers, and she was still a fallen angel. Her relationship with the Horsemen had been antagonistic, and even though she'd chilled out since regaining her wings and mating Reaver, mending relationships had been a glacial process.

To Logan, she'd always been his cool grandma, blood kin or not.

"Yeah. Cara has her hellhounds out looking for Lilith, and the Horsemen are gathering intelligence inside Sheoul. But I had an idea about how we could help."

Ky nodded. "Shoot."

"What if someone in IT could use Lilith's DNA to track her? You know, like the devices StryTech made for cops to track humans."

Those were nifty little things that detected human skin cells and scent like bloodhounds did. Since introducing the devices, police organizations around the world had seen their arrest and solved-crime rates skyrocket.

"Can't hurt to talk to Cyan and see if it's possible. I assume you're willing to donate the DNA sample?"

"Yup."

"Excellent. Let me know how it goes." Kynan stood, a clear dismissal. As Logan pushed to his feet, he added, "The exchange with

The Aegis seems to be going well. Have you heard any complaints or problems?"

"Nah. A couple of our people and theirs have butted heads, but it's nothing we can't handle." He looked down at his comms to check the time. After he gave some blood, maybe he'd see if he could get Eva assigned to him for a training session. He hadn't seen her yet today, and they'd left things in a weird place last night.

He couldn't even imagine what she must be thinking.

He sent in a request for a schedule change for Eva as he left the office, and when the confirmation came through while he was getting his blood drawn for the DNA sample, he swore he filled the vial in two heartbeats.

Eva had a headache, a hangover, and a lot of regrets.

She'd practically attacked Logan last night. Then she'd seen him attack another woman but in a completely different way.

Logan's ex is a demon. She has to be.

And how weird was it for her to be keeping her fingers crossed that Logan's ex-girlfriend was a demon because the alternative—that he attempted to choke out a human ex—was seriously not cool.

On top of everything else, she'd slept like shit. Nightmares about Logan's ex morphing into a hideous, leathery monster and killing her in dozens of different ways plagued her sleep. Her only consolation was that at least they'd been normal, anxiety-induced bad dreams, not the kind that nightmare demons forced into your head. The kind that caused night terrors and injuries. And sometimes death if one didn't wake before they died in the dream.

Thoughts about her dreams and last night with Logan tumbled through her tired brain in a loop during the morning spent digging through DART's historical archives and poring over the ancient texts in their library. The Aegis had a larger and more extensive trove of books, but DART had a few that were so rare or remarkable they were locked behind unbreakable glass. When Eva asked the library supervisor if she could see the tomes, he'd politely refused, telling her that very few, even at DART, had access to those books. The best Eva could do was get a picture through the glass to send back to her superiors.

Lunch in the cafeteria was uneventful except for how her heart leaped into her throat when a guy who looked like Logan walked past the coffee station.

Keeley, whose sharp warrior eyes never missed anything, leaned over to whisper, "You're staring. Did you think that guy was Logan?"

Eva sipped her coffee, which was a thousand times better than the brew at Aegis's HQ. "Of course, not."

"Uh-huh." Keeley went back to snarfing her fries. "So, did anything exciting happen last night?"

"What?" Eva nearly choked on her coffee. How did Keeley know? "Logan and I didn't do anything."

Keeley stopped slogging a fry through a puddle of ketchup and looked up at her. "Logan? You were with him last night?"

It was Eva's turn to be confused. "No. I mean, he brought my tablet to the hotel. And then his psycho ex showed up. And get this…I think she's a *demon*." A guy walked by with a cinnamon bun that smelled amazing. As soon as he passed, she pressed her friend for more information. "What are *you* talking about?"

Keeley dropped her fry and snagged a napkin. "I'm gonna need to know more about the demon ex later." She tapped on her tablet and handed it to Eva. A three-dimensional holoplatform featured a news snippet, a leaked story about The Aegis choosing a new spokesperson. According to the report, they'd made their decision.

"So, they didn't call you last night?" Keeley asked.

"To tell me I got the job?" The bottom of Eva's stomach dropped out as she scrolled and tapped in a hasty search for more information. "No."

Keeley stabbed her salad with her fork. "Well, I talked to Stefani this morning. She wasn't contacted either."

Thank God. "Maybe it's just a rumor, then."

"Nah." Keeley swallowed the bite of greens and pushed her plate away. "I'll bet you hear from them today. You know the job's yours, right? They won't give it to Stefani."

Eva wished she could be that confident. "I hope you're right. I'd rather lose the job to *anyone* but her."

"The job is yours," Keeley repeated, hauling her purse into her lap and pawing through it. "Trust me. Your parents are really important to The Aegis." She pulled out a tube of lipstick. "They know where all the bodies are buried."

"Seriously?" Eva stared at the other woman. "You think the only reason I'll get the job is because my parents are The Aegis's lawyers?"

"No," Keeley said quickly. "Of course, not. You earned it, and Stefani is a twatweasel. But if you were both equally qualified, you'd have an edge over her." Keeley dabbed lipstick onto her bottom lip. "I'm just trying to get you to stop stressing. Job's yours."

"I hope you're right," Eva said, gathering her bag. Everyone was supposed to meet in the auditorium after lunch if they didn't get assignments before then, but she wanted to get in a quick walk beforehand. She had a lot of nervous energy to burn off and a lot on her mind that might shake loose with a little fresh air. "But I don't like the idea that my parents could have anything to do with the decision at all. I worked too hard for anyone to think it's less than deserved, and you know that'll happen. Just listen to the rumors about Maja."

Keeley smacked her lips together as she tucked her lipstick into her purse. "I heard she gave Elder Hammond a blowjob for his vote."

Cringe. "See, that's what I mean—"

"Fuck off, man."

"You fuck off."

"Wanna take this outside?"

Wrenching around in her seat, Eva turned around and groaned. At a table across the room, some DART guy was in Carlos's face. Sig and Mason shoved to their feet and moved toward the trouble, and…oh, shit, this wouldn't be good.

"That DART dude is a jerk," Keeley muttered. "He's been all over Carlos and Sig today."

"Did Sig start it?"

Keeley's grin was sheepish. "Yeah. But still, that guy won't let it go."

"Come at me, bro," Sig said, knuckling his chest and getting in the DART guy's grill.

Eva leaped to her feet. "Sig! Carlos!"

"Knock it off!" Draven's roar shut everything down.

All eyes turned to him as he slammed a lunch tray onto a nearby cart. He moved through the cafeteria like a shark, weaving around tables and scattering onlookers.

"Not here, assholes." He shoved his way between the warring parties and pointed at two empty tables. "Sit your butts down. All of you." He jabbed his finger at each of The Aegis's people, one by one, ending with Eva. "You should all be getting afternoon assignments momentarily. Until then, behave."

A cacophony of chirps from Eva's and her colleagues' comms went off as if on cue. Thank God. The distraction cut through any remaining tension, no doubt aided by Draven standing there like a drill sergeant, ready to pummel anyone dumb enough to start shit up again.

"Oh, cool," Keeley said. "I have a meeting with DART's personnel management team." She gathered her things and stood. "What about you, Eva?"

"It should be a meeting with DART's media team…" Eva frowned down at her device. "Wait, no. Holy shit. I have one-on-one combat training."

"With who?"

Her pulse fluttered with excitement and more than a little anxiety. "With Logan."

"Ooh, lucky you."

"Yeah," she murmured. "Lucky me." Feeling like a teen being called to the principal's office, she threw her bag over her shoulder. "I have to go. I'm supposed to be there in fifteen minutes, and I need to change."

"Have fun." Keeley gave her a teasing wink, which Eva pretended not to see.

It only took her a few minutes in the locker room adjacent to the gym to put her hair up into a ponytail and change into a pair of khaki green sweatpants, a white Aegis T-shirt, and sneakers. When she was done, she hurried to the main facility, where Logan was waiting on the mat, his muscular upper body bare, his black sweats hanging loosely around his slim waist. His back was to her as he pounded on a practice dummy, his tan skin stretched taut over sculpted muscles that flexed and rolled with every graceful move.

"So," she called out. "How many strings did you have to pull to get me here?"

"None." Logan swung smoothly away from the dummy, and she drew in a sharp breath as his eyes zeroed in on her like an eagle. "I just asked. You need the training."

Man, everyone was full of insults today. "I told you, I've had plenty of training."

He strode toward her, his bare feet not making a sound on the floor mat. "You had the bare minimum."

"That's because I'm not out in the sewers fighting demons like most Guardians."

"You should still be prepared. Everyone in The Aegis has a target on their back, and you're a public figure. I can't believe you haven't had a dozen attempts on your life already."

She wasn't going to tell him that she had, indeed, had a couple. But that was back in her journalism days, and it certainly wasn't a dozen.

"Why do you care?"

He looked perplexed, his brow furrowed, his head canted just a teeny bit to the side, which was adorable because she doubted that he got flummoxed often. "It *was* you I was kissing last night, right?"

Sure. Before he weirded out and disappeared with another woman following a physical altercation. "So kissing equals caring?"

"You think I kiss a lot of females I don't care about? I might not know you very well, but I wouldn't have stayed as long as I did if I didn't like being with you."

His words made her stomach flutter, and she suddenly felt like she was back in high school talking to Tim McKinney, the star basketball player and total studmuffin.

Then an image of Logan in the hall with the skank she assumed was his ex popped into her head, and the flutters turned sour. Squaring her stance, she crossed her arms over her chest.

"What happened with that woman in the hall?"

The pale flecks in Logan's eyes glittered with stark warning.

"She's dangerous, Eva." He stepped onto the center of the mat and gestured for her to join him. "Really dangerous. That's why what happened last night can't happen again. She'll do whatever she can to hurt me. No one around me is safe."

His tone sent a chill up her spine as she moved closer, just beyond his reach. "She's a demon, isn't she?"

"Did you really think I'd throw a human woman against the wall?"

"Of course, not." Well, now she felt like an idiot. "I mean, I hoped not. Is she the jealous type?"

He snorted. "I'm pretty sure she *invented* jealousy. Literally." He gestured for Eva to come closer, but she stood her ground. If he was going to give her a beatdown, he would have to work for it. "Look, I don't want to talk about her. But I do want to give you a fighting chance against her, or someone like her."

"Again, why do you care? You don't even know—"

Suddenly, he was against her, his chest to hers, in a move so fast she'd only seen a blur. Her heart pounded violently against her breastbone, and her breath jammed in her throat as she looked up at him, his handsome face mere inches from hers.

"I've seen a lot of pain and death in my life, Eva. It's in my job description. But that doesn't mean I like it. Believe it or not, our goal here is to save humanity. Not watch it be destroyed by evil."

"I do believe it," she said breathlessly. "I believe you want to help people, but why me? Why me, specifically? Mason and Benji aren't exactly the best fighters in The Aegis either, but I don't see them here."

"They're assholes." Blunt, but accurate.

"They can be."

His voice dipped low, as dark and silky as the luxurious Belgian chocolate hot cocoa she'd had for breakfast. "And I don't want to fuck them."

She drew in a hot, harsh breath at the honest, raw jolt of his words. "But you just said we can't be together because that demon is a danger to me."

"Yeah, well, my head and my dick are in two different places." He shoved a frustrated hand through his hair and stepped back. "And if all goes well, the demon won't be a problem for long. In the meantime, you need to stay out of her crosshairs and work on defending yourself. So, let's get to work."

Chapter Eleven

Two sweaty, achy hours later, Eva was as exhausted as she'd ever been. Logan was a good teacher. Instinctive, patient, and encouraging, he'd focused on defensive moves more than offensive since, in his words, "most demons will have the upper hand against you." Insulting, but true. She had neither the speed nor the strength required of a warrior. Although, he'd sworn that she could, in time and with effort, develop both of those things to a much larger degree.

She just wasn't sure she wanted to put her focus there. She wasn't a total couch potato; she jogged two miles five days a week and did yoga every other day. But The Aegis hadn't hired her to be a fighter.

However, she had to admit that if Logan was the one teaching the classes, she might be more tempted to hone her battle skills.

Grateful to be off her watery legs, she sank onto a bench and chugged half a bottle of water. He didn't even look winded.

"You did great," he told her as he removed the cap from his own water bottle. "You're getting the hang of the elbow strikes and scrot-hooks."

She had to laugh at the scrot-hook. Using a knuckle to jab behind a demon's junk was brilliant. Who knew so many of the most common demons had hyper-sensitive spots in fairly easy-to-reach places? Was Carlos aware? If so, he hadn't taught her that in any of their training sessions.

"Scrot-hooks can be debilitating, but you gotta watch out for the spray." Logan took a swig of his water.

"Let's hope I never have to watch out for that." She shuddered. "Getting drenched in demon funk is not something I want to experience. Ever."

"It's not fun." He wiped his mouth with the back of his hand and then set the bottle on the bench. "Depending on the species, the stench can cling to you for days, no matter how much you shower."

"Speaking of a shower, that sounds like heaven right now." She revised her thought. "A shower and a nap."

"Did you not sleep well last night?"

"Bad dreams."

"Because of the nightmare demon?"

She fumbled her bottle and caught it just before it spilled all over her legs. "Excuse me?"

"I saw the protection glyph."

Dammit. She'd assumed he'd seen it through the slice in her shirt the last time they'd sparred, but she'd hoped he would think it was something less personal. Like the Cookie Monster, or Mickey Mouse, or the name of an ex.

"And you just happened to know what it was?"

A sheepish flush of pink spread across his cheeks. "I might have searched through DART's database this morning." He sank down cross-legged on the mat in front of her, his knees brushing her sweatpants. "What happened?"

"It's not a big deal." She really didn't want to talk about this. The bottle in her hand started shaking, so she steadied it on her thigh. "It was a long time ago."

He nodded thoughtfully. "When I was twelve, I went with some friends to a sleepover at Draven's house. One particular breed of nightmare demon is attracted to groups of people sleeping. I guess we won the lottery that night. The demon linked all our dreams together and tried to make us fight to the death."

"Holy crap." She gripped the bottle so fiercely it crinkled under her fingers. "What happened? Obviously, you're not dead."

"Before any of us were killed, my, ah, dog broke in and woke us."

He broke in? "You mean he barked and woke you?"

"What?" Logan blinked. "Oh. Yeah. He barked." He reached out and gathered the loose laces on one of her shoes. "It was all kinds of fucked up, but it only happened that once." He looked up at her as he tied a neat bow. "But you? It must have happened more than once if you got inked to protect yourself." When she nodded, he gave her foot a gentle squeeze. "How old?"

"I was in first grade."

He swore softly. "I'm sorry."

She wanted to hate his pity. Pity was one of the reasons she never told anyone about the nightmares or the demon that had haunted her since shortly before her sixth birthday. But he was the first person she'd met who could relate even a little to what she'd gone through.

And, truthfully, it felt good to have someone attempt to comfort her. She couldn't remember the last time anyone had done that. She'd been raised by a mother and father who were from the buck-up-and-stop-whining school of parenting. And she was pretty sure The Aegis invented it, because you could get your arm bitten off by a demon, and the response would be, "*That must have hurt, but you have another arm to fight with, so get back out there.*"

So, yeah, for the first time, she wasn't tempted to change the subject.

"Thank you," she said. "The ward keeps the demon from entering my dreams, but it doesn't keep it away."

He scowled. "What do you mean? You see it?"

"No." She shivered. "But I can feel it when I'm sleeping. It's like it's tapping on the walls of my dreams, trying to get in. Wakes me up a lot, and sometimes I have night terrors. I kind of hate sleeping." She spent a fortune on undereye concealer, eye masks, and cucumbers.

Toying idly with her laces, he contemplated that for a moment. "Has anyone watched you sleep? To see if the demon is physically nearby?"

She looked up sharply. "What do you mean? It could be standing by my bed all night?" Holy shit, she was never sleeping again.

"It's pretty unlikely," he said. "Most species haunt their victims through a psychic link from inside Sheoul."

Okay, that calmed her pulse down a little. "When my parents first began suspecting that I was being stalked by some sort of evil entity, they contacted The Aegis, and they said a demon's spirit was haunting me, not a physical demon. They sent one of their people to tattoo the ward around my navel."

It had been terrifying and painful, and she'd kept her eyes closed the entire time. Afterward, though, her parents had taken her for pizza and ice cream, and it had been one of the few times they'd showered her in cuddles instead of buck-up bullshit.

He nodded. "That's where a lot of demons enter and exit. But if it was a spirit, why didn't they contact DART? We could have trapped it and saved you a tattoo."

Huh. "You know, I didn't think of that. I'll have to ask my parents." She snorted. "Not looking forward to that conversation. They don't like being reminded that their lives were disrupted for ten months, even though the whole thing is how they ended up partnering their law firm with The Aegis."

"They're upset about the inconvenience to *them*? You're the one who was probably so tormented you couldn't sleep. It only happened to me that one time, and it was a month before I could sleep a full night through."

"Did your parents think you were nuts?" Like hers had, until she began to get up in the mornings with cuts, bruises, and even a broken wrist. At that point, they finally set up a camera to catch whatever was going on.

His fond smile gave him a boyish charm, but there was nothing boyish about the deep rumble of his voice when he spoke.

"They took turns staying up with me. Mom would make cookies or popcorn and we'd watch old movies. Dad liked to drag me to the gym and make me work out until I fell asleep on the mat. Then he'd sit there all night while I slept."

"Your parents sound really cool."

"They're good together. My sister and I had happy childhoods. Lots of travel and big events with the extended family. What about you? Do you have a big family?"

"Not really. I'm an only child and both of my parents are kind of estranged from their families. They both came from money, but neither set of grandparents approved of my parents' marriage, so no one talks to anyone. It's sad and stupid."

The door at the far end of the gym opened, and loud voices filled the space as Carlos, Sig, and Benji filed in. Carlos waved, Benji nodded. Sig gave her his lame *whattup* gesture.

They all headed toward the weapons room.

Eva checked the time. "I should probably go. I've got a lot of meetings tomorrow to prep for."

"That's no fun." Logan pushed to his feet in a single, nimble motion and flipped a nearby basketball into his hands with his foot. "I don't know if you noticed the insanity outside—"

"You mean the massive crowds, horses, and people with crossbows dressed in medieval costumes?"

"That." Logan bounced the ball from hand to hand and squared up with the basket on the other side of the gym. "It's Ommegang. Big yearly festival. You should check it out after work. And the Grand Platz and Mannekin Pis are not to be missed while you're in Brussels."

"Are you offering to show me around?" The moment the words were out of her mouth, she cringed. "Sorry, forgot about your evil ex-girlfriend."

He hurled the ball, and she wasn't surprised to see that, even at this distance, he made the shot. "You should still go. I can meet you in your room afterward. I'll make sure I'm not followed. But you should get a new room on a different floor."

She wasn't sure she'd heard him right. "Meet me afterward... for...?"

"Just sleep, I promise," he said, and she couldn't decide if she was relieved or disappointed. "I'll hang out in one of the chairs while you get some rest. I might be able to capture your nightmare demon."

She swallowed tightly. What he was offering was incredible. To finally be free of that thing and no longer dread sleeping or need to take a pill to sleep at all...it would be a miracle.

"You...would do that?"

"It's nothing I don't do for a living."

He looked like he was about to say something else when Carlos jogged up to them carrying a wicked-looking edged blade.

"Hey, man, I don't suppose you can show me how this thing works?"

"Sure thing." Logan turned to Eva. "See you later. Text me after the festival."

He winked, and her belly fluttered all the way to the showers. Man, she hadn't had it this bad for a guy in years.

If she had, she couldn't remember, because Logan had just reduced every guy she'd ever been with to faceless wastes of time.

"You're going to stay the night with Eva to *watch her sleep?*" Draven laughed—harder than necessary to make his point, in Logan's opinion. "You expect me to buy that bullshit?"

Logan threw some money onto the pub table he'd been sharing with Shanea and Draven for the last two hours as he waited for Eva's text. His comms had just lit up with her message and new room number.

"Just sleep." Logan grabbed the bag his cousin Leilani had dropped off and scooted his chair back on the uneven floor planks of the historic Belgian building. "Shit's too complicated for anything else."

"Because she's human?" Shanea's two dozen bracelets jingled as she reached for her hard cider. "Or because she's an Aegi?"

Draven drained his ale. "Human." He signaled the server for another. "Logan got hardcore screwed over by a human back in our college days. I warned him not to tell her who he was. Humans can't handle that kind of shit."

No, they couldn't. Even the ones who had a thing for vamps or werewolves drew the line at demons. As Logan found out.

Shan idly tapped on her glass with a long, black-lacquered nail. "So, don't tell her."

"I'm not sleeping with her unless I tell her, and I'm not telling her, so I'm not sleeping with her. Simple."

"Why do you have to tell her?" Shanea asked. "I mean, you're just having fun, right?"

Right. But not being entirely human seemed like one of those things that would make him an asshole if he didn't disclose it upfront. Like, he could see himself posting to *AITAH* on a media site and asking if sleeping with someone without telling them he was part demon made him an asshole. And being told that, *yep, you're an asshole.*

"Because she'll find out who I am eventually, and she'll freak the hell out. I learned that lesson the hard way."

"Boy howdy, did he ever," Draven said. "That bitch tore his heart out and ran it through a woodchipper. Total carnage. Like, if that had happened to me, it probably would have triggered my demon."

Logan punched his buddy in the shoulder as he stood. "It would not. You're tougher than that."

Draven had sworn he'd never let his emotions overcome his willpower to remain in human form and live a normal life in the earthly realm. Like Logan, Draven had been raised by loving parents who'd taught him how to live among humans the way their kind had done for millennia—as long as nothing triggered their inner vengeance demon.

No one wanted that. The gentlest of them, once triggered, became Ufelskala Tier-Five demons, existing solely to deliver vengeance. Their first victims were those who triggered them. After that, they doled out gruesome vengeance for those who hired, summoned, or asked them. For their entire thousand-year lifespan.

Logan could think of few fates worse than that.

Draven gave him a skeptical eye roll. "Heartbreak is the reason most vengeance demons lose their shit."

Shanea covered his hand with hers and gave him the biggest, sappiest puppy-dog eyes. "Which is why I swore I would never hurt him."

"Aw, how cute," Logan said, his voice carrying an unwelcome thread of bitterness. He was happy for his friend, but damn, he'd love to have what Draven and Shan had. What his parents had. What all his aunts and uncles had. "Maybe you two should come with me and get your own room."

Draven kissed his fiancée. More cuteness. "Speaking of hotel rooms, aren't you worried that Lilith will show up?"

Logan shifted the shopping bag to his other hand. "Nah. Eva moved her room to the fourth floor next to the stairwell. And I'll cover my tracks and make sure I'm not followed. Plus, I think Lilith's focus is on my cousins right now." He held up the bag. "When Leilani brought the blouse for Eva, she said someone broke into her flat and decorated her bedroom in erotic demon art."

Shanea's pierced eyebrow arched, the little gold ring glinting in the candlelight. "What's erotic demon art?"

"I made the mistake of asking that question too," Logan said. "Turns out, it's a bunch of genitals strewn around. Nailed to the walls. Glued to the ceiling. Things like that. Limos said it sounds exactly like something Lilith would do."

"Holy shit." Draven grimaced. "That's messed up."

After seeing Lilith's artistic and sexual tastes in her shrine, Logan agreed with Limos. "Limos and Arik are insisting that Lani stay with them until Lilith gets taken out."

"Well, if you need anything, let me know." Draven grinned. "And let me know how much you *sleep* tonight with Eva."

There was no point in trying to convince his friend that nothing was going to happen, so he left the pub, the sound of Draven's and Shanea's laughter following him out.

He hurried to the hotel, taking an indirect, winding route while keeping an eye out for anyone who might be tracking him. He arrived at Eva's door without incident, if he didn't count the demon spirit he'd captured a few blocks away. The thing had been darting between unsuspecting restaurant patrons seated outside, sucking their energy or brainwaves or whatever, when Logan casually tossed a *decipula* between tables and watched the screeching fiend get slurped into the trap.

Every diner was completely oblivious to the drama, and that thing had been *loud*.

The hotel room door opened just enough for Eva to peek out. "Password?"

He held up the bag. "New blouse."

"That's correct." Smiling, she swung open the door and stood there in a fluffy, knee-length white robe that made him wonder what she was wearing underneath. "You may enter."

He brushed past her and handed her the bag. Like a giddy child, she dug through it and pulled out a tissue-wrapped parcel.

"Ooh, this is nice," she said as she unfolded the blouse. "It's nearly identical to the one you sliced up."

"I gave it air vents. You were hot and sweaty. I did you a favor."

She laughed and pulled a box from the bag. "What's this?"

"I picked it up today." He dropped his backpack next to the chair where he'd be spending the night. "Thought you needed a souvenir from Brussels."

She opened the box, and her full lips parted in surprise. "It's beautiful," she breathed as she lifted the delicate gold necklace with her fingers.

"It's a yellow iris. The city's symbol."

"I love it." She held it out to him. "Help me put it on?"

He took the necklace and waited for her to turn around. "Your robe's collar is in the way. Can you tug it down?"

"Better." She dropped the robe to the floor. The white fluff pooled around her bare legs. Long, bare legs that went on forever, all the way to the hem of her sapphire satin sleep shorts. She wore a matching tank top with thin spaghetti straps he could bite through with his teeth.

Lifting her hair, she waited.

Reaching over her head, he settled the necklace around her slender throat. The scent of gardenia soap wafted off her smooth skin as he fastened the clasp.

"I had one of DART's mages infuse it with a ward that'll repel succubi." Although, probably not one of Lilith's strength. Still, a ward couldn't hurt.

"Your ex is a succubus?" She swung around, her eyes flashing with surprise.

"Something like that."

"What happened between you two?"

Geez, how often in one day did he have to discuss this? "Let's just say she couldn't accept who I am. I made the mistake of trusting her with something personal, and she couldn't deal." Of course, he wasn't talking about Lilith, but his ex had already taken up some headspace thanks to Draven, so he ran with the truth, even if it wasn't about the female Eva was talking about.

"She sounds like a huge bitch," she said. "I'm sorry you have to deal with her stalker ass now."

"Yeah." His gaze fell to the iris resting at the neckline of her top, just above her breasts. She was braless, and the outline of her nipples pressing against the silky fabric, nearly made him groan. Instead, he tore his gaze away and gestured to his pack. "I should brush my teeth and get ready."

"Of course." She glanced down at her comms. "It's past my bedtime, and I'm still jet-lagged." Her teeth caught her bottom lip, a pensive expression creeping into her face. "How is this going to work, anyway?"

He snared his pack. "You sleep, I wait. If the demon's spirit shows up, I'll catch it."

She climbed onto the bed, giving him a tantalizing glimpse of her perky ass before she swung her legs under the covers. "How will you know it's here? Some fancy DART equipment?"

"It's not fancy, and you shouldn't hear a thing."

"How long will you wait for it?"

"As long as it takes, Eva." He swung the pack over his shoulder and headed to the bathroom. "As long as it takes."

Chapter Twelve

Eva wasn't even close to being asleep when Logan came out of the bathroom and settled into the chair next to the bed. Leaning back, he stretched his long legs in front of him and crossed them at the ankles.

"You okay with the light off?" he asked softly.

"Yep."

He reached over and flipped off the reading light, plunging the room into darkness. A few seconds later, her enchanted Aegis tattoo kicked in, allowing her to see shapes and shadows other humans couldn't.

"Logan?"

"Yeah."

"Thank you. Even if you don't catch the demon, I appreciate that you're willing to do this."

"I'll catch it, Eva. If it doesn't show up tonight, then the next night. Or the next. I won't give up, I promise."

Her heart thudded so fiercely she swore the bed rattled. When was the last time someone had made a promise like that to her? One that was instantly comforting and made her feel safe? Probably when she was a kid, terrified of having the symbol tattooed onto her belly, and her mom had held her hand and promised that everything would be okay.

Eva had believed her parents, and for the most part, things *had* been okay. In fact, shortly afterward, the family law firm went international, and her parents took on The Aegis as clients. They'd moved from their upper-middle-class neighborhood in Boston to an ultra-wealthy suburb outside DC. She'd gone to elite schools, got great grades, and was eventually accepted into the prestigious new School of Journalism and Mass Communication at Yale. The demon had been mostly forgotten.

Except at night, when Eva's sleep came in fits and starts, her dreams interrupted by the fear that a demon was scratching to get in.

"Logan?"

"Yeah."

"I know you work in the Spirit Management department, but I'm not clear on what you do. The Aegis doesn't have one." Probably because The Aegis hadn't found a way to reliably and efficiently collect and imprison souls.

"I mostly hunt and trap demonic spirits. I perform a lot of exorcisms too."

The Aegis had Guardians who specialized in exorcisms, but since most humans were possessed by living, physical demons, the goal was to free the human and send the demon back to Sheoul. If the entity possessing the human turned out to be a spirit, DART's Spirit Management team was called in to handle it.

"What drew you to that job?"

She heard him shift in the chair. "I thought you were jet-lagged." His voice was low, soothing, and teasing at the same time.

"I am." She yawned, her body proving her words. "But I'm concerned about your qualifications."

He chuckled, and she wished she wasn't facing the far wall. She'd have loved to see his smile. Closing her eyes, she imagined it. Ah, he had the most kissable lips…

"I knew from birth that battling demons in some way was my destiny," he said, and her eyes popped open. Destiny? "I guess I always figured I'd work for DART since half my friends and family do."

"You have family at DART?"

"A cousin. Scotty. You might have met her. The rest, the friends, are pretty much family too." He shifted again, the soft rasp of his shirt or pants against the upholstery sounding stupidly erotic. It made her wonder what sound the chair would make if she straddled him, her satiny pjs the only thing between his skin and hers.

"Okay, but why Spirit Management? What made you want to catch the spirits of dead demons?"

There was a long silence, filled only by the increasingly loud thud of her pulse in her ears. Finally, he inhaled. Exhaled. Spoke softly.

"I discovered I had a talent for it. But the story involves college and a girl, and I don't want to talk about it."

Disappointing, but she understood. "It's okay. I guess I should try to get some sleep. But, Logan?"

"Yeah."

"Will you wake me up after you catch the demon?"

"Sure. But why?"

"I don't know," she said honestly. "I guess I just want to see if I feel any different. Thank you again. Good night."

"Sweet dreams."

She hadn't had sweet dreams since the day the nightmare demon took them from her. Thanks to Logan, she now had hope, and for the first time in years, she fell asleep the moment she closed her eyes.

Logan didn't have long to wait.

Eva had barely been asleep for an hour when he felt the telltale tingle of a spiritual presence. He rolled the *decipula* around in his palm as he watched her breathe. His nocturnal vision was excellent, thanks to Lilith's demon DNA. Could be Reaver's too, he supposed. Some angels could apparently see as well in the dark as they did in the light. No doubt his grandfather was one of them.

Eva snored lightly, an adorable catch in her throat. For just a moment, he wondered what she'd do if he told her the truth about himself. Would she freak out?

Of course, she'd freak out. The question was, how much? Not that it mattered. He wasn't giving his heart to a human ever again. Especially not one who worked for The Aegis. That was a mistake he wouldn't make twice.

Eva's breath hitched. Took on a new, frantic rhythm. Logan stilled. Watching. Waiting.

Out of the darkness, a blurry, transparent form took shape. A disembodied torso with long arms and claws. Floating above that was a spiked skull with a malformed jaw and a mouth full of sharp teeth.

"Damn," he whispered. "You're an ugly bastard."

The thing didn't appear to hear. It floated toward Eva, its claws outstretched. Drool dripped from its gaping mouth onto the comforter. And Logan cursed. Until the bedding was washed, anyone sleeping in this room would suffer nightmares. He'd have to take it with him when he left.

Logan bounced the soul trap in his palm and planned the perfect toss. Head shots were best to minimize having to listen to them scream.

"Head shot, it is..."

The demon's head cranked around with a hiss. "You can see me?"

In answer, Logan flicked the trap at the fiend. Lightning-fast, it evaded the head shot, but the little marble caught the base of its torso.

"No!" it screamed as the trap sucked in its blurry body. It clawed at the device, it's long arms flailing. "We did not agree to this!"

We? Agree to what?

The demon's spirit wailed so loudly Logan winced, his ears ringing painfully.

And then it was gone, and the marble plopped to the bed, its work done. He tucked it into his pocket with the other from tonight and then threw his bag over his shoulder.

Eva sighed softly into her pillow, and the slightest smile turned up her lips. What was she dreaming about? He didn't want to wake her, but he'd promised. So, he went down on his haunches next to the mattress and laid his hand on her shoulder.

"Eva?"

"Hmm?" Her eyes flickered open and settled into slits. "Logan?"

"It's me. The demon is gone."

He expected joy. A smile. Something other than the sudden tear that beaded in the corner of her eye.

"Finally," she whispered. "Finally, I can sleep."

Her lids dropped, and so did the tear, and then she was snoring.

Chapter Thirteen

Eva got the best night's sleep of her life.

She barely remembered Logan waking her, but she knew the moment she woke up that the demon that had haunted her for over twenty years was gone.

It was as if a weighted blanket had been tossed off the bed and now, she was sleeping on a cloud.

She owed Logan so much. So, so much. Although she'd have to ask what he'd done with the comforter.

She was so alert and awake that she passed on her morning coffee and drank water with lemon instead. Then she left a message for her mom. She couldn't wait to tell her the demon was gone. She no longer cared why her parents didn't contact DART about capturing it a long time ago. The thing was in the past, and that was where it would stay.

After that, she met with a former Aegi named Tayla at DART HQ, which had been…unpleasant.

"I'll bet The Aegis tells you I betrayed them." Tayla stood near the window of *her Special Investigative Unit office, her arms crossed over her chest, her green eyes spitting fire.*

Eva kept her voice even, conducting the meeting like an interview because it was. She was even recording the conversation. "We're taught that you were supposed to blow up a demon hospital, but you didn't because you were seduced by an incubus who slaughtered several Guardians."

"They were killed in battle, fair and square because they were trying to kill us,"

she snapped. "And I didn't fail to blow up the hospital. Your precious Aegis set me up as a suicide bomber. So fuck off with that shit."

Suicide bomber? How ridiculous. "I'm sorry, but I don't believe they intended for you to kill yourself."

"Then you're delusional. Everyone is expendable to The Aegis. Everyone."

Nope, it had not gone well at all.

Now, she was settling her nerves on one of DART's two outdoor patios. Well, she was *attempting* to settle her nerves. Maja had placed a holocall thirty seconds after Eva sat down with a much-needed coffee. She hoped the Elder would spill the beans about The Aegis's choice for their Chief Spokesperson, but if the woman knew anything, she kept the information to herself. She was more interested in discussing DART.

"How many demons have you seen?"

I don't know. Everyone looks human.

"How well trained do their people seem to be?"

Very.

"Have you met the traitors, Kynan Morgan and Tayla Mancuso?"

I met Tayla.

She'd only seen Mr. Morgan in passing. And from the way everyone at DART talked about him, he was an excellent boss who ran a tight ship. They said he was liberal with praise, fair with criticism, and unforgiving of incompetence. He certainly didn't sound like the man who had betrayed The Aegis, stolen its treasures, and sold it out to demons and the Four Horsemen of the Apocalypse.

When Eva said as much, albeit a little more gently, Maja's reply had been, "Not all villains wear black hats."

Eva didn't mention that Kynan had been wearing a black DART baseball cap at the time she'd seen him.

"One last thing before I go," Maja said. "Will you be available for Jennifer to do a short Q&A with you tomorrow night? We want to post something about the joint project with DART. She'll send the questions to you today. Nothing hardball. It's going to be a puff piece to show the world that we're one big, happy demon-fighting family."

"Are people going to believe that after the Boston incident?"

Maja waved her hand as if shooing a pesky fly. "We're trying to get that out of the headlines. Turns out that lady walking her dog near the scene got video of one of our guys stumbling out of the building and shouting that his partner was dead just as two DART agents arrived. It destroys the narrative that DART took forever to get there and cost the life of an Aegi."

Unsure how to respond, Eva merely nodded. She'd been around the media world long enough to know that was how things worked. Everyone wanted to put forth a narrative that made them look good. The first version of events usually got traction, and even if it turned out to be completely wrong, there would always be a percentage of people who wouldn't see the new information or would believe the new information was fake or a lie, even if it *was* the truth.

So, she wasn't surprised. But she *was* disappointed. The Aegis held itself above all others as the guardians and defenders of humankind. The keepers of truth. The just and righteous.

Everyone is expendable to The Aegis. Everyone.

Shoving Tayla's condemnation aside, Eva finally replied. "I wasn't aware we'd put that out there."

"We didn't," Maja said. "But that was the takeaway by several media outlets."

Of course, it was. Most likely by design. And The Aegis would let that narrative ride until forced to correct it in a statement that would be buried so deep few would see it.

"So, will you be available?" Maja asked.

Eva checked her schedule and nodded. "I'll take a look at the questions and get back to Jennifer if I have any concerns."

Maja smiled. "Excellent. You are all doing a great job. We'll talk later."

The feed went dark, and Eva started when Keeley appeared across the table from her.

"Oh, hey. I didn't see you."

"Sorry, it sounded like you were wrapping things up with whoever you were talking to."

"I was." Eva glanced at the time. "We've got twenty minutes before the group session upstairs. Wanna grab something quick to eat?"

"I actually came to ask you the same thing. I hate walking around here by myself. People look at me like I'm a pile of demon shit they almost stepped in. It's so rude."

She gathered her things and stood. "Imagine what DART's people are putting up with at Aegis HQ."

"Well, *they* deserve it," Keeley said with a snooty sniff. "We don't."

Eva had noticed the dirty looks and insults spoken under people's breath, but none of it bothered her. She had a skin toughened by a structured upbringing and a career in the public eye. Heck, her emails had to be screened before she read them because she got so many whackos sending her disturbing shit, from insults and threats to marriage proposals.

A few glares wouldn't register on her annoyance meter at all.

They headed back inside, and as they strolled through the wide corridors, Keeley nudged her with her elbow.

"So…how did the workout with Logan go yesterday? I saw you leaving the gym, and it looked like you got taken to the mat a few times."

"I did. And it was about as humiliating as you'd think."

"Humiliating…and…?"

Eva's cheeks heated at the memory of being pinned beneath Logan. Only it wasn't embarrassment making her face feel sunburned. It was lust. Pure, unadulterated lust.

"I don't want to talk about it." Or the fact that he'd been in her hotel room again last night.

"Hmm," Keeley teased. "Must have been good."

Eva sighed as they turned the corner. A buttery cinnamon scent mingled with the heady aroma of DART's freshly brewed coffee made her stomach rumble.

Raised voices interrupted her drooling, and she paused, waiting for Keeley to catch up. "Does that sound like Sig? And Carlos?"

Keeley gave up digging for whatever she was looking for in her tote and hurried to catch up as another round of shouting fired up. "Definitely Sig. And Benji too. I think they're in the cafeteria fighting with people again."

"A Guardian is dead because of you," Sig bellowed. "I want to know who was there."

A chorus of "fuck offs" rose, and then the sound of crashing furniture. Broken glass. And fists on flesh.

"Oh, shit." Eva sprinted to the cafeteria entrance, Keeley on her heels. She skidded around the corner, thankful she was in flats today.

"*Demons!* They're fucking demons!"

She came to a hard stop, barely avoiding being brained by a thrown chair. And then came a sound that chilled her to the bone. One she'd only heard once during a grisly live demonstration last month. But it was a noise she'd never forget.

Ch-pop! Ch-pop! Ch-pop!

Silence stretched. Then came the screams. And the blood. It streamed and pooled from the two shredded bodies on the floor, two DART people. Two *demons*.

Holy shit, Shanea was a demon? And Noah? She'd seen both of them just an hour ago, looking perfectly human. Now, Shanea had black horns, and Noah had scales on his ruined face.

"What the—?"

Sig stood there, the new Aegis pistol in his hand. His stunned expression slowly morphed into a mask of horror as he realized what he'd just done. Benji, Carlos, and Mason had frozen in shock, their wide eyes shifting between Sig and the two dead demons.

Everyone had frozen.

And then Sig charged for the exit.

"Sig!" Carlos yelled as the cafeteria erupted in shouts and screams once again.

"Fucking Aegis!"

"Kill those fuckers!"

Oh, shit.

"Run!" Mason grabbed Eva and Keeley and flung them toward the side door.

Threats following them, they ran, everyone scrambling after Carlos, who sprinted toward a crowd down the street.

"This way!" Carlos called out as they ducked and weaved through festival chaos. Costumed horses pulled carts, and people in medieval garb danced through the streets. And thank God for all of it.

Eva ran next to Keeley, who maneuvered better in heels than Eva did in flats.

"Thank God for whatever this festival is," Keeley shouted over at Eva as they passed a band of colorful jesters playing instruments Eva had never seen. "It's gotta be Divine intervention. We have right on our sides."

Keeley was trying to be comforting, but her words just settled in the pit of Eva's stomach.

A *lot* of dead Guardians had had right on their sides.

Logan, thank you again for what you did for me last night. I don't know how to repay you, but I was thinking maybe I could start tonight by buying you dinner. I know there's the whole vengeful demon ex thing to worry about, but I'm sure you're creative enough to find a way we could still get a bite to eat. What do you say? ~Eva

Logan glanced down at the text that had popped up an hour ago on his comms. He hadn't replied yet and wasn't sure *how* to reply. Because while he was creative enough to find a way to have dinner without worrying about Lilith, that would involve telling Eva the truth and taking her somewhere crowded, like Paris, Milan, or somewhere remote and accessible only by donkey or Harrowgate.

That would never happen. Which was yet another reason he should shut this shit down now before his heart got too involved.

Might be too late.

Fuck that. It wasn't too late. He and Eva just had to let things cool down.

Maybe Lilith will die today.

Awesome, but that didn't solve the problem of Eva being human. And an Aegi.

Suddenly, klaxons blared, shrieking from every alarm in the building. His comms unit screeched.

CODE 2: CAFETERIA.

Code 2? Multiple casualties? What the hell? He was out of his chair and office in three strides. The open hallway looked down onto the first floor and magnified the sounds of shouts and screams from below. He ran for the stairs, taking them three at a time. The moment he hit the landing, Logan summoned his sword.

Armed security forces charged toward the cafeteria, where a crowd had gathered. A few people ran out the side exit while others righted furniture or just stood around staring at the smashed dishes. Broken chairs. Blood splattered everywhere.

And two bodies lying on the floor.

Logan could barely process the sight of Blade, his *dermoire* glowing, pumping his healing juice into Noah's shredded remains, and Mace performing CPR on Shanea. Half of Shanea's head was gone, and with every pump of Mace's fists, blood spilled out of her mouth.

"No," he rasped. "Noah. *Shanea.*"

How? How could this have happened?

Blade cursed and wheeled around to Shanea, his boot slipping in her blood. Mace backed off as Blade clamped his hand down on what was left of one of her arms.

Blade's attempt was pointless; Logan could see it in the male's grief-stricken eyes. But he had to try. Logan got that. He so got that.

A piercing, agonized roar silenced the room. Draven shoved people aside, mowing others down as he rushed to his fiancée. He dropped to his knees, tears streaming from his eyes.

"It's okay, baby. It's okay." But behind him, Blade shook his head. He hadn't really needed to.

"What happened here?" Kynan rushed into the cafeteria. "What the fuck happened?"

"It was the Aegi," Cyan snarled, her violet eyes damp with tears. She and Shanea had been BFFs for years. "They have a weapon, some kind of gun—"

"Impossible," Mace said. "Bullets can't kill vampires and demons."

Mace was right—mostly—and yet, two people were dead, and none of them belonged to the few demon species vulnerable to human bullets.

"I hate to tell you this," Cyan snapped, "but they did. Somehow, bullets killed them."

"Where are the Aegi?"

One of the cafeteria servers pointed at the side door with a trembling hand. "They took off through there. Cowards."

Kynan nodded. "Okay, everyone split up. We're going to find those assholes."

Mace raised his hand. "One question—"

"Alive," Kynan interrupted. "I want them all, and I want them alive."

"But—"

Kynan rounded on Mace, but when he spoke, it was to everyone. "Right now, The Aegis is the asshole in this situation. If we kill a bunch of Guardians out of revenge, we're the asshole, and the world will turn on us. We have to be better than they are. But trust me," he growled, "they're going to get what they deserve."

Chapter Fourteen

Somehow, Eva and her team were able to lose their pursuers without losing each other.

Carlos led them through some narrow streets and then down a cramped, gated tunnel. At the end, a door led them into a small house.

They stopped inside the building, breaths heaving.

"Where?" she gasped, looking around at the empty living space. "Where are we?"

"It's an old Aegis cell house. It's no longer used, but it's available for anyone to lay low if they need it."

"How the hell do you know this shit?" Sig asked between panting breaths.

Carlos closed the door and engaged the locks. "Eva's our mouthpiece, Benji's our tech specialist, and you're Daddy's spoiled frat boy spy, but I'm our tactical and security lead. The moment you killed those DART people, this became my operation." Carlos cuffed Sig in the head as he turned away from the door. "And I research *everything* before I go on assignment. Don't get in my way, kid. Now, tell me what the fuck that was back there."

"They were demons," Sig said sullenly. "Didn't you see them?"

"I saw." Mason coughed, wheezing as he tried to catch his breath. "Shanea. Her eyes. So red. And her skin…" He shuddered.

"It went pale and transparent. It was so gross," Sig said. "And that guy, I swear he grew fangs."

"He did," Carlos snapped. "He was some sort of lizard mother-fucker. And you shot him. You shot two damn DART agents." He reached out and snatched the pistol out of Sig's jacket pocket. "You fucking idiot! Do you know what you've done?"

"They were going to kill us," Sig whined. "They started it. It was self-defense."

"Self-defense, my ass." Carlos thrust the weapon at Eva. "Put this in your bag. And then we all need to calm down and get our stories straight."

"They were *definitely* going to kill us after I wasted their people," Sig muttered.

"Shut it, Sig." Carlos tapped on his wrist comms. "I'm going to report this and get instructions."

Eva peeked out the window while Carlos contacted his handler. She could call hers, but Carlos and his Elder had been designated as the initial contact team in case of emergency.

The alley was empty of everything but an orange tiger cat that was clueless about the drama playing out inside the building. Eva stood motionless, watching for anyone with two feet—or hooves.

She heard the telltale beep of a holocall and turned to see Elder Philip's balding, life-sized projection standing in the room.

"What happened?" he barked.

Carlos filled him in with a few additions from Sig, Mason, and Benji. By the time they were done, the Elder was furious. His vulgar verbal storm made everyone but Eva shrink back. She was already plastered against the wall.

She looked out the window again. An elderly lady shuffled down the cobblestone path toward them, and Eva's heart nearly stopped beating. The lady could be a demon in disguise. Or a shifter of some sort. Every step closer brought Eva nearer to panic, but finally, just as she was getting ready to raise the alarm, the woman entered a house a couple of doors down. The cat meowed. Eva released a shaky breath.

Philip's cursing stopped, but he was no less angry. "Where are you idiots now?"

"The old Antwerp House," Carlos said. "A few blocks south of DART."

"A few blocks? They'll find you. You need to get out of there."

"Excuse me," Eva said, stepping away from the window, "but shouldn't we go back? We should clear this up with DART instead of running. Running makes us look guilty."

Philip turned to Sig. "You claim this was self-defense? Can DART prove it wasn't?"

"Probably not." Sig ground his jaw. "I mean, their people turned into demons. We had the right to defend ourselves."

"Who started it?"

No one said anything. Philip turned to Eva. "Eva?"

"By the time Keeley and I got into the cafeteria, it was over. I didn't see anything, sir."

"Sig started it," Benji blurted, ignoring Sig's glare. "He started mouthing off about DART being responsible for Robert Lynch's death in Boston."

Philip swore under his breath. "Who threw the first punch?"

"Their guy. Noah," Mason said. "It went to hell after that."

"Okay, let me convene the Elders. Hold tight. I'll get back to you as soon as I can. Stay safe." His feed died, and he winked out.

"Man, we're fucked," Mason said.

Eva peeked out the window and let out a strangled curse. Two people she recognized from DART were moving toward the building, their heads on swivels, their eyes scouring every stone and blade of grass. The cat scurried into a bush.

"It's DART," she whispered. "We're *really* fucked."

"I swear, Sig, I'm going to beat your ass if we survive this." Carlos rushed over and looked out. "Pretty sure the big dude is a werewolf. The back door," he snapped. "Everyone. Now! If we get separated, we meet at Ashford House in Ghent. And get the silver ends of your stangs ready. Werewolves don't die easily, even in human form."

Chapter Fifteen

In all her life, Eva had never been as afraid as she was right now. She ran with the group, ducking in and out of alleys and blending in with the crowds of tourists and festivalgoers.

"This way," Sig called out, gesturing to a taxi van down the street. "Hurry!"

They scrambled after him, doing their best to move quickly but without drawing attention. Eva cursed when a horse-drawn carriage cut her off, and she had to stop, trapped between the conveyance and a herd of people exiting a chocolate shop.

Suddenly, a hand came down on her elbow, and she nearly screamed.

"Eva? Eva Tennant?"

She wheeled around, hand clenched around her stang inside her tote, expecting to come face-to-face with a DART demon or something. Instead, a smiling fifty-something woman carrying several shopping bags greeted her.

"Oh, my gosh, it's you! Can I get a selfie?"

Her companion, a woman with twice as many bags, looked her up and down before exclaiming, "It *is* you. I saw in the news that you were here on some kind of exchange program with DART."

"Ah, yes…" Eva kept moving, but her colleagues were already loading into the van. "Yes. I'm sorry, I have to go—"

Sig closed the sliding door, and the taxi pulled away from the curb—without her. Those *jerks*.

Holy shit, she was in trouble. Panic frayed the edges of her control, threatening to send her spiraling into paralysis. She'd always rallied easily under pressure, but right now, her brain raced, and the noise all around her was deafening.

"You have no idea how much I've been looking forward to your updates."

"You're so much prettier in person."

"I hear Jennifer is stepping down. Are you going to be the next Aegis Chief Spokesperson?"

She blinked at the women. "What?"

Their confused expressions grounded her a little, enough to take a deep breath and plaster on a shaky smile. She was supposed to be representing The Aegis, and these people were taking pictures and videos. It wouldn't look good if she was panting and acting squirrelly.

"Oh, I really am sorry," she said. "I'm on my way to a meeting. I'm sure you'll be hearing about how The Aegis and DART exchange is going *very* soon, and—"

Logan.

Oh, dear God. He was parting the crowd like a crocodile through water, his gaze dark and fixed on hers. His shoulders rolled under a fitted black tee, and his biceps flexed as he clenched and unclenched his fists.

She almost wished anyone else had found her, partly because she hated the disappointment in his expression, but mostly because no one else would have made her pulse pound like it was. Like her veins would burst at any moment.

It was pointless to run, and truth be told, she didn't think she could. Fight, flight, or freeze had kicked in, and the soles of her shoes might as well have been frozen to the sidewalk.

Somehow, she found her voice long enough to say to the crowd, "And here's my escort to the meeting."

Swallowing, she walked calmly toward Logan, hoping no one could tell that her knees were wobbly.

"Let's not make a scene," she murmured as he seized her upper arm.

"Let's not make demands," he growled through clenched teeth, but he did flash the people a friendly smile as he guided her in the direction of DART headquarters. He yanked her aside once they were away from the crowd. "Where are the others?"

"I don't know."

His lips peeled back from his teeth in a silent snarl. "You just killed two of my friends. Do *not* bullshit me."

"I didn't—"

"It doesn't matter who pulled the fucking trigger, Eva." He tugged her back onto the sidewalk. "You have a lot of explaining to do."

Her wrist comms beeped, but before she could take the call, Logan's long fingers encircled her wrist, holding her as firmly as cuffs. He clicked the clasp and slipped the device into his pocket. "You don't get to talk to anyone."

Still gripping her wrist, he started walking again.

"Excuse me? You don't have that kind of authority. You're not a cop."

"In most countries, we actually *do* have authority over demon-related incidents." He halted, swinging around to face her in one swift, smooth motion that made her almost run into him. "But okay. Do you want the police involved? Do you want an international incident? Because right now, we can keep this contained. But the moment you go to the cops…"

The whole world knows. He didn't need to finish the sentence, and he knew it. He'd made his point. And his point was…*you're screwed.*

Logan struggled to keep his jaw from locking up as he frog-marched Eva back to HQ. The image of his mutilated friends lying on piles of organs and in pools of blood on the cafeteria floor kept flashing in his head, keeping his fury stoked, and his jaw tight.

He glanced over at her as they neared the rear entrance. "I want to know about the weapon. Bullets don't kill most demons."

Eva looked straight ahead, avoiding his eyes. She was wearing the top he'd given her. And the necklace.

"I think it best to say nothing until I speak with The Aegis."

"I see. You said you didn't kill Shan and Noah. Who did?"

Her chin came up in stubborn defiance. "Again, I think it best to say nothing until I speak with The Aegis."

He smiled darkly. She wasn't going to speak with The Aegis, but she *was* going to talk. DART employed one of the best, if not *the* best, interrogators in the human realm, and he just happened to work from out of the Brussels office.

Blade met them at the door, his normally brown eyes gone gold with anger. "Bring her downstairs," he said. "Holding cell one."

"Holding cell?" Eva gasped. "Are you serious? Do you honestly think I'm a threat?"

Crimson forks of lightning spiderwebbed through Blade's eyes, a measure of his growing wrath. Blade was pretty laid back and slow to anger, but when the red shit streaked into his irises, watch out.

"Throwing you in a cell isn't to protect *us*, lady," he growled. "It's to protect *you*."

Logan casually put himself between Blade and Eva. Not that he was worried about the guy. Blade, once triggered, was truly a demon, but murdering defenseless humans wasn't his thing.

But Eva didn't know that, and clearly, the reality of her situation was starting to sink in. Until now, she'd practically reeked of defiance. And maybe a little arrogance. But she abruptly lost some swagger, and the sharp scent of fear overpowered her orchid perfume that probably cost as much per bottle as the wine he'd bought the other night.

Flanked by both Logan and Blade, shoulders hunched, and gaze fixed on a future that must have looked bleak, she said nothing during the short elevator ride to the basement. She even remained quiet as he took her tote and opened cell one, which had been designed for low-threat beings like humans and were-creatures on non-full-moon days.

He shoved her inside, and dammit, he actually felt bad when she banged her elbow on the doorframe. Cursing his stupidity, he slammed the door shut.

"Is she the only one we've got so far?"

Blade didn't take his eyes off her. "Every available agent is out looking for them. Kynan's pissed, man. I've never seen him like this. He's been on the phone with the Aegis Elders, and there's been a lot of yelling. He's threatening to go to the World Council on Supernatural Governance if this was an assassination."

Whoa. Taking this incident to the WCSG, a global committee that oversaw the funding and operations of DART and The Aegis, would stir up a lot of shit, and make matters even worse. Logan doubted Kynan would actually do that. But then DART had never faced anything like this before, and Kynan wasn't the type to back down from a threat.

"Does he think this was some sort of Aegis plot?"

Blade shrugged. "Would explain why one of them had a weapon like that when they were specifically told not to have anything but their stangs."

"This wasn't an assassination," Eva said from the middle of her cell. "It was a stupid accident. Whoever fired it wasn't supposed to even have the weapon."

Blade pounded a frustrated fist against Eva's cell door, and she jumped backward. "An accident? Are you fucking kidding me?" He pivoted on his heel and stormed toward the elevator.

"Blade, wait." Logan caught up with him. "Where's Draven?"

Blade didn't appear to hear him. "This is so fucked up, man. Draven and Shanea were supposed to get married in a few months. I just got fitted for my tux last week."

Logan was going to be the best man. His throat swelled with grief. He'd known Draven since their third-grade year at Hellmouth Academy, a school started with funding from the Horsemen and Underworld General to educate supernatural children who lived in the human world but, for whatever reason, couldn't attend human schools.

Draven and Logan were like brothers, and when Draven proposed to Shanea two years ago, no one had been happier for him than Logan. He had to be distraught. Destroyed. Completely out of his mind.

Logan grabbed the sleeve of Blade's leather jacket, halting him in his tracks. "Where's Draven," he repeated. "I need to be with him."

"He's probably hunting the Aegi. No one can get ahold of him."

"Shit." Logan stepped inside the elevator. "If he catches one, it's gonna get ugly."

"That's what we're afraid of." Blade followed him inside.

"No. *Really* ugly." Logan looked into the elevator camera/mic. "Lobby." He turned to Blade. "You know he's a vengeance demon, right?"

"Yeah. I know. But his species doesn't go Ufelskala Five until they've made what? Half a dozen vengeance kills?"

"Six. Yeah. There are six Guardians involved in Shan's death. He's not going to stop with the shooter. And all it takes is him killing one to start the process."

Blade went still. "Oh, shit."

"We have to find him, and we have to find him *now*."

The elevator came to a smooth halt, and Blade swung back to the doors. "Find the other Aegi, we find Draven. Good thing we have Eva."

"Yeah," Logan said. "Great."

"Hey." Blade stopped in the middle of the hallway. "What's wrong?"

Nothing, really. Just the female I really liked but can't be with is sitting in a cell for killing my friends. No big deal.

Logan was going to say precisely none of that. "I just don't think Eva's going to make it easy. She won't give up her people."

"Oh, yeah, she will." Blade's lips curled into a rare, dark smile. "Just wait until she meets my brother."

Chapter Sixteen

Eva wasn't in the cell for long.

Five minutes after Logan slammed the door, a woman who didn't offer her name escorted her to a slightly larger room with two chairs and a metal table in the middle. What made this room even more different was the symbol near the exit that Eva didn't recognize.

The woman sat her down at the table, told her to wait, and left without answering any of her questions.

"Why am I here?"

"What's going to happen?"

"Are you deaf?"

Eva stewed for a minute, fidgeting with the necklace Logan had given her as she tried to translate the strange symbol. He probably regretted giving the gift to her—and banishing the nightmare demon.

And kissing her.

With a groan, she plopped her forehead down on the table. "Thanks, Sig," she mumbled into the metal.

The door creaked open, and she nearly jumped out of her skin. A dark-haired male Seminus demon entered, his resemblance so similar to Blade's that she knew they must be brothers. The differences were subtle but somehow significant. From her brief glimpses, the sleeves of glyphs on their right arms seemed identical, but the symbols at the top, their personal marks just under their jaws, were different. Blade's was a broken sword, but this guy's was a line. A flat, horizontal line.

This guy's hair was also an unkempt mop, so unlike Blade's short, neat waves. And his eyes might have been the same chocolate brown as his brother's, but they were hard as diamonds. The biggest difference was in his expression. She hadn't spent much time with Blade over the last couple of days, but with the exception of his understandable rage, the times she'd seen him, he'd been smiling or laughing.

This guy didn't look like he'd smiled or laughed in his entire life.

"Eva Tennant," he began as he tossed a file down onto the table with enough of a crack to make her jump again. "I'm Rade. I know you think the smart and loyal thing to do is to keep your mouth shut until you talk to The Aegis or get a lawyer. But you're wrong. We need information from you now, and it can't wait."

"I'm sorry, but I—"

"I wasn't done." He sank down onto the empty chair, all rudeness and flexing arm glyphs that disappeared under his black T-shirt sleeve and popped back out on his neck. "One of the people you killed has a fiancé who is right now hunting your colleagues. When he catches them—and that isn't an *if*, he *will* catch them—they will die horribly. We need to know where your colleagues are so we can get to them before he does."

He was trying to scare her. He might even be telling the truth. But she wasn't going to spill her guts so easily.

"They are all trained demon hunters," she said. "I'm sure they're capable of taking care of themselves."

Rade looked at her with pity. Pity! "Draven's a vengeance demon. A *tormentus* demon. Do you know that species? No? They are born looking and acting like everyone else in the human realm. They live their lives without humans ever knowing they're the fire chief down the road or the kindergarten teacher in their kids' classroom. Most live good, decent lives. Until tragedy strikes. When that happens, they lose themselves. They become...monsters. The kind of monsters you Aegi believe all demons to be. Right now, he's redeemable. But once he makes his first kill, it's kind of a trigger. He'll kill another, and another in his pursuit of vengeance. And he won't stop until you're all dead. And that's not even the worst part. The worst part is how he'll do it. I'm not going to waste time explaining. Your imagination can take care of that. Just tell me where they are."

Cold sweat drenched her palms as she clenched them in her lap. He was definitely trying to scare her, and it was working. She had to put more effort into keeping her voice strong and steady.

"If I can't contact my supervisor," she said, "I'd like to speak to

Kynan."

"He's busy dealing with the firestorm you started."

"Then Arik."

"Busy."

"Logan?"

"No."

"Is he busy too?" she asked, her frustration with this jerk making it a little easier to hide her anxiety.

Rade just stared, his cold, dead eyes making her want to shiver. But she'd been trained for this very scenario, and she stared right back. She had a right to demand access to the top DART personnel. It said so in the exchange program paperwork, which she'd read carefully, thanks to parents who had imparted on her the importance of going over a legal document with a fine-tooth comb and a critical eye.

Section 4, paragraph C stated specifically that in the event of an interagency conflict, she must be allowed to speak to either DART's Director, Kynan Morgan, or its Deputy Director, Arik Wagner. And she wasn't going to back down.

"I know my rights, and—"

The door swished open again. Logan entered like a storm cloud, bringing a crushing pressure and plummeting temperature with him. For a moment, she wondered if she'd be better off with Rade.

"It's okay, Rade. I got it." His voice was clipped. Rough. Charred around the edges.

Rade bowed his head and slipped out. "I'll be in the hall when you need me."

When. Not *if*.

Eva suppressed a shiver.

As soon as the door closed, Logan rounded on her. "You asked for me, I'm here. So, what do you want?"

"I want to speak to my supervisor."

"We've gone over this. It ain't happening. Is this a game to you, Eva? Are my dead friends a joke to you?"

"No!" She stood, on the brink of going to him…for what reason? No clue. She had no idea why it was so important that he believe her. Whatever relationship they'd had—or might have had—was as dead as Shanea and Noah after today's tragedy. She needed to stop reacting with emotion and act like the calm professional she was.

"Of course, not," she said, lowering her voice and her body back down to the seat. "I'm sorry this happened. This exchange was supposed to bring our agencies together. Now, it's probably irreparably damaged."

"You think?" He inhaled deeply, and when he spoke again, his voice was calmer. "You can make this better. Answer our questions. Tell us where your colleagues are and if that weapon we found in your bag killed Noah and Shanea. No one else needs to get hurt."

"Is that a threat?"

"I was talking about Draven and your colleagues but take it however you want. Rade will get the answers out of you one way or another."

She went cold all the way to her fingertips. "You think you're so superior to The Aegis, but you would torture me?"

"Neither the Geneva Convention nor the World Council on Supernatural Governance have classified what Rade does as torture. Yet." He must have sensed the twinge of fear that speared her gut because he lowered his voice and sounded almost comforting as he said, "We're not after your pain, Eva."

Oh, good," she said with enough snark to conceal her fear. "I just got a manicure. Wouldn't want to lose those nails." She glared up at him. "I won't betray my people."

"You are betraying them by not telling us where we can find them," he snapped. "There's a really pissed-off vengeance demon looking for them, and I promise you, they won't die well. If you're counting on that new secret weapon killing him, think again. He's smart, resourceful, and he knows what scares people. His species makes *Soulshredders* tremble. *Fallen fucking angels* avoid them. Tell me where your people are." He planted his palms on the table and leaned close. "Please. I have to find Draven."

The worry in his eyes bled through the anger, and she felt her resolve slip. But it didn't matter. She couldn't help him even if she wanted to. "I can't tell you where they are because I don't know," she admitted. "They got into a taxi and left me behind."

"Unbelievable." He barked out a bitter laugh. "Your colleagues are dicks. But you still should have some idea where they went. We know of two Aegis safe houses in Brussels. Which means there are half a dozen we *don't* know about."

"Just let me talk to the Elders. Please. If they say it's okay—"

"We've tried talking to the Elders." He slammed his fist on the desk in frustration. "They won't tell us jack shit. It's like they don't care that you are all being hunted." Cursing, he backed away from the desk and studied the ceiling before looking down at her again. "Last chance, Eva. Please, don't make this difficult."

She leaned back in the chair and stubbornly crossed her arms over her chest. "You know my answer."

He gave her a disappointed shake of the head. "I guess I do." He opened the door and paused at the threshold. "Don't fight Rade. It'll hurt if you do."

The door closed quietly behind him.

Logan's chest felt cold as he watched Eva from a viewing area behind the interrogation chamber. She sat stiffly in her seat as Rade prowled around the room, occasionally throwing her softball questions meant to lower her guard.

But after she gave her legal name—Eva Marie Tennant—her town of residence—Washington, DC—and the reason she'd joined The Aegis— "Because they wanted me"—he turned up the heat.

As expected, she shut down.

Logan couldn't blame her. If he'd been in her situation, sitting in a chilly room and being grilled by Aegis assholes, he'd clam up too. He wouldn't believe anything they told him, and he certainly wouldn't give up his friends' locations or that of the safe house. So, he got it.

But that didn't make him any less pissed about the situation. All he wanted right now was to find Draven, and he needed her help to know where to start. He'd deal with his grief over his lost colleagues and his complicated feelings for Eva later.

Rade stepped up next to the table, looming close to Eva and forcing her to sit back and look up at him. Everything the guy did was calculated and deliberate. Blade liked to say that his brother didn't even take a piss without first weighing the pros and cons. He meant it as a joke, but it was probably true.

"Do you know what a Seminus demon is, Ms. Tennant?"

"You're incubi. Sex demons," she said matter-of-factly. She even managed to not look uncomfortable in that awkward position. Impressive. Logan had seen people piss themselves at this point during questioning. "Generally classified as Ufelskala One demons until a transformation at the age of approximately one hundred makes you fertile, insatiable, and violent. Each Seminus demon has one of three…gifts, as you probably call them. All meant to make their female partners pregnant, whether they want to be or not."

Rade cracked a rare, amused smile that disappeared as quickly as it had appeared. It was creepy as fuck when he smiled.

"Right out of the textbook," he said. "You did your research. Bet you were an A-plus student, weren't you? Teacher's fucking pet." She stiffened at his mocking tone. "But do you know what else we use those gifts for?"

Her chin came up even more in that infuriatingly defiant way of hers. "For killing, I assume."

"Is that all you think demons do?"

She let out a dramatic sigh. "I don't think were-creatures are inherently evil. They're human most of the time. But demons? I hope you don't expect me to believe that benevolent demons exist."

"You're an Aegi. I would never make that mistake."

She crossed her arms over her chest, making the little iris pendant on her necklace rest just above her cleavage.

Rade better not have noticed that too.

The thought flashed through Logan's brain before he could stop it. Because what the hell? Of course, Rade had noticed. He noticed everything. Plus, he was a sex demon. They definitely noticed shit like that.

But why did Logan care so much?

He was losing it over this female.

"Explain it to me, then," Eva said. "I'm open-minded. But the fact is, demons are Satan's creations. They are literally forged by evil, using evil powers."

Cocking his head, Rade studied her. She probably thought he was being cordial. Logan knew him well enough to know the guy didn't do cordial. He was mentally mapping her mind, planning his route once he got inside her head.

"Do you believe that evil humans exist?" he asked quietly. Politely. Disarmingly.

"Of course."

He turned away, clasped his hands behind his back, and started pacing. "Then doesn't it make sense that good demons would exist? Why would you think there aren't aberrations in the demon world, just like there are in the human one?"

Eva actually blinked in surprise, then frowned. She hadn't thought of that, had she?

"Just so you know," Rade continued, "our Seminus gifts can be used to kill, but they can also be used to heal. I'm sure you've heard of Underworld General Hospital. It's run by Seminus demons. My father, Shade, is one of them."

"Oh, I'm very familiar with your unholy medical center." She watched him pace, her knee bouncing faster each time Rade started back toward her. "Your Special Investigative Unit Director betrayed The Aegis for the head doctor there. Tayla got dozens of Guardians killed. When new Guardians are in training, they learn all about how that event put The Aegis on a bad course. One that ultimately led to Kynan Morgan and Regan Matthews plotting with the Horsemen to destroy the organization. So, yeah, I don't think that evil healing other evil equals good." She sat back in her chair, but her knee still bounced with anxious energy. "Is that why I'm here? To get lectured about how demons are really good guys?"

"You people are taught a load of shit, but I don't give a fuck if you think we're good guys or not. I just wanted to explain my particular gift."

He continued to pace the length of the room. Ten steps, then a pivot. Ten steps. Pivot.

"Most of my family uses their gifts to heal injuries or make the body perform optimally so it can heal itself." Ten paces and a pivot. "They can also make a heart stop as easily as they can make it beat."

Five paces. Stop.

"But my gift is different. I can get inside the mind." He pivoted. Looked her directly in the eye. "The mind is like a puzzle. I can see when pieces are missing, and sometimes, I can patch shit up. I can ease mental trauma and take away bad memories."

He moved around behind her. Slowly. Casually. Eva swallowed, and a fine sheen of sweat bloomed on her brow.

"I can see thoughts." His hand came down on her shoulder, and she flinched. "And secrets." He bent down so his mouth was mere inches from her ear. Her chest heaved with deep, rapid breaths as her anxiety built.

Son of a bitch. Logan didn't like this. At all.

His palms were growing clammy.

"What I'm saying, Ms. Tennant, is that I will get the answers to my questions whether you tell me or not. And while I'm in there poking around, I'll get a lot more than that."

The coldness centered in Logan's chest thawed in a wave of heat. Angry heat. He'd known Rade his entire life. Knew what the demon was capable of. But the reality of it happening to Eva sat like acid in his gullet.

"You can't." Eva might be terrified inside, but her voice was strong, and Logan wanted to cheer her on. "I'm protected against psychic attacks."

Rade released her and moved around to the front of the desk. Logan felt like he could finally breathe again.

"You mean your Aegis tattoo? The one that also gives you night vision and masks the sound of your heartbeat?" Rade shook his head. "I can get around that without breaking a sweat."

Suddenly, he lunged across the table, his hand clamping down on Eva's wrist. She yelped in surprise as he put his face in hers, his lips pulled back in a snarl.

"Tell me where the safe house is," he growled. "And tell me about the new Aegis weapon."

Eva's terror was clear, from her trembling hands to the pulse fluttering in her throat. But damn if she didn't lean into Rade's space, put her free hand between them, middle finger extended, and grind out, "Fuck you."

"You should never throw out an invitation like that to a sex demon." Rade's voice was dark velvet, both a threat and a statement of fact, and real fear broke Eva's mask of defiance.

Logan knew better. He knew there were lines even Rade wouldn't cross. Probably. But Eva didn't know that, and Logan's throat closed at the primal fear welling in Eva's eyes.

Damn you, Rade.

Rade's arm lit up as he engaged his gift. "Last chance." He hooked the garbage can with his foot and dragged it closer.

She glared right through the terror. "Go. To. Hell."

"Where do you think I'm going on my next vacation?" The symbols on Rade's arm went from a soft glow to radioactive brilliance.

Eva yelped and then clenched her teeth, fighting against what Rade described as something akin to a battering ram slamming into a portcullis. How badly it hurt depended on the strength of the mind or the mental wall around it.

"Bastard," she hissed. She squirmed and fought to free herself from Rade's grip. Her fist came around hard, and for a moment, Logan cheered her on.

Hit him! Punch how I showed you—

Rade's other hand snapped out, catching her wrist, and she screamed as the demon broke through The Aegis mind shield.

No!

Logan couldn't deal with this. There was a better way. There had to be. He lunged for the door, but Kynan intercepted him.

"What are you doing?"

I'm letting my emotions get in the way of our work because I'm an idiot.

"I'm going to try one more time to get her to talk."

"Logan, you know this is the best way. For her too." Ky was using his *dad voice*, the one that usually got people to settle down and make the right choices. Or, at least, the ones Ky wanted them to choose. It wouldn't work this time. "We get the information, and she doesn't get branded as a sellout or traitor."

Eva sat motionless, her face pale, her eyes glassy and brimming with unshed tears. Rade was inside her mind now, pillaging every scrap of knowledge he could find, and depending on how much care he used as he traversed the trillions of memory pathways, she could be reliving trauma at a painfully accelerated pace.

Logan had seen Rade operate dozens of times, had watched the demon pull out information gently and not so gently. He'd seen him tiptoe through fragile memories and bulldoze through others, leaving behind permanent damage. The guy was so good dozens of intelligence agencies and militaries around the world called him in. He'd trained with all the biggies too—the CIA, Mossad, CSIS, SVR, SIS. He'd even spent time with Hell's intelligence arm, the Intelligence Ministry of the Profane.

He'd needed a little downtime after training with IMP.

So, yeah, watching Rade work was like watching an artist paint a masterpiece. But for some reason, Logan wasn't in the mood for art today. Not when Eva was the canvas.

Eva started struggling again, but Rade's grip on her arm was solid, and she let out a cry that made Logan think of an animal caught in a leg trap.

He whipped open the door. "Sorry, boss, but I need to try again. I'll get her to talk."

For an agonizing second, Logan pondered what he'd do if Kynan tried to stop him. Thank fuck it didn't happen. Ky let Logan go, and in a dozen steps, he was inside the room with Rade and Eva.

The stench of fear and flowers permeated the room, slamming into Logan like a punch to the face.

"Release her," he barked at Rade. "Now."

Rade shot a confused glance over at the glowing wall glyph as if for guidance, even though he couldn't see Kynan through it. After a moment, he shrugged and backed off.

"What's going on?"

"I'm taking over." Logan put himself between Rade and the desk, and Rade's eyes narrowed.

"Did Kynan order—?"

"No," he said, gesturing at the door. "But you can talk to him if you have a problem."

Rade grunted, probably deciding a pissing contest wasn't worth it. "Whatever." He glanced back at Eva. "But you only need to find out where her colleagues are. I already got what she knows about the weapon and bullets." He paused, clenching his fists and shaking his head. "Fuck, man. Just…fuck."

A lump of foreboding formed in Logan's gut. "Stryke?"

Rade's eyes flashed with disappointment but also acceptance. Like everyone else, he'd probably suspected that his estranged brother's company had been responsible for the new tech that'd killed their colleagues.

Wordlessly, Rade slipped out, leaving Logan with Eva. His gut took another hit when she looked at him with something akin to hatred.

"What's next? Waterboarding? The rack? Should I actually regret getting that manicure last week?"

"Nothing so dramatic. But now you know what Rade can do. He's the best in the world, and he'll get the information." He gentled his voice, practically pleading with her. "He doesn't need to come back. Tell me what we need to know."

"How dare you?" she snapped. "How dare you pull the good-cop, bad-cop routine on me? I will never, ever give up the location of any Aegis cell or safe house." She planted her fists on the desk and surged to her feet, practically hissing like a cat. "That demon might as well come back and start slicing up my brain because I will never betray my people."

Damn her. He understood her loyalty. Admired it. Friends and family were everything. But she was missing the bigger picture.

"Eva," he said, keeping his voice measured, though it wasn't easy. Too much was riding on this. People's lives. Draven's soul. Logan's heart. "Please. You don't think Rade will stop at the local cell locations, do you? He'll dig around until he finds all your secrets. All the Aegis offices. All Aegis weapons."

"No, he won't. He might have been able to bypass the shield protecting my mind, but this"—she tugged down the waistband of her skirt just enough to reveal a knot tattoo—"protects certain information differently."

Interesting. He knew all Aegi were marked with a glyph that gave them some protection and enhancements, but that wasn't it. Of course, now he wondered where *that* one was located.

"Okay, so what *certain information*?"

She looked a little smug. "The kind low-level Guardians don't have. But those of us who know more about the inner workings of the agency get this protective glyph. If anyone tries to access particular areas of the brain, certain information…"

"What? What happens?"

"There are land mines. Booby traps to disable the invader. And, sometimes, the person with the information. Rade was talking about how the mind is like a puzzle. Well, the pieces that hold the most sensitive information will self-destruct if accessed through magical means, and neither of us will get out of it unscathed. We call them land *minds*. Kinda clever."

She could be lying, but he doubted it. The Aegis liked martyr shit, and they wouldn't hesitate to sacrifice their people to protect themselves. Rade was a master mind-bomb defuser, but Logan would rather not put him in a situation where he might trigger an explosion inside Eva's head.

"Look," she said, sounding suddenly tired, "I know how important Draven is to you—"

"Do you?" Hearing her use Draven's name sparked instant, hot anger. It wasn't logical, and he knew it. But, dammit, she and her colleagues were the reason Draven's life had been ruined. "Do you really?" He tapped his comms and flicked open the video images file. He found the one he was looking for, and suddenly, the room became a wooded, sunlit park.

"We're at a barbecue at Draven's folks' place," he told Eva. "Draven just asked Shanea to mate him."

The couple was alternately kissing and laughing, and then Draven left his new fiancée to come over to where Video Logan stood. Eva watched with curiosity as Draven gave Logan a hug.

"Congrats, man," Logan said. *"You don't deserve her."*

Draven laughed. "I know. And she wants like, a dozen kids. I can't wait."

"Draven loves kids." Logan smiled at the memory as he spoke to Eva. "He and Shanea were going to have their mating ceremony and then start pumping out little ones as soon as they got back from their honeymoon in the Caymans. They'd have made great parents."

Cyan came up behind Shanea and tapped her on the shoulder. Shanea, always jumpy, popped her demon *as she liked to put it. She sprouted horns and claws as she spun around in surprise. Then she laughed and hugged Cyan so hard it lifted the platinum-haired technomancer off the ground.*

"See, Shanea's automatic response to pretty much anything was to go demon," Logan told Eva. "But she was harmless. Her skin was tough as titanium, but her claws were kind of rubbery. Her species is hard to kill, but they aren't good fighters. They have a great defense but no offense. Kind of like armadillos. She wasn't a threat to your people, but they killed her anyway."

"I want you to be my best man," Draven said to Video Logan. "You're my best friend and my brother, and there's no one I want more."

Logan remembered that day so clearly. Remembered how choked up he'd gotten, and how happy he'd been for his buddy.

Eyes stinging, he flicked off the holovid. "When we were kids," he said, hoping Eva hadn't caught the hitch in his voice, "we swore we'd never get married. We were going to be lifelong bachelors and spend our days fighting bad guys and doing dangerous shit like jumping out of airplanes and climbing glaciers. But then he found Shanea, and I swear, the day he met her was the day he knew she was The One." He looked over at her. "His life is ruined, Eva. He's dying inside. I would be too. So would you. Help me find him."

For a moment, she looked like she might cave. She glanced down at the desk, her shoulders hunched, her hands clasped so tightly her knuckles turned white. "I'm so sorry, Logan. Maybe I can—"

The door crashed inward, and Kynan burst into the room. Logan's breath seized at the sight of his boss, his expression grim and haggard, his eyes bloodshot.

"It doesn't matter anymore." Kynan's shredded voice hung in the air, drenching the atmosphere in foreboding. "We don't need to find the Guardians."

Eva shot to her feet, propelled by fear for her friends. "Why not?"

"Because," Kynan rasped, "Draven found them first."

Chapter Seventeen

Eva couldn't breathe. Could barely think. If Draven had located her colleagues…oh, God.

"What did he do? Where is he?" The hope and fear woven through Logan's voice hit her hard, especially after seeing that holovid. Logan loved his friend, and his friend was hurting.

She shouldn't care. Draven was a hellspawn. An especially horrible hellspawn. But his deep affection for Shanea and Logan had been obvious, and Eva felt sorry for a demon for the first time in her life.

But she also feared for her friends, and she had a feeling there wouldn't be any winners even if they caught Draven.

"We don't know where Draven is." Kynan reached up and scrubbed his hand over his face before turning to Eva. "I'm sorry, Eva. He killed two of the Aegi. We don't know who they are yet. There wasn't enough left to identify them."

Her stomach, which had already been roiling, let loose. Scrambling, she heaved into the little metal garbage can next to the desk.

That's why Rade put it there.

Logan appeared at her side, pulling her hair back and pressing a tissue into her hand. Through the retching and gasps for air, it struck her as an oddly kind gesture from someone who clearly despised her. Or, at least, despised her employer.

"I'm sorry," she croaked as she wiped her mouth. "I don't usually…" She retched again. The embarrassment, on top of the horror, anger, and adrenaline, left her shaking and on the verge of a meltdown.

As if losing her breakfast in front of Logan and Kynan wasn't bad enough.

How had this gone downhill so fast?

She'd been sent on this mission to prevent an international incident. Now, four people were dead, more were missing, and she was part of the worst kind of international incident.

"Do you know where the others are?" Logan asked Kynan as she tried to clean herself up. But there was no way to dab away the stench of humiliation.

"No," Kynan said. "But I spoke with an Elder who says they're on their way to a safe location."

"There is no safe location if Draven is after them." Logan let go of her hair, his touch gentle as he arranged it over her shoulders. Again, with the surprises. "And he would have gotten the Guardians he killed to talk. He probably knows where all The Aegis's secret locations are."

"I doubt it," she offered, her voice sounding like it had been sandpapered. "Most of the super-confidential knowledge is held by the Elders alone. I doubt anyone on my team knows about the most highly guarded locations. Me included. They learned their lesson after—" She bit her lip to keep from saying, *"They learned their lesson after Kynan betrayed them."*

The Director's glare said he knew exactly what she'd almost said. "Draven might not know top-secret shit, but that doesn't mean he didn't get information that could put him on the trail of the Guardians who got away."

This just kept getting worse and worse. And who knew what info Rade had lifted out of *her* head?

"What happens next?" she asked. "Do I get to go home?"

Kynan shot her an are-you-kidding-me glance. "Not until The Aegis releases our people."

"The Aegis is holding them?" Logan raised his voice enough to echo through the room. "As prisoners? Fuck them. They can't do that."

She tapped on the braces mounted on the desk meant to hold restraints. "You're holding me prisoner."

"Our people didn't do anything wrong," Kynan snapped. "And until I get assurances that whoever is responsible will be held accountable, you're staying here."

Logan raked a frustrated hand through his hair and swore. "The Aegis won't like that."

"So I found out when I talked to Elder Hammond."

Eva would have laughed if she wasn't so busy trying to keep from crying. Kell Hammond was a humorless, hardheaded former Marine who didn't negotiate with terrorists or anyone else.

"What do they want?" Logan asked.

"They want Draven's head. His literal head. And they won't release our people until they have it. And they want Eva back. They'll give up one of our guys for her, but that's not good enough. I want them all. They gave us one day to either give her up or find Draven."

"Or?"

"Or they go to the press and tell the world that one of our pet demons is rabid and on the loose." Kynan slammed the side of his fist against the wall. "It'll be the end of DART."

How had the last twelve hours gone downhill so fast?

DART had been fighting an uphill battle for decades when it came to employing supernaturals, and the one golden arrow they had in their quiver of arguments was that no DART agent had ever gone rogue. There had been a handful of investigations, sure, especially when civilians had been injured during the course of a battle between DART and dangerous supes. But for the most part, they'd kept their supernatural employees clean and out of the spotlight.

This would reverberate through every anti-demon entity in the world, and it wouldn't matter that an Aegi instigated the incident. News that a vengeance demon was slaughtering demon slayers would be devastating to the organization. Even if it didn't completely destroy them, public approval would plummet, and funding would dry up.

Logan could already visualize the protests filling the streets, stirred into frenzies by a media that made its money by fueling hate and sowing division. It would be The Aegis's wet dream.

They definitely couldn't give up Eva. She was the only leverage they had.

"If you let me go, I promise to do what I can to get your people released." Eva's proposal sounded sincere, but Logan doubted she had that much sway with the Elders.

"Sorry, Eva," Kynan replied, "but we can't do that. Not yet. We need to find another way."

Logan scoured his brain for ideas and rejected them one by one as too stupid, too outrageous, or too dangerous. Except…shit. He had a card he didn't want to play, but they were out of options, and Draven's life was on the line.

Reluctantly, he turned to his boss. "Can I talk to you outside for a minute?" Kynan agreed, and as soon as they stepped outside, Logan put down his ace. "Let me talk to them."

"What, you have some special backdoor into The Aegis's leadership?"

"Ah…yeah." At Kynan's raised eyebrow, Logan's cheeks heated. "I dated one of the Elders back in college."

Kynan, who was rarely surprised by anything, blinked. "Say what?"

"Maja Weso. She wasn't an Elder when we dated. She wasn't even in The Aegis. I met her in one of my demon archaeology classes." Logan had taken the class mainly for the easy A, as well as to see how ridiculous the lessons would be. Turned out the human who taught it had been extremely knowledgeable, so much so that Logan suspected Professor Sheeron was a demon.

The class had been interesting, but what he'd really gotten a kick out of was the students. Some took the course out of curiosity, like Maja. Others needed it for the new degrees available in a handful of demon-centric studies. Students of both categories came at the class from two different angles—about a quarter had neutral to positive attitudes toward supernaturals, while the rest went the other direction to varying degrees.

Logan hadn't liked the latter much.

But Maja had been on the fence, leaning a little more toward finding supernaturals to be fascinating, and she'd been open to giving them a chance. So, she'd taken the class as an elective on her journey toward a psychology degree.

"Was it serious?" Kynan asked.

"Yes."

"Did it end on good terms?"

"Not at all."

"Then what makes you think you'll even be able to speak to her, let alone get through to her?"

"She's smart, and she's curious. She'll want to know what I have to say." Or she might tell him to go fuck himself and the hellhound he rode in on. He'd give his attempt fifty-fifty odds.

"Okay, let's give it a try." Kynan tapped on his comms unit, and Logan's beeped. "That's the direct number to the Elders. You'll tell the person who answers who you want to talk to, and they'll either connect you or they won't. They're assholes."

"Thanks. I'll let you know how it goes." Logan ducked into a vacant office next to the interrogation room and propped his hip against the dusty desk. He looked down at the number. It pulsed on his watch screen like a heartbeat.

Shit. Was he really going to do this? Was he *really* going to contact his ex after more than a decade and have a conversation that was already inherently volatile? He'd hated her for a long time, and it had actually been Draven who'd pulled him out of the dark place he'd gone after she shredded his heart.

He'd healed, but the hurt and betrayal had left one hell of a scar.

By the time he tapped the number to dial the Elders, his mouth was as parched as the Scorched Wastes in Sheoul's Horun region.

Not that he'd ever been there. But he'd heard his aunt and uncles talking about it.

A virtual screen popped up from his comms, and a middle-aged woman with frosty gray eyes and a severe blond bun stared at him from what he guessed was her office. "To whom may I direct your call?"

"Maja Weso."

She looked down and typed something. "And you are?"

"Logan. Logan Thanatos."

Her eyes skipped up and flared wide before she put on the cool mask again. "Is she expecting your summons, Mr. Thanatos?"

"It's just Logan. And she's definitely not expecting this."

"One moment please." The screen went black.

Logan fully sat down on the desktop, his gut churning more than it should be. What if Maja rejected his call?

What if she didn't?

He took a deep breath and thought about Eva in the other room. How close had she been to the two dead Guardians? And how involved was she in the deaths of DART's two dead agents? Witnesses had pinned the shooting on Sig, and Logan was inclined to believe Eva's story about Sig possessing the weapon illegally because the guy was a world-class douche. But how much did she support what he'd done? How far had she gone—and would she go—to protect him?

The screen flickered, and his heart did the same as Maja materialized in front of him. She looked like he remembered, still wearing her thick brown hair tucked behind her ears, her wispy bangs sweeping at the edges of her green eyes. The years had sculpted her cheekbones and jawline a little more, making her even more striking. Figured. She couldn't have a missing tooth or a few wrinkles?

"Hello, Logan," she said, her gaze wary but not glowing with blistering hate. He hoped he could pull off the same.

"Maja."

There was a heartbeat of awkward silence. Then, "You look good," she said. "You haven't aged a day."

He didn't know if that was a dig at his immortality, but he figured he'd play along. "Ditto."

She gave a skeptical snort. "Flattering, but you literally stopped aging at what…twenty-five?"

"Give or take a year," he said with a shrug.

Her lips, glistening with fresh pink gloss, thinned into a hard line. She still didn't like hearing the truth. "Since you're calling from a DART comms signature, I assume you work for them. I should have known. And I assume you're calling about the incident."

"Incident." Unbelievable. "Your people killed two of ours."

"And your people killed two of ours," she shot back. "We're even."

"Oh, come on, Maja." Anger, fresh and hot, sparked from the cold, dead ashes of their relationship. "It's not even, and you know it. But we can prevent more deaths. Draven won't stop until he finds everyone involved."

"Draven? As in, the Draven you roomed with in college? He's a demon?" She let out a bitter laugh. "Of course, he is. I don't know why I didn't put that together when you told me who you were."

She'd probably been too busy trying to kill Logan to consider Draven's demonic status.

"Look, I know you hate me—"

"I don't hate you, Logan."

"Really? Because the last time I saw you, you were pretty clear about how you felt. I loved you. I trusted you with my secrets. And you let demon hunters set a trap for me."

She hadn't even gone to The Aegis. Nope, after her attempt to stab him in the gut failed, she'd given up his location to a bunch of local yahoo Guardian wannabes who made it their mission to rid neighborhoods and schools of anyone who wasn't one hundred percent human.

She stiffened, her posture taut and defensive, and he braced for her hot temper. But a few heartbeats later, she bowed her head in contrition. "I did. But that's because you betrayed me. You betrayed me hard, Logan."

"Betrayed you? By not telling you the truth of who I was?"

"You took away my choice. I should have had the right to choose if I wanted to sleep with a supernatural being. I thought you were human. You kept the truth from me."

"And you went and proved why I was right to do it."

But he did understand her anger. He was far enough removed now that he could see why she'd been angry. But she'd gone far beyond merely *angry*.

All he'd wanted back then was to feel normal. To have a college experience that included study groups and frat parties and sporting events. He hadn't expected to fall for Maja, and by the time he did, it was too late to reveal the truth. Then she started hanging with increasingly anti-demon friends, and telling her became even harder. When she expressed interest in joining The Aegis, he'd come clean, desperate to dissuade her and prove that she was wrong about his people. About him.

She huffed. "What did you expect? I'd just told you I was thinking about joining an anti-demon organization. Springing that your father is one of the Four Horsemen of the Apocalypse on me was an asshole move. You should have just broken up with me."

"Yeah, stupid me, wanting to fight for a relationship with the woman I loved and who I wanted to understand me." The past slid into his mind, and with it, so much anger. Pointless anger. He wasn't here to rehash shit. He shook his head to clear it. "None of that matters anymore. All I want is to find Draven and prevent more deaths. I'm hoping you can help."

Maja took her time considering what he'd said, no doubt to make him squirm.

"First," she began, "you can assure me that Eva is okay."

"She's fine. I'm sure we can arrange for you to talk to her when you and I are done."

"And what is it you want? We've already told Kynan we're not giving up your people until your pet vengeance demon is dead."

"Draven isn't a pet," he snapped, as angry at himself as he was disgusted by her cavalier attitude. What had he ever seen in her? "He's a decent male who lost the love of his life. He's angry and in pain.

Wouldn't you be?"

"I wouldn't go on a killing rampage," she said. "*I'm* not a demon."

He wished he could reach through the holoscreen and strangle her. "Maja, we need time. A day isn't enough. If you get your people to safety, it won't be a problem."

Maybe.

She thought about that, took a sip of whatever was in the mug on her desk. Nodded.

"Tell you what. We'll give you one of your people and four days. One day for every Guardian who's alive. And for every Guardian we lose, we strike a day."

"Oh, come on—"

"That's the deal. And I don't want Eva locked up in some DART dungeon."

"We don't have dungeons."

She ignored that. "One more thing. I want *you* to be responsible for her. You'll be her bodyguard twenty-four-seven." Maja held up her finger to shut him up when he started to protest. "If you want more time, that isn't negotiable. You know Draven better than anyone, and if anyone can keep Eva safe from him, it's you and your godforsaken mutt."

Godforsaken mutt? Sure, Cujo had phased into Logan's room when Maja tried to stab him, and the canine had nearly eaten her, but still.

"Fine," he ground out. "Now, tell me about the weapon that killed our people."

She smiled. "Respectfully, fuck off. You already know more than you should. Let me speak with Eva now."

"Respectfully, fuck off."

"It's part of the deal. Take it or leave it."

Join The Aegis with me. Repent and reject your demon family or I walk. Take it or leave it.

Those had been her last words to him. The last thing she'd said before she revealed his presence to the group that thought they could capture him.

Fuck you.

He wanted to say that to her again, just like he'd said it after she gave him the ultimatum.

But her current request wasn't unreasonable. It might even show Eva that DART was willing to work with her and The Aegis to save lives.

"You get five minutes."

She made him wait a heartbeat before saying, "Fine. Nice seeing you again, Logan. I expect to hear that Draven is neutralized, and Eva is on her way home shortly. Bye."

Maja winked out of the room.

He cursed to himself, but it felt hollow. He'd gotten DART more time…but he'd also gotten himself a babysitting job.

And there wasn't a curse word strong enough for that.

Chapter Eighteen

So, it turned out that Kynan Morgan, ex-soldier, former Aegis member, and current Director of DART, wasn't a psychotic megalomaniac.

Eva supposed he could be hiding his inner scumbag, but from everything she'd seen, he was nothing like the stories she'd heard from colleagues and learned from Aegis records.

He had, in fact, ordered her a sandwich and coffee from the cafeteria and sent someone to a nearby store for toothpaste and a toothbrush. He'd escorted her to the bathroom so she could brush her teeth and clean up, and now he was sitting across from her in the interrogation room as she picked at her ham and cheese baguette.

"You're not what I expected," she told him, and he snorted bitterly.

"I'll bet. My divorce from The Aegis was messy, and you've probably only gotten my ex's side of the story."

"Which ex?"

One black eyebrow climbed up. "You did your homework."

"Everyone knows the story of how you and your wife ran a cell of Guardians until she cheated on you," she said bluntly. Kynan struck her as someone who appreciated straight talk, and she was too tired for tact. "Then you hooked up with a demon, got some demon friends, and betrayed The Aegis to the Four Horsemen."

"The Aegis betrayed *me*," he said. "And they betrayed the Horsemen."

"So, you take no responsibility for any of it?"

Kynan gazed at the weird symbol on the wall for a minute as if gathering his thoughts. "I was a toe-the-line Guardian." He absently ran his fingers over the scars on his throat. "I hated demons, and I bought into The Aegis ideology. And I made a lot of questionable decisions because winning a war means doing distasteful shit. Sometimes, the collateral damage is…too much."

"So, you're sorry you left?" She forced herself to take a bite of the sandwich, even though she wasn't hungry. Her head was pounding from Rade's mind scramble, and her stomach still roiled, but she hoped getting something in it would settle it down.

"I'm sorry I didn't do it sooner." He sat back in his chair and watched her chew her food. "You aren't like the rest of them. Don't let yourself get caught in the quicksand, or you'll find yourself doing things that will go against your moral fabric."

Her journalist's brain sensed a huge story there. But before she could attempt to pry, the door swept open, and Logan popped his head inside.

"Boss? Can I see you for a second?"

For some reason, the sadness in Kynan's expression deepened when he looked at Logan. It only lasted a second, and then he was up and heading toward the door.

"Be right back," he said to Eva.

They were only gone for a couple of minutes, during which time she finished her sandwich and the coffee. As she was wiping her mouth, Logan came inside with a portable comms unit.

He placed the flat, coaster-sized device on the table.

"I'm putting you on with Maja. You have five minutes." He pointed to the red button on one corner of the unit. "Push that, and it'll make your conversation private and engage your implant's security scrambler."

"Thank you," she said, grateful that he was finally allowing her to speak with an Elder.

He nodded and left. A heartbeat later, Maja popped up on the holoscreen in front of her, looking frazzled but concerned.

"Eva, it's good to see you. My end of the conversation is secure. Is yours?" When Eva nodded, the Elder relaxed a little. "Are you okay? Are they treating you well?"

Eva wasn't sure how to answer that. Rade and his interrogation had been terrifying, and her head still throbbed. But even worse, it had been a violation, a theft of her private thoughts. What had he seen? What did he know? And how was she supposed to sort through all of that with words? There were none.

"Eva?"

She shook her head. "Right. Sorry. I'm okay. But I don't know what information they might have gotten from me during the interrogation with that demon bastard."

Maja scowled. "What demon?"

"Name's Rade. He's a Seminus demon."

Maja went still for a moment. "I've heard stories about him. He's the guy every government agency in the world calls when all else fails to break someone. Did he get inside your head?"

As if in answer, pain streaked across the top of her skull. She could use a couple of aspirin. "Yeah. Logan stopped him, but he still got some info. Definitely got some stuff about the Smiter. They suspect StryTech made it. They're probably dissecting it right now. Carlos put it in my bag, so I had it when DART caught me."

Pursing her lips, Maja nodded. "They were bound to find out we had it eventually." She exhaled on a soft curse and shifted focus. "Do you know if the demon got anything about our locations?"

"Didn't sound like it, but he could have kept that to himself in front of me."

Eva rubbed her gritty eyes, completely wiped out. It was as if all the day's events, the grief, and the panic, hit her all at once. She just wanted to crawl into a bed and cry herself to sleep while hoping she'd wake up and find that all of this had been a nightmare.

Even if that meant the nightmare demon was still haunting her.

"Do you know who Draven's victims are yet?" Eva asked.

"We just heard from Keeley. Everyone got separated when they were attacked. She saw Sig get away, but his comms unit was damaged, so it makes sense that we haven't heard from him yet. Keeley is on her way to the airport in a taxi...wait." Maja looked over at something and turned back. "Hammond's on the line with Sig. He's on a train to a safe house in Ghent. We'll extract him as soon as possible and get him back here. We've had no contact from Mason, Benji, or Carlos."

Eva's gut clenched. "I need to be there. I need to—"

"You're staying. We gave DART more time, but we're not giving up their people in exchange for you. I'm sorry, Eva, but listen to me. This is a golden opportunity for us. And you."

"Golden..." She sat back in the seat, stunned and numb. "Being held like a prisoner by demons and werewolves and who knows what else is *golden.*"

"I know, and I don't like this, either," Maja insisted. "I don't trust any of them. But I do believe they can keep you safe."

"Safe?" Eva gaped at the Elder. "From one of their own colleagues?"

Maja held up a hand in a calm-down gesture. "I understand how it sounds, but they know Draven, and they know how to counter him. In the meantime, you have a prime opportunity to get a look at DART's operations from the inside. We've never had that before. You can find their weaknesses, learn about their weapons, their allies…we might not have this kind of chance again."

"But—"

"It'll be okay. Logan will be personally responsible for you."

The hell he will. "That's insane. His buddy is a *demon.* As good as Logan is in the gym, how is he supposed to keep me safe from that?"

Maja stared. "You don't know?"

"Know what?"

"About Logan."

And right then…holy shit…it clicked.

Logan. That was the name of the child born to an ex-Aegi named Regan and the Horseman known as Death.

Shock stole her breath. And her energy. And her ability to think. Her hands grew clammy.

"Eva? Eva. You okay?"

"So much makes sense now," she mumbled, more to herself than Maja. His fighting ability. The demon ex-girlfriend. His ability to catch the soul of her nightmare demon. The fact that he somehow got to Boston from Brussels pretty much instantly.

Yes, it made perfect sense.

But her feelings on the matter did not. As an Aegi, she should be angry, shocked, appalled, and sure, there was a little of that.

But as a woman who had spent time with him, she couldn't help but be a little curious about what a man like that would be like in bed.

Chapter Nineteen

"Anyone got anything? Anything at all?"

Logan sat in one of DART's conference rooms with a handful of his colleagues, his gut churning with worry over Draven. It had now been fourteen hours since the shooting and Draven's disappearance, and no one at DART had come up with a single lead.

Seated at the far end of the twenty-seater table, Blade shook his head, flinging bits of bone, flesh, and scales from his dark hair. No doubt he had an interesting story to share.

"We got nothin'. We hit every one of Draven's favorite haunts. As far as we can tell, he hasn't even been back to his apartment."

"Yeah, I went by there too," Logan said. "It was crammed with boxes. I knew Shanea was moving in, but I didn't realize she was basically already living there."

That had been a punch to the gut. Shan and Draven should be unpacking boxes, arguing over where her gaudy pink lamp should go, and then making up for hours on the frilly comforter she'd put on the bed.

"Fuck those Aegi," Mace growled, his clothing flecked with the same gore Blade sported. "They're getting what they deserve."

"Has anyone talked to Draven's parents?" Scotty kicked her boot up on the chair next to her and scowled at the bloodstains on her jeans. She, Mace, and Blade must have been in one hell of a fight. "Do they know what's going on?"

Logan scrubbed his hand over his face, but he couldn't scour away the memory of talking to Draven's mom and dad. "I went to their place to tell them."

"Shit," Mace breathed. "That must have been hard."

"They're devastated."

Thinking Logan had come for a social visit, Draven's folks had been thrilled to see him. Offered tea and cookies. He and Draven had been connected at the hip since they were kids, and Logan was like a second son to them. Draven's mom had screamed and collapsed when he told them the news, and his father had been on the verge of joining his son in a murderous rampage.

It had taken Logan an hour to talk Martin down, and if not for the fact that Draven could still potentially be saved, the guy might have gone full vengeance demon.

"But this can be reversed, right? Their species has some sort of ritual they can do to stop the transformation if it hasn't been completed, yes?" Scotty played with the end of her braid. Her long, red hair had mostly come out of the bands that held it, and she was only making it worse. "As long as he doesn't kill everyone he's after."

"Sure," Logan said. "But it's not easy. And the closer he gets to the complete transformation, the more of him will be lost, even if his parents *can* reverse it."

"We'll get him, Logan." Scotty leaned across an empty chair and punched him in the shoulder. "We won't let you or his parents lose him."

"Thanks, cuz." He punched her back. They'd done the routine for as long as he could remember. It was silly, but ever since she was two and he was six, she'd toddled around behind him, just dying to get in a punch every time she saw him. It was a thing now. If she stopped, he'd miss it.

He knew because Chaos used to climb Logan like a tree at least once every time they were together. Logan was a teen for most of the kid's short life, and he'd been annoyed.

Now, he'd give anything to be bothered like that again.

"Dude," Mace said. "We done for now? I gotta shower. I'm covered in Blighter guts."

"Same," Scotty said.

"Bastards led us down a rabbit hole looking for Draven," Blade said. "They hadn't seen him in months, but they thought it would be funny to lie and say they saw him at an evisceration club in New

Oubliette."

Yikes. Formerly known as Australia's Northern Territory, The New Oubliette region was one of the worst, similar to its namesake counterpart in Sheoul. An anything-goes meat grinder with little oversight.

Scotty wiped some grayish-red bits off her cheek with the back of her hand. "They basically sent us there to be slaughtered. Total trap. Dickheads were going to get paid for sending the pit fresh blood." She looked at the gunk that came off her face. "Ooh, that's not from a Blighter. That's a Khepri scale." She tucked it into her pocket. "They're fun to put in water. They glow for hours."

"Is that how Limos makes the ocean glow at her night parties?" Mace asked.

"Yep. Just this one could light up an Olympic-sized swimming pool."

Logan really didn't care about demonic illumination, and he still had a million things to do before he could catch a few hours of sleep and get back to looking for Draven. He wished Cujo could help track the guy down, but the canine's ability to move unseen in the human realm was limited. Cujo wasn't sitting idly by and doing nothing, though. Aunt Cara had put a dozen hellhounds, including Cujo, on Lilith's trail. So far, they'd come up empty, but they were good trackers, and they'd hopefully find something useful soon.

"You guys clean up and get some rest," Logan said. "I gotta grab Eva."

Blade's dark brows popped up. "The Aegi? Why?"

"I'm her babysitter. She's been locked up in a cell all day. I figure she can stay in one of our guest rooms."

"Screw that." Mace shoved angrily out of his seat, and Logan tensed. The demon was liberal with his right hooks. "You gotta be kidding. Draven and Shan are—were—our best friends, and you want Shan's killer sleeping in our house?"

"Sig killed them, Mace. Not Eva."

The fury flickering in his eyes said he didn't care who pulled the trigger. "She ran with the rest of them. Innocent people don't run."

"Let her rot in the cell," Blade said, coming to his feet, as well, but with a little less vitriol. "It's what she deserves."

No, she didn't, but these guys hadn't been around her. They wouldn't give her the benefit of the doubt, and Logan wasn't going to waste his breath trying. He had a better argument anyway.

"She's not safe from Draven in a cell," he said. "Until StryTech updates our security software with his species' DNA, he can get past the demon detectors. But our place is warded to keep everyone out, and I've already changed the code to our private Harrowgate so Draven can't use it. I texted you all the new code an hour ago."

"Fuck that shit." Pivoting on his heel, Mace went for the door. "I'm outta here."

Blade and Scotty took off with him, but as they were leaving, Scotty gave him one more punch in the shoulder for fun.

"See you tomorrow. I'm going to check one more place for Draven."

"You're covered in guts and scales."

She waggled her brows. "Where I'm going, it won't matter."

"Then I'm going with you," Blade said gruffly.

"You guys gonna be okay?" Mace asked as he spun back around. "Because I promised I'd play some retro games with Crux tonight. I'm already two hours late."

"Go," Blade said. "We'll be fine."

They all went their separate ways, and Logan headed for the block of cells that currently held only one resident.

Eva.

Eva had spent over eight hours pacing. Well, pacing and thinking. And then pacing some more.

Oh, and peeing. The DART people supplied her with as much coffee, soda, and water as she wanted, and since she'd had nothing else to do, she'd drunk a lot. Which meant asking for an escort to the bathroom *a lot*.

Kynan came to hang out twice. He was friendly enough, but she knew what was up. Their chats were soft interrogations. She couldn't even be upset because she was just grateful that Rade wasn't getting into her head again.

He'd brought her a video too. Security footage of the cafeteria incident made it clear that Sig had killed two people not in self-defense but in cold blood. Yes, he'd been freaked out, but neither Shanea nor Noah had made aggressive moves, even though others in the room had been throwing punches. Shanea had transformed into a hideous beast, and Noah had hissed, his mouth revealing shockingly huge fangs, but they hadn't attacked.

Sig had fired the weapon needlessly. He'd either been looking for an excuse to kill a demon, or he'd been a coward who shot first and ran later. No wonder everyone at DART stared daggers at her. Only Kynan and Logan had treated her with any kind of decency.

God, she hoped Logan had found Draven. Obviously, she wanted her colleagues and her to be safe from his wrath, but she wanted him to be safe too. He didn't deserve the destruction Sig had brought down on him.

And look at that; she was actually sympathetic to a demon.

Even more shocking, she had feelings for someone who was part demon. One-quarter demon, one-quarter angel, and half-human, to be exact.

She was still stunned by the knowledge of what—and who—Logan was. The story of his birth was basically a legend in The Aegis. While there was the official version and a few variations told by conspiracy theorists and people with secondhand knowledge, they all boiled down to a prophecy. One The Aegis believed made Logan the central character in preventing his father's Seal from breaking. And in the mess, Kynan and Logan's mother, Regan, had betrayed The Aegis, resulting in the Horsemen slaughtering Aegi and nearly destroying the organization.

It made her wonder what Logan had been told about those events.

She also wondered where he was. She hadn't seen him since he'd set up the conversation with Maja. After she'd hung up with the Elder, Blade had taken her to the cell, shoved her inside, and locked the door.

"I met your mom," she'd told Blade on the short walk from the interrogation room and cell. "I liked her. Didn't she teach you better manners?"

"Didn't yours teach you not to murder people?"

"I didn't—" She'd snapped her mouth shut because arguing would do no good. These people hated her, and she had to admit that if the same thing had happened at The Aegis HQ, she and every Aegi would have treated the DART people like POWs—way worse than she'd been treated.

With the exception of Rade. Fuck that psycho mind-rapist.

The sound of a lock clicking had her spinning around as the door opened. Her breath caught at the sight of Logan, standing there with her tote dangling from his fingers, looking like he had earlier in black pants, a black shirt, and big boots. His blond hair was grooved as if he'd raked his fingers through it, and a fine shadow of scruff softened his chiseled jawline.

Now that she knew he wasn't fully human, she eyed him, looking for any hint of demon or smidge of angel.

But all she saw was a tall, striking man with dark hollows under his bloodshot eyes. Exhaustion and worry were written all over his face.

They didn't find Draven.

"We need to talk."

Her heart sank. No good conversation ever started with those four words.

"What's going on?" she asked, steeling herself for the worst. Another round with Rade? News that another of her colleagues was dead?

"I'm taking you someplace safe." He handed her the tote. "But I need to tell you something first."

Her sunken heart stopped. Just seized in her chest. "Did someone else die?"

"No," he said quickly, and a flood of relief nearly made her knees weak. "Draven is still out there, but as far as I know, he hasn't found any more of your friends." He clenched his fists. Unclenched. Tucked his hands into his pockets.

"Logan?" she prompted, and he cursed.

"I told you I was human," he said. "But I didn't tell you the rest."

"Oh, that." She shouldered the tote. "Maja already told me."

It was as if a wall slammed down between them. His eyes became chips of ice, and his jaw tightened so much she expected to hear his teeth crack.

"And?"

"And what?"

"What all did she tell you? Do you regret what happened the other night? Do you think I'm a monster too?"

"Whoa," she said, holding up her hands as if they could protect her from his venom. "Who the hell damaged you?"

She couldn't accept who I am. I made the mistake of trusting her with something personal, and she couldn't deal.

Oh. Oh, damn. *This* was what he'd been talking about in the hotel room when she asked why he and his ex had broken up. His bitch of a demon girlfriend had probably rejected his human side. Or the angel in him. Either way, she'd done a number on him.

He'd expected Eva to freak out too, and it broke her heart.

"Listen," she said softly, "I'm a big girl. I don't kiss anyone I don't want to kiss." Wariness crept into his gaze as if he expected her to add a *but* to the conversation. There would be none of that. "I definitely wanted to kiss you…and I'd have taken it further if you'd let me. I'm not ashamed of that, Logan."

Her cheeks heated at the admission because…holy shit, she'd just confessed way more than she wanted to. To a supernatural being.

And yet…the shock of it all was…underwhelming. The truth was that she'd always wondered what being with a non-human would be like. She'd grown up in a world where supes were out in the open, so even though they were generally despised, they weren't complete rarities. Some were even celebrated. Demons like Stryke, the CEO of StryTech, who had as many groupies as he had enemies. Or J.R. Chance, a movie star who spent full moons in a werewolf containment system rigged with cameras so his fans could watch him even when he was all furred out. Women loved him. *Begged* him to bite them.

Which was illegal in every country except Australia.

Logan didn't move. Didn't blink. Maybe she'd crossed a line. She had no idea. But what she knew for sure was that she didn't want this tension between them.

"I mean, it might have been nice to know who you were," she said with an exaggerated casual shrug. "But that's on me. I should have done some research. Would have been great to know one thing, though."

His eyes narrowed as if he suspected a trick. "And what's that?"

"Kynan brought me dinner and mentioned that you like mayonnaise on your fries. I'm sorry, but that's gross. If anything makes you a monster, it's that."

He blinked. Stared. And she kicked herself for attempting a bit of humor to lift the pall of the hell they'd been through today.

"We're in Belgium," he said finally, one corner of his mouth turned up in the sexiest hint of a smile she'd ever seen. "You gotta have mayo on your *frites*."

"It's ketchup or nothing." Tension dispelled, or at least tamped down, she tapped her tote, which felt lighter than it had. She suspected they'd relieved it of the Smiter gun. "Where are we going?"

He stood aside and gestured for her to exit. "My place."

"Where's that?"

"Sydney. I need to—"

"Sydney?" Her heart stopped, and she nearly stumbled as they walked down the hall. "Sydney, Australia?"

Ever since the continent had been ceded to demons by the entire world, few humans stepped foot there. Few *decent* humans, anyway. It was, however, a popular destination for corrupt, power or wealth-hungry individuals and evil sickos.

That said, the states formerly known as Queensland and New South Wales were relatively safe. Ruled by Ufelskala Tier-One and Tier-Two demons, New Horun and New South Horun were, on the surface, not much different than when humans occupied the country. Sydney was especially well-managed and open to human visitors.

"Do you know another Sydney?" he asked.

As a matter of fact, yes. "There's a Sidney, Nebraska, you know."

"Why the hell would I live in Nebraska?" He guided her to a nondescript door in an area of the building she'd never seen. It opened into an empty cobblestone courtyard with a nine-foot stone wall topped by iron spikes.

"My grandparents were from there." The courtyard was weird, only about twenty feet by twenty feet. It was empty except for a twisted iron arbor fastened to the back fence. "And it would make sense for your place to be in Nebraska. No one would look for demons in the middle of nowhere."

Grunting, which she took as a reluctant acknowledgment that she'd made a point, he pressed a quarter-sized bronze disk into her palm. "Here, hold this."

"Why?" She pocketed the coin. "What are we doing?" She glanced around, confused as hell. "Where *are* we?"

"We're taking a Harrowgate to my place."

The hell they were. "Humans can't go through them. We'll die unless we're unconscious." She took a couple of wary steps back from him. "Are you planning to knock me out?" Because screw that.

He gestured to her pocket. "That's what the coin is for. StryTech made them so we can transport humans through the gates."

She dug the disk out of her pocket. Both sides of the rich bronze metal were smooth and shiny. One was blank, while the other had been embossed with a spiral symbol. She ran her thumb over the glyph, horrified by the implications of its existence.

"So now demons can kidnap humans and transport them alive to Hell for their own sick and demented purposes?"

"StryTech gave us exclusive access to them," he said, "and they came with a shit ton of restrictions and rules." He glanced up at the cloudy night sky. What time was it, anyway? "I think they even track their usage. Each is numbered and accounted for, and if any are lost or stolen, they'll be deactivated."

"Interesting." She eyed the archway, her stomach rebelling a little.

"It's perfectly safe," he said, moving toward it.

"I'm not worried about the Harrowgate. It's"—she made an encompassing gesture with her arm—"everything. You're taking me through a demon portal to a demon continent because I'm in danger from a vengeance demon. It's...a lot."

"I know." He took her hand and led her to the archway. "And it's about to be a lot more."

How comforting.

Willing her sandwich to stay down, she stepped with Logan into the archway. Darkness swallowed her a heartbeat before glowing symbols and maps lit the uncomfortably close black walls. Thank God she wasn't claustrophobic. She watched Logan tap a bunch of symbols as maps expanded or shrank, depending on what he touched.

Seconds later, an archway appeared, and she stepped out of the darkness into a well-lit warehouse filled with boxes, equipment, and even a couple of vehicles.

"What is all this?"

"We have a lot of room," Logan said as he guided her to a door on the far side of the building, "so we let our families store shit here."

Outside, they crossed a beautifully maintained, parklike yard full of ponds, sprawling trees, and water fountains. At the end of the pathway, a sprawling, three-story mansion wrapped in decks overlooked a pool with a waterfall.

They mounted the steps of a patio with an outdoor kitchen that could handle a party for fifty.

"Wow." She craned her neck to check out the lazy river and slide on the far side of the building. "You said *we*. Do you have roommates?"

"Yep." He held the door open for her. "Some you've even met."

She nearly groaned. If she'd met them, then they worked at DART and hated her.

This was a terrible idea.

They took a hallway to an enormous living room that reminded her of a hotel lobby. She groaned again. Sure enough, she recognized one of the two demons lounging on the couch, playing video games on a TV that took up an entire wall.

Mace raised his hand in greeting but kept his eyes on the screen. "Yo."

"I think you know Mace," Logan said to her. He gestured to the other guy. "That's Crux. Blade and Rade's younger brother."

Neither of them seemed to be paying any attention.

Logan moved around the couch so he partially blocked their view. "Hey, can you guys keep an eye on Eva for a few? I need to run by her hotel room and grab her stuff."

"Wait, what?" Eva stepped closer and lowered her voice. "You're going to leave me alone with demons?"

"Demons with excellent hearing," Crux muttered.

"They're cool," Logan reassured her. "They're not going to steal your soul or drink your blood or anything. They're incubi, but they won't touch you. I promise."

Yeah, well, she hadn't had the greatest experiences in the world with sex demons so far. Rade was a sadistic bastard, and Blade was just a bastard. "I'm not sure—"

"Oh, bloody hell, lady," Mace said, stretching around Logan to mow down some enemies with his rifle. "Do you wanna fuck?"

"What?" she blurted, completely taken aback. "No. Hell, no."

Mace shrugged. "Then Logan's right. We won't touch you. Take a seat, grab a controller, and kick some old-school *Call of Duty* ass with us. I'll probably kill you in the game, though." He shot her a look. "Seeing as how I can't kill you in real life and all."

"See?" Logan said. "They're not going to hurt you. I'll be back in a little while. If you get hungry or anything, the kitchen is down that hallway. Help yourself to whatever you want." He gave Crux and Mace pointed looks. "You two behave."

He left before she could argue, and she just stood there, unsure of what to do, until Crux picked up a controller and tossed it at her.

"Have a seat." He gestured to a chair near him. "I'll show you how to play."

Having nothing else to do and no argument to make, she sank down and let them explain the game to her. Crux turned out to be pretty nice. Sparing with his words but nice. Mace was much freer with words, mostly of the four-letter and insulting variety.

She caught on quickly, racking up a body count that was sort of cathartic once she got into it. Mindlessly mowing down enemies gave her a chance to burn some nervous energy and take her mind off the tragedy and violence going on in the real world all around her.

Weird how a violent game could be so relaxing, so—

Suddenly, Crux threw down his controller and leaped to his feet. She nearly screamed.

"Anyone want a soda or beer while I'm up?"

Mace flicked his hand dismissively, and Eva shook her head, unable to find her voice. The kid flung himself over the back of the couch in a single, effortless leap and disappeared into the kitchen.

"He's like a squirrel on crack," Mace muttered. "You get used to it. Mostly." He jammed his finger on a rapid-fire button. "Yes! Got the bastard."

She glanced over at him as he lounged on the couch in black sweat shorts and a Foster's T-shirt, his tan skin contrasting with the cream leather. She'd only seen him in passing at DART, and she'd known the moment she laid eyes on him that he was a Seminus demon. They all looked like they were made to play the starring role in a romantic action movie.

"I'm surprised you're playing old-school games."

"Oh, dude." He hit the pause button and turned to her, making the personal glyph below his jaw, a bird in flight, flap its wings. "We have a sweet mixed-reality game room where we usually play, but we gotta get some rest and didn't want to get too amped, you know? Too bad you suck at this."

What a jerk. "You say you have a mixed-reality room?"

"A killer one." Crux sauntered back to the couch with an armload of snacks and drinks. "We even have racing and jet chairs."

Oh, things were definitely looking up. She hadn't sat in a jet chair in years but doubted she was rusty. "Do you have any games with torpedo racers?"

"Duh." Mace popped open a bag of cheese puffs. "Why? You wanna try a race game?"

Welp, the Elders had wanted her to play dumb, hadn't they?

"I'd love to try." She batted her eyes, all innocence and enthusiasm. "I've heard so much about them."

Crux grinned at Mace. "This is gonna be fun."

"Killing a noob? Nah. But killing an Aegi? Let's do it."

Suckers.

"Tell you what," she said, looking between the two demons, "let's play two against one."

Mace snorted. "What, you and Crux against me?"

"No." She set aside her controller. "*You* and Crux against *me*."

Crux laughed into his can of soda. "Puny human thinks she can beat us."

She wasn't going to beat them. She was going to *destroy* them. "Wanna make it even more interesting?"

"How's that?" Mace asked warily.

"A wager. Whoever wins four out of seven games can claim a favor from the loser. Or losers."

Mace and Crux exchanged glances. "Deal," they said in unison.

Fools. She might not be a match for them physically, but she was more than a match for them in her own way.

She would make them kiss her puny human ass.

Chapter Twenty

Logan barely held in a chuckle as he slipped inside Eva's hotel room. The Sem boys were probably driving Eva nuts. They were harmless—mostly. Crux was young, nerdy, and hadn't yet gone through the sexual maturity ordeal that his species went through in their twenties. And while Mace was a deadly fucker with no filter or impulse control, he wasn't into sexual assault.

On the other hand, if a female showed any interest in him at all, he was incapable of saying no. And the females always showed interest because he was handsome, fit, and constantly pumping out Seminus fuck-me pheromones.

Suddenly, Logan's amusement died a bitter, ugly death at the realization that he'd just left Eva with a demon whose mere presence made females horny.

If he touches her, he's dead.

Shit. Logan was a dumbass. He wouldn't destroy his friend over a female.

An image of Mace and Eva tangled on the couch made him revise that thought and shove it from his head. He'd get her stuff and get back before anyone could tangle *anything*.

Closing the door behind him, he thanked Eva for being so tidy and making his job easier. The way she dressed, organized, and kept every hair in place spoke of someone who was a bit of a control freak, and he didn't mind that at all.

As a control freak himself, he understood the need to dominate the environment around you, and keep situations in check. Letting one's guard down could end badly. Uncle Ares had drilled that into him from a young age, but he'd learned hard lessons all on his own too.

He carefully folded her clothes and tucked them into her suitcase. He even folded her panties into neat little triangles. His mom, who had battled with OCD her entire life, would be proud of his attention to detail. But she'd be less than thrilled at the direction his mind went as the silky fabric slid over his fingers.

He could imagine stroking the lace design all the way around Eva's waist before feathering his fingertips lower, cupping her ass as he followed the seam between her cheeks. The elastic leg opening would provide no defense against his fingers.

Or his teeth.

A growl erupted from his throat as he shoved the last pair of underwear into the suitcase. He was such an idiot. The world was falling apart, and he was having an erotic experience with a pair of panties.

Now was not the time to get involved with anyone, let alone someone from The Aegis who worked directly for his ex-girlfriend.

It seemed, though, that employment by The Aegis was the only thing Eva and Maja had in common. Eva's reaction to his heritage had been the exact opposite of Maja's, and he'd been so stunned by it that it had taken time for his brain to process.

I definitely wanted to kiss you…and I'd have taken it further if you'd let me. I'm not ashamed of that, Logan.

Fire had shot through his veins at her admission, and had they been anywhere but at work, he would have taken her in his arms and tested her words.

And it would have been a mistake.

The universe was gearing up for Armageddon, and life in all the realms would only get worse. Humans hadn't quite caught on yet, either. So many couldn't see beyond their lifespan to want to make the kinds of sacrifices needed to prepare. Even *if* they believed that Satan was fated to be freed from his prison in less than a thousand years, humans had a cavalier, let's-pass-this-down-to-the-next-generation attitude. Few cared that Satan's release would trigger the events leading to the final battle between good and evil, Heaven and Hell, with Earth as the battleground. They wouldn't be around to see it, after all.

But Logan would. His family would. And he *did* care. He definitely didn't need to fall for a human who would die and leave him mourning for centuries.

He cleared out the last drawer and grabbed her toiletries from the bathroom. They were already packed neatly, so he was finished with the bag zipped closed a minute later. Time to go.

But as he did one last sweep of the hotel room, the hair on the back of his neck stood up. The high-level warning shot down his spine and through his veins in a rush of adrenaline. Instinctively summoning a sword, he swung toward the door as it crashed in.

Wood splinters bounced off Logan as the door, twisted on its frame, crunched into the wall behind it.

Through the cloud of dust and the rain of wood shards and paint chips, Draven strode inside. A frigid blast of air accompanied him, so biting that the room's furnace kicked on.

"Kynan's got you raiding those assholes' rooms before The Aegis can get here, huh?" Draven asked casually, amiably, as if he hadn't just lost his fiancée and gone on a killing spree. As if his eyes hadn't turned black, the pupils ringed by a crimson glow. As if he didn't have wicked steel-gray claws now instead of fingernails.

Oh, buddy. Just...fuck.

"Yeah," Logan said, just as casually, even though he was dying inside. Draven had once told him that the only way to get through to a partially transitioned *tormentus* demon was to stay calm and appeal to their old selves. Their decent selves. "They took off so fast they might have left behind other weapons or something."

"I punished two of them." Draven's twisted smile creeped Logan out. It would creep out Draven too, if he'd just look in the mirror behind him.

"I know. You did what you felt you had to do." Logan eased a little closer. He'd always been the stronger of the two, beating Draven handily when they sparred. He didn't want this to devolve into a fight, but he couldn't let the guy go, either. "But that's enough."

"Enough? They killed Shanea!"

Logan released the sword and let it fade away. He didn't need it. He'd never need to use it against Draven. Never. "And they will pay for what they did—"

"I'm going to make every one of them pay," Draven growled.

"At what cost?" Logan struggled to keep the urgency out of his voice. *Never let a demon know you're desperate,* as Ares liked to say. "You'll become the very kind of demon we've been fighting. You'll become a monster, Draven. You'll lose yourself and your family. You've got to stop this. Right now."

"But I don't want to stop. I want to know where the rest of them are." He studied his claws. "Do you know where they are?"

"The Aegis won't tell us."

"I don't believe you." Draven looked up from his hand. "Just tell me if they're out of the country."

"Draven, I swear I don't know." Very casually, he clasped his fingers together, moving his right hand close to his comms. He needed to get DART here ASAP.

"Then I'll have to raid every Aegis house in Belgium until I find them. I'll leave a bloodbath in my wake, Logan. You know I will." He glanced at Logan's hands. "Don't even think about alerting DART."

"I'm not," Logan lied. Fuck. Draven knew him way too well. "But come with me back to HQ. You're not in trouble. DART will stand behind you. Those Aegi started it. We have it on holocam. They murdered two of our people. Everyone understands why you did what you did."

Logan didn't have to lie about that. They all got it. There wasn't a person at DART who wouldn't go homicidal if their loved one was murdered. But this would become very public very soon, and the world wasn't ready to see a DART agent get demonic revenge, especially if the targets were human—ones the world saw as heroes in an organization that stood as a bulwark between good and evil.

No, Draven on a bloody rampage wasn't a good look for DART at all.

"Okay, how about this?" he continued, reading Draven and the conflict in his expression. Logan was getting through to him. "Let me take you to your parents. They're worried about you. They can bring you back to the real you. Because this…this isn't you."

Draven swallowed. When he spoke, his voice trembled. "But it *is* me. It's me without Shanea."

"It hurts, I know." Logan eased even closer. He'd take his buddy down if he had to. Draven would thank him later. "But we'll all help you through it. Let me call your parents."

For a long time, Draven just stood there, his eyes glazed with unshed tears, the crimson rings flickering.

I have him.

Then a door slammed at the end of the hall, and Draven snapped out of his…humanity. That was the only word Logan could think of. One moment, Draven's skin had lost its gray tinge, and the red light in his eyes had dimmed. The next, they lit up like fires again, and blue veins spread across the backs of his hands as he curled them into fists.

"Help me," he growled.

"I will," Logan swore. The pain in Draven's voice wrecked him. He reached for his friend, ready to take him to his parents. "I'll do anything. You know that—"

"Help me get justice," Draven roared, his teeth elongating, sharpening. "*Help me slaughter those who took everything from me!*"

Agony and hatred filled the room like acidic steam. It stung Logan's eyes and skin, corrupting his thoughts and very soul as he actually considered Draven's plea. He didn't know if it was some sort of effect Draven's species had, or if it came as a result of Logan's breeding. Maybe Draven's evil side was connecting with the demon DNA inside Logan that came from Lilith. Whatever it was, it called to him. Made him want to cause suffering and death.

Family is not to be fucked with.

"I want to." No lie. It was no fucking lie. The truth of it seared his gut. His heart. His soul.

Draven held out his hand. "Take it, brother." His voice became smoky and rumbling, scraping the deepest pits of Hell. "Let's lay waste to the human filth that plagues this world. We won't stop with the fuckers who took Shanea from me. We'll be vigilantes. Righting wrongs the humans do to us. It's you and me against the world. Just like when we were kids, except we now have the power to really take out the bad guys. We'll be real-life heroes."

The demon on Logan's shoulder whispered in his ear, telling him to join his best friend on the noble mission.

The angel on his other shoulder, the one he imagined to be his grandfather, whacked him upside the head and threatened to put him over his knee.

Somehow, even though he hadn't seen Reaver in forever, he heard his grandfather telling him he loved him. And to get his head out of his ass, or he'd sic grandma Harvester on him.

In some ways, Harvester was far scarier than either Reaver or Lilith.

As if merely thinking Lilith's name was a summons, she appeared in the doorway, her skintight black leather bodysuit revealing far more than any grandson wanted to see.

Draven wheeled around to her. "Lilith," he spat, sounding like his old self, and for the first time, Logan was actually glad to see her.

This could be the break Logan needed. They'd fight Lilith together, on the same side. Surely, Draven would remember the DART agent he was. And if he still didn't, Logan could beat his ass and haul him to his parents' place for the reversal ceremony.

Lilith cocked her head and eyed Draven. "Weren't you at the club the other night? With my grandson? You look different." She waggled her brows suggestively. "I like." She turned to Logan. "Did you really think changing rooms would fool me? I knew you'd come back for that bitch in heat."

Draven gave Logan the side-eye. "What is she talking about?"

"Don't listen to her. Lilith's been stalking me. She followed me here when I returned a tablet to Eva."

"Did you?" Lilith tapped her chin and affected a thoughtful expression. "Because you seemed a little busy with your tongue in her mouth."

"*Liar.*" Draven, squared to go one-on-one with Lilith, spun around to Logan with a snarl. "Tell me she's lying. You can't be fucking one of the Aegi who killed Shan."

"Come on, Draven. You're taking the word of Lilith—"

"They killed the female I love!" Draven shouted, and Lilith's eyes sparked with life as she realized what was going on here.

"Oh…so *you're* the one who killed The Aegi today," she purred. "I can help you, dear boy."

"Don't listen to her," Logan warned his friend. "Don't do it. Draven! You've known me and my family your entire life. You know what she's done. You've heard the stories."

Draven looked between Logan and Lilith, his tortured gaze softening and hardening depending on who he focused on last.

Lilith's slender fingers drew down the zipper at her cleavage, revealing plump breasts. Her fingernail scratched across her skin, opening a paper-thin cut from which blood began to well.

"Taste me," she whispered, "and I'll make all your dreams and nightmares come true." Her voice became a drone. "You do for me, and I'll do for you."

Draven drifted closer. Logan put himself between them and slammed his hand into his friend's sternum.

"Draven! Dammit. Shanea wouldn't want this!"

For a second, a mere gazillionth of a second, Draven hesitated. Deep down, he knew the truth. He knew the female he'd loved would not want this. He knew that the old Draven wouldn't want this either.

But the vengeance demon inside Draven *did* want it.

And it was stronger than the old Draven.

"Give me what I want, Lilith," Draven breathed, "and I am all yours."

Triumph lit Lilith's face.

Draven struck out, knocking Logan into the dresser as if he was a gnat. Logan recovered, throwing himself at Draven like a linebacker.

But in a blur of motion, Lilith wrapped her slinky body around Draven, shot Logan a seductive wink...and phased out of the room, taking his best friend with her.

Chapter Twenty-One

It only took half an hour and five games for Eva to win the best of seven battles. She'd let the boys win once out of pity.

The outer space game projection faded, leaving her sitting in the soft-floored room instead of inside a triple-engine starfighter. Crux and Mace stared like they'd never seen her before.

She winked. "Gotcha."

"What. The. Fuck?" Mace shoved out of his chair. "How the hell did you do that?"

"Dude," Crux said, his broad grin and mussed hair giving him a charmingly boyish look. And wasn't it weird to think of a demon as boyish? And charming. "That was awesome."

They filed out of the room and toward the living room, Mace shaking his head. "I did not see that ass-kicking coming."

"And," she said cheerily, "now you owe me a favor."

Mace grumbled as he plopped back down on the sofa. "You cheated."

"Well…I might have failed to mention that I was the number-one player in the world back in college. Oops."

Crux laughed and gave her a high five. "Well played. And kinda hot. You think you'll be around in a few months? Maybe a year?"

Confused, she looked at Mace, who shrugged. "He can't have sex until his transition. He's due for it any day now." Leaning back against a couch cushion, he threw his feet up onto the coffee table. "But until then, he can only window shop."

She had no idea how to respond to that. She did, however, need to pee.

"I don't suppose someone could point me to a bathroom…"

Mace grabbed a video game controller. "There's one down the hall behind you. It's just off the kitchen to the right."

"Thank you." She hiked it to the bathroom, closing the door as the sound of booted feet rang out. Hoping it was Logan, she cracked the door so she could hear better.

"Mace." Logan's voice rang out. "Where's Eva?"

"Bathroom. And, man, your girl is a gaming badass. Not that I'd ever tell her that. But it was hot. If she weren't an Aegi, I'd—"

"Shut it. We have a problem." His voice lowered, and she had to strain to hear. "A huge fucking problem. I just texted Blade and Scotty. I saw Draven while I was picking up Eva's things."

Eva's breath caught.

"Holy shit," Mace said, voicing what she was thinking. "What happened? Did you talk him down?"

"No. I thought I had him. Then guess who showed up."

There was a pause. And then, "No fucking way. You can't be serious." Obviously, Mace knew who Logan was talking about.

"Yeah. I am. I'm guessing she was there to harass me, but she realized she could use Draven, and he fell right into her trap. I don't know what he'll be willing to give up about me, us, DART…"

"He wouldn't." The conviction in Mace's voice gave her hope. "Not Draven. He lasted three days in a Necromancer's dungeon once, and he didn't give up jack shit."

Another moment passed. When Logan finally spoke, he sounded defeated. "You didn't see him. You didn't see him, man. He's almost gone. His demon has a solid grip on him."

"What do we do?"

"I called his parents on the way here. They've got a ritual ready to go. They're putting out a call to everyone they know to be on the lookout for him and to bring him in hogtied if they have to."

Mace let out a frustrated curse. "Who all knows about Draven's new unholy alliance?"

"Just Scotty and Blade. Figured I'd tell everyone else when I got here."

Mace mumbled something about someone being in their room and someone else being at work at a hospital, but she didn't catch the names.

"What about Kynan? And the Horsemen?"

There was another long pause. "I don't want to get them involved. You know how they are. Especially Dad and Ares. They're not going to care that Draven is our friend. They'll kill him. Let them focus on her for now. Draven is DART's business."

"Okay, so what about Kynan?"

"I'll tell him tomorrow at the party."

Mace's voice lowered, and Eva had to strain to hear him. "And Eva? Whatever you say to her will get back to The Aegis. We don't need our rivals knowing we've got bigger problems."

Bigger problems than a rogue vengeance demon bent on slaughtering Aegi?

"She needs to know about Draven. I'll decide about the rest later."

So, Draven had apparently hooked up with a female demon. Logan said he thought she'd been there to harass him, so was Draven's new BFF Logan's ex?

Figuring she would be missed soon, she hurried to use the toilet and wash her hands, then loudly opened the door and clomped down the hall.

Logan stood in the living room with her two suitcases and her Louis Vuitton duffel slung over his shoulder. He swung around, and she drew a breath at the way he smiled when he saw her.

"Logan. You're back." Dolt. Obviously, he was back.

"I think I got everything." He cocked his head toward the staircase. "C'mon, I'll show you to your room." He gave Mace and Crux a wave. "Night, guys. Mace, see you in a couple of hours. And get some rest. Trust me, we don't want to face Draven tired."

Mace flipped off Logan, who shook his head and started up the stairs. When Eva offered to take one of the bags, he turned her down and kept climbing, which gave her a great view of his butt. He should always wear those black tactical pants. Although she'd love to see him in jeans too.

And in nothing.

The erotic image stole her breath and her coordination, and she stumbled on the top step. If not for the industrial steel railing, she'd have taken a header right into Logan's juicy ass.

Then I could bite it.

Did he like being bitten? And why was she thinking this way?

Because you spent the last hour with sex demons.

Right. This entire residence was probably permeated with incubi pheromones, and depending on how many lived here—

A shirtless Seminus demon wearing only a pair of shorts appeared from a hallway at the top of the stairs. She nearly collided with him as he beelined for the balcony landing.

"Excuse me—"

Rade.

Instant, stark fear shot down her spine. She took an involuntary step backward, out of the range of his hands and his mind-fucking weapon.

"*You.*" She glared at Logan. "He lives here too?"

"Get over it, lady." Rade rubbed his muscular chest as he sauntered over to a wooden pedestal centered on the balcony overlooking the padded game room where she'd kicked Blade's and Crux's asses. "I was just doing my job. Nothing personal."

"Maybe it wasn't personal for *you*," she snapped.

"Isn't that what I just said?" He swiped an ornate jade vase off the pedestal and started down the hall.

"Wait," Logan called out. "We need to talk."

Not slowing, Rade swung the vase into the air. "Hit me up in half an hour."

"I despise him," she muttered as he disappeared into a room and slammed the door.

Logan stared down the hall after him. "He can't help how he is."

"Why? Because he's a species of demon predisposed to being assholes?"

He chuckled, but an underlying sadness weighed down the amusement. "He was kidnapped as a baby, and when his family got him back, he wasn't the same. Long story. Let's just say he's nothing like his brothers. Which isn't to say they aren't assholes. They are. For different reasons."

"Crux seems sweet," she said. "Blade is a jerk. How many brothers are there?"

"Crux is the younger brother, one of a set of twins." Logan glanced down over the railing at the game room. "He just turned twenty-two. Rade and Blade are two of triplets. The other is the CEO of StryTech."

Whoa. "Stryke? *Stryke* is their brother?" And Runa's son.

Holy shit. *Seriously*, holy shit. Blade and Rade had both reminded her of someone—each other, she realized. And Stryke.

The reclusive trillionaire known around the world as *the demon Steve Jobs* had built an empire with his combination of genius and technology—technology that had gifted the world its best defenses against demons. Humans both loved and feared him, and he was largely credited for humanity's growing tolerance for underworlders. He was the poster boy for the argument that some demons were good. Detractors insisted that his gifts of demon-detecting machines, soul traps, and anti-demon weapons were surely a trick, even as they used and praised the technology.

Hell, The Aegis was one of his biggest customers.

Logan turned away from the iron railing. "Yeah. Good old Stryke."

Ouch. Big story there. "Do you guys see him a lot?"

There was a moment of pause, as if he was deciding how much to share.

"It's okay," she said. "I don't mean to pry."

Except she did. She was curious, not just about Logan's life, but also the private lives of demons. She'd told Logan she hadn't really thought about whether or not demons could love, and she was ashamed now to realize that she'd never thought about their lives at all. They were the *others*, people from a world of pain and evil whose lives were so different from those of humans that it wasn't worth thinking about. Heck, a good percentage of humans were convinced that demon lifestyles involved nothing but sacrificing virgins and drinking the blood of infants. Surely, demons that ate people didn't do dishes, vacuum, or take family vacations to the Grand Canyon.

"No, it's fine. It's just that a bunch of family shit went down a while back, and Stryke pretty much cut everyone out of his life." He made an encompassing gesture. "This was his first compound. He gave it to all of us after he moved his company to the Sydney high-rise."

"Wow." Now the odd architectural blend of modern house and industrial building made sense. She strolled around the balcony, with its four hallways shooting off in an X pattern. The balcony, she realized, was the center of the building. The heart of it.

Pictures lined the walls, and she paused to look at one taken at a beach. She recognized a slightly younger Logan, hanging out with a couple of people she didn't know. But she definitely knew who the three Seminus demons nearby were. Blade, Stryke, and Rade. Clearly, they were brothers. All had black hair, although styled differently, chiseled jaws, and good looks that should be illegal. But Rade had one thing the other two didn't.

Ice-cold eyes.

She moved to another photo in the collage, obviously taken at the same event, and saw a dark-haired boy. "Is that Crux?"

Eva swore the temperature in the room dropped thirty degrees before Logan answered. "That was Chaos. Crux's twin."

"Was?" she asked softly.

"He died fifteen years ago. A week after that picture was taken. He was only seven."

"Oh. I'm sorry for your loss." It was an automatic response, said a million times during a career that made poking around in dark places mandatory. How many times had she exploited others' pain to get a good story? Interviewing the survivor of a tragedy was freaking gold.

I'm sorry for your loss.

"Are you?" The doubt in Logan's voice was like a lash, sudden, stinging, and coming from out of nowhere. "Chaos was a demon. Your people would have killed him without a second thought."

Ah, so it wasn't from out of nowhere. He'd just remembered that she worked for the enemy of his people.

"I really am sorry," she said, hoping it sounded sincere and not rote. "Is that what happened? Did The Aegis kill him?"

"If The Aegis had killed him, all of you would be extinct by now."

The anger and pain in Logan's words chilled her to the bone. He wasn't speaking in hyperbole. He was stating fact. And for maybe the first time in her life, she decided to stop digging and let something go, no matter how much she wanted to know what'd happened to Chaos.

And yet…one thing niggled at her, and the journalist in her *couldn't* let it go.

"You said he was seven. Fifteen years ago. So, he was born twenty-two years ago?"

"Yeah, why?"

"Because according to our sources, not a single demon has been born for almost three decades. Not since the destruction of Sheoul-gra."

"So The Aegis knows about the zero birth rate?" He nodded thoughtfully. "Interesting."

"I find it even more interesting that two demons were born during that time. With Sheoul-gra no longer holding and reincarnating demon souls, how were they born? Are their souls…human?"

"We don't know. No one has ever been able to sense what's inside them."

"Maybe they have no souls," she offered.

He dismissed that with a shake of the head. "People sensitive to souls can feel the presence of one, but they can't determine the type."

"Are you?"

"Am I what? Sensitive to souls?"

She hoped that wasn't a rude question, but now that she'd asked, she might as well get an answer. "Your father stores the souls of those he kills in his armor, and your mother can repel souls. I just thought maybe you inherited—" She drew a quick breath as a thought occurred to her. "My nightmare demon. You were able to catch it, even though it was a spirit, because you can see souls, can't you?"

He watched her carefully, gauging her reactions. And it made her want to beat his ex for making him so wary of telling her personal details.

"Again," she said, "you don't have to answer." She gestured to the table where the vase had been, looking for a change of subject and mood. "Why did Rade take that, anyway? Is it a priceless artifact? Was he afraid I would steal it?"

The tension seemed to melt from Logan's taut body. She'd definitely made the right choice to focus her questions elsewhere.

Another lesson from her lawyer parents.

Logan started down the hallway directly across from the one Rade had taken. "It's for sex."

"Oh," she said. Because, of course, a Seminus demon would need sex. Except... "Wait. Did you say sex?" At Logan's nod, she paused, unsure how to process this. "He has sex with a vase?"

He stopped at the third door on the right. "You ever watch *I Dream of Jeannie*? It's like a super classic TV show." He tucked her carry-on under his arm and reached for the door handle.

"I only saw the reboot that came out a few years ago. Are you telling me a genie lives in that bottle and Rade has sex with her?"

"Masumi isn't a genie." He turned the doorknob. "She's a species of succubus that can only survive by hooking up with Seminus demons. She has two vases. One is here for all the guys, and Stryke has the other."

Damn, that was fascinating. "Does she live in both simultaneously, like in an alternate dimension?"

"Exactly." He swung the door open and gestured for her to enter. "Her vases are a big Tardis. When a Sem summons her, she either comes out, or they can transport inside."

"Wow." She stepped through the doorway and found herself not in a bedroom but an apartment, complete with a living room and small kitchen. The place would have been stark if not for the pictures of family scattered on the end tables and shelves, and the bookcase loaded down with a few knickknacks that looked like ancient artifacts, several thick books, and some magazines. A hoverboard and surfboard sat propped against some whimsically painted exposed pipes, each done in a different primary color that brightened the place.

And in the middle of the living room was what looked like a giant dog bed.

"Oh, my God," she blurted, suddenly remembering a detail that had been added to what little The Aegis knew about the children of Thanatos and Regan Matthews.

The son is bonded to a hellhound.

"You have a hellhound."

"Don't worry." He took her luggage to the bedroom on the left. "He knows better than to eat anyone in this house."

"Great." She wasn't sure she was as comforted by his words as he probably thought she'd be. "That's just…great."

At least the bedroom was cheery, with a sliding glass door that allowed plenty of light and access to a covered patio.

He set her luggage on the floor and plopped her bag into the chair in the corner. "I'll sleep in the spare bedroom down the hall."

She stopped him as he turned to the door. "Why not give me the spare bedroom?"

"This one has a private bathroom," he said. "I didn't think you'd want to traipse up and down the hall in a strange place in the middle of the night."

Aw, how considerate. But the idea of being in the room alone tonight left her unsettled. "Aren't you worried I'll try to escape or something?"

He shot her an amused look, and she wondered if he saw through her clumsy attempt at getting him to stay. The couch looked comfy. So did the giant dog bed, actually.

"And where are you going to go? We're on a continent owned by supernaturals. You take one step outside this compound and you're in demon territory with no way out. Draven will be the least of your problems."

"Right." She hadn't been serious, not really, but now the reality of her situation crashed down on her. She truly was out of her element, and all of a sudden, her body became aware of the stress the day had put on her.

"You okay?" Logan's concern touched her, bringing the stress even more to the forefront.

"No, I'm not," she admitted, too tired to feign strength. "I've been on the run, captured, there's a demon after me, and friends have died. I just want to go to bed. And I don't want to be alone."

There. She'd said it. The truth sat there, hanging between them. She wasn't ready for Logan to go.

"If you're sure." He gestured to the living room. "I can take the couch."

Not good enough. She'd still be alone. Taking a deep, bracing breath, she told him exactly what she wanted. She'd never been shy.

"I want you to sleep in the bed."

"I'm not letting you take the couch," he said, and she almost laughed at how utterly oblivious he was. It was kind of adorable.

"I wasn't planning on it."

Logan's eyes flared as he finally caught on. Then they darkened and narrowed. His jaw set hard, the muscles twitching along the bone. "That's not a good idea."

Closing her lids, she whispered, "I know."

She didn't need to open her eyes to read the sudden electric shift in the room. The air felt thick with desire, but no more so than his smoky voice.

"I don't want to be right next to you," he growled, "keeping my hands to myself—"

"I don't want you to keep your hands to yourself." She stepped into him. At this point, it was all or nothing, and she liked to gamble. "I want them on *me*. All over me."

Holy shit.

Logan couldn't believe this was happening. He looked down at the beautiful, exhausted female standing so close her heat scorched his skin through his T-shirt.

"It's not a good idea," he repeated. "Bad enough I couldn't control myself during combat training when we only had one demon to worry about. Now, we have an international incident, and a vengeance demon after you."

The heat in her eyes cooled a little, but she was still throwing off a carnal fever that he wouldn't be able to ignore even if he wasn't one-quarter sex demon.

"Exactly. We could wait for a perfect time, but when will that be?" Her fingers trailed down his shoulder, leaving tingles everywhere they touched. "I heard you talking to Mace earlier. About Draven and someone else. Your ex? The demon?"

He hadn't been sure how much to tell her about that, but in the moment, he couldn't deflect. Her life was on the line, and ultimately, The Aegis was well aware of who Lilith was and what she was capable of. Them knowing she was an active threat might not be the worst thing ever.

"The demon who has been stalking me isn't my ex-girlfriend. She's Lilith. *The* Lilith. My grandmother."

The color leached from Eva's face. She swallowed. Hard. And then sank down onto the end of the bed. Instinct had him wanting to step back in preparation for a blow to the face.

But Eva wasn't Maja. Still, his shoulders tightened as he waited for her reaction. And maybe a knife to the gut.

"Oh, my God," she whispered. "She's real? I mean, of course, she is. I just thought...I don't know what I thought. Your grandmother is *Lilith*. The most infamous succubus ever." She frowned as she considered what he'd told her. "Why would your grandmother be stalking you?"

"Long story. Basically, she's always felt that the Horsemen were disappointments because they aren't evil psychos. Then my uncle Reseph, who you would know as the Horseman known as Pestilence, killed her right after I was born. When Azagoth destroyed Sheoul-gra and released the billions of souls back into their physical bodies, she came back. She's been plotting revenge for decades and chose now to reveal herself."

She rolled her bottom lip between her teeth and thought about that. "How dangerous is she?"

"Take whatever you've heard and multiply it by twenty on the atrocities scale," he said. "We all hate her. But if it makes you feel any better, my paternal grandfather is an angel. I know you guys know who Reaver is."

That didn't seem to make her feel better.

"Reaver." She stared blankly at him. "He slept with Lilith and created the Four Horsemen. Not much is known about him after that except that he lost his wings and then got them back after he saved the world from an apocalypse." She shook her head. "Wow. I think...I think I'm having trouble processing all of this. I sound like an Aegis encyclopedia."

"I know what you must be thinking—"

"No, you don't." She shoved to her feet, her eyes flashing as if she hadn't looked ready to pass out just a couple of moments ago. "I've always been a risk-taker. I'm not as afraid of things as I should be. I was a journalist before I joined The Aegis, a reporter for some very anti-demon networks."

"I'm aware," he said. "I did a little research."

She gave him a firm nod. "I wouldn't respect you if you hadn't." She turned and paced to the sliding door to look out over the compound's extensive grounds. "I've had stalkers. I even had a death threat when I exposed a vampire colony near a Houston elementary school." She swung back to him. "But this is different. There's a lot going on. I'm in real danger, and it's kind of crazy, but it's sort of making me feel like I need to burn off some energy. You know, live life to the fullest. In case I'm going to die. Is that weird? Is it weird that I want a handsome, powerful man to give me a night of pleasure to forget all the shit?"

No. No, it wasn't weird. Because he had just had one hell of a shitty day too, and right now, losing himself in a hot, willing female might be the last chance he had for a respite before all hell broke loose. He had a terrible suspicion that things were going to get very fucking real, very fucking soon.

But she'd called him a man. Men were human. He needed to know for sure, one hundred percent, that she truly understood who he was. He couldn't deal with morning-after regrets.

"We can have a night," he said, his voice hoarse and needy. "Just a night."

"Okay," she whispered, taking a step closer.

"But first, tell me you're okay with what I am."

Her dark brows knitted in confusion, but a heartbeat later, they arched as she understood what he was asking.

"What you are," she said, taking another step, "is unexpected. And exciting. And a little scary." Another step. "*Who* you are is someone who cares deeply for friends and family. I know what I'm getting into, and no matter what happens between us, I won't use your DNA against you."

A sense of relief loosened muscles he hadn't realized were tense.

They met in a tangle of limbs and mouths.

His hands went straight for her blouse. His fingers tore at the buttons, but as the first one popped, she stepped back. "Wait. I mean, I don't want to wait, but…"

"It's okay," he said. "I have condoms."

"No, not that. I'm on the pill." She looked down at her clothes, rumpled and splashed with blood. "It's just that it's been a long, sweaty, bloody day. I really could use a shower first."

"Funny, so could I."

It was a race to the shower, their clothes coming off as they scrambled toward the bathroom. Logan couldn't even regret not being able to strip her because watching her peel out of her underwear was the highlight of his damn life.

That. Ass.

Eva got to the bathroom first, and she skidded to a halt on the tile floor just before she reached the fully open shower stall.

"Wow." Her dark hair spilled around her shoulders and swung against her spine as she took in the wall of mirrors, the heated towel racks, and the waterfall feature in the tub. "It's like a spa."

"Stryke has expensive tastes. He had all six master suites designed for comfort."

"Did he expect a dozen people to take a shower at the same time? Because you could fit that many in there. There are four showerheads."

"And six in the walls." He hit a button on the pad on the wall, and every showerhead spurted hot water. "What can I say? Stryke likes his luxury."

"I have so many questions," she breathed.

"Later." He hooked her around the waist, bringing her hot body against his so they were skin to skin. Breasts to chest. His hard cock pressed into her soft belly. "Much, much later."

Chapter Twenty-Two

Eva hadn't been nervous about sex since she'd lost her virginity in college. Even then, she didn't remember being nervous. More like anxious. She'd wanted to be done with it already. Her friends had talked about sex as if it was the greatest thing ever.

Eva had found it to be messy, painful, and not that satisfying.

It had gotten better as she got older and dated guys with more experience, and it had been great with her ex. She'd finally understood the hype. But nerves? Never. Men didn't make her nervous.

At least, they hadn't until Logan.

He's not a man.

And he was *magnificent.*

His tongue flicked across the seam of her lips, seeking more, and she opened, giving him what he wanted. Right now, he could have *anything* he wanted.

Lust flowed through her like hot honey, making her body languid as he wrapped one arm around her waist and the other beneath her butt. With a sexy growl, he lifted her against him and sank down onto one of the benches, settling her on his lap.

"This is probably really stupid," he said against her mouth.

"Agreed." She grinned. "But it's gonna be fun."

He chuckled, his chest rubbing against her sensitive breasts. Her nipples were on fire, begging for his touch. As if he knew, he dropped his palm and cupped one. His thumb stroked inward, making light, slow passes that had her arching into his hand as she straddled his thighs.

His cock stood erect, pressing into her belly, and she loved how his breathing hitched when she rocked against it. She shifted, putting her core so close to his thick shaft she could feel its heat on her aching flesh.

Tendrils of steam swirled around them, leaving glistening drops on Logan's skin. She licked them up as she kissed her way along his strong jawline. He threw his head back against the tile and let her nibble her way down, following the sinewy tendons that jutted starkly from his extended neck. When she reached the crook of his shoulder, he moaned and pumped his hips upward, grinding his cock against her center.

"You feel so good," he murmured, his voice husky, thick with passion.

It was *such* a turn-on.

She wedged her hand between them and brushed her finger across the crown of his cock. "So do you."

"Ah…keep doing that."

"This?" She circled the cap with one finger. "Or this?" Taking him in her fist, she made a twisting motion around the head while her thumb flicked across the slit.

"Oh, Jesus. *That!*" He gasped. "Do…that."

The sight of him, surrendered completely to intense pleasure, took her lust up a few notches. This powerful, masculine, rock-hard being had been brought to his knees by a few kisses and erotic touches.

Smiling, she licked a few glistening drops of water off his shoulder. "You taste good," she murmured. "Makes me want to bite you."

"Do it." He squeezed her buttocks and hauled her even closer as he began rocking against her core. "Bite. Hard."

"I knew you liked it that way."

"I've never liked it until this minute," he growled. "Put your mouth on me. Now."

She shivered at the command in his tone, even as she rebelled and dug her fingernails into his shoulder instead of her teeth. She'd never been one to take orders well. Her mother called her *spirited*. Her father called her *feisty*.

Logan called her a vixen and pushed her face into his chest.

"Make it sting."

She did. She bit his nipple. Hard.

His shout echoed off the walls as he hauled her up and impaled her on his thick shaft. Then it was her turn to shout as he stretched her slick channel and lowered her slowly, one erotic inch at a time. Pleasure spread through her pelvis and all the way to her breasts, and she was acutely aware of his fingers digging into her ass, his palms massaging deep into her muscles as he settled her, fully seated, onto his cock.

"Are you okay?" he rasped, sliding his hands up to her waist.

It struck her that his question was sweet, a little check-in with her, even though it wasn't needed.

Lifting her head, she locked gazes with him. He watched her, the banked heat in his eyes taking a back seat to curiosity. She had no idea what possessed her to take his face in her palms, because despite the fact that he was deep inside her, that action seemed even more intimate.

"I am," she said softly. "Are you?"

He appeared to think about it for a minute. Everything went quiet and still. The only thing caressing her skin right now was the swirling steam.

"Yes. I don't know about later, but right now, the world is shut out and there's only you."

Be still my heart.

That might have been the most romantic thing any guy had ever said to her. And they weren't even a thing. This wasn't a relationship. It was a release of a bad day and a mental-health break. It was a reminder that as shitty as things could get, there were still basic pleasures that made life worth living.

"Now," he said with a wink and a smile that would have charmed her panties off if she'd been wearing any, "fuck me."

She didn't need to be told twice.

Bracing her knees on the bench and her hands on his thick shoulders, she lifted herself until she felt the cap of his cock nearly come free, then sank down hard. He barked out a curse, and she did it again…and again. Faster and faster, until he was panting, his hands clutching her waist so hard she'd have bruises tomorrow.

He wedged his hand between them and captured her clit with his wet thumb, rolling it gently on one side, just the way she liked it. How the hell did he know exactly how to touch her, how much pressure to use?

She moaned, her body jerking as the delicious tension inside her built.

"You're so close," he murmured against her ear. "I can't wait to feel you come around me."

Oh, yes.

"And later, I want to taste you come on my tongue."

His graphic words, his thumb, his shaft pulsing inside her...it was too much. She exploded with a shout before slapping her hand across her mouth.

"Scream, baby," he grunted. "All the bedrooms are soundproof."

She freaking loved that. She let loose with a scream that would have been heard a mile away if not for the sound insulation. Everything came out as her orgasm peaked: intense pleasure, aching sorrow, and helpless anger. The release tore her apart, and as Logan joined her, his body bucking, his strong arms crushing her to him, tears stung her eyes.

Yes, this was sex. Incredible, hot, steamy sex. But it was more than that. It was a reminder that life was unpredictable, painful, and wonderful.

Sometimes, all at once.

Logan held Eva close, listening to her breathing, feeling her pulse as her heart beat against his chest. He hadn't had shower sex in years, not since college.

Not since Maja.

He wiped his ex from his thoughts and concentrated on the woman on his lap. She smiled down at him like a cat with a bowl of cream and then stretched, her long, toned arms flexing upward and lifting her breasts into the perfect position to kiss.

"Mm." She wrapped her arms around his shoulders and pressed a kiss into his scalp. "That was awesome."

"Was?" He lifted her to her feet and stood. "We're not done."

Her eager smile was enough to have him soaping them both up in a hurry. Her curvy body was slick under his palms, and she practically melted every time he dipped his soapy finger through her folds. He couldn't wait to replace his finger with his tongue, and he considered dropping to his knees right now.

The thought made his cock hard again. Not that it ever took much. Thanks to Lilith, he had sex demon DNA, and it made itself known in the form of arousal on demand and multiple orgasms.

He lapped water off her neck and shoulders and drank from the rivulet that cascaded between her breasts. The sounds she made, little hushed whimpers, drove him lower, until he was on his knees, and his mouth was inches from where he wanted it to be.

She watched him, her gaze hooded, her mouth parted in anticipation.

"Not yet," he said, planting a tender kiss on her hard belly. He traced the tattoo around her navel with his tongue, following the swirls and lines as she whimpered with need.

"I'm so grateful you've made the tattoo irrelevant," she murmured. "But I like what you're doing with it."

He smiled against her skin. He liked it too. But now that he was able to get a good look at it…it wasn't what he'd originally thought. The top half that he'd seen was definitely a ward against the demon that had been terrorizing her. But the bottom half…he had no idea.

Didn't matter right now, though. He committed it to memory and filed it away as a mystery to solve later.

Way later.

He dragged his tongue over to the knotted tattoo she'd said protected sensitive information from mental invasions. He couldn't soothe what Rade had done to her, but he could soothe her in other ways.

Turning her so her chest and stomach were pressed against the tile, he admired her firm ass.

Oh, and there, low on her spine, was the Aegis shield tat he knew she'd hidden somewhere on her body.

He was so going to kiss that.

Steam rose, swirling between her legs and around her slim waist as hot spray splattered on her smooth skin. Rivers of crystal-clear water streamed down her back and buttocks, and he leaned in, catching them with his tongue. He followed the streams all the way to the backs of her thighs and down the crease of her ass until he was throbbing, desperate to be inside her again.

Palming his cock, he gave it a vicious squeeze. *Shut it down, big guy. We have time.*

He refocused his attention on Eva, pressing a lingering kiss into the shield tattoo. She shuddered at the touch of his lips at the shallow divot where the valley of her buttocks met the pointed base of the symbol. He licked her there, drawing sexy little whimpers with every lap of his tongue.

Finally, he couldn't take it anymore. Shoving to his feet, he shut off the water and wrapped her in a towel before grabbing one for himself. "There's a hair dryer in the drawer—"

She dropped the towel and jammed her hands on her hips. "Do I look like I want to dry my hair right now?"

He discarded his own towel. Her gaze fell to his hard cock, and when she looked up at him, the heat in her eyes had turned to flame.

"What do you want?" he asked roughly.

"Your tongue in my pussy. It's all I can think about since you mentioned it. And I'm really impatient."

In a flash, he was on her, kissing her as he pushed her to his bed. The backs of her legs hit the mattress, and she fell backward with a playful squeal that drew out the starving predator in him. He pounced, lifting her legs so he could dive between them and feast the way he'd been fantasizing about since he first laid eyes on her.

Mouth watering, he lowered to her plump, smooth flesh. A growl escaped him as he kissed her there, dipping his tongue into her slick heat. She tasted like the sea, and him, and the primal urge to mount her roared through him.

Fucking her in the shower hadn't been enough. He wanted to take her. To cover her with his body, his scent. He wanted to have her at his mercy as he drove into her, and he wanted to watch her face as he made her come over and over.

But first he'd make her come in his mouth.

He speared her with his tongue, fucked her with it until she began to rock against his face. He slowed things down for a second and lapped at her, long, deep strokes from her entrance to her clit that made her moan and tug on his hair. He gave her a couple of flicks with the tip and then plunged inside her again, tasting her essence as deeply as he could.

"Yes," she cried, her gyrations growing frantic, her nails digging into his scalp. He felt her stiffen, and her flavor became electric as her climax took her. He brought her to the height, but as she came down, he shifted to her clit, sucking lightly as he dipped a finger inside her to replace his tongue.

She came again, screaming his name and digging her heels into his back. When she hit the peak, he lunged up her body and entered her, feeling her inner muscles clench and draw him deep.

Hooking her ankles around his ass, she clung to his shoulders, pulling at him as if she couldn't get enough.

"Faster," she whispered. "Come in me."

Yes. "Mother of…" He came with a roar, his pumping spasms

driving her to yet another high. Which triggered another for him. He went willingly, letting her drain him over and over. Now, he knew why males went happily to their deaths between the legs of succubi like Lilith.

Sex with Eva was bliss, and he didn't want it to end.

It did, though, and he collapsed on top of her, unable to move a muscle, barely able to breathe. He let himself bask in the afterglow because, too soon, the real world would get in bed with them, and he doubted he'd have time to be blissfully exhausted like this again for a long while.

Chapter Twenty-Three

Eva lay panting in a state of post-coital bliss, her body spent, her heart pounding so hard she was sure Logan could hear it as she curled against him with her head resting in the crook of his shoulder.

"Thank you," she breathed. "I needed that."

His deep chuckle made her head bounce. "Thank you? Like I provided some service?"

She popped him playfully on the chest. "That's not what I meant, and you know it."

"Hmm." He shifted so he could look down at her. "You thirsty? I got water, seltzer, cola, and beer."

"Water would be great. Thank you." She wriggled off him so he could get up, and then she admired his seriously fine ass as he walked out to the kitchen and snagged a couple of waters from the fridge.

Then she admired his front as he sauntered back, naked, his hard body moving like a piece of living art. He threw himself down onto the mattress and stretched out on his side as he handed her a bottle.

"So, you said you had questions," he said.

"Small talk?"

He propped himself on one arm and used his other hand to make shivery little trails along her shoulder. "Pillow talk."

"Is that your favorite way to communicate with a woman?"

"Well, it's not the *worst* way."

She laughed as she unscrewed the bottle cap. Why did he have to be so irresistible? She really wanted to be done with him when this was over because she had a feeling they were in for a lot of shit—shit that would probably be easier to deal with if she didn't like him.

Or if she at least didn't drool over him.

"Well, when you talked about liking luxury, it made me wonder if that's how you grew up."

"You mean you weren't briefed on every aspect of the Horsemen and their lives as part of Aegis training?" Underneath the husky, post-sexual drawl was a note of bitterness.

"Yeah, I was," she admitted. "And I knew a little from back in my news days and from reading the Four Horsemen graphic novels, but I've always wondered how true everything I heard and read was."

There was a long stretch of silence. And then a quiet, "What did you hear?"

It was her turn to be silent. She hadn't thought this would be a sensitive subject, but now it occurred to her that he'd grown up in a completely different world, one in which most humans hated or feared his kind. One in which his mother had betrayed The Aegis and triggered a war between the two agencies.

She needed to tread carefully.

"I heard that all the Horsemen are richer than God, and that you grew up in a castle in Greenland. I just assumed that if you lived in a castle and were rich, you'd have lived a life of luxury."

He snorted. "Castles are chilly, no matter how much money you have. And I inherited my mom's human weakness for being affected by extreme heat and cold. I was always freezing. But we didn't want for anything. And since my dad can cast personal Harrowgates, we could go wherever we wanted pretty much whenever we wanted. I mean, I could too, as long as Cujo took me, but when I was a kid, I wasn't allowed to go anywhere unless it was to my aunt's or one of my uncles' places."

She shook her head. She was still freaked out by the fact that he had a pet hellhound. She'd never seen one and wasn't sure she wanted to. By all accounts, they were violent fiends that liked to sexually ravage their prey before eating it alive.

"So, you can't cast your own Harrowgates, but you can travel with Cujo?"

"As long as I'm touching him, he can take me wherever I want to go."

How cool was that? She hadn't had a pet growing up at all, let alone one that could take her anywhere she wanted in the blink of an eye.

"How do you communicate with him?"

He shrugged. "We communicate everything through images or emotion. I can call him in my head, but actual words are sometimes tricky." He took a swig of his water. "Did you travel much when you were growing up?"

She nodded. "My parents love to travel. They didn't have much time because they were lawyers at a big firm, but at least twice a year, we'd go to Europe or the Bahamas or something. Gave me a love for exploring new places and cultures. Where did your parents take you?"

"It was usually just me and my dad. He took me all over. Lunch in Tokyo or dinner in Berlin. Things like that."

That. Sounded. Amazing. If she could travel anywhere in seconds, she wouldn't stop exploring new places and eating new things. "Where were your mom and sister?"

He took a long drink of water before saying, "My sister doesn't like to travel, so my mom usually stayed home with her."

"Doesn't like to travel? Why not?"

A couple of heartbeats passed as if Logan was trying to decide how—or if—to answer.

"Amber is, as my parents put it, an empath of remarkable strength. Being around people she doesn't know is hard for her, especially crowds. She gets sensory overload. Actually, she gets overloaded by a lot of things."

Well, that wasn't in The Aegis's broad library of knowledge. Very little was known about any of the Horsemen's offspring, actually, and most information they did have came from the rumor mill and unreliable sources.

"So, she doesn't ever leave the house?"

"She does, but she only visits my aunt's and uncles' places. She loves Ares' Greek island. She'll go there just to hang out on the beach all day or to chill with our cousins. But trying to get her to go anywhere else is almost impossible."

"That must be so hard for her," she murmured. "So, she still lives at home? Does she have a hellhound too?"

"She lives at home, and no, she doesn't have a hellhound. I only have one because it was orphaned when Pestilence killed its parents."

The stark reminder that the world had been very close to total destruction cast unwelcome clarity on her post-coital haze. The real world was just on the other side of the wall surrounding the compound, and she wasn't ready for it yet.

"How old is Amber?" she asked, desperate to stay engaged in pillow talk, as if that would keep everything else at bay.

He arched an eyebrow. "You mean there're some details about my family's life The Aegis doesn't know?"

"Shocking, I know." The Aegis knew of Amber's existence, but they only had a broad idea of her age.

"She's thirty," he said. "Three years younger than I am. But she looks like she's twenty. We immortals age slowly and then stop aging at around twenty-five or thirty."

"You suck."

He laughed. "If it makes you feel any better, since my mom is human, I get hurt easier than my dad, it takes longer to heal, and according to the angels I train with, I can die." He paused to take a drink, but she was still trying to wrap her head around the fact that he trained with angels. *Angels.* "Fortunately, my bond with Cujo helps me heal faster than I would without him. My sister and I both broke our arms when we were kids, and mine was almost fully healed before my parents could even get me to Underworld General. But it took four days for my sister's arm to heal because she refused to go to the hospital, and she wouldn't let a doctor touch her. She's so stubborn."

"Still. Four days to heal a broken arm? That's amazing. Does she have a job or any interests?"

"Oh, yeah. Hell, yeah. She's interested in everything. If she's not writing, she's reading. Or trying new recipes. Or using the game room to go places virtually."

"So, she's a writer?"

He hesitated for a heartbeat and then gave the tiniest shrug, just a twitch of the shoulder, really, as if he'd decided it was okay to keep talking. "She's actually a bestselling author, but she writes under a pseudonym. And, no, I can't tell you what it is. You can ask her about it if you want when you meet her tomorrow."

She sat up so fast she whacked her cheek into Logan's chin. "Ouch. What? I'm meeting her?"

"You're meeting everyone," he said. "It's a big family get-together. We do it once or twice a month. It's at Limos's place this time. We were going to cancel because we're concentrating on finding Draven and Lilith, but I guess everyone figured we could meet tomorrow and share info. So, it won't be a party as much as a battle-planning session. With burgers and beer."

Oh, God. Her stomach was already churning with nervous energy.

The idea of meeting not just one Horseman but all of them, plus their kids and friends…she might actually throw up for the second time in twenty-four hours.

"Your family is going to hate me."

He took her hand so tenderly her heart fluttered. "They have reason to despise The Aegis, but they have no problems with humans. All the Horsemen's mates are human."

"What about you?" It suddenly occurred to her—now that she knew who she thought was Logan's ex was actually his lunatic grandmother—that the ex he'd spoken about must have been human. "Your ex was human, wasn't she? And clearly, she didn't react well to finding out who you were."

"She exposed me to a local demon hate group and got me expelled from college." He threw his head back into the pillow. "That was after she tried to stab me.

"What a bitch. How long were you together?"

"Almost a year." He tossed his empty bottle into a trash can near the door. "I guess I should have told her sooner. I just didn't think she'd freak as bad as she did."

She stroked his arm, letting her fingers play along the hills and valleys of his hard muscles. "When I asked how you discovered you had a gift for capturing spirits, you said it involved a girl. Was it her?"

He snorted. "Yeah. Before college, the only thing I could do was summon a sword." Suddenly, there was a sword in his hand. *So cool.* "But I was at a restaurant one night with her, and I saw a demon's soul floating around our waitress." The sword disappeared, and he dropped his hand to hers. "I kind of freaked out. And I couldn't tell her the truth, so she thought I was drunk or high or something. We had a huge fight. Almost broke up. I wish we had."

His ex sounded like a controlling twat. "Why couldn't you tell her? What was her attitude toward supernaturals?"

"She was curious at first. Not hostile. I should have told her at the beginning, but I wasn't sure I could trust her. Then she started hanging out with radical anti-demon groups and going to Aegis-hosted events. I got worried about how she was talking about not just demons, but weres and vamps too. Then, one day, she suggested that The Aegis should have imprisoned the Horsemen and held them until Armageddon, and I had to tell her the truth. Wanted to convince her that we aren't all monsters. I mean, she'd known me for a year. She *knew* I wasn't a monster, you know?"

"Do you still love her?"

"She tried to stab me and have me captured by extremists."

"That's not a no. Maybe you're into that kind of thing."

His deep laughter shook the bed. "No. Hell, no."

She liked that answer. "But you're still angry?"

He blew out a breath. "I was for a long time." He twined his fingers with hers. "But I think I've finally made my peace with it." Leaning over, he kissed her, a fleeting, tender kiss that made her eyes sting with the emotion that passed through it. "Thank you."

"For what?"

"For accepting who I am."

"Oh, Logan," she breathed, cupping his cheek in her palm. "I—"

Suddenly, someone pounded on Logan's door.

"Dammit, Logan!"

Eva squeaked in surprise and tugged the blanket up just as the door burst open, and Rade charged toward the bedroom.

"Why didn't you tell me Lilith got—what the fuck?" He looked at Eva, shook his head, and took off, slamming the door closed again.

"Shit." Logan kissed her, a quick peck, and then rolled out of bed and tugged on a pair of sweatpants. "Get some sleep. I'll join you later."

She was asleep before the door closed.

Son of a bitch.

Today had been one of the shittiest days of Logan's life. But his time with Eva had at least dulled the edge of the knife currently carving out his chest. The one engraved with Noah's and Shanea's names being wielded by Draven and Lilith. Now real life had violently intruded on the brief piece of heaven he'd found with Eva.

And he was pissed.

He'd truly thought that sleeping with her would be a mistake, but it hadn't been. They both needed to remember what they were fighting for. Life. Family. Love.

Yeah, he was supposed to be focusing on making sure the world didn't burn before Satan was released, but he'd been so wrapped up in preventing Armageddon that he'd neglected his needs. He'd let old wounds fester, and for the first time in years, he felt like he finally found some relief.

Then Rade had to go and ruin everything.

Logan pounded on Rade's door and then burst inside without waiting for an invite, just as Rade had done to him.

Rade pivoted from the fridge, kicked the door shut, and slammed his unopened bottle of iced coffee on the counter. "What the shit, man? You're fucking the enemy?"

"She's not the enemy, Rade." Logan gave the door the fridge treatment with his foot.

"Well, she's sure as hell not our friend." He strode to the computer and waved Logan over. "I looked into your little fuck buddy after the interrogation. Have you seen her work?" He punched a button, and a clip of Eva during her time as a journalist in Houston popped up.

"Much-needed legislation regarding the rights of businesses to refuse service to known werewolves is being discussed a thousand miles away in the nation's capital today," Eva said from outside a courthouse in Houston. *Behind her, scores of protestors held signs demanding First Amendment rights for business owners and calls to send all were-people to reservations. "This comes as those who succumb to moon fever three nights a month demand to be identified as human rather than werewolves, claiming the label, no matter how accurate, unfairly reduces them to a disease, and exposes them to harassment and discrimination."*

"Eva," the guy at the news desk said, *"do these people deny that their disease is contagious?"*

"They acknowledge that the werewolf virus can be transmitted, but they claim it can only happen through a bite or a scratch while they are in their beast forms."

The news guy nodded thoughtfully. "And yet they have no proof."

"Some early studies have shown that the lycanthropy virus is dormant and non-contagious while the infected are in their human forms, but so far, there is no official declaration or recommendation by the World Council on Supernatural Governance about how to proceed with the treatment of werewolves in society."

"Thank you, Eva," the guy said. *"What a world we live in. News Twelve will be back after these messages."*

Rade pressed a few more buttons as the newsfeed blinked away. "And check out these articles she wrote. *Demon Neighbors: Protect Yourself with Household Items You Can Use as Weapons.* She goes on about how demon-on-human crime has increased, and what humans can do about it."

Logan frowned. "I remember that. A dude in Phoenix broke out of his werewolf containment unit and slaughtered a half-dozen people in his neighborhood. The next day, some *ter'taceo* kid went full demon on a group of kids who were bullying him." That bloody event had ended with the ten-year-old boy being put down by The Aegis. "Humans changed a bunch of laws after those two incidents."

Those years had been a tense time in human/demon coexistence. Things were still volatile, but the ceding of Australia to demons had relieved a lot of tension. The country had already been largely destroyed during the first near-apocalypse, and humans gave up trying to rebuild when Azagoth wiped out Sheoul-gra and set loose billions of demons. When it became clear that humans would never be able to send all demons back to Sheoul or destroy all vampires and were-creatures, a global coalition came together to address the problem. By officially relinquishing Australia to demons—with strict conditions—the temperature on the planet had dropped from boiling to a high simmer.

"Oh, and here's a good one," Rade said. "She's talking to a demonology professor and asking if someone with as little as one percent DNA should be considered a demon when it comes to legislation. When he said nothing less than twenty-five percent should be subject to law applied to demons, she argued." Rade swung around to Logan. "Dude, you're twenty-five percent demon. So, tell me she's not the enemy."

Okay, yeah, that stung. But would she have slept with him if she still believed that shit? "Those were all from years ago—"

"Not all of them. There's one from last year that's all about your parents. And she works for the fucking *Aegis*." He shoved away from the desk and headed back to the kitchen, his voice getting louder with every step. "You know, the people who killed Shanea and Noah? The people who want to eradicate our kind?" He swiped up his cold coffee and rounded on Logan with a growl. "The people who tried to kill you and pretty much everyone we know?"

"I get it, Rade. I know the deal. I don't need to be reminded every damn second. But give Eva a break. She was tormented for years by a nightmare demon. She's got as much reason to hate demons as we have to hate The Aegis."

Rade's stare was practically hot enough to leave scorch marks on Logan's skin. "I don't care."

No, he probably didn't. But he didn't usually get this worked up about anything. Something was off.

"Rade, man, this isn't like you. What's going on? Did you bust into my room just to tell me about the dirt on Eva?"

Rade popped the top of his beverage with a violent flick of his wrist. "I wanted to know why you didn't tell me about Lilith and Draven. What the fuck?"

"You were busy with Masumi. I was going to tell you as soon as you were free."

"So, you thought you'd get busy with the Aegi in the meantime? I'd expect that of Mace, but you?"

Logan stared at his friend. This was bizarre. Rade's emotions usually read like a cardiac flatline. He was rarely happy or furious. Shit rolled off him, and even if it didn't, he wouldn't notice. Nothing got to the guy. He was ice on top of ice. On top of more ice.

"Jesus, man," Logan muttered. "Seriously, this isn't you. What's really going on?" Abruptly, pain flickered in Rade's eyes, ruthlessly quashed a second later, but Logan had seen enough. "Son of a bitch. It's Stryke, isn't it?"

Rade slammed his bottle down on the counter so hard Logan was surprised it didn't crack. "Sabre's forensic lab analyzed the weapon that killed Shan and Noah. The pistol and bullet casings are made from a metal found only in Sheoul, and the bullets are packed with a fluid Sabre says is enchanted blood, but he can't identify it or the enchantment. He thinks it's possibly of Divine origin. The weapon was definitely developed by StryTech." Rade looked down at his feet with a subtle, sad shake of his head. "I was hoping what I got out of Eva's head was wrong."

"Dammit," Logan snapped, angry at the confirmation, even though they'd all suspected as much. The Aegis couldn't have pulled off the development of that kind of advanced weaponry, and no weapons manufacturer or tech company even came close to what StryTech could invent.

Others tried, but they merely copied or piggybacked on StryTech's products and research. Advancements in human technology had largely stalled over the last thirty years, the focus instead turning to ways to combat, identify, or use demons. And StryTech had led the way since the beginning.

"Why the hell is he arming our enemy?" Logan cursed again. "I know he's all about giving anyone who wants them weapons to destroy demons, but this is too much. DART should have had sole access to that weapon."

"He should have at least told us about it," Rade said, his voice rumbling with barely restrained anger. "The fucker couldn't even be bothered to warn us, his *family*, that The Aegis possessed guns that could kill us!"

That was definitely a dick move. No matter what had gone down between Stryke and his family after Chaos's death, there was no excuse not to give them a heads-up. "Have you tried contacting him?"

Rade barked out a bitter laugh. "Are you fucking kidding me? It takes him weeks to respond to my communiques. And that's if I'm lucky. You think he's going to want to talk to me when I'm mad? Blade has tried too. Nothing. We're his damn brothers—we're triplets—and he acts like we're as unimportant to him as the nameless guy who delivers lunch to his high and mighty tower office."

"Screw him." Logan glanced around the undecorated apartment in an attempt to refocus his thoughts. Too bad there was nothing to look at besides the bizarre artsiness of the gray and copper pipes crisscrossing the ceilings and scaling the walls. Rade didn't believe in personal touches. The guy lived an extreme minimalist existence. The industrial nature of the building suited him, as well as the stark white walls and exposed pipes with odd angles.

"I wish I could do something to help," Logan said, "but he won't have anything to do with me, either. The last time I went to see him in his office, it didn't go well."

"When was that?" Rade propped his hip against the island, his posture relaxing a little, shifting from angry and defensive to angry and tired. "I can't believe he let you in."

"It was a couple of years ago. Remember when we had that birthday bash for you and Blade? I went to invite him so we could celebrate all your birthdays. Maybe take a step toward mending some fences. Figured if I invited him in person instead of over an email or text or something I could convince him. When he said no, I said some choice things that got me kicked out of there."

"What did you say?"

"It doesn't matter." Logan glanced over at the only personal touch in the apartment, a family portrait on the desk, taken a few months before Chaos died. Before everything changed. "What I said was true."

You're still a selfish piece of shit whose selfishness got your brother killed.

Logan should have expected a violent response, but he'd been angry, too balls-deep in his own pain over that day that he didn't see the blade coming. It stopped in mid-air, one millimeter from his pupil, hovering there like a spear.

"Get out," Stryke roared. "Get the fuck out! Guards!"

And that was when a half-dozen armed goons had emerged from who knew where, and *escorted* him out of the building. It was a lot more humiliating than Logan liked to admit.

Rade moved to the couch, his steps wooden. He sank down, braced his arms on his spread thighs, and gazed at the concrete floor. Logan had known the Sem his entire life, and aside from the blur of days after Chaos's death, Logan had never seen the male this distressed. Usually, the guy was a solid shard of ice. There had been times when Logan wondered if the thing he'd lost during the time the demon had him was his soul.

"How's Blade doing?" Logan asked. "Have you talked to him?" He didn't need to ask about Crux. They all left him out of shit involving Stryke.

Rade didn't look up. Just talked to the floor. "I don't need to. I can feel him. He's as fucked up about this as I am."

"What about Stryke?" Logan sank down onto the ottoman across from Rade. "Can you feel him?"

"Stryke cut us off a couple of years ago."

Whoa. How did Logan not know that? As Seminus demons, Blade, Rade, and Stryke could sense each other. But their mother was a werewolf, and the triplets had inherited some of her traits, including telepathy among themselves on nights of the full moon.

"What do you mean, he cut you off?"

Rade finally looked up, his eyes weary and bloodshot. "He found a way. He was so desperate to be rid of us that he used his company to sever our connection. And not just the werewolf one. The Sem one. So, it affects Crux too. None of us can sense him. I think that even if he died, we wouldn't feel it."

Logan ground his molars. What an ass. "One of the things I told him last time I saw him was that he's a selfish piece of shit. But he's worse than that."

"I don't get it," Rade said. "How can he be so self-centered? How can he not know that he's killing our parents with his bullshit? I feel bad for Mom. And Crux. He's just a kid. He needs all of us."

A heavy silence expanded in the room, an uncomfortable companion to Rade's misery. Logan sensed that the guy needed to be alone. He definitely wasn't the type to want a hug or some shit.

"I'd better go," Logan said. "Eva's probably wondering where I am."

Rade snorted. "Just be careful. I don't trust her."

"You don't trust anyone."

"True. But I was inside her head." He set his bottle down on the coffee table and leaned back into the couch cushions. "She's dedicated to her job. She'll choose it over you."

"It was sex, Rade. You of all people should get that. I didn't ask her to marry me. It's just sex."

"*Just sex* can get people hurt too," Rade said quietly, and the pall of Chaos's death fell over them once again.

If Stryke hadn't gone off with that girl, leaving his little twin brothers alone—

Logan had to get out of there.

"See you tomorrow." He paused at the doorway. "You going to the get-together?"

"Nah." Rade stretched and relaxed with his hands clasped behind his head. "I volunteered to help the FBI interrogate a demon they think is spying for China or Russia or something."

Figured. Rade usually found a way out of Horsemen and Sem family gatherings.

"Okay, have fun."

"Will do. I always love a difficult case."

Logan shook his head as he shut the door. That guy had issues.

But didn't they all?

Chapter Twenty-Four

Eva was used to waking up in strange places. Her job required a lot of travel, so she'd gotten accustomed to dealing with jet lag, long hours, and living out of a suitcase.

But waking up in a strange house full of demons was a first. She'd slept hard and had only awakened because the aroma of coffee had overpowered her dreams.

Or, more accurately, her nightmares.

But she couldn't even complain about them because there had been no demon scratching or banging on the surface, trying to get in. Her nightmares had been the garden-variety sort, normal, everyday bad dreams of things like The Aegis hiring Stefani and firing Eva.

Stretching and yawning, she rolled over and found a covered platter and a carafe of what had better be coffee on the nightstand. Inhaling deeply, she moved the lid aside and nearly groaned in delight at the fresh fruit, sweet pastries, and various cheeses and breads on the plate. A note floated to the floor, knocked off when she tried to set the lid aside.

She picked it up and smiled at the block letters and Logan's crisp signature.

EVA,

I'M OUT LOOKING FOR DRAVEN. I'LL BE BACK BY TWO, AND WE'LL LEAVE FOR LIMOS'S PLACE. SEE YOU SOON,

Logan

P.S. IF CUJO SHOWS UP, IGNORE HIM. MOVE SLOWLY. NO EYE CONTACT. DON'T TALK TO HIM. AND DEFINITELY DON'T TOUCH HIM. HE KNOWS PEOPLE IN THE HOUSE ARE OFF-LIMITS, BUT LET'S NOT TEST HIM.

Great. She really hoped the beast didn't show up without Logan. She'd never been very comfortable around dogs, and the idea of coming face-to-face with a giant, evil dog made her flesh crawl.

She ate quickly and then hurried out to the kitchen to drop off the dishes. As she turned back to the bedroom, a low, serrated growl turned her marrow to water.

Oh, God.

Very slowly, she angled her body toward the living room. And there, crouched on the enormous dog bed, was a pitch-black beast the size of an SUV. Its gaping maw full of sharp teeth could swallow her whole, all the way to her waist. Drool dripped from its jaws onto its massive, clawed feet.

Frozen to the floor by terror, she averted her gaze.

I exorcise you, spiritus diabolica!

The hellhound snarled, and she felt a hot breath against the back of her neck.

I exorcise you, spiritus diabolica! Oh, please, please go away.

Cujo stepped around her, his flaming crimson eyes boring into her as if daring her to look at him. He sniffed her face, and she nearly gagged at the stench of his breath.

Then, suddenly, he disappeared.

Relief sapped her strength, and she sank heavily onto the couch. She just needed a minute for her heartrate to return to normal. Up until now, it had been pretty easy to forget that Logan wasn't an ordinary guy, and this wasn't an ordinary situation.

Coming face-to-face with one of Hell's most vicious creatures was a hardcore reminder that she wasn't in Kansas anymore. She glanced around, needing to be grounded in something normal. Anything.

That bow and quiver of arrows hanging from pegs on the wall were pretty unremarkable. Exquisitely crafted but otherwise normal.

So was the stuffed lion on the shelf. Although the contrast of a deadly weapon and a child's toy next to each other was odd. Seemed fitting for Logan, though. He was a warrior, confident and powerful.

And yet, he had a funny, tender side and a fierce love for those in his inner circle.

It made her wonder about his childhood, especially because everything she'd learned about his parents had been less than complimentary. A father who was responsible for thousands of years of atrocities and the murders of countless Aegi. A mother who betrayed The Aegis and facilitated the deaths of her colleagues. How could two people like that raise someone like Logan?

Shaking her head, she pulled herself together and got moving. She showered, dressed in a casual blue-and-turquoise sundress and jeweled sandals, and then, as she rummaged through her things for her comms device Logan had confiscated, he showed up.

His boot treads were light across the concrete floor and throw rugs, and she tossed her tote aside onto the bed as he stepped through the bedroom doorway. Holy…wow. He'd stolen her breath from the moment she'd seen him and every time after, including now.

At well over six feet of lean muscle, he was so damn hot in tan cargos and a black button-down that her nipples tingled in an echo of how he'd taken them in his mouth last night.

"Hey." She tried to play it cool as if she didn't feel any morning-after awkwardness. "I don't suppose you know where my comms unit is?"

"Sorry," he said. "DART kept it. But if you need to contact someone, you can use mine."

Of course, she could use his. All conversations would be recorded. She hated the truth of that, and she hated that by bringing up DART, Logan had dropped them back into the real world so abruptly.

"Thank you. I need to call my parents later. And thank you for breakfast." She gestured through the doorway to the living room. "I met Cujo when I took the dishes to the kitchen."

"Really." One blond eyebrow arched. "Well, you're still here and in one piece, so I guess everything went all right."

"I don't think he likes me, but I'm still alive, so I guess that's a win." She fidgeted with her pinky ring, needing some way to diffuse the nervous energy eating at her like acid. "Anything on Draven?"

"Not much. Someone claimed to have seen him at a club in Perth, but if he was there, he took off before Mace and I arrived."

Damn. "Did you at least get some sleep? You didn't come back to bed."

"I checked in on you when we got back a couple of hours ago, but I didn't want to wake you, so I caught some Zs in the spare bedroom."

Disappointment left a sinking sensation in her belly. She had no idea why since what he'd done had been considerate and thoughtful. But what if there was another reason he'd slept elsewhere? What if he was done with her now that they'd had sex? Or worse, what if he'd spent the night with that trollop in the genie bottle?

She stopped herself, hating the direction of her thoughts. This wasn't like her. She'd never been the jealous type. Not ever.

This guy was making her spin out of control, and she wasn't sure she liked it. Or maybe she liked it too much.

Definitely too much spinning.

"Okay, well—" She broke off as he tugged her against him. One second, he'd been on the other side of the room. The next, he was holding her in his arms and kissing her senseless.

He tasted like toothpaste and a hint of mocha.

"That," he said roughly as he broke off and stepped back, "was because I don't do morning-after awkwardness. I don't treat females like they were just a lay, and I don't treat sex like it was nothing. I'm not like my roommates. Even if we never hook up again, know that I didn't just use you and throw you away, okay?"

Good...God. She'd dated a lot. She really had. Mostly nothing serious, and she hadn't slept with all her dates, but she'd been around the block enough to know that Logan wasn't your average guy. Again, she wondered how someone raised by one of the Horsemen of the Apocalypse and an Aegis traitor, someone whose DNA was at least a quarter demon, could be so...charming and relatable.

"But," he said, his tone taking on a grave note, "we play for opposite teams, and I've told you more than I should. Don't screw me over, Eva."

Ah. There was the demon. Except that wasn't true, was it? He was being reasonable. She felt the same way.

"We've both shared a lot. So, let's not screw each other over. Agreed?"

He gave her a guarded nod, which she completely understood, given what his heinous bitch of an ex had done to him. "Agreed." Taking her hand, he slid her a panty-melting smile. "Let's meet the fam."

Eva had been to Hawaii a handful of times, and she'd always loved the laid-back lifestyle that sucked the tension right out of a body.

But she didn't think she'd ever been as tense as she was right now, at the thought of meeting demons, maybe some angels, and definitely biblical legends.

The Elders would shit themselves when Eva finally got the chance to tell them about this.

Logan led her down a sandy path toward a bungalow on stilts with an incredible wraparound deck and stunning views of the jungle and ocean. A broad-shouldered mountain of a man with short reddish hair tended a pit fire in the grassy side yard, and her mouth went as dry as the sand under her feet.

"Is that…War?"

"He prefers Ares. He won't be War until his Seal breaks." Logan pointed to a tiki bar closer to the beach, where a woman with long black hair and a bright yellow-and-green-floral sundress was mixing drinks. "That's Limos. She always takes charge of the alcohol. And she puts pineapple in everything, so if you don't like pineapple, get a beer."

Wow. Famine was a bartender. Eva recognized the man next to her too. The Deputy Director of DART, Arik Wagner, was a human who somehow managed to steal the Horseman—Horsewoman?—away from Satan and marry her.

"And you know Arik," Logan said. "Did you know Runa is his sister? She might be here later, but I think Shade has to work. He's a paramedic at Underworld General." He gestured for her to follow him to a group of women seated around a table with a pitcher of margaritas. "Eva, this is Amber, Raika, and Dawn. And you know Scotty from DART." He turned to the group. "Do you guys mind if she hangs with you for a few minutes? I need to talk to Ky."

"No problem," Dawn said, her resemblance to Kynan so pronounced that Eva didn't have to ask if she was his daughter. "But you can't just dump your new girlfriend on us without giving us the scoop."

"There's no scoop," Eva blurted. "And I'm not his girlfriend."

"Ooh, snarky," Raika said. "I like it. But there's definitely a scoop." The way she looked at Eva, as if seeing right through her, was unnerving as hell. So was the way her long black hair didn't move in the breeze. At all. "You a werewolf? Logan likes the furries."

"Funny, Raika," Logan muttered.

"No, it's not funny." Scotty slammed her margarita glass down so hard alcohol splashed onto her skull-print tank top and denim shorts. "She's *human*. And she's one of the Aegis scumbags who killed Shanea and Noah."

"Back off, Scotty," Logan said. "She didn't pull the trigger. She wasn't even there when it happened. So, chill the fuck out."

The fact that Eva didn't pull the trigger didn't seem to matter to Scotty, who tugged on her thick ginger braid and shot Eva a look that sent a chill up her spine.

"Shanea was my friend."

God, Sig had caused so much pain. Eva wished she could do something, but all she had to offer was her sincere condolences.

"I'm very sorry for your loss," Clasping her hands together, Eva tried to communicate sincerity. "I'm genuinely—"

"Oh, fuck off," Scotty snapped. "I'm glad Draven is hunting every one of you down and taking you apart slowly. I hope—"

"Scotland!" Logan grabbed her by the arm and yanked her aside. "Let's see if we can find Mace or Blade. They're probably looking to start a volleyball game." He pointed to the remaining three women. "Be. Nice."

As Logan and a sulky Scotty walked away, Raika gestured to a seat across from her. "I'd apologize for Scotty, but we all loved Noah, Draven, and Shanea. And frankly, I think we're all pretty wary of Aegi."

"And we're pretty wary of you." Eva took a seat. "So maybe we can start over?"

Dawn nodded. "I don't know what you've heard about us, but we're all pretty normal. I mean, we're not psychos or anything."

Dawn seemed okay. She'd gotten Kynan's black hair and denim-blue eyes, and she was free with her smiles. She had interesting tats on her wrists, ankles, and neck, though. They were similar enough to the one around Eva's navel that she couldn't let it go.

"Can I ask about your tattoos? Do they repel demons?"

"Nah. They're restraining glyphs." Dawn skimmed her fingertips across the linked symbols around her wrist. "They keep my inner Soulshredder contained."

Ice-cold terror dropped into the pit of Eva's stomach. Soul-shredders could see scars, both mental and physical, and they used their Satan-given talents to open old wounds. Long-lost cousins of nightmare demons, Soulshredders haunted their victims for years, terrorizing them, hurting them, and driving them insane.

And Dawn had one of those inside her.

Amber glanced at Eva and then back at her sketchbook. "You scared her, Dawn."

Recalling what Logan had said about Amber being an empath, Eva took a deep breath and forced herself to settle down. And made a mental note to temper her emotions in front of his sister.

"Dawn probably shouldn't have said we're regular people and then dropped her Soulshredder DNA thing on you." Raika took a sip of her margarita and then licked salt from her lips. "Look, we're all either immortal or have some sort of demon in us. But we just want to live like everyone else. No one wants to harm anyone, and most of us are dedicated to protecting the world from evil. That's The Aegis's goal too, right? So, let's just chill and get back to gossiping."

"I'll drink to that," Amber said, raising her glass but not actually drinking. Instead, she went back to sketching in her notebook.

"Oh, my God," Raika said, gesturing with her Solo cup at a red-haired woman who resembled Scotty so much they must be sisters. "Aleka's doing it. She's actually flirting with Sabre!"

"I told you." Dawn continued to play with her tattoo. It was just so strange that part of Eva's was almost a perfect match and yet had the opposite effect with demons. "She broke up with that asshole she was dating, and all she can talk about is Sabre. She's had a crush on him for years."

"Excuse me," Eva said, tats forgotten. "Aleka is Scotty's older sister, right? And who is Sabre?"

"Yes, Aleka and Scotty are sisters." Raika poured from the pitcher into a clean cup. "Their parents are Ares and Cara. Sabre is Eidolon and Tayla's son. You probably know who they are."

Eva absolutely knew who they were. She took the cup and downed half of it to calm nerves that were probably broadcasting a lot of information to Amber. "So, he's related to Blade, Mace, Rade, and Crux? He's a sex demon?"

Dawn nodded. "They're his cousins. You can see why this is so amusing. He'd be crazy to lay a hand on Ares' daughter."

"Hilarious, right?" Raika's glossy hair billowed softly around her shoulders now. But the breeze had died down, and no one else's hair stirred. Who *was* this chick? At this point, Eva wouldn't be surprised if her father was Hades. "Aleka'd better not let her dad see her batting her eyes at Sabre."

"Oh, damn," Dawn muttered, and everyone looked at the dark-haired, athletic guy walking along the shore with a tall, busty blonde in a thong bikini. "I keep hoping he'll dump her skanky ass."

Amber uttered a soft curse and scribbled harder.

Raika leaned toward Eva and said in a conspiratorial voice, "That's Talon. Sometimes we call him Stewie to annoy him. He's also a Seminus demon, and we hate his bitch of a girlfriend. She's a fallen angel. Real piece of shit." She jerked her chin toward Amber. "And Amber there has been in love with him since she was born."

Amber shot Raika a dirty look. "I'm not in love with him. And it doesn't matter because he treats me like his little sister."

"Then maybe," Raika said, "you should put on a slinky black minidress sometime."

That earned Raika another glare. "A slinky black dress would look pretty silly at a beach party."

Dawn squeezed a lime wedge into her cup. "You know what wouldn't look silly at a beach party? A bikini. Show him you're more than Logan's little sister."

Amber gave Dawn the finger and then shot the fallen angel a scorching glare before diving back into her notebook. What was she doing, anyway?

"Shorts and tees are acceptable beachwear," she muttered.

"Not if the tees are baggy, and you're trying to catch the eye of a hot sex demon." Raika sat back in her chair. "I'll bring you some swimsuits to try. Or…we could go shopping."

Amber didn't look up. "I'm not going shopping."

"Excuse me. But, Amber…you're Logan's sister, right? So, Thanatos—Death—is your father?" At her nod, Eva frowned. "Would he be okay with you dating a sex demon?"

Raika choked on her drink. When she was done coughing, she laughed. "Oh, my God. Are you kidding? He'd castrate the poor guy and make him eat his own dick. And then he'd hang him from the castle walls to deter anyone else from touching Amber."

Right. Regular people. They weren't insane at all.

Amber sighed. "He would not. He loves Talon. Wraith is Dad's best friend. He'd never hurt Wraith's son."

"Uh-huh." Raika rolled her eyes and gave Eva a no-way shake of the head. "Are you wondering about anyone else here?"

Eva took a sip of her drink, which turned out to be a pineapple margarita. "Well, I don't know your story."

"Oh," she said brightly. "My mother is an angel, and you'd probably know my father as the Grim Reaper."

Of course, he was.

Eva drained her cup and grabbed the pitcher. "I recognize your name now. The Aegis has been pronouncing it wrong. They call you Ree-kuh."

"*Ree-kuh*? Like I reek? Rye-kuh is not that difficult. Morons." She shrugged at Eva. "No offense."

"None taken." She set the pitcher down. "Are you really tasked by Heaven to gather the souls of the demons your father set loose on the world?"

"Sounds a little judgy," Amber said quietly. And yeah, it might have been. But Raika's father was the reason the human world was dealing with so many demons and demonic spirits.

"It's okay," Raika said. "I get it. She's only heard one side of the story." She shifted to face Eva. "Do you know why my father destroyed Sheoul-gra?"

"Publicly, The Aegis's official take is that it was the first real sign that the Apocalypse was near. Azagoth destroyed Sheoul-gra to release all the demons to be Satan's army."

"That's ridiculous. Ugh." Raika's eyes narrowed. "And unofficially? What do you guys *really* think?"

None of this was secret information. Not exactly. But she still hesitated, tucking her hair behind her ear as she bought herself a moment to unpack The Aegis's internal stance on the topic.

"We know that Satan has been imprisoned," she said carefully, not wanting to offend the Grim Reaper's daughter in any way, "so it doesn't make sense for Azagoth to have released the demons in Sheoul-gra. Not yet. There are two theories. That he released them to wage war on the current King of Hell, Revenant, is probably the most popular. The second is that Revenant wanted them released for his own purposes, but no one knows what that could be."

Raika laughed. "Not even close." She glanced over at Amber. "Should I tell her?"

Amber shook her head. "That's not to be revealed to the world yet. And it's going to be one of my plot twists."

Right. Logan had mentioned that his sister was a writer.

"Anyway," Raika continued, "after Dad released the souls, Heaven punished him by cursing me to spend my life catching the worst of the worst demons he freed. Demons like Lilith. I capture and deliver them to Hades, who stores them while he rebuilds Sheoul-gra."

"It's being rebuilt? By Hades?"

Amber plucked a red pencil from the caddy next to her notebook. "Plot twist."

There was so much The Aegis didn't know. No wonder Maja had been so anxious for Eva to stay with Logan. These people were a treasure trove of information. Her unprecedented access to the Horsemen and their families would secure Eva's career in a million different ways. She could even see a book deal in her future.

Her parents would be so proud. She'd be invited onto talk shows and to speak at events. She'd make a documentary that would earn accolades and millions. The kind of success she'd always dreamed of would become reality.

And you'd hate yourself for it.

Shame stabbed her right in the chest. How could she even think about exploiting these people? With a couple of exceptions, they'd been good to her and were nothing like The Aegis described.

She shot a covert glance at Amber, hoping she hadn't felt Eva's guilt.

But Amber's gaze bored right through her. Dammit.

Raika tapped Amber on the shoulder. "Hey. What are you looking at?" She frowned and tapped harder. "Amber? Shit."

"What's going on?" Eva caught Amber's pencil as it fell from her frozen fingers.

Dawn hurried around the table and sank down next to Amber. "She's having a vision."

Logan hadn't mentioned that his sister had visions. "What does she usually see?"

"She doesn't talk about them, and even if she did…" Raika shrugged. "Sorry, but there are things we don't want getting back to The Aegis."

Yeah, Eva got that, and the shame flooded back. Forget fame and fortune. What should she tell The Aegis about *any* of this?

"How often does this happen?"

"I don't know," Dawn said. "This is only the second time I've seen it. It's been years since the first time. She came out of it kind of confused."

Amber gasped, her gaze still locked in place, but not *on* Eva. Through her. "There's trouble," she whispered.

"Trouble?" Raika prompted. "From who? Lilith?"

Amber turned to her, and Eva wouldn't have described her expression as *confused*. No, that face was etched with fear.

"Amber." Raika snapped her fingers in front of Amber's face, getting her attention. "What's going on?"

"It's Heaven," Amber croaked. "Bad things are happing in Heaven."

Chapter Twenty-Five

Reaver strode down the pristine halls of the Archangel Complex, wondering if he looked like everyone else moving toward the auditorium.

Confused.

Harvester squeezed his hand and gave him a tentative smile. "I know Archangel business is overly shrouded in secrecy, but an urgent call for ranking members of all angelic Orders is kind of strange."

He nodded. "Especially just hours before the Council of Orders Summit."

She squeezed his hand again. "I'm sure it's fine. In any case, you will be seeing your family soon. I know it."

Harvester was rarely optimistic, which meant she really *didn't* know it. She was as worried as he was that the Archangels would go back on their word to finally allow him to visit the human realm and his family. Six months was far too long, even if time moved differently in Heaven.

They entered the open-air, five-thousand-seat auditorium and filed toward the front.

On the stage, thirty-nine Archangels stood in matching golden robes, looking stern and serious. Only one was missing, but Reaver was certain that Metatron would appear at any moment. Sure enough, a few seconds later, he materialized on the stage, but instead of moving to the speaker's position, he stood aside as Michael came forward.

"Fellow Celestials," Michael began, "thank you for coming. We brought you here to discuss a threat to not only us but also the very Heavenly order."

Murmurs rose from the thousands of people seated in the room. Once they died down, Michael continued.

"It has come to our attention that a small contingent of malcontents from other Orders have been undermining our rule, and worse, this group of dissenters may be plotting a coup to take away the Archangels' rightful place as Heaven's supreme leaders."

Reaver sat forward in his seat. This was interesting. So was Michael's choice of words. "*Rightful place.*" Other angelic Orders had taken turns ruling, but never for long, and certainly not for thousands of years. Archangels had been in charge almost constantly since the beginning of time, with only a few brief periods of power being wielded by others. But the other Orders' reigns had been disastrous, and despite having some of the fewest members of all the Orders, the Archangels had always taken control again, most recently after the Sheoul-gra disaster. Archangels were the only Celestials to be named to their Order by God Himself, instead of being born into it, and thus were considered *blessed*, or *chosen*, and given power simply because of who they were. They were the elite, the rock stars of the Celestial world, and the ones most humans knew of…which was all by the Archangels' design.

They had a great marketing team.

At the front of the chamber, a male stood, his silver hair flowing around his shoulders. He could have chosen any color for his long mane, so the fact that he'd gone with silver said he wanted everyone to know how ancient he was. Or maybe how wise—or at least how wise he *believed* he was.

Michael gestured to the male. "The Ruling Body recognizes Pi-Zeus, First Celestial of the Order of Dominions."

"I do not believe that a *small* contingent of dissenters is questioning the Archangel rule," he began, his voice carrying with crystal clarity and authority through the enormous space. "I believe the numbers are significant, and I speak for my Order when I say that we want change. The human realm is in decay, and your pathetic *leadership* is letting it happen. You should never have been allowed to take control from the Thrones after the Sheoul-gra disaster. It was more your fault than theirs."

Michael's eyes darkened. "Is that so?"

A female in jeweled robes stood, and a dozen of her companions came to their feet with her. "I am Lucinala, Sixth Celestial of the Order of Virtues. We have seen a radical, rapid decay among humanity, and also on the planet itself. Humans are destroying the oceans and the air. They're driving plants and animals into extinction. Crops are failing, and people are starving. Yet we do nothing about it. Therefore, we align with the dissenters."

Interesting. Reaver took in the room, the quiet whispers, the nervous shifting. On the stage, the Archangels began fidgeting.

Michael cleared his throat. "Who else stands with the dissenters?"

The entire contingent of Principalities and Thrones joined the Virtues and Dominions, and shock turned the Archangels' faces pale. Reaver thought he might have lost some blood in his face too, when his Order, the Powers, stood for the dissenters.

A Throne stood. "I, Zaphkiel, First Celestial of the Order of Thrones, call for a Convention of Celestials to determine a new Ruling Body."

Gasps filled the theater but were quickly drowned out by cheers.

"This is rather unexpected," Harvester murmured in Reaver's ear. "But I do believe it isn't a surprise to many in here."

Reaver agreed with his mate's assessment. The smirks and shifty gazes from more than a few of those in the audience made clear that something was in the works.

Uriel, a senior Archangel and ginormous douchebag, joined Michael at the front of the stage. "This is ridiculous. We will not stand down. We held a Convention of Celestials after Azagoth destroyed Sheoul-gra, and we agreed to give the human realm a century to sort out their issues with demons on their own."

"Fool!" Pi-Zeus shouted. "We agreed to non-interference and no more memory wipes. We did *not* agree to let demons take over an entire continent, and we certainly didn't agree to let humanity sink so far into depravity that they not only allow demons to live among them but facilitate it."

Cheers erupted.

"They have fallen faster than we imagined while you have been sitting around drinking ambrosia!" someone called out over the din. "Did you know that demons have been born with human souls? It's madness!"

The guy was being an alarmist jackass, but he wasn't entirely wrong. While no demons had been born with *demon* souls since Azagoth destroyed Sheoul-gra, a few, like Crux and Chaos, had been born with human souls. The twins had been considered miracles among demons.

And while Chaos was already dead, they could never know about Crux. If anyone learned that his soul was human, thanks to his human-werewolf mother, he'd be targeted for death by any number of entities. Demons, humans, and angels all tended to destroy what they didn't understand. Kill first, dissect later.

"Metatron!" someone else called out. "You are our Creator's mouthpiece. What say you?"

Reaver held his breath as his uncle came forward, the sheer power of his mere presence quieting the room. "I say that we trust God's plan."

"Well, maybe He could let us in on that plan," Lucinala snapped. "Because *trust God's plan* is all we hear from you."

"And yet, you haven't listened." Metatron's voice, calm and measured, rang out. "None of you have. You have interfered when you shouldn't, and you've sat idly by when action was called for. We agreed to let the human drama play out without dipping our wings into it beyond what is routine."

"Was it routine to allow Reaver and Gabriel to conspire with Azagoth to destroy Sheoul-gra?" A Power from near the front shoved to his feet. "Was it routine to give them mere slaps on the wrists?"

A chorus of "No!" exploded in the seats and echoed around the colosseum.

"You protect them!" someone shouted, and shit, the Archangels had better get this under control.

"Silence!" Michael bellowed, his words booming in waves through the space, amplified by his angelic power. A golden glow surrounded him as he lifted into the air, his wings splayed wide in a display of authority. "We will abide by the agreed-upon timeline."

Suddenly, Pi-Zeus shot into the air with a great flap of his sienna wings. His aura churned around him in the form of fiery rings. "We cannot afford to wait. Call for a Convention of Celestials *now*. We demand new leadership!"

Metatron's deep voice rang out, as calm as Pi-Zeus's was frantic. "And who," he said, "do you propose should replace the Archangels as the Ruling Body?"

Michael laughed. "Let me guess. The Powers? They're our best defense against demons and powerful warriors, but they have proven incapable of governing."

Uriel sneered. "No, my guess is the Dominions. They can govern, but power goes too quickly to their heads. Last time they were in charge, they had temper tantrums resulting in great floods that God got blamed for in every culture with flood lore."

"Yikes." Gabriel cringed dramatically. "You Dominions were in the doghouse for a long time for that one." He bared his teeth at another delegation of angels. "Nope. My money is on the Principalities. You guys still haven't learned that you shouldn't coup."

"How dare you?" Suroth, the head of the Order of Principalities, shot into the air, lightning sparking from his multicolored wings. "We have atoned for the actions of a handful of our people—"

"A handful?" Uriel barked. "Ninety thousand of your Order sided with Satan against God. No other Order lost even half that. You are forever tainted. No amount of inspiring spirituality in humans can make up for that."

Reaver stood and addressed the fiery redhead. "Suroth. Why would the Principalities be dissatisfied with the state of mankind and the Archangels' leadership? Humans are aware of the existence of angels and demons. Their conversions to religion have been unprecedented. You should be overjoyed. Your yearly quotas to bring religion to humans have been hundreds of times higher than at any other time in history."

Suroth hissed. "At what cost? The knowledge of demons living amid humans has also caused chaos and a disturbing rise in Satanism. Evil and sin are growing as quickly as faith in a higher power is. We can't keep up, and we lack the guidance from on high to deal with it. We need new tools. New weapons. The Powers can't spare time to help us anymore."

"Enough!" Zaphkiel rose above everyone, his wings aflame, his aura writhing with orange lightning. "We Thrones have the votes to take control. Stand aside, Archangels."

Oh, shit. The Thrones, Dominions, Virtues, Powers, and Principalities together numbered in the tens of millions. And even if the Seraphim and Cherubim stood with the Archangels, there were fewer than a thousand on their side.

They needed the Order of Angels to stand behind them, or the Thrones would succeed in a hostile takeover.

Michael's thoughts clearly went in that same direction, and he spun to Teleri, leader of the Angels. They were what humans might think of as common angels. Guardian angels. They lived and worked among humans, disguised as humans, each managing several human souls at a time.

And there were a billion of them.

"Teleri. Where do you and your brethren and sistren stand?"

Teleri stood, her sapphire robes swinging around her hips. "We choose not to take sides."

"Of course, not," Uriel snapped. "Your neutrality is cowardly." He glanced over at the Memitim delegation of three. "And you?"

Hawkyn stepped forward, his serious expression so like his father's. "It seems we weren't consulted about this little rebellion the way everyone else was." More than a little anger seeped into his voice. The Memitim were regarded by most as the dregs of Celestial society, and more than a few in Heaven believed they shouldn't even be considered angels. "I will consult with my fellow Memitim before I commit to one side or the other."

Disappointing. Memitim numbered in the thousands, and their muscle would be welcome. But Reaver understood Hawkyn's reluctance to blindly choose a side for his Order. Especially given that his—and every Memitim's—father was Azagoth, who had caused all this tension in the first place.

"This is wrong," Metatron said. "This is not how it is done. You all agreed to let a century pass—"

"Things have changed," Zaphkiel argued. "We demand a Convention of Celestials."

"*I said no!*" Metatron roared.

"Do you speak for God or yourself?"

Tension winged through the air, and Metatron, who Reaver had rarely seen angry, suddenly seemed fifty feet tall with the wingspan of a jumbo jet. "What if I say I speak for God?"

"Then let us hear it in His voice," Suroth called out.

"That's not how it works."

"Funny, that's how it has worked in the past." Zaphkiel slapped his palms together and held them in front of his face. "Oh, Father, if we displease you, let us hear in your own voice, through your vessel, Metatron."

Every eye turned to Metatron. Fury blazed in his eyes, red-hot and stormy. All around him, lightning sparked and sizzled. The tempest grew, filling the auditorium with electric tension that skittered across Reaver's skin.

Uncle Met was about to unleash the power of the Almighty, crack some skulls, and drive angels to their knees before him.

Anticipation built, ramped up to the boiling point. Harvester's nails dug into Reaver's palm. Silence was heavy, and fear was a sharp bite in the nostrils.

And then…

Nothing. The storm passed as Metatron slowly descended back to the stage, his eyes still burning with fury.

And defeat.

Reaver's chest felt like it had caved in. This was…not good.

"Looks like God's plan is non-interference, after all," Zaphkiel said. "I'll take that as a sign that He supports our cause." He waved his hand with a smirk, and suddenly, the auditorium filled with warriors from the Order of Powers.

Reaver squeezed Harvester's hand. "Stay here. If things get ugly, get out. Go to Limos's place."

Harvester barked out a laugh. "Sure."

"I'm serious."

"I know you are." She sighed. "But you're asking me to run from a fight. It's as if you don't know me at all."

"I'm not asking," he growled. "I'm *telling*."

"Has that ever worked on me?" She rolled her eyes and crossed her arms over her chest, completely unaffected by his command. "Do you even *know* me?"

Yeah, he'd screwed up. Shouts of anger and insults rose from the front as the Powers moved in. "Just…don't get killed."

"That, I can do."

Reaver kissed her and then shot into the air, his golden wings that made him unique among Celestials cutting through the room with a whisper. He landed next to Metatron as Powers surrounded them.

"Camael." Reaver pushed through the crowd to the leader of the Powers. "What are you doing?"

Camael grabbed him by the arm and pulled him aside. "You need to choose sides. Right now. I know Metatron raised you, but you belong with us. With your Order."

"You can't do this. You all agreed to a timeline. This is a damn coup."

Camael snarled. "The Archangels have given us no choice! They refuse to call for a Convention, so this is the result. Stand with us, Reaver. I can make sure you are given a fair trial."

"A fair…*what*?"

Something clamped around his neck, and he went numb from the top of his skull to the tips of his toes.

Camael patted his shoulder, but he couldn't feel it. "I'm sorry,

Reaver. You and Gabriel, you went too far when you helped Azagoth. The Archangels have allowed you too much freedom and not enough structure. It's not your fault, it's not as if there's another Radiant around to guide you. We will explain that to the Throne's tribunal when they investigate your involvement in the Azagoth fiasco. With any luck, they'll go easy on you." He nodded to a couple of battle angels behind him. "Take him to containment."

Oh, no. *No.*

This was bullshit!

Harvester scanned the room, her mind working furiously. Her instinct was to pop her wings and do a strafing run through the auditorium, blasting every fucking asshole who was in on the coup. And a few decades ago, she'd have done just that. She'd have caused death and destruction and wouldn't have regretted a thing.

But mating Reaver and getting her wings back had taught her a measure of restraint. Going off half-cocked could make things far worse for Reaver, and it could leave her in chains, as well. And that could happen anyway, if those who captured Reaver and Metatron thought she was a threat to them too.

She had to get out of here.

Even though she assumed the traitors had restricted everyone's ability to flash out, she tried. Sure enough, nothing happened.

Fuckers.

"Verrine."

Her heart jumped into her throat at the sound of her angelic name coming out of Zaphkiel's mouth. Drawing on her powers, she wheeled around to the Throne.

"Where are you taking my mate?"

"I think you know the answer to that." He flapped his wings. "We won't hold him indefinitely. We just need to find a way to…neuter him a little."

"*Neuter* him?"

"We can't keep allowing him to run around with all those powers.

Radiants were meant to be controlled, not given freedom. But don't worry, we will give him his powers back when the Apocalypse is nigh. Right now, we need to make sure you don't cause trouble."

"So, you're imprisoning me too?"

"No, but you are restricted to Heaven. You will not be allowed to travel to the human or demon realms."

"Excuse me? I need to be able to communicate with the Horsemen—"

"You are no longer their Watcher. You have no need to see them."

"They're my family, asshole." She shoved aside a Power who tried to play peacemaker and get between them. "They're Reaver's children and grandchildren. I definitely have need to see them."

"And seek their help to move against us?" He grabbed her arm. "I don't think so. We're temporarily blocking all travel between realms."

"*Release her!*" A great roar shook the building, accompanied by a blinding flash of light and a clap of thunder so powerful it blew everyone yards away from the epicenter.

Which was Reaver.

Harvester picked herself up off the floor and glared at Zaphkiel as she shot into the air. "Fool! No one touches me. Did you not learn from Raphael's mistake? Now look what you've done."

A swarm of angels attacked Reaver, who had somehow freed himself from his restraints, but he remained in the power restrictor. Harvester threw a bolt of lightning into the crowd, scattering them. She did it again and again, but supporters of the old regime were outnumbered ten to one, and as an army of Powers and Thrones came at her, she had one last play.

If she couldn't get help from the Horsemen or, better yet, Revenant, she could at least send a message. She stroked her fingers over the Gaiaportal pendant Amber had given her.

I saw this in a vision.

As the traitors reached her, Harvester shot upward, gathering speed and summoning every drop of power she had. She shot through the top of the dome, hundreds, maybe thousands, of angels on her tail.

Her wings beat furiously, keeping her at the front of the pack, but she could feel the desperation from the other angels as they began to realize where she was going.

"Don't do it, Verrine!" Zaphkiel screamed. "Do not!"

A searing bolt of angel fire struck her thigh and put her into an uncontrolled dive. She spiraled between two great ivory pillars twice as tall as Burj Khalifa, pulling up a millisecond before she crashed into the crystal pool at their bases.

She put on a burst of speed, barely avoiding another bolt of angel fire. And another. And ten more.

They came at her as she dodged and weaved through the air on her way to the Gaiaportal.

"Don't do it!" Zaphkiel screamed again. "Harvester! It will kill you."

Would it? Perhaps.

But it would also send a message.

She just had to hope it got to the right people.

Chapter Twenty-Six

"Aleka!" Logan jogged up to Sabre and Aleka as they huddled together under a tree beyond the view of the house.

Sure, it looked like they wanted to be alone, but they also looked like they would be sneaking off in a few, and Logan needed to talk to Aleka first.

She leaped away from Sabre, her cheeks pink with embarrassment. As if he gave a shit that she was hot for the Seminus demon. They'd just better hope Ares didn't catch them.

"Hey," she called out, all nonchalant. "What's up?"

He dug a slip of paper out of his pocket and handed it to her. "I was wondering if you could research this for me."

She stared down at the sketch. "What is it?"

"It's a tattoo. One half is a ward against a nightmare demon, but I don't know what the other half is, and I couldn't find anything relevant in DART's database." Granted, he'd only performed a cursory search. His time after leaving Eva in bed had mostly gone toward finding Draven. "I was hoping you could use your resources at the museum to find out what those symbols mean."

"Sure." She frowned down at the drawing. "Part of it looks kind of like Dawn's restraining glyphs."

Now that she said that, he realized she was right. The differences were subtle but still seemed to be from the same magical family. Restraint, containment, tethering. But pairing something like that with magic that also repelled didn't make sense.

Aleka shrugged and tucked the slip of paper into her small crossbody purse. "I'll let you know what I find."

"Thanks." He gave Sabre a friendly fist bump and then found Kynan coming out of the surf with his board.

"Water's great," Ky said as he shook out his hair, flinging cool droplets everywhere. "You getting in?"

"Nah. I didn't bring my suit." Logan picked up a mollusk shell and tossed it into the waves, which was as close as he was getting to the ocean today. "Can we talk?"

Kynan snapped into pro-mode, propped his board in the sand, and listened to what Logan had to say.

He was not happy to hear that Draven had devolved so much. He was even less happy to hear about the dangerous complication of adding Lilith to the mix. And he definitely didn't want to keep the new information from the Horsemen.

"If anyone can help us find Lilith and Draven, it's them," he argued. "And they're among the few people in existence who can defeat her. I know you're worried about Draven. We all are. But the Horsemen need to know what they're up against in their hunt for Lilith."

Dammit, Kynan was right. So, while he took off to consult with the Horsemen, Logan headed back to Eva.

He kicked through the hot sand and considered summoning Cujo to play with Aunt Cara's hellhound, Hal, who was frolicking in the waves, probably trying to catch a shark. Logan could properly introduce Eva to the mutt. He felt bad that he hadn't been there when she'd run into him. It must have been terrifying. Having grown up in a household from the time he was only a couple of weeks old, Cujo was friendlier than most hellhounds, but he was still an unpredictable asshole sometimes.

If that introduction went well, he'd let her meet his parents.

He almost stumbled in the sand at the thought. He'd never introduced his parents to a female. And now he was thinking of throwing a human Aegi at them? His father would be happy to see every one of them exterminated, and his mother had disavowed the organization before he was even born.

Still, his parents were pretty cool. Usually. Meeting Eva shouldn't be *too* awkward.

Hopefully.

"Hey, Eva," he called out. The females were all gathered around his sister, and at first, he thought they were looking at her sketches. Then Scotty's barely audible curse carried, and he realized something was wrong.

Amber.

His sister had turned the milky gray color of a carnage maggot, her gaze lost somewhere beyond the human realm as she swayed in her seat.

He sprinted to her, the other females parting to make room for him. "Amber? Hey, sis. Are you okay?"

Her tortured moan wrecked him. He'd been her self-appointed protector from the day she was born, and it killed him to see what the visions put her body through. Some were rougher than others, but even the mildest episode often left her with a migraine and nausea.

He'd cleaned up a lot of puke and blood over the years.

He sank down next to her and took her hand. "It's okay. I'm right here. Everyone is here for you."

"I saw the sky bleed," she whispered.

Everyone automatically looked up. "Nothing but blue sky, hon," Dawn said.

He brushed Amber's hair back from her eyes. "Her visions don't usually manifest for weeks. Sometimes, months."

But he'd learned that the intensity of the postictal phase, as Eidolon called the immediate aftermath of a vision, was an indicator of the timing. The sooner her vision was to become reality, the worse the toll it took on her body.

Eva sat down on Amber's other side and dabbed at her upper lip with a napkin. "Her nose is bleeding."

"At least it's not her ears." Or eyes.

"She said something about Heaven." Dawn reached blindly for her drink. "Oh, shit. Her ears." She slapped her hand over her mouth. "Her *eyes.*"

As if his words and thoughts had triggered it, blood began trickling down her cheeks. Suddenly, she went taut, her jaw clenched.

"Seizure. Get Eidolon!"

Raika took off, shouting for the doctor as Eva helped him ease Amber to the ground. But she screamed and wrenched away before he could position her the way Shade had shown them. He heard the distinct crack of bone and the tear of flesh as a gash sliced through her biceps. Another in her thigh. And again, in her calf.

Logan's heart bled as much as her wounds. "Eidolon!" He shouted. "Hurry!"

"Blood in the sky," she rasped, gripping his hand as if he was her lifeline. "Blood in the temple. Blood in the vessel. *Bloodintheskybloodintheskyyyy!*"

Then Eidolon was there. Everyone was there, including his mom, who must have run at full speed despite being pregnant and wearing flip-flops.

"Regan," Thanatos growled as he caught up to her. "You should not be running—"

Darkness fell across the beach in a wave of shadow. Logan looked up as black clouds rolled in from nowhere and boiled.

Eidolon barely spared the sky a glance as he gripped Amber's arm, shooting her full of healing energy.

Overhead, lightning spiderwebbed through the clouds, and thunder shattered the air.

"Oh, my God," Regan breathed. "Tempestus demon. Not again."

"No, sweetheart. It's not a demon." Thanatos wrapped his arm around her and held her close, the love for his mate something Logan had admired his entire life. His parents gave as much comfort to each other as they did their children. Eva watched too, and he wondered what she was thinking. "I don't know what it is, but it's not a demon."

The doctor moved around from Amber's head to her torso as Logan's parents crowded close. His mom's eyes were glassy with tears, and the concern in his dad's put hollows beneath them.

"How is she?" Regan's voice trembled.

"She's going to be okay." Kneeling at Amber's side, Eidolon channeled more healing energy into her. "She seized so hard she broke some bones and tore muscle and ligaments, so I want to keep her out of it for a little while. She doesn't need to be feeling this." He shouted for Mace, who was already on his way over. "I need you to keep her unconscious for a few minutes."

Mace went to his knees opposite Eidolon. His *dermoire* lit up as he sent his gift into Amber. His ability was different than the doctor's, allowing him to affect bodily function, like slowing the heart or speeding up the production of adrenaline. Although he preferred to use his gifts against enemies, completely stopping their hearts with a quick zap.

Fear for Amber edged into frustration and anger. She didn't deserve this shit. Why did her visions come with pain? And why did they always have to be so vague and cryptic?

A low rumble crawled across the sky as it grew even darker, taking on a crimson cast.

"She said she saw blood in the sky." Eva wandered a few feet away, her eyes glued to the storm. "Do you suppose she meant the red clouds?"

Suddenly, a bolt of lightning stabbed downward. Eva froze as the burst of energy engulfed her in a millisecond of blinding light. But there was no crack of thunder. No heat. There was, in fact, no sound at all.

Not from the wind, the ocean, or Limos's alternative rock station blaring from concealed speakers mounted in the trees.

"Eva!" Logan shouted, but the void swallowed the sound.

It felt like minutes, but only a heartbeat passed, and Eva was walking toward him, blinking and looking shell-shocked.

He rushed to her and gripped her shoulders tight, ready to catch her if she fell. "Are you okay?"

"Yeah. Fine. Everything got bright and tingly. Was I struck by lightning?"

Logan really had no idea at this point.

Thunder crashed, and a warm droplet struck his face. Dammit. Rain was the last thing they needed.

"That's weird." Frowning, Eva brushed her finger over the raindrop on his cheek. "It looks like blood."

Abruptly, the sky let loose. Red rain pelted them in a torrential downpour, drowning the pristine beach in crimson gore.

"Everyone take cover!" Logan gathered Amber in his arms as his father helped rush his mom for the cover of the tiki bar's covered seating area. "Come on, Eva!" he called out, and they hurried through the warm downpour. Once under the roof, he eased Amber into a chair, holding her until Eidolon and Mace had her under their care again.

Eva looked freaked out, but no more so than anyone else. Taking her hand, he looked out at the carnage. "What *is* this shit?"

Talon put the back of his hand to his mouth and swiped it with his tongue. "It's blood."

Grinning, his girlfriend leaned into him and lapped hungrily at the rivulets flowing down his neck and shoulders. Fallen angels had no class.

Gently, Logan wiped blood from Eva's brow. A grateful smile trembled on her lips. "Are you sure you're okay?"

"I'm fine. I don't think the lightning hit me."

"That's good," Logan said. "But maybe we should have Eidolon look at you when he's done with my sister." Eva had definitely been struck by *something*. But what?

Blade jogged up, dripping wet and looking like Carrie on prom night, his gaze glued to his comms. "No reports of anything out of the ordinary anywhere else. It's just us." He frowned. "No, wait. This is weird. It happened in Jerusalem too. Someone got a video of a localized storm over Temple Mount."

He flicked the video into the air, and they all watched a storm dump blood rain on a shrine with a gleaming gold dome.

The camera panned, and Logan's jaw dropped. The rain was falling on a building, and one building only.

"Ow, wow," Eva murmured. "It's the Dome of the Rock, a place of immense historical and religious significance. It's even associated with end-of-times prophecies. That can't be a coincidence."

"It's Lilith," Scotty said. "It has to be."

"This is too big for Lilith." Ares had armored up, his sharp eyes assessing the threat. "It's got to be Revenant."

Eva eased up next to Logan. "Could it be Satan? Could he have broken out of his prison?"

An uneasy silence hung in the air. Escape shouldn't be possible, but the suggestion was enough to freak everyone out. The impossible had happened before.

"It's not Satan." Reseph's voice was hoarse, spoken through lips that dripped with blood.

"How do you know?"

His hands trembled at his sides until Jillian took them in hers and held them steady. Held *him* steady. Only after he'd grounded himself in his mate did he speak again.

"I've tasted this blood before." He swallowed sickly and looked up at the sky. "It's Harvester's."

Shock rolled through Logan in a seismic wave. Harvester was invincible. She'd survived horrors most couldn't even imagine. And as Satan's daughter, she was more powerful than most angels.

"No," Scotty rasped. "Not G-ma."

Everyone looked up as the black clouds faded away as quickly as they'd come, leaving behind a stinking, steaming nightmare of a scene.

"Holy shit," Limos said. "What has happened in Heaven?"

Chapter Twenty-Seven

Eva's mind was having a hell of a time trying to process this. They'd just been drenched in…angel blood? Actual blood from an actual angel?

Seriously?

The journalist in her had many questions. The rest of her was terrified and of the opinion that this was way above her pay grade. The Aegis freaking *owed* her.

Desperate to gain some measure of control before she lost her ability to cope, she cleared her throat.

"Excuse me." Eva's heart raced as a group of the most powerful beings on the planet turned to her as one. "You're talking about Harvester, the angel also known as Verrine? Wife of Reaver? Are you sure?"

Ares swiped his finger across the little crescent-shaped scar on his neck, and his armor melted away, leaving him in swim trunks once again. "If Reseph says it's her blood, it's her blood."

Reseph stumbled out of the shelter, his gait unsteady as he trudged through the sand. He stopped a few meters away and threw back his head.

"Reaver!" he roared at the sky, his voice drenched in pain that made Eva's heart clench despite knowing that this guy, as Pestilence, had given Satan himself a run for his money when it came to cruelty and body count. "*Father*! Where the fuck are you?"

Logan respectfully averted his gaze from his uncle. "Reaver and

Harvester have been MIA for a few months," he explained to her. "No one has been able to summon them. And now…" He looked up at the sky as if silently calling for them.

Amber had come to, and tears rolled down her face. Next to her, Scotty dabbed at her eyes and then ran toward the house.

Eva took his hand and gave it a comforting squeeze. "Logan—"

He shook his head, subject closed, and then led her over to the people she already knew were his parents. "Eva, this is my mom and dad, Thanatos and Regan."

In Eva's line of work, she met a lot of bigwigs. Politicians. Entertainers. Even a few world leaders. She never got tongue-tied and was rarely anxious.

She was so nervous right now that she would have asked about a bathroom if she could form the words.

Thanatos was still in his armor, one arm wrapped around Regan, supporting her against him. His pale-yellow eyes reminded her of a hawk, sharp and merciless. He said nothing, but Regan smiled. Barely. Still, Eva was going to call it a win.

"Hi, Eva." Regan's hand fell to her rounded belly. "Sorry we had to meet under these circumstances."

"I agree. But it's good to meet you. Logan speaks very highly of you both." A ray of golden sunlight spread over the beach in the distance, and she stared in awe as the clouds dissolved like cotton candy in the wind. "Oh, wow. Look."

As if by magic, the sticky blood that had coated everything melted away, disappearing as if it had never been. Their clothes weren't even stained. Was this happening in Jerusalem as well?

"I've seen some weird shit," Thanatos said, "but this is next-level weird. Humans are going to freak out."

The Horseman was right. Eva was on the verge of doing it right now, and she had a front row seat. How was the world at large going to handle this event?

With a growing sense of urgency, Eva wheeled around to Logan. "Can I borrow your comms? I want to see what's coming out of The Aegis."

He unclipped his device from his wrist and passed it to her. She secured it quickly and then flipped on the eye screen, allowing her individual implant chip to operate Logan's device. Instantly, her brain was flooded with video and photos from people near Temple Mount.

She used the eye tracking to turn on The Aegis app and let out a silent growl at the sight of her boss, Jennifer, speaking with Stefani at her side.

That should be me, dammit.

"*…to be clear,*" Jennifer was saying, "*we don't know the origins of the phenomenon, nor do we know if the substance that fell is blood, let alone to what—or whom—it belonged. We are calling for calm at this time.*" She nodded at a reporter with her hand raised. "*Molly Baker from BBC.*"

Eva would bet a million dollars that she knew what Molly would ask.

Molly stood. "*Is there any chance this may be a sign that Satan has broken free of his prison?*"

Ding, ding. Winner. Reporters asked the question every time something big happened. Every. Time.

Of course, that had been Eva's first question to the Horsemen, as well.

"*We have no reason to believe the apocalyptic timeline has been altered.*"

Standard answer.

"*But the Dome of the Rock and the entirety of Temple Mount are central in some apocalyptic prophecies. Surely, this bizarre occurrence isn't a coincidence.*" Molly again.

Jennifer's smile was somehow both comforting and condescending. "*Molly, how often is the Dome of the Rock the site of some sort of disturbance? It's a historical site of great importance and powerful energy. It's highly doubtful this event is in any way a precursor to any kind of apocalyptic activity.*"

She'd made it sound so ho-hum and run-of-the-mill. Jennifer was truly talented at that.

"*Could this be a sign from God?*" another reporter called out. "*Or a punishment?*"

"*We have no reason to believe the phenomenon is of Heavenly origin,*" Jennifer said, completely in sync with Eva as she mouthed the rote response. "*Ladies and gentlemen, we ask again that everyone remain calm while we investigate—*"

"*Will you be working with DART to get to the bottom of this?*"

Eva saw the surprise of an unanticipated question in Jennifer's expression. But she was a pro at this, and Eva doubted anyone else watching would have noticed the slight flare of her eyes or the split-second glance at her prepared notes before she recovered with a reassuring nod.

"*We will use all the resources and assistance available to us,*" Jennifer said. "*Now, if you'll excuse me, I'm going to get the latest information. I'll be back with you shortly.*"

Eva clicked Jennifer's call code without thinking, but at the second unanswered tone, an incoming call blared in her ear.

Maja.

Quickly, she disconnected the line with Jennifer and opened the line with Maja as she retreated farther back, away from the Horsemen and their families.

"Maja," she said in a hushed voice. "It's good to hear from you."

"Did you see the news?" Maja sounded as frazzled as she looked.

"Ah, okay…yes, I saw what happened at Temple Mount. The same thing happened at Limos's place. That's where I am right now."

"Oh. It happened there too? Interesting." Maja said the words, but her voice conveyed anything but interest. The Elder was rattled. She reached somewhere off to the right, and then there was a glass and a bottle of vodka in view of the screen. She splashed three fingers of alcohol into her glass with a trembling hand.

"Elder Maja? What's going on?"

"Are you safe?"

"Of course, she's safe. She's with me."

Eva nearly jumped out of her skin at the sound of Logan's voice behind her. Holy shit, how had he snuck up on her like that?

"Oh, hey. I was just talking to—"

"Maja. Yeah, I know. I can't see her, but I can hear her."

She stared at him for a second. He knew Maja well enough to know the sound of her voice?

Maja knocked back a gulp of vodka. "Turn on the public view and let me talk to him."

Baffled, Eva turned the screen from private to public, and a 3D image of Maja in her office popped into the space in front of them.

"A Guardian was found dead," she said, and Eva's lungs seized. *No, no, no.* She didn't want to hear any more… "Mutilated. The body impaled on a church spire in Brussels. It's all kinds of public."

"Draven." Logan scrubbed his hand over his face. "Ah, damn."

"Who…?" Eva croaked. Swallowed. Found her voice. Barely. "Who was it?"

Maja's eyes glistened with unshed tears, and Eva's chest caved in. *Please, don't say Keeley.* "It was Keeley," she said in a husky, two-pack-a-day rasp. "Dammit, it was Keeley."

Eva wasn't sure how she didn't break down. She'd spent her entire life behind a professional mask, starting at age three while competing in beauty pageants. She'd been trained to maintain a neutral expression by parents who were experts at withholding emotion.

But right now, this was all too much. Her job was on the line. People she knew and cared about were dying. Her life was in danger.

And she was being babysat by the son of Death.

Who she had feelings for—way more than she cared to admit.

"Eva."

Numbly, Eva jerked her gaze to the Elder.

"Eva, I have to go. We'll talk later."

Maja's image blinked out, but Eva kept staring into the space where her boss had been.

"I'm sorry about your friend," Logan said softly.

Behind him, Scotty snorted.

Eva didn't know what came over her. Grief, anger, or the toll the last couple of days had taken on her, it didn't matter. Rage bubbled up, hot and acidic, charring the edges of her control.

"Are you?" she shouted at all of them, tears burning her eyes and the humiliation of that making everything even worse. "Are you really sorry? Why haven't you found Draven yet? Why aren't you out there looking for him? All of you."

"We are, Eva." Logan shot a glare at Scotty before taking Eva's hand and leading her to a bench that faced the shoreline. "DART is using all its resources to locate him. But now that he's hooked up with Lilith, it's more complicated."

"Why?" His level voice and logical words penetrated her fury, and she dialed it back a notch. But that didn't stop a tear from rolling down her cheek. "I don't understand."

"Draven's species resides in our world. We know him. We know where he likes to hang out. We should have been able to find him by now." He swiped a napkin off the bar top and handed it to her. "But Lilith is a product of Sheoul. She knows every corner of it. If he's with her, he's a million times harder to find. DART doesn't have the kind of reach in Sheoul that we do here. Most DART agents are human and can't go there."

"But you can, right?" She dabbed at the tear and then caught another that escaped. Dammit. She hated being so vulnerable on a normal day, but here among strangers and in a strange place after a strange event…she was honestly surprised she hadn't curled up in a fetal position yet.

He shook his head. "My cousins and I are all half human and one-quarter angel. We can use Harrowgates and stand being in Sheoul for a few minutes, but we get sick if we're there too long." He gestured to Ares and Reseph. "The Horsemen and the Sems are already looking for Lilith, but—"

"It's like trying to find a hot dog that doesn't contain assholes," Mace said, pulling up next to Logan.

Okay, she got it. She was being unreasonable. But none of this sat well with her. She was a person of action, someone who confronted problems instead of hiding from them—or instead of standing around crying.

"Then let me help. Give me a comms device. It doesn't have to be mine. I'm great at research. Or I can consult with a demon law firm. I know the language. Just…please. Let me do something."

Logan and Mace exchanged glances, and then, in a shocking move, Mace shrugged, unclipped his comms, and handed it to her. When Logan looked at him like he was a loon, he shrugged again.

"I've got another one at home. And I owe her."

"I'm going to need more information," Logan muttered. "Later."

She hid a smile as she handed Logan his comms and clipped Mace's around her wrist. That demon wasn't so bad.

Seemed weird how easily that thought came to her.

"What's going on?" Kynan asked as he approached. "What's The Aegis saying about the blood rain?"

"I don't think they know anything," Eva said. Even if they knew the blood belonged to an angel, there was no way they'd know to whom it belonged or how—and why—it rained down on a single building.

Logan scrubbed his face, suddenly looking tired. The guy was probably running on fumes and fear, and if they'd been anyplace else, Eva would have hugged him.

"But things just got even worse," he said. "Draven killed another Guardian. The female, Keeley."

Kynan closed his eyes and threw his head back with a frustrated curse. "We're running out of time."

"I think we're already out." Logan's voice was grim. "This time, Draven put his victim on public display. It won't be long before she's identified, and the media learns she was one of the DART/Aegis exchange members."

Kynan swore. "And then The Aegis will tell the world that one of our people is a killer."

Chapter Twenty-Eight

Shit just kept getting worse, and Logan was tired of playing defense.

It was clear Kynan felt the same way, and he cursed in a couple of different languages as he tapped at his comms device. "I need to reach out to the Aegis Elders." He frowned. "Speak of the devils. Hold on."

Kynan wandered off, speaking to whoever was on the line, and Logan sank down next to Eva on the bench. She was rubbing her bare shoulders and looking around as if she couldn't focus on any one person or thing.

"You okay?" he asked for what had to be the millionth time. "Are you cold?"

"No." She offered a shaky smile. "I'm fine. I just…" She inhaled deeply. "It's nothing. How can I help?"

"You can tell me if Kynan was right," he said. "Will The Aegis get in front of this with their spin?"

"I don't know. Maja didn't tell me their plans."

Even though he'd expected Eva to be careful with the information she shared, disappointment flared in the pit of his stomach.

"I think you *do* know."

Her head snapped up to his before she averted her gaze and sighed. "She didn't share their strategy, but my guess is they'll want their side of the story out before you make yours public."

Bastards.

"What *is* their side of the story?"

"I honestly don't know, Logan." Reaching out, she gave his arm a little squeeze. "I'm telling you the truth."

Call him a fool, but he believed her.

"Hey, Logan! Eva!" Kynan waved at them from where he stood with Mace, Blade, and Scotty. "Can you please join us?" When they approached the group, Kynan addressed everyone. "The Aegis has decided to give us our people back."

Nope, not suspicious in the least. Logan didn't bother keeping the skepticism out of his voice. "In exchange for…?"

"Eva."

"Oh, thank God," she breathed. For some reason, that struck a nerve. Which was ridiculous. Of course, she would want to go home. But did she have to be *so* relieved to get away from him?

"Why?" Scotty played with her braid. "That makes no sense."

"I'm guessing they're planning to make the situation public," Kynan said, "and don't want to be seen holding hostages. They're going to get ahead of this before we do."

Which was pretty much what Eva had told Logan.

"That's what you get for trusting those assholes," Blade said.

"Hey," Eva said irritably. "From our side, *you're* the assholes."

Scotty bristled, but Logan held up his hand in a settle-down gesture. "Chill out. Eva just lost a friend."

"Yeah?" Scotty shot back. "So did we."

"Enough," Ky barked. "There's a lot of pain going around, okay? We're all feeling it. Deal with it on your own time. Right now, we have to make a prisoner exchange. I'm going to ask Ares to take Eva to DC and then gate our people back to Brussels. Logan, Maja asked for you to be there too."

Logan did not like the speculative look Eva gave him. "Why does she want me there?"

"No idea." Kynan tapped something on his comms.

Mace, dressed in cargo shorts and a busy blue-and-green Hawaiian shirt, looked up from making designs in the sand with his toes. "It's probably a trap."

"Maja assured me it isn't," Kynan said. "But I don't believe anything they say. That's why Ares will be there, and Logan has Cujo for backup."

"Cool." Mace grinned. "I hope Cujo gets a nice lunch."

"Those are my people you're hoping get eaten," Eva said, but she sounded way less annoyed by Mace than she had been with Scotty.

"I know." Mace grinned even wider. Had to hurt his face.

It took a few minutes to collect Ares and coordinate the meeting point with The Aegis, and then Ares opened a gate and he, Logan, and Eva stepped out inside the old Washington Nationals' stadium.

Several people waited at the other end of the field. The six DART agents came forward, followed by Maja and two others Logan assumed were Elders, and about a dozen Guardians, all armed to the teeth.

Ares closed his gate and then opened another directly to DART's courtyard, waiting as Logan and Eva moved toward the Elders.

"Are you calling in Cujo?" Eva asked, pausing in the middle of the field.

Logan didn't take his eyes off the Aegi coming toward them. "Not unless I have to."

At least one of the Aegi probably had the new Aegis weapon, and Logan had no idea how it would affect him or Cujo, so he'd rather keep his hellhound out of it unless absolutely necessary. Besides, Cujo was a little unpredictable around humans, and he didn't want to be responsible for starting another international incident.

"Well, I guess this is goodbye," Eva said, and he felt a twinge in his chest.

He didn't want her to go. He risked a glance at her, which was stupid because it made him want to grab her hand and dive back through the gate Ares held open for the DART agents.

"I guess so," he said with a casualness he didn't feel.

Eva gestured to Logan's colleagues. "I'll wait until they're all through." She winked at him. "In case Mace is right, and it's a trap."

He smiled, despite not feeling very cheerful at the moment. "You can't blame us for thinking that."

"No, I can't. I'd have thought the same thing about you," she admitted, her expression turning pensive. "Before. I'm not sure I'd think that now." She smiled up at him. "You've surprised me, Logan. All of you have."

"You've surprised me too."

The way she looked at him, like a dark-eyed temptress, made his breath catch, and his cock twitch.

"When all of this is over…" The longing in her voice matched the yearning inside him, and he wanted her to finish the sentence, to say that when it was over, maybe they could find each other. Do things the right way.

But she never got the chance. Maja busted in and ruined everything.

She was good at that.

"Hi, Logan." Maja held out a scrap of braided leather. "I just wanted to give you this."

A pang of recognition stole his breath. He'd thought he'd lost that. Holy shit. He'd ruined his relationship with Stryke over that—well, partly, anyway. Mostly, the problem with Stryke was that he was an insufferable jackass.

"You had it this whole time?"

She had the good grace to look chagrined but offered no apology. "I know it meant a lot to you."

"And yet you took it."

Maja just shrugged and turned to Eva, who was looking between them, brow furrowed. "Eva, you ready to head back to HQ?"

Eva's mouth opened to say something…and then her jaw dropped, her eyes shooting wide as she finally put shit together.

This wasn't uncomfortable at all.

Eva recovered quickly and smiled politely. Suspiciously politely. Logan knew that look. It was the one his mom gave his dad when she was trying to keep from killing him in public.

"Can I talk to Logan alone for a minute?" she asked.

Maja hesitated, her speculative glance bouncing from Eva to Logan. "Sure. We'll wait."

"One second." Logan tucked the bracelet into his pocket. "What is The Aegis going to say about Keeley and Draven?"

"Nothing." Maja looked him dead in the eyes and lied, just the way she had all those years ago when she'd said she loved him, then tried to ruin his life. "We're going to stall for time. You need to get Draven under control, and now."

Spinning on her heel, she marched away.

Eva waited until Maja was out of hearing range before rounding on him. "So. You and Maja?"

He reached up and massaged the back of his neck where the muscles had suddenly gone painfully tight. "Yeah."

"She's the ex from college who couldn't handle the truth about you?"

"Yeah."

Eva blew out a breath. "Shit."

He shrugged because it was all in the past. And truthfully, much of the reason for that was thanks to Eva.

"Humans don't tend to react well to finding out who I am. Aegi especially despise me, and it's not even because of my demon blood. It's all about my parents."

"I'm sorry," she said after a moment. "It's not fair. You shouldn't be judged for their sins."

He blinked. "Their sins?"

She looked at him like he was an idiot. "I mean, the history of the Horsemen is written in blood. Literally. You should see some of our books. And your mom…" She shook her head. "She betrayed The Aegis and your dad. Your parents' story isn't exactly an enemies-to-lovers romance."

What a load of shit. Sure, his father wasn't a saint or anything, but Eva was way off base about his mom and The Aegis's role in what happened when he was born.

"I'll give you the part about my dad." Thanatos had thousands of years of atrocities behind him, and there was no sugarcoating that. Sitting through history classes at school had been a special kind of hell. "But my mom didn't betray The Aegis. They betrayed *her* when they tried to kill me."

One dark eyebrow arched. "Is that what they told you?"

He really did not like the turn this conversation was taking. "You have a different version of events?"

She appeared to consider her wording, finally deciding on, "Every Guardian learns Aegis history, and trust me, that whole thing with your mom, Thanatos, and you is a three-day course all by itself. I actually did an hour-long Aegis TV special about it last year. Won a Hellfire Journalism Award."

He hoped he wasn't supposed to congratulate her. "Okay, I'll bite." He crossed his arms over his chest and waited for whatever bullshit she was about to spew. "What's The Aegis's side of the story? How do you guys spin being tricked by Pestilence into attempting to murder me?"

"Tricked by Pestilence?" Their gazes met, and her expression softened, sparking another stupid desire to take her into his arms and dart through Ares' gate before her colleagues could stop him. "Look, let's not do this. It's not important, and we've got a lot more urgent things to worry about."

"Agreed."

She cast a furtive glance at her Aegis buddies, her eyes narrowing at Maja before turning her attention back to him.

"I—" She shook her head as if clearing her mind of the words she'd been about to say, and a wall seemed to slam down between them. In an instant, she became the professional, no-nonsense Aegi he'd met that first day. "I'd appreciate it if you could arrange to have my things delivered from your place." She unhooked Mace's comms device with two mechanical, precise motions, and handed it to him. "Please thank Mace for me again. Take care, Logan."

As far as dismissals went, it wasn't a *fuck you*. But it sure felt like it as he watched her go, his emotions popping off in every direction like fireworks. She'd just pissed him off. But he didn't want her to go. She worked for the enemy. But she hadn't felt like the enemy last night in bed.

Dumbass. It's for the best. Draven is in trouble, the sky is raining angel blood, and Lilith is trying to hurt everyone you love. Eva is nothing but a distraction.

It was true. All of it. He had to forget Eva.

But first, he was going to find that damn award-winning video.

Chapter Twenty-Nine

Reaver had spent time in Hell. A lot of time. Well, it had *felt* like a lot of time. If you weren't a demon, a day seemed like a year in Sheoul.

But in most regions of Heaven, no one noticed the passing of time. Mainly because it was just that awesome.

Unless you were being held in a Heavenly prison made from the minds of dozens of Celestials.

Physically, Reaver was hanging by his arms from threads of spun crystal connected to every Archangel except Metatron and Gabriel. He didn't know where they were, but he'd seen the others connected to the threads, and their powers channeled into one single purpose.

Keeping Reaver imprisoned.

Back when Reaver had been gifted the rare, coveted, and ultimate angelic status of Radiant, he'd been told that, as the most powerful angel in existence, he couldn't be brought to heel or destroyed by anyone or anything save Satan, God, and the Council of Orders.

They weren't going to destroy him—Metatron would be needed for that, and there was no way Uncle Met would agree. But apparently, Metatron wasn't needed to *imprison* Reaver, and it didn't make him feel any better that the Archangels were also prisoners, forced by the crystal threads to channel their power into a brig crafted from their thoughts and nightmares.

Some of these Archies were seriously messed up.

Didn't matter. Reaver ran, swam, flew, and crawled through every scenario thrown at him. He'd been swallowed by giant flaming space grubs, ripped apart by millions of eyeless frogs with razors for claws, and chased by oily demons with swordlike penises. He'd lived through scores of nightmares now, but he welcomed them.

He learned from them. He'd discovered that if he looked hard enough, he could determine the owner of the nightmare. Once he knew that, he could manipulate the dreams and draw the owner out. Sometimes, that meant a better scenario. Other times, he could interact with whatever Archangel was running the show.

Currently, Michael was hosting a mind-numbingly boring scene of endless black sand. Two suns beat down on Reaver as he trudged across a featureless plane, his bare feet red and split like overcooked hot dogs.

The nightmare might not be real, but the pain was.

"What the hell, Mikey?" he shouted. "Why is your mind here?" And where *was* here? Wasn't Earth.

"Reaver?"

He looked down at a green crablike creature near his plumped feet. "Michael?"

The crab waved one of its six pincers. "Why are you here? And why are you a polar bear?"

"I'm not a—" Reaver looked down at himself, and…yep, he was a polar bear, and they were now on a frozen tundra. Thanatos's castle was in the background.

Why?

He looked down at the Michael crab. "We're in prison. You're linked to everyone but Metatron and Gabriel to create a cell strong enough to hold me. If we all come together at once, we can break it."

Michael Crab waved all of his pincers. "Why does this sound familiar?"

"Because this is the third time I've told you. Right now, is when we usually get thrown out of your dream, so we need to make it quick. Fight against the shit in your head. Keep your thoughts happy. Stay aware that this is a prison."

Suddenly, Michael himself was standing there, his eyes burning literal fire. "I remember now. The coup. The Thrones, and—"

"Yes, that. Listen, we don't have time. I need you to—"

Reaver gasped, sucking in great lungsful of air. It was bright. Nothing but light. He'd been yanked out of Michael's dream and into another.

He frowned. This didn't seem like a nightmare, though. There was too much sensation. Pain. Cold. The smell of sweet fruit. He looked up, and yes, he could feel the crystal threads biting into his wrists. He hung where the Thrones had left him suspended in the middle of a ring made from the Archangels.

He couldn't get a sense of how long he'd been trapped in Archangel head hell, but he didn't expect to. Heavenly prisons cut you off from the angelic network, Heavenly energy, and mate bonds.

And that was the worst of all of this. He could deal with the nightmares. He could handle not having a sense of time. He could even live without the strength of the Heavenly energy. What he couldn't live without was Harvester, and being unable to feel the bond between them was torture beyond anything these bastards could do to him.

A slice of brilliant blue cut into the blazing white. Three figures emerged. He squinted, unable to discern any facial features. A pair of flaming wings cast off orange lightning. Okay, that was Zaphkiel.

Suddenly, the light faded into a field of brilliant greens dotted by flowers of all the colors in the universe, some that human eyes couldn't see until they were here in Heaven again. It was the Meadow of Azna, near where Revenant's presence had left scars.

Zaphkiel approached, his lightning now tamed and sizzling only through his wings, and Reaver could finally make out Suroth. Between them, bound by the wrists and ankles, his wings strung up in golden twine, was Gabriel. His long mane, streaked in all the colors of mankind's hair, hung in matted ropes, and his eyes glowed with hate.

"Bastards," Reaver growled, disuse leaving his voice as fragile as ancient parchment. "You have no right."

"But we do," Zaphkiel said. "The Thrones are in charge now. We're going to fix what the Archangels have ruined."

"You should never have been elevated to Radiant," Suroth said. "The honor should have gone to someone better suited to handle the great responsibility of so much power."

"Like you?" Gabriel snarled. "Idiot."

That earned Gabriel a backhand from Suroth that snapped the Archangel's head back so violently Reaver heard the crack of vertebrae.

"We don't relish this, Reaver," Zaphkiel said in a voice tinged with regret. He genuinely believed they were doing the right thing. Which made him dangerous. True believers could justify anything. "But we must do what's necessary to restore balance to all the realms. Balance is what the Creator intended, yet you and Gabriel betrayed that by helping Azagoth destroy Sheoul-gra while the Archangels sat by and did nothing.

We must repair the realms before the Final Battle, and we haven't much time."

"The realms will balance themselves." Reaver struggled against his restraints, but they were as effective as they were painful. "The Archangels put it on the right path. Hades is rebuilding Sheoul-gra. Angels are training the Horsemen's offspring. Raika is hunting down the worst of the demons Azagoth released. The human realm doesn't need your interference."

"There shouldn't have been a need to rebalance the realms!" Zaphkiel snapped. "Demons should never have been allowed to take over an entire continent. The Archangels failed in their leadership, and it is up to the rest of angeldom to right their wrongs. And as soon as we uncover the names of every individual who assisted you and Gabriel, we will begin the process of weeding out the traitors in our midst."

"Tell him, Gabby," Suroth said. "Tell Reaver the news."

"Bite me."

"News?" Icy sweat bloomed across Reaver's skin. Any news these bastards wanted him to know wouldn't be good.

Averting his gaze, Gabriel shook his head. "They want me to tell you because, I don't know…punishment? They're cowards."

This time, Gabriel's bone-breaking backhand came from Zaphkiel. "Tell him."

Gabriel slowly lifted his gaze to Reaver's, and Reaver's heart clenched. This news was worse than *not good*. It would be devastating.

"No," Reaver breathed. "My children? Harvester?"

Gabriel flinched.

"*Harvester?*" Reaver struggled against his restraints, not caring that his wrists were starting to bleed. "Tell me!"

"I'm sorry, Reaver," Gabriel rasped. "We don't know where she is."

For a moment, Reaver almost laughed with relief. If they didn't know where she was, she was safe. She'd probably escaped before they shut down Heaven's borders.

"Finish it," Suroth prompted. "Tell him why."

Sudden anger, fresh and hot, flared in Gabriel's eyes. "Because Zaphkiel chased her into the Gaiaportal," he growled.

"The Gaiaportal isn't operational. It's sealed."

"She broke the seal." Gabriel clenched his fists. "At the same time, blood rained down on *Ilhum a'Aral.*"

Ilhum a'Aral. The angelic name for what humans called the Dome of the Rock. The site at which angels had arrived or departed when the

Gaiaportal was operational.

"I still don't—"

Gabriel closed his eyes. "We're no longer in the prison," he said, his voice heavy with emotion. He made an encompassing gesture. "This isn't a mirage. We're in the Meadow of Azna."

Reaver looked around at verdant fields stretched into purple mountains. A herd of unicorns frolicked near a forest of fluffy trees.

"Cool. The prison was getting stale. But what the fuck does that have to do with Harvester? I…no." The meadow wobbled as Reaver began to comprehend Gabriel's meaning. "*No!*"

Agony swelled inside him, filling the hole in his soul where Harvester had been.

He hadn't been able to feel the bond with her while in prison. But if she were alive, anywhere in the universe, he should be able to feel her now. The space she'd occupied was hollow.

His beloved mate, the female he'd hated and loved, loved and hated, over and over, was gone.

Chapter Thirty

Logan had Ares gate him back to the compound in Sydney. It was hard to believe it had only been four hours since he and Eva had left for Limos's place. Felt like days.

Sabre was there, angrily tossing back shots of Scotch while Mace and Blade looked on.

"What's going on? Why isn't everyone still at Limos's?"

"Party's over, man," Mace said. "Turns out dead Guardians and Harvester going through a juicer are fun killers."

Logan's body moved before his brain caught up. In the blink of an eye, he had Mace against the wall, his forearm pinning the demon by the neck.

"That is my grandma you're talking about," he snarled. "Have some fucking respect."

Mace shot a glance at Blade, who shrugged. "Don't look at me for help. You asked for it."

"Sorry, man." Mace slowly held up his hands in a show of surrender. "It's cool."

No, it wasn't cool. Logan was in the mood to take someone apart, and right now, Mace was practically begging to be that someone.

"I really am sorry," Mace said, sincerely this time. "I always liked her. She didn't take shit from anyone."

"Come on, you two," Sabre said between swigs of Scotch. "There's more important shit to worry about."

Blade swiped the bottle away from Sabre. "Everyone has assignments. All the Horsemen are working on hunting down Lilith and Draven." He jammed his other hand between Mace and Logan, and Logan reluctantly released Mace. Blade had always been the peacekeeper, designated driver, and idiot wrangler of the group. Hell, he was probably the only reason Mace wasn't dead after pissing off the wrong person by now. "Kynan is back at DART HQ with Arik, Tayla, and Decker. They're playing some kind of chess with The Aegis. He told us to get changed and get back there." He used the bottle to point at Sabre. "Then we found this moron doing his best to drink himself into oblivion."

If it were Mace, Blade, or Rade doing that, Logan wouldn't question it. But Sabre wasn't one to drown his sorrows in anything but a good fight. The Soulshredder DNA inside him made sure of that.

"What's going on?" Logan put himself outside Mace's punching range. "Didn't you leave the party with Aleka?"

"Yup." Sabre swiped the bottle back from Blade. "And no, I don't want to talk about it."

"Lotta that going around," Logan muttered.

"Why so glum?" Mace asked him. "Someone kick your dog?"

Blade looked over at Mace. "You think someone's going to kick a hellhound and survive it?"

Logan shook his head. "It's just something Eva said about my parents. It's psycho bullshit, but I can't get it out of my head."

"Told you." Rade came into the kitchen, silent as a snake, and they all nearly jumped out of their skins. "Told you she was full of shit."

For a moment, Logan considered letting all of it go. But he was already hopped up on anger, and he'd always been one to stick his hand in hornets' nests, so what the fuck?

"I want to see that video you have. The one Eva made about my parents."

Rade's shrewd eyes narrowed at him, but he tapped his comms and threw the holovid up into the space between them.

The clip, twenty-three minutes of outrageous lies, spewed by the female he'd slept with, the one he'd actually wanted to get to know, left him and his friends—even pissed-off Sabre—stunned and silent.

Mace broke the silence with a nervous laugh. "Dude, that's so whacked. Have you heard any of that stuff before? From your cousins or anything?"

It took a second for Logan to respond, his mind too busy trying to wrap itself around the fucked-up shit he'd just seen. "No. Never."

Rade stuck his head in the fridge. "Just ask your parents about it."

Blade barked out a laugh. "Yeah, sure. What's he supposed to say? *'Hey, Mom, did you roofie dad to get prego? Dad, did you put Mom in the dungeon and threaten to kill her after I was born?'*" He rolled his eyes. "Great dinner conversation."

"I'm not talking to anyone about this," Logan snapped. "It's not true. I'm not going to insult my parents by investigating it. I have other shit to do. Like getting Stryke to meet with me."

Everyone went quiet and still. The mere mention of Stryke always weighed down conversation.

"Good luck with that." Sabre chugged more whiskey.

Yeah, it wasn't going to be a good time. "I used to think it was difficult dealing with Stryke back when he was just a cocky asshole who always knew he was the smartest person in any room. But after Chaos…" He trailed off, not wanting to go there.

Logan had always liked Blade, and while Rade could be a jerk, he didn't mean to be. But their brother Stryke was always an arrogant ass, and he'd gotten even worse after Chaos died. Gone was the insufferable playboy genius. In his place was a cunning, stone-cold male with the dark aura of a predator.

Rade finally snagged a bottle of water from the fridge. "Stryke's a dick. What kind of asshole runs away when things get tough?"

"He didn't run away." Blade squared his stance in front of Rade. "We *pushed* him away."

"*You* pushed him away." Rade jabbed his finger at his brother. "You blamed him for what happened."

Logan had seen this movie before, and it deserved *all* the rotten tomatoes. All these years later, and no one had sorted their feelings on how much blame for Chaos's death to place on Stryke's shoulders. Time to shift away from the blame game.

"Hey," he said, casually moving between the brothers, "have either of you heard from him lately? Might be easier to get in touch with him through you than it would be going through his administration."

Tension diffused, Rade twisted the cap off his water bottle. "He hasn't seen anyone in the family in years. What makes you think he'll want to see you now?"

"Trust me." Logan dug into his pocket and pulled out the leather bracelet. "He'll see me."

"Oh, shit," Mace reached out and took the scrap of leather, turning it over in his hands as he studied the intricate weave Chaos had made with his own little fingers. "I thought you didn't have it."

"I didn't. The person who had it gave it back to me today."

Sabre punched the cork into the bottle and set it aside. "Is that...*the* bracelet?"

"The one Chaos gave to me for safekeeping and Stryke demanded I give him after he died? Yep. This should get me a meeting. Hopefully, right away. We need to know more about the Aegis weapon. Maybe—"

His comms buzzed. Aleka. Out of respect for Sabre and whatever had gone on between them, Logan excused himself and answered her call from the living room.

"Hey," he said as she appeared in front of him. "I didn't expect to hear from you so soon."

Aleka spoke to him from her office at the British Museum in London. "I had some energy to burn off. Plus, we all got called in for an emergency meeting. My team will be looking into why blood fell on Temple Mount. We haven't confirmed that it's Harvester's yet. Since all the blood is gone, no one has a sample." Sadness shadowed her green eyes. "I hope she's okay. And Grandpa too."

"I know. I'm worried about them too. I've missed watching Harvester needle our parents."

She smiled fondly. "And Grandpa Reaver always took her side. Anyway," she said, "the reason I called is that I found your mystery glyphs, and I consulted with one of my colleagues who specializes in ancient magic." She held up the drawing he'd given her. "So, the top side repels nightmare demons and keeps them from influencing dreams. Usually, that would be the only ward needed or used. But in this case, someone added glyphs that also tether the demon to an individual."

Logan sucked in a harsh breath. "Why would someone want a demon both attached to them *and* repelled?"

"Good question. Which is why I consulted with Linda. It turns out that the symbols are species-specific, and the demon attached to this tattoo is a symbiote. They feed off the nightmares they create, but in return, they grant their host good luck. What's interesting is that the owner of this tattoo probably no longer has nightmares, but they'd still benefit from the luck, and so would whoever was responsible for the tattoo. In fact, Linda thinks several people are reaping the luck rewards."

So, Eva was being used as some kind of...luck cow? Fury sizzled in his veins at the thought that someone—probably her parents—had saddled her with a demon and lied about it, all for personal gain. Eva hadn't had a good night's sleep since she was six years old, which had to affect her health. He was shocked she was even lucid.

"What would happen if the demon was captured or killed?"

Aleka sat back in her chair. "Uh…nothing good. There'd be an immediate reversal of luck. Really bad luck, to make up for all the good shit. It would detonate on an accelerated scale, potentially affecting everyone around the former host. Twenty years of good luck would turn into like, five days of shit luck, and might even end in death."

Logan felt the ground shift beneath him. He'd captured the demon the night before Sig killed Shanea and Noah.

Had all of that happened because of him?

And *how the fuck* could things get worse? It didn't matter how angry he was at Eva for all the lies she'd told about his family. Right now, he just needed to make sure she didn't die.

And then, once she was safe, he'd prove her wrong about his family.

"Logan?" Aleka tapped on her desk. "Yo. You were spacing." She eyed him in that unnerving way her father did. "Does this nightmare demon problem have anything to do with that Aegi you brought to Aunt Limos's place today?"

"Yeah." He swallowed and ran his hand through his hair. "I fucked up, cousin. The demon was a spirit. I trapped it the other night. Before everything went to hell." A potential fix popped into his head. "I'll release it. It's in storage, but I can—"

"You can't," Aleka broke in. "I mean, you *can*, but it won't help. Once it's separated from its host, the bond is broken."

Anger and panic winged through him. "How can we stop the bad luck? There has to be a way."

"I don't know," Aleka said. "I'll get back to you." Her feed cut off, and Logan sank heavily onto the arm of the sofa.

"Logan?"

Lost in his head and caught off guard, Logan snapped his head up so fast his neck cracked. "Ouch, shit. Hey, Crux. 'Sup."

The kid cocked his head and looked at him, his baggy sweats falling low on his narrow hips, and his size-large *Hella Good* restaurant tee hanging loosely on his thin frame. He'd fill out and look like his brothers after his sexual maturation phase, but right now, there was little resemblance. Even his coloring differed from theirs. The triplets had gotten their father Shade's black hair, dark eyes, and tan skin, but Crux was fairer like his mother, and he'd gotten her caramel hair and light eyes.

"You okay?"

"Yeah," he lied as he opened a link to Eva's comms unit. She might not have a new device yet, but her chip implant would accept and store his message until she got access through any comms device she connected to. "Just tired."

Crux jammed his hands into the pockets of his sweats. "Don't bullshit me. Nobody will tell me what's going on, but I know it's bad."

A virtual keyboard popped up in front of Logan. "They're just trying to keep you safe until your transition. Be a kid while you can. You have a five-hundred-year lifespan, and that means four hundred and seventy-something years of adulthood. Play video games and watch junk on TV. Things will get hectic soon enough."

"Everyone tells me that." Crux shot him the finger and a droll look. "Got something original?"

Busted. "No. Sorry, kid. I got nothin'." He started typing out a message to Eva.

"Are you messaging that Aegi?"

How the hell had he known that? "I have some information she needs."

"Oh. I liked her."

Logan looked up. "Really?"

"Yeah." He shrugged, his bony shoulders rolling under the oversized shirt. "I go to school with a lot of humans who don't know I'm a demon because, well, you know."

"Too well."

Crux shrugged again. "She was cool, you know? I mean, after she got over Mace asking her if she wanted to fuck."

The kid was twenty-two years old *and* a demon, and Logan couldn't help but want to scold him for using the f-word.

That was what happened when your mom was human.

"Yeah, she was cool," Logan muttered as he marked the message as urgent and sent it off.

"You gonna see her again?"

"I don't know," Logan said.

"Do you want to?"

Logan didn't even have to think about it. Because yeah, he did.

But would he?

Chapter Thirty-One

So, saying goodbye to Logan could have gone better. Way better.

And Eva had so many questions. Like, why was she not as excited to be back home as she should be? And why did she want to punch Maja in the face?

Well, she knew the answer to the latter question, but she considered the answer to the former as she and Maja trudged through one of the gazillion underground tunnels that ran under the streets of the nation's capital. The walk so far had been mainly silent, but when Maja slowed and let the escort get a little farther ahead, Eva braced herself for questions she didn't want—or know how—to answer.

"You okay?" Maja's voice was quiet, but even so, the tunnel amplified it enough that those up ahead surely heard.

And would people stop asking if she was okay? It was yet another of those questions she didn't know how to answer.

Finally, she settled on, "It's just been a long couple of days."

Maja nodded. "Sounds like things didn't end well for you and Logan."

Bingo. Stuff she didn't want to answer. "What do you mean?" she asked, even though she knew.

"I heard you arguing," Maja said. "Did you guys…?"

Eva let the question hang for longer than necessary. If she had to be uncomfortable, so did Maja. Who had also slept with Logan. Grr.

"Did we what?"

"There's no delicate way to ask this, so…are you involved?"

"We are definitely not involved." Not anymore. "He just didn't like finding out that his parents have lied to him for over thirty years." The escorts unlocked a steel door and held it open for them. "I shouldn't have said anything," Eva said as they entered the underground level of Aegis headquarters. "I should have let him believe that his parents had some sort of fairy-tale romance. Poor guy. He actually thinks we tried to kill him."

Maja's silence sent an inexplicable stab of doubt into Eva's gut. She kept hoping the Elder would offer some sort of explanation, but the thunderous silence continued until they stopped at an elevator, and she punched the *up* button.

"I have a meeting right now," Maja said, "but let's meet in an hour, and you can brief me on everything that went on while you were with DART and Logan. Your parents will be there, and I'm sure they're looking forward to seeing you."

"Sure," Eva said as they stepped inside the lift. "Where are Sig and Carlos?"

"They're here." Maja smashed the third-floor button, and the doors closed, leaving their escort to take the next elevator. "You'll all stay in the DC Guardian quarters until the threat is neutralized."

"Shouldn't we be someplace secret? The entire world knows about this place."

Maja shook her head. "If you three are in a secret location, it won't stay that way. Besides, this is the most defensible location we have. Welcome back."

Yeah. Sure.

"Thanks." Eva should probably track down Jennifer, but for the first time in her life, her career wasn't in the forefront of her mind.

Logan had taken up that space, and Maja's reaction to the story about his parents niggled at her. It might be nothing. It might have something to do with Maja's past relationship with Logan.

But it could also be something else. And after years of following her instincts as an investigative journalist, she knew she should look into it.

She glanced at the time on the elevator's control panel. If she hurried, she could get in forty-five minutes of research before she met with Maja again. She could catch up with Jenn later.

Maja got off on the third floor, and Eva took the lift down to the underground level where the library and artifact center sat deep inside the complex, protected from physical and magical attacks by layers of security from locked doors and guards to wards. It was like a gauntlet, and it always gave Eva a thrill. She loved research, and when the research material was cloaked in mystery and protocol, it added more fun.

At the very end of the gauntlet, a gray-haired Guardian named Tobey sat behind a desk, his fingers flying over the three screens in front of him.

"Hey, Tobe," she said.

He looked up with a smile. "Hey, Eva. Haven't seen you in almost a month. Heard you were on the DART exchange team." He shook his head. "Terrible what happened. I hope those freaks are shut down. The Aegis can do everything DART does."

That...wasn't entirely true. People argued that The Aegis could replace DART, but right now, The Aegis wasn't set up to capture demonic spirits or handle forensic investigations the way the Demonic Activity Response Team could. They were usually called in when a demon was suspected of a crime, where The Aegis handled larger attacks and clear demonic incursions. Plus, like it or not, DART did employ demons, which often gave them unique and more effective methods when it came to dealing with demonic activity.

But it wasn't worth her time to argue with someone on Team Destroy DART.

"Well," she said politely, "hopefully it will be resolved quickly. There's been too much tragedy on both sides."

"Both sides." He laughed. "That's cute. But they need to pay for what they've done. Haven't you seen the video?" Tobey pinched his fingers on the screen, made a throwing motion, and a life-sized, 3-D holovid popped up in front of her. Suddenly, she was standing in the DART cafeteria again, surrounded by DART and Aegis people.

"I've seen this, Tobey..." She trailed off as Shanea and Noah shifted into their demon forms, just as she'd seen them do in the video Kynan had shown her. But then everything went off the rails. Shanea and Noah attacked Carlos and Mason, completely unprovoked. Sig rushed in to separate them. Then, when Shanea raised her clawed hand for what looked like a potentially fatal blow, Sig shot her, totally justified in his actions.

But...that wasn't what happened. This wasn't right. Or was the DART video the one that wasn't right?

"Tobey, where did you get this?"

"It popped into my newsfeed. Like, five minutes ago."

After the prisoner exchange. After Ares and Logan left the ball field. Quite the coincidence.

"Did *we* release it? Surely, DART didn't."

Tobey reached for his coffee. "It's not an official release. It's from a whistleblower blog. They claim someone from DART leaked it."

Ah, whistleblower media. She'd loved it when she reported stories for the *pro-human* news outlets she'd worked for. There were always good conspiracy theories or so-and-so-is-really-a-demon stories to dig into.

But she didn't love this. One of the two videos she'd seen had been altered. She didn't want to believe that either agency would do that, but it was entirely plausible that the DART video she'd seen was original and had been leaked and then altered by an independent actor. Someone sympathetic to The Aegis or who had an ax to grind with DART.

Troubled by all the various scenarios, she waved away the holovid. She'd deal with it later. "Tobey, I need to get into the historical archives."

"Which section?"

"Twenty-first century."

Nodding, he flicked his fingers over one of the screens. "Topic?"

"The Four Horsemen."

His fingers flew again, and then a door on the right slid open. "You should have access to almost everything."

She paused. "Almost?"

He nodded again. "Looks like there's material related to the Horsemen in the secure vault. You'll need an Elder's code to get into it."

"Okay, thank you."

"No problem."

The door slid closed behind her as she walked through the aisles of material gathered during the current century. Most were digital files of pictures and articles, but there were also shelves of books and videos of every press conference given by The Aegis's media department.

She used the tablet mounted to the research table to scan the entire vault for topics related to the Four Horsemen of the Apocalypse, and specifically Regan Matthews and Logan.

Hundreds of files popped up on the screen, including several related to Regan, and one of Logan…that were locked away inside the secure vault.

Dammit.

She quickly scanned the available materials for information related to Regan's assignment as Thanatos's Aegis liaison, but there was nothing out of the ordinary. It was all the stuff every Aegi learned. The stuff she'd told Logan.

Well, that was all she could do.

Although...

Nah. She couldn't. She couldn't lie to an Elder.

Could she?

She thought about the look on Logan's face when she'd basically called his parents liars. And the look on Maja's face when Eva had told the Elder about it. Something was off.

And she'd done worse to get a story.

Before she lost her courage, she used the library's comms system to send a message to Maja, asking for permission to enter the south vault because it contained files related to the Dome of the Rock. Eva had no idea if that was true or not, but she'd bet Maja wouldn't question it, given today's blood-rain event. And sure enough, the Elder shot her a code.

Armed with the code and high on adrenaline, Eva hurried to the vault and activated the code lock. The door popped open with a soft hiss.

Oh, man. She'd give her right arm to spend just twenty-four hours in here. Heck, a couple of hours would be gold. How many secrets were filed away? And why?

She quickly dug through the materials related to Regan, most of which were service records, medical charts, and mission details.

Eva knew little about Logan's mother beyond the basics given during Aegis history orientation and the bits and pieces she'd picked up here and there. Everyone knew Regan was something known as a Camborian, born to two human Guardians, but her father had been possessed by a demon at the time her mother conceived. The Aegis had put her father down, and her mother had died by suicide after giving birth.

Regan had bounced from Aegis foster home to Aegis foster home as her powerful abilities manifested—spirit-defense abilities that had made her the perfect choice to work with Thanatos, who held power over souls.

But... Eva's pulse picked up as she read an account by an Elder named Lance, who had been slaughtered by Thanatos a few months later. He wrote that Regan had initially refused the assignment.

A mission to seduce Thanatos and get pregnant with the Horseman's baby to avert an apocalypse.

Okay, that was new information. The official version of the story was that the pregnancy was Regan's idea and not endorsed by The Aegis. But according to this, she was sent there to seduce the Horseman because The Aegis believed the resulting child would prevent the Apocalypse. When Thanatos found out what she'd done, he imprisoned her, and then new information came about and—

Dear God.

Eva slapped her hand over her mouth as she read the rest.

Oh, holy shit.

Holy, holy shit.

Logan was wrong about his conception, but he'd been right about The Aegis.

"Oh, Logan," she whispered. "I'm so sorry."

StryTech Tower, a shiny diamond rising from the center of Sydney, was both formidable and delicate, a work of art designed and built by a collaboration of demon and human architects and contractors. Somehow, it managed to be both creepy and elegant, forbidding and welcoming, a brilliant feat of one-of-a-kind engineering that wouldn't look out of place in either Heaven or Sheoul.

Logan strode to the entrance, past fountains and parklike green spaces where people on breaks strolled with their lunches from one of three food trucks in the square. Logan actually stopped and considered hitting the taco truck, or maybe the Aussie pie truck, but his stomach was a little too unsettled. Which definitely made the Sheoul food specialty truck a hard pass. Eyeball blood aspic wouldn't sit well, even on a settled stomach.

He kept an eye out for security personnel but doubted Stryke would make them obvious. No, there would be layers of concealed security, from wards and traps to invisible demons, and demons disguised as humans. The one exception was the sixteen-foot-tall, red-eyed, pitch-black devil standing near the corner of the building, its malevolent gaze taking in everything and everyone. It wouldn't move unless it sensed danger.

Logan made sure he didn't think any murderous thoughts.

The front doors opened, and he walked through a state-of-the-art demon detector. He passed, but then Stryke had made sure none of his tech flagged Horsemen or Seminus DNA.

At the front desk, he gave his name and was immediately escorted to the nearest elevator. A big male wearing sunglasses held his hand over the control panel, which lit up with floor numbers and demonic symbols. The guy pressed a combination of the symbols, and the elevator began a smooth ascent.

"You didn't press a floor number."

"No."

Friendly dude. After way too many uncomfortable seconds, the doors slid apart, and Logan stepped out into an open floor of windows. Logan had heard that the mirrored glass all over the building was bullet and magic proof, and there was no reason to believe it wasn't. Stryke wasn't only brilliant and wealthy, he was prepared.

The white marble floor was etched with more demonic symbols. Logan didn't recognize any of them.

Ahead, behind a wall of desks and lab equipment, Stryke was talking to a familiar male who appeared to be in his late fifties, his expensive suit perfectly pressed, his shoes shiny, and his red face glistening with sweat. Another guy, younger and sweating even more, stood next him.

Stryke didn't so much as look Logan's way as he stood slowly, his gaze locked on the man in front of him.

"Chancellor," Stryke began, "I don't give a shit if you spent too much money on our competitor's demon detection systems. We aren't giving you a discount for stupidity. We gave you a quote, and you went with the other guys, which was your prerogative. But then you badmouthed us publicly, saying our system is overpriced. So, if you want our *inferior* product after all that, you'll have to pay full price for it. And if you jerk me around again, I'll double the price and cut in half the number of demon species it can detect. Do you understand?"

"Yes, I understand," the guy said in a German-accented voice.

Holy shit. Now, Logan knew why the man was familiar. He was the fucking German chancellor. Just standing in front of Stryke with his head down, sweating bullets and swallowing like he was trying to choke down a plea for mercy.

"Well, I don't understand," the other guy said. "One of the reasons we chose the other company was because they offered free updates when they have new demon DNA to add to the detection database.

Now, you're offering free updates, but not for us?"

"William," the chancellor snapped. "Let it go."

"Yes, William," Stryke said, his voice velvet-smooth but edged with warning. "Let it go."

"Go to hell—"

Suddenly, two of the symbols on the floor flared orange. Two nine-foot Ramreel demons materialized on top of the symbols, their massive horns rising out of their skulls and curling over their heads. Their dinner-plate-sized hooves clacked on the tile as they lumbered toward the piss-their-pants-terrified humans.

"Escort my friends to the Sales department. Use William's blood to sign the contracts."

William lost all color in his face as he and the chancellor were all but dragged past Logan to the elevator. Only after the doors closed did Stryke seem to notice Logan.

"Logan." He looked down at his desk as Logan walked across the bare expanse, his boots thudding on the shiny tiles. "Right on time."

"I know what a stickler you are for punctuality." Stryke had always been obsessive about being on time, and he got seriously annoyed when people were late. He glanced back at the elevator. "Sounds like the Germans were not happy with your competitor's work."

"No one is. Most people who buy their inferior tech eventually come crawling to us."

"Probably because of your winning personality."

"No," Stryke said, completely ignoring—or not recognizing—the sarcasm. "It's because our DNA library is more than triple Demonovation's. There's been a rise in Nightlash attacks since they figured out how to disguise themselves as humans, and Demonovation doesn't have their DNA on file. It's bringing a lot of their customers to us. Of course, they're accusing us of orchestrating the attacks in order to steal their customers."

"Are you?" Logan honestly wouldn't be surprised. Stryke was obsessed with protecting the world from demons and had an achieve-the-goal-by-any-means-necessary kind of mentality. So what if a few innocents died if that meant saving many more?

"If we were," Stryke said, "I wouldn't tell you."

"There was a time you used to trust me."

"There was a time when it mattered."

Ouch. Logan wandered over to the bank of spotlessly clear windows and looked out at the Sydney Harbor Bridge. "Thank you for seeing me."

"You have my brother's bracelet. You knew I'd want it."

Logan pivoted to the demon. "You could have asked me to mail it."

"Would you have done it?"

"No."

"Exactly." His finger flew across a pad on his desk, and the symbol closest to him began to glow. He stood as a Harrowgate shimmered into existence over the symbol. "You wanted a face-to-face meeting. Let's go."

Logan had no idea where they were going, but he had no reason to think Stryke would lead him into a trap, either. Stryke's business dealings and ethics were sometimes questionable, but he was, ultimately, playing for the good guys.

Probably.

"Where are we going?"

"My place."

"Cool." He followed the demon into the Harrowgate, where Stryke slid his finger over one of the handful of symbols.

The door opened onto a covered patio of stone and rough-hewn timber. Logan stepped out of the gate into air that smelled like fir and berries. A forest spread beyond the house in every direction, as far as the eye could see. The lulling sound of running water drew him to the railing, where it looked out over a river below.

"I thought you lived in your building's penthouse." Logan had seen about a million pictures and videos from there, where Stryke held social events and often gave interviews.

"Everyone thinks I live there," he said. "By design, of course."

"But you really live here?"

"Yes." Stryke looked out at the craggy mountains and rolling hills that seemed to be untouched by human—or demon—hands. "And I'd appreciate it if you'd keep that to yourself. Very few people know about this place."

"Where are we?"

"We're in the Canadian Rockies. My house and property are invisible to human eyes and warded against detection from satellites and both Heavenly and Sheoulic beings."

Of course, it was.

"Come inside." The sliding door opened automatically for Stryke, and Logan was impressed to find that the interior was as grand as the outside.

Pristine wood floors broken by cabin-themed throw rugs and rustic furniture extended through the open floorplan all the way to the wall of windows at the back of the house, beyond which was a parklike yard with a pool, hot tub, and an outdoor shower.

Stryke had always had a book in his hand as a kid, and his love for reading was obvious in the rows of full bookcases and shelves placed creatively around the rooms. Canoes had been converted into bookshelves, as well as sets of skis and even snowshoes. Only one shelf was bare of books. The only thing on its rough-hewn surface was Masumi's second jade vase.

Stryke made a beeline for the bar and splashed whiskey into a couple of lowball glasses. "So. Where did you find the bracelet?"

"Long story." Logan pulled it from his pocket and slid it across the bar top.

Stryke's expression hardened, became a carving of stone, but his eyes couldn't hide the sadness as he gingerly took the bracelet with his fingers.

"Chaos," he whispered.

Guilt tore at Logan with Cruentus-sharp claws. He'd blamed Stryke for Chaos's death, even though it wasn't really fair. Yes, Stryke had been charged with watching the twins that day. And he'd made a mistake, for sure, by leaving them alone on a theme park ride while he hooked up with a popcorn stand attendant. But no one could doubt that Stryke had loved his little brother, no matter how cold and distant he'd grown since the boy died. Seeing the pain in his eyes knocked Logan down a little. Stryke had paid a steep price for his error in judgment.

It was just that Chaos had paid more.

It wasn't often that Stryke revealed vulnerability, and Logan could practically hear his uncle barking in his ear.

Now is the time to ask him anything you want. His guard is down. Strike fast, kid.

"Stryke…can I ask you something?"

The Sem carefully and precisely placed the whiskey bottle onto its assigned position in the lighted liquor cabinet. "I can't stop you."

Logan's fists clenched in frustration. The Sem had always been hard to talk to, even before he morphed into the broody dick he was now.

"Do you know much about my parents?"

"Like what?" Stryke handed Logan one of the lowballs. The way it made his fingers sting told him the glass had been made from Sheoulic sand.

"Like how they got together."

"Why would I know anything about that?"

"Dunno. You have access to resources I don't. I heard some disturbing crap from someone in The Aegis, and I'm feeling it out."

"From that human female you're saddled with?"

"*Was* saddled with." Except it hadn't felt that way. He'd enjoyed being around Eva. At least, as long as she wasn't trying to make him doubt his parents and their entire relationship. "How did you know about her?"

Stryke drew a dart from the basket on the end of the bar. "I have an active network of informants."

"Did your spies tell you that one of your weapons killed some of our people?"

"No." Stryke flung the little missile at a dartboard hung below the skull of a horned demon that must have been the size of a water buffalo. "Kynan did." Bullseye.

Logan scowled. "Kynan said he hadn't heard from you."

"He hasn't. I heard from him."

What an ass. "So, you got his message and didn't respond?"

Stryke tossed another dart. Bullseye. "I've been busy."

I've been busy?

What the hell? Too busy for family? For friends?

The last few days' events, the conversations and lies, the blood and death...all of it sat on Logan like an overburdened mule. The weight of it rubbed painfully, and now it felt like the load was slipping, becoming unbalanced.

And his temper was going along for the ride.

"People are dead, you son of a bitch," he growled. "Because of your weapon. And Draven is on a rampage I'm not sure he'll come back from."

Stryke paused before taking another dart. "I didn't know about Draven."

"His fiancée was one of the people killed."

"So that was why Kynan wanted DART's demon detector software upgraded with *tormentus* DNA. I had a tech take care of that a few hours ago." Gripping the dart in his fist, Stryke stared blankly at the board. "I'm sorry."

Logan believed him, but it wasn't enough. Sorry didn't bring people back from the dead.

"If you were really sorry, you'd give us something we can use to stop him." Determined to get this jerk to give up the goods on The Aegis's secret demon-killing pistol, Logan pressed harder. "What's with the new Aegis weapon, Stryke? And why did you give it to them but not us?"

Unfazed by Logan's anger and still clutching the dart, Stryke fetched what looked like a child-sized pistol from a glass cabinet on the far side of the room.

"It's called a Smiter," he said, handing the gun to Logan. "It's invisible to most metal detectors and weapons sensors. The pistol and bullet shells are constructed from metals found only in Sheoul. If DART gets the fragments analyzed, they'll find that out."

The pistol weighed practically nothing, its black surface as smooth as glass. It looked fragile, incapable of the kind of destruction Logan had seen in the cafeteria. "It's at Sabre's lab as we speak." He handed the thing back to Stryke.

Stryke inclined his head. "I would expect Ky to send it to the best."

"What's inside the bullets that makes it so lethal to demons?"

"That," Stryke said, "is a secret." He placed the weapon back in the case. "The reason I gave it to The Aegis instead of you is because they contracted it. And they provided the sacrifices required to bring it to life."

Logan stared at the guy. "Sacrifices?"

"It's exactly what you think," Stryke said as he finally unloaded the dart. Bullseye. "DART would never have asked that of its people. But The Aegis?" Stryke shrugged. "They're True Believers. They'll gladly offer up their blood for the cause."

Holy shit. Talk about dedication. And brainwashing. "How much blood?"

Stryke waved his hand in dismissal. "I'm not discussing my business with you. You've brought the bracelet. Thank you. Are we done?"

Jackass. "Do you have any questions for me?"

"No." Stryke popped the darts out of the board and repositioned himself to go again.

"Nothing? You don't want to know how your family is doing? Your mom? Dad? Not even Crux?"

"I thought you were leaving." Fucking bullseye.

"Are you for real?" Logan closed his fist around the stinging lowball glass and let the pain soak up some of his anger. He was on the verge of jamming every one of those darts down Stryke's throat. "Crux misses you, though for the life of me, I have no idea why. He'll be going through his change soon, and where will you be? Hiding in your mountain paradise?"

Stryke remained unmoved. "Don't be dramatic. He has Blade, Rade, and all his cousins." He gestured to the lonely jade vase on the shelf. "And Masumi. She'll guide him through it."

"You're a selfish piece of shit, man."

Stryke snorted. "That again? You don't have an original insult? You're losing your touch, Ponyboy."

Ponyboy. Logan hadn't heard that nickname since he was a teen. The Sem boys had called him that. All of them except Stryke. Stryke had considered it to be demeaning.

"Dammit, Stryke!" Logan shouted. "Work with us! Make a fucking effort to ensure your friends and family are safe. It wouldn't hurt you to ask us how you can help more. We need better soul traps. We need a way to track down Draven. We need you to give a shit about us, you asshole!"

In a sudden, lightning-fast motion, Stryke launched a dart. It missed the bullseye and hit the wall.

"Fuck you." He rounded on Logan, red embers burning in the black of his eyes. "I do care!"

"Then you should've warned us about the Aegis weapon." Blood pumping hotly, fists more than ready to start pounding, Logan got up in the demon's face. He hadn't tangled with Stryke since high school, either in battle-training or in a real, knock-down brawl, and he was ready to make up for lost time. "Good people are dead because of that weapon, and we're about to lose Draven too." He jabbed the demon in the breastbone, ignoring the other male's warning growl. "This is on *you*."

It wasn't entirely fair. Logan knew that. Didn't care. He needed to release the fury and pain inside him, and Stryke had been number one on Logan's list of people who needed an ass-kicking for years.

They were nose to nose, eye to eye, and then Stryke smiled, even as the crimson flecks spread in his eyes, forming a spiderweb of fury.

Baring his teeth, he ground out, "Why don't you go ask your dad how your mom got knocked up?"

Shock hit Logan like a sucker punch to the throat. Then, Stryke hit Logan with a real sucker punch to the throat.

It. Was. On.

Logan was faster, better trained, and stronger. But Stryke made up for it with a complete lack of self-preservation. It was another change in him since Chaos's death. He'd always been a better-than-average fighter, but he'd known when he was outmatched, and he would put his effort into defense.

Not this time. He fought aggressively, no-holds-barred, like a male daring the other to kill him. The surprise factor alone gave Stryke an edge for a few seconds.

Blood splattered on the shiny wood floor with every brutal punch.

Logan got in a powerful blow that knocked Stryke into the bar and gave Logan a second to breathe. Deep in the back of his mind, Cujo whined, sensing Logan's pain. Normally, the beast would flash to him, but clearly, Stryke had warded his property to prevent unauthorized and unexpected demons from popping in.

I'm fine, buddy. The hound's concern faded.

Stryke stumbled to his feet, and Logan sent a roundhouse kick to the demon's face, taking him down again. "You said you didn't know anything about my parents."

Dabbing blood from his mouth, Stryke sat up and laughed. "I lied. I know everything. Now, get the fuck out."

As much as Logan wanted to go for another round with Stryke, he had shit to do.

And first up was a conversation with his parents.

Chapter Thirty-Two

When Logan arrived at his parents' place, Wraith and his son, Talon, were just leaving.

"Hey, man." Wraith gestured to the blood on Logan's shirt and face. "You look like hell. Work or pleasure?"

He snorted. "Pleasure. Guy had it coming." He looked down at himself as the last of his bruises faded and the cut on his lip sealed. Being able to draw healing power through his bond with Cujo was awesome. He'd be pain-free of even his worst wounds within minutes. Stryke would feel that fight for a couple of days.

Hilarious.

"Any news about Draven?" Talon asked.

"Nothing. He's dropped off the face of the Earth. I've got Cujo looking for him, but it'd probably be easier to find a lost halo in Hell."

"I've been looking for him too," Wraith said. "Mace and I are meeting with the *tormentus* Council in an hour. If we can get their help, it widens the net."

Interesting. Demon Councils rarely wanted to help anyone. "Why would they do that?"

"I used to hang with one of the Council members," he said. "She...owes me some favors."

"I'll bet," Talon muttered. "And why Mace?"

"Because he knows about my past with her, and he asked me."

"How does he know about that, and I don't?"

Wraith's blue eyes flashed, sparked by years of friction between him and his son. "Maybe if you'd hang out with us more often, you'd know."

It was time to seek an exit ramp because this was going to devolve quickly. Talon and Mace had hated each other since they were kids, and Wraith's relationship with Mace was a giant wedge between Wraith and Talon.

Technically, Talon and Mace were cousins *and* brothers, and they were as unalike as any two Seminus demons ever were. Talon had also taken after his uncle Eidolon both in mannerisms and career, while Mace was basically a clone of Wraith—reckless, cocky, and dangerous, making matters even more volatile.

Not that Talon wasn't a lethal motherfucker too. As Wraith's son, he was a badass fighter, trained in multiple disciplines from the time he could walk. But it wasn't long before little Talon preferred playing with toy scalpels instead of throwing knives and hanging out at Underworld General instead of the dojo.

On the other hand, Mace soaked up everything Wraith—his biological father—had to teach. He'd had no interest in anything even remotely healthcare-related, much to his parents'—Lore and Idess—disappointment.

"So," Logan said in an attempt to change the subject. "Why were you guys here?"

"I came to see Thanatos," Wraith said. "I didn't know Talon was here until I was leaving."

Talon nodded. "I was just dropping off a book for Amber. I was supposed to bring it to the party, but with the Draven shit going on, I forgot."

Amber and Talon shared a love of fantasy novels and had been swapping books and discussing them for years. Talon swore to Logan that the only *fantasy* involved in their relationship was in the books, but sometimes Logan wondered if Amber felt differently. For Talon's sake, Logan hoped he was wrong. Nothing good would come of any male who tried to date Amber.

"I'm sure she was happy to get it."

"Nah." Talon frowned. "I think she's mad at me. I haven't had much time to hang with her."

"Maybe if you didn't spend all your spare time with your new girlfriend, Amber wouldn't be so upset," Wraith offered, and Talon rolled his eyes.

"I've been busy at work," Talon said. "And, yeah. I get it. You don't like her. We all get it."

No one liked Talon's girlfriend. Sometimes, Logan thought even Talon didn't like her. Mace was sure Talon was only with her for sex and to piss off his father, and Logan was inclined to believe that.

"She's a fallen angel," Wraith growled. "You can't trust them. Not ever."

Talon let out a frustrated sound somewhere between a snarl and a shout. "I'm so tired of this shit." He nodded at Logan. "See you later."

He teleported out of there in a blink. Lucky guy hadn't had to use a Harrowgate since his first maturation phase when his birth mom's ability to teleport manifested.

"I do not know how to deal with that kid," Wraith said, staring into the empty space where his son had stood.

"You're very different people."

Wraith smiled sadly. "He's better than me." He clapped Logan on the shoulder and headed toward the Harrowgate Thanatos had installed outside the walls. "See you later. Your dad is in his workshop. Tell your mom I said hi if you see her."

"Will do."

Still jacked up on adrenaline-fueled anger, Logan tamped down any misgivings he might have had about confronting his parents over something so heinous and obviously untrue. He'd clear the air about this bullshit, proving Eva and Stryke wrong, and then he'd find Draven.

Easy.

He strode across the courtyard to the old stone building his father called his *male cave*. He'd spent thousands of years honing his woodcarving, leatherwork, and weapons-making skills, and he'd entertained Logan as a kid for hours on end with his art.

Logan had even tried his hand at working with leather, making a saddle, bridle, and reins for Cujo.

Cujo hadn't been *at all* receptive to being ridden like a horse.

Logan found his dad bent over his workbench, pounding on a strip of iron.

Thanatos looked up as Logan approached, the two blond braids at his temples swinging against his cheeks. "Hey, Logan. Perfect timing. I could use a hand."

He peered around his dad at the workbench. "What are you making?"

"It's a weapon. For you to use against Draven."

And just like that, he got another sucker punch to the throat. "I don't need a weapon for that."

"You're no fool, son." Thanatos's voice was grim, hitting home the reality of the situation that Logan hadn't wanted to think about. "You know you might."

Okay, maybe. But only as a last resort. There was still time to bring his friend back. "What makes this weapon special?"

Thanatos held up a smooth, curved piece of wood, its sharp, pointy tip fashioned from what looked like crimson glass. "Limos gave me this."

Logan drifted closer, drawn to the eerie light that seemed to pulse inside it. More than light, it was power. The way it whispered to him, with vile descriptions that somehow stroked his pleasure centers in all the wrong ways, said it was evil power.

"What is it?"

His father ran his finger over the stone. "It's all that's left of Bones."

"A stone?"

Thanatos nodded. "When a hell stallion or mare dies, their essences are compacted into a single stone. In a way, they leave their power behind. These stones are rare, priceless, and powerful." He placed the piece on the bench. "It'll deflect Draven's mental and telekinetic attacks. But it won't just deflect them. It'll send them back to him at half-power. So be careful if you want him alive."

"I'm not going to need it at all."

"Why? Because Draven won't hurt you?" His dad laughed. "Sometimes, I forget how young you are."

Not this again.

Generally, his dad was cool. He'd been a great father. Strict but fair, and as willing to play catch with Logan as he'd been to have a tea party with Amber and her stuffed animals.

But the guy liked to play the I-know-better-than-you-do-because-I'm-ancient card every chance he got.

"I'm thirty-three. I know I haven't been alive for thousands of years, but I'm not naïve. I studied demons and battle tactics in school. I've trained my entire life with angels and demons. And I've had you, Limos, Ares, and Reseph breathing down my neck constantly. I might as well be hundreds of years old with all the knowledge I have."

His dad snorted and turned back to his project. "The universe doesn't care about your hundreds of years' worth of knowledge. You're a child on the scale of our existence."

Logan watched his dad run sandpaper along the wooden handle of the weapon. He'd always been good with wood. Had even hand-carved Logan and Amber's cradle—a cradle that would soon rock another baby to sleep.

"Dad?"

Thanatos didn't look up from the workbench. "Yeah?"

"I have a question."

"Shoot."

He paused, then blurted, "How was I conceived?"

"Sex," his dad said, not missing a beat. "We had this talk when you were, like, eight. When you caught me and your mom—"

"Yeah, I know. I don't need to relive that." Logan's pop wasn't making this easy. "But I mean...*how*?"

His dad tossed the sandpaper aside and grabbed a woodworking tool. "That particular night, I was on the bottom, and your mom was on top—"

"Stop! Criminy." Logan shook his head, hoping to prevent any traumatic images from forming. Catching them going at it like rabbits when he was eight was more than enough mental damage. "I'm serious."

Thanatos scraped gently along the edge of the weapon. "So was I."

"Stop it!" Frustrated, Logan jammed his hands into his pockets and started over. "Dad. Can we talk? Please?"

The scrapes slowed and became deliberate. Calm. But Logan wasn't buying the act. His dad had set aside the sandpaper and went to a more familiar tool. A comforting one. "We're not discussing your conception."

Logan's palms grew damp. Sure, his dad could be protecting the intimacy of his marriage, but he could also be hiding something. Also, if he wanted to protect the intimacy of his marriage, he shouldn't have said that thing about Logan's mom being on top.

Because...gross. Logan could have gone his entire life without that knowledge.

"Fine. I'll talk. You can nod yes or no."

"No." Thanatos's grip on the scraping tool turned his knuckles white as the strokes along the edge of the wood came faster. Became less precise. Fat slivers and wood chips started to fall to the floor, out of place among the finer dust from earlier scrapings.

Now was probably not the time to do this, but there would never be a *good* time. So, what the hell?

"Did Mom trick you into getting her pregnant?" He vomited the words, sickened to even speak them.

Thanatos went utterly still for ten deafening heartbeats that made Logan sweat. Fifteen. Twenty. When he finally spoke, his voice was low and rough. "Who told you that?"

"Is it true?" Logan asked. It didn't matter where he'd gotten the information. What mattered was the truth.

With controlled, precise movements, Thanatos placed the scraper on the workbench and turned to face Logan. His pale-yellow eyes drilled into his son with a rare intensity. "It's complicated."

Which wasn't a no. In fact, it was practically a yes.

"The way I heard it, it was pretty simple," Logan said, his voice suddenly hoarse. "Mom seduced you, drugged you, and used you to get pregnant. Then she ran off, intending to give me up. You kidnapped her and held her prisoner until I was born. At which point, you intended to kill her. Is that the gist?"

Logan's voice was shaky now and growing hoarser as the pain in his father's expression confirmed it all. "You told us Mom came to work with you, and you fell in love. You didn't mention anything about her restraining you with poisoned wine. I don't remember anything in your syrupy love story about how you threw her in a dungeon. And I definitely don't remember you saying that Kynan and Gem were supposed to raise me after Mom hid her pregnancy from you so she could give me up to them."

"Logan," Thanatos said tightly, his fist clenched hard around the scraping tool. "That is not the whole story—"

"It's not? Because you look really fucking guilty right now."

"Guilty about what?" The door swung open, and his mom strode in, a plate of food in one hand and a beer in the other. "Hi, Logan. Do you want to stay for lunch? I made plenty. Where's Wraith?" She looked between them, confused. "Ah…did I interrupt something?"

"No." Thanatos dropped the tool and started toward her. "Logan was just leaving."

"I'm not going anywhere." Logan blocked the exit. They weren't going anywhere either. "Not until you tell me the truth."

"The truth about what?" his mom asked.

"Logan—"

"My conception," he blurted before his dad could finish his sentence.

The plate of sandwiches fell from Regan's hand and shattered on the floor. "Logan," she whispered. "No."

His world splintered like the plate. It *was* true. What Eva had reported was true. He stumbled back and bumped into the wall.

"Oh, my God, Mom," he croaked. "Why? How could you—?" He looked at his dad, whose face had gone almost as pale as his mom's. "And how could you forgive her? *Did* you forgive her?" A thought struck him, and he blurted roughly, "Is she still a hostage? Has all of this…this family shit been a lie?"

"No, Logan," Regan said, her voice thick and raw. "Of course, not. I'm not a hostage, and the details of that don't matter. It was a difficult time with Pestilence on the loose and trying to break the rest of the Seals, and we all made a lot of mistakes."

She reached for him, but he wheeled out of reach, unable to bear her touch.

"Mistakes? You were going to give me away! You told me you fell in love. That I was wanted. You didn't say I was wanted as a tool for The Aegis! You didn't tell me Dad had no choice in the matter! Did The Aegis really try to kill me, or was that a lie too? What about Amber? Did you get Dad drunk to get her?" He was on a tear now, beyond caring that his words were stabbing at his parents like daggers. He gestured at her softly rounded belly. "Did you poke a hole in the condom for that one?"

Regan cried out, her face ashen, and Logan knew he'd gone too far.

"Logan!" Thanatos roared. "Enough! We can talk about this when you can process information like an adult instead of a child."

"No, we can't." Logan backed toward the door, his head spinning, his heart aching. "This isn't something I ever want to discuss again."

He escaped, a mix of shame and righteous anger fueling his exit. He practically ran to the courtyard, where Cujo was pacing the walls, drawn by Logan's distress.

When the big beast saw Logan, he zoomed over in a literal flash, bringing with him the faint odor of brimstone. His big tongue slathered Logan's cheek, probably more to lick off the blood from the fight with Stryke than to offer comfort, but Logan appreciated it anyway.

"Let's go," he rasped. "I don't care where—"

His comms unit buzzed. An urgent message from Kynan.
HQ. Hurry. It's Draven.

DART headquarters was in a state of disarray, unlike anything Logan
had ever seen. It mirrored his emotions. And his thoughts.

Everything in his life was mangled, from his childhood memories to
his relationship with Eva to his friendship with Draven.

And now DART.

He charged through the lobby and nearly bit it when his boot
slipped in a puddle of blood.

"Logan!" Blade jogged toward him, Mace on his heels. "You just
missed him. No fatalities, but he fucked some people up."

"How did he get in?" Logan took in the carnage, and hard as he
tried, he couldn't tell how many people had been injured. "The demon
detector was upgraded. It should have set off alarms."

Kynan approached, escorting a team of medics from Underworld
General. Most of the victims were probably human, but DART had
decided long ago to keep shit quiet and avoid human hospitals when the
agents were injured. Besides, UGH's demon medicine was far more
advanced than the humans'.

After the personnel dispersed, Kynan joined them, and for the first
time in his life, Logan couldn't stand the sight of the human. He'd
always loved Ky like a second father, but finding out that he'd plotted
with The Aegis to be his adoptive *first* father wasn't sitting well.

"I just spoke with a StryTech technician to find out what went
wrong," he said. "Apparently, they failed to mention that the detector
won't activate for Draven's species until they're fully transitioned."

"Which won't happen until every Aegi involved in Shanea's death is
dead." Logan swore, as much out of anger with Kynan as the situation.
"Why was he here?"

"We don't know. We weren't aware he was in the building until I
got an alert that someone had accessed some sensitive files. I've got
Cyan going through the security logs right now."

"Sir!" Nikko Masters, a sixty-something ex-cop and one of Kynan's first human agent hires decades ago, ran up to them, nimbly avoiding the blood puddle Logan had stepped in. "Chuck Verinn's dead."

Stunned, Kynan wheeled around to Nikko. "Chuck was working today?"

"No, he was late, so I sent someone to check on him." Nikko tapped his comms, and another human agent, Stan Geardon, popped into view in front of them. "Tell them, Stan."

Stan shook his head. "I'll show you." He stepped aside and angled his view device to a bed, where Chuck's battered, naked body lay sprawled in the tangled sheets. "He looks…"

"Like he's been fucked to death," Mace finished. "Died with a smile on his face."

"It was Lilith." Logan's mouth flooded with bile at the knowledge that his grandmother had done…*that*…to a colleague. "It had to be. She's working with Draven, and she could have gotten the information he needed to break into the files."

"I saw Draven battling to get out of here after he was discovered," Blade said. "He wasn't trying to kill anyone." His broad shoulders drooped as he took in the bloody scene all around them. "He held back. It was our Draven. It *was*."

"And yet he's working with Lilith," Kynan said, his emotional pain making his voice even rougher. "And now the question is…"

Logan's chest constricted around his heart as if protecting it from the reality that he was losing his best friend. And from the devastating understanding that whatever Draven was after, it wouldn't be a good thing for Eva.

"What information did he get?" Logan murmured. "And how is he going to use it?"

He needed to warn Eva. But of what? She knew Draven was hunting her and her colleagues. And if she got his message, she knew her luck was on a downturn. She was in the safest place she could be right now.

She'd be safer with me.

"You okay?" Kynan eyed Logan, taking in his blood-flecked clothes. "You look like you went a round with—"

"Stryke," he said sharply. "I went a round with Stryke. And no, he didn't share anything useful about the Aegis weapon."

"You saw Stryke?" Kynan swore. "You shouldn't have—"

"Shouldn't have what?" Logan snapped, his anger bubbling up again, all fresh and hot. "You don't get to tell me what I can't do. You're not my dad. Your scheme failed."

"Scheme? What are you talking about?"

"I *know*, Kynan. I know what went down when I was conceived." He jabbed his finger in his boss's face. "And I know what part you played, asshole."

Kynan's eyes flared, and he took a surprised step back. He went very quiet, and so did everyone nearby. Mace and Blade watched, wide-eyed, and Nikko, who had been about to leave, froze mid-stride.

"We need to talk about this, Logan," Kynan finally said, calm—but calm the way Ares was when digging deep for control. "I have to make some calls, but after that, we're talking." He stepped close again, his expression as serious as Logan had ever seen it. "And yes, I can tell you what to do because I'm your damn boss." He gestured to the alcove where visitors sat. "Meet me there in half an hour. And while you're waiting, calm your ass down."

Kynan wheeled away from Logan and strode toward the elevators. Next to Logan, Mace whistled.

"Dude. I thought you didn't believe Eva's story."

"I didn't. Until I talked to my parents."

"So, it's true?" Blade waved to one of the medics. His father was in charge of Underworld General's paramedic department, so Blade had grown up with most of them. "Well, welcome to the club."

"What club?"

"The Parents Meeting In Fucked-Up Ways club. What, you never heard how my parents hooked up? Or Mace's? And talk to Talon sometime about his parents. Holy shit."

"You guys are demons. Your parents are supposed to be into fucked-up shit."

"Your dad is half-demon and fated to turn into a homicidal maniac when his Seal breaks," Mace pointed out. "And your mom got caught up in The Aegis's brainwashing. There's a lot to unpack there. At least listen to their side of the story."

He didn't want to. He'd told his father as much. But his idiot friends, the ones who usually went off half-cocked and who Logan often had to talk down, made sense.

And if *they* thought he needed a brake check…

Logan might have screwed up big time.

Chapter Thirty-Three

Eva was still reeling from the new version of events surrounding Logan's conception and near death, as well as her agency's involvement in it, when she strapped on a new comms unit and got a message from Logan.

Her heart skipped a beat when she saw the alert, and then it skipped a few more when she saw it was urgent.

She hadn't expected to hear from him so soon after parting. Maybe it was an update on Draven.

Slinging her tote over her shoulder, she opened the file as she walked down the main Aegis corridor toward the room where she'd be meeting with several Elders and her parents.

The message appeared to be an update on her tattoo. Weird. Maybe—

She gasped. How could…how was it possible…?

"Oh, my God," she whispered, coming to a shocked stop in front of the meeting room door. "What the hell?"

The door swung open. "Oh, Eva," Maja said. "I was just going to get some coffee. Want anything?"

I want you to spill hot coffee all over yourself.

"No, thank you," she said absently. "I'm good."

Maja gestured to the table where Elders Dmitri, Hammond, and Sig's father, Lukas, sat, their eyes focused like lasers on Eva. "Have a seat. Your parents will be here soon."

Good. Because they needed to have a serious conversation.

Eva settled in at the table in silence, her mind spinning with the events of the last few days. By the time Maja returned and took a seat, Eva was ready to get this over with.

Maja smiled from across the table. "Thank you for meeting with us."

As if she'd had a choice. "Of course. But I'd rather be doing something to find Draven. What is The Aegis doing about him?"

One eyebrow arched. "You know we're supposed to be asking the questions, right?"

As far as admonitions went, it was mild. But still, it pissed Eva off. On top of everything else, her confidence in her employer had been shaken, and now she wondered what else they were hiding.

"Sorry," she said, even though she wasn't. But she had to play the game if she wanted that promotion, right? Bitterness coated her tongue and her words. "It's been a rough couple of days."

"I know," Maja said. "We're all upset and furious over the slaughter of our people."

Eva looked up sharply. "Did you see the leaked video of the incident?"

"Appalling." Anger turned Lukas's normally pale face bright red all the way to his thick blond hair. "Sig shouldn't have had the weapon, but it's a good thing he did. He saved you all. It was exactly as he said it happened."

Saved us all? The asshole had said that?

Eva scowled at the Elder. "That's not what happened, though."

The Elders exchanged glances. Maja braced her elbows on the table and leaned forward. "What do you mean?"

"I mean, I was there."

"And you saw everything?" Maja asked.

"Well, no, but I saw DART's video, and it matches up with what I *did* see."

Maja seemed relieved. "They must have manipulated it before you saw it."

"I don't think so. They didn't have time."

"They employ demons," Lukas explained as if Eva was a toddler. "I'm sure it didn't take one of them any time at all to tamper with the video."

Maybe, but her gut said no.

"It's just that—"

The door opened, and her parents entered. Torn between wanting to hug them and ask why they'd saddled her with a nightmare demon, she clenched her teeth and smiled politely. She could wait until the right time.

And the right time would be soon.

"Honey, I'm so glad you're back." Her mom hurried over to hug her, and then she was engulfed by her dad's strong arms.

"We were worried about you, Pumpkin." He gave the Elders a stern look. "She's staying here until that demon bastard is killed, right?"

Maja nodded as Eva's parents settled into chairs next to her. "This is the safest place in the world for her."

No, the safest place would be with Logan.

The thought just popped into her head as if it had every right to be there. And as if it were true. It couldn't be. Because, surely, in a complex full of Aegis warriors, in a city that Freemasons and Aegi had designed to repel Satanic forces, she was in the safest place she could be.

"Now that we're all here," Elder Hammond began, "let's go over everything that happened while you were at DART. We'll start at the beginning."

Eva settled in for the interrogation. When the Elders said "everything," they meant it. And when Elder Dmitri asked if she was on her period on any of the days, she decided that *everything* was bullshit.

"Excuse me? That is none of your business."

Maja reached across the table and laid her hand on hers in a comforting gesture. "I know Dmitri could have been a little more delicate about something so personal, but it really is important. A lot of demonic spells involve the usage of menstrual blood. Other spells are either more or less effective depending on a female's cycle."

"So you think DART did something weird to me? Based on my menses?" Eva stared at the other woman. The other woman who had slept with Logan and then betrayed him and broke his heart. "Are you kidding me?"

"Let's move on." Maja cleared her throat and shot the others a pointed look. "Next question."

Lukas looked down at his notes. "Were you involved in any sexual acts with any DART employees?"

Eva had anticipated that question. Leave it to Sig's creepy father to be the one to ask it. No problem. She was practiced at this—at staying calm in the face of challenging questions and hostile questioners. And she'd given her fair share of half-truths and vague responses.

She could do this.

"I've told you everything relevant to my stay at DART. I wasn't on my period, and I didn't eat anything weird or see any demonic rituals."

But she hadn't told them about the hotel. Or Logan. Or Lilith. Or Harvester. And she wasn't even sure why.

Elder Dmitri drummed the table with his fingers. "What does DART know about the blood event?"

"They didn't exactly keep me in the loop." It was true enough. "What does The Aegis know?"

"Very little. The liquid disappeared without a trace. But," Maja said, "we got a report from the contractor who runs the Temple Mount's demon detection system. The rain splashed one of the sensors. Before the sample disappeared, the machine identified it as blood. According to the tech, the system went haywire, saying the blood belonged to all species…and none."

"Huh."

Hammond spoke up. "One of our historians thinks it's a sign from God, warning us that the barrier between Hell and Earth is weakening."

Lukas snorted. "The historians always say that. They think everything is weakening the barrier between us and Hell."

"Demons have taken over an entire country and infiltrated our schools, stores, and governments." Dimitri slapped the table angrily. "Newsflash, the barrier is already weakened. You talk as if blood falling from the sky on top of a holy place isn't a big fucking deal."

"Obviously, it's a big deal," Maja said calmly. "And we need an answer *now*. The entire world is waiting for our analysis. We might want to come up with something fast before people start panicking."

"From what I've seen in the media," Eva said, glad to have the focus off her and her time with DART and Logan, "people are looking to NOAA and NASA and other agencies for answers. As long as people believe it might be a natural phenomenon, like a flock of birds getting squeezed by an atmospheric rarity or something, it'll buy some time."

"This isn't natural," Dmitri said. "It's Satanic. And it might be exactly what we need to finally convince all the idiot demon lovers out there that it's time to exterminate them instead of letting them live among us."

Lukas glanced at the wall clock. "Let's discuss this later." He gestured to Eva. "Is there anything else we should know about your time with DART?"

"As a matter of fact, yes." She turned to her parents. "I got rid of the nightmare demon while I was there. Logan captured it in a trap. I'm free."

It wasn't her mom who reacted first. It wasn't her father, either.

Lukas's strangled, "What?" accompanied a shove back from the table as he stared at her, wide-eyed and stunned. "You did *what?*"

Before Eva could ponder Lukas's bizarre reaction, her mom grabbed her forearm. "Eva, darling. What are you talking about?"

Eva jerked her arm out of her mother's grip, too upset by all the secrecy and deception from every direction to stand anyone being that close to her. "You said the tattoo would keep the demon out of my dreams. You didn't tell me it would also tether it to me. Why? Why would you do that? For the luck? Is that really why I haven't had a decent night's sleep in over twenty years?"

"Pumpkin," her father said, "The Aegis assured us the demon wouldn't be able to harm you and would bring you good fortune. Don't you think that was a fair trade?"

"No!" She gaped at her father as if he were a stranger. "Did you not hear the part about me not being able to sleep? That demon was always there. It didn't cause nightmares, but it damn sure influenced them. It scratched at the edges of even my good dreams, and I woke up in terror multiple times every single night. It tormented me my entire life."

"And look where you are, darling," he said, clearly not hearing a word she'd said. "You've had a successful career, and you're going to be the new Chief Spokesperson for the world's premier demon management agency. It seems like a small price to pay."

Maja coughed. "I was going to tell her that." She turned to Eva. "Congratulations. Right after this meeting, you'll meet with Jennifer for a press conference."

Eva didn't have time to digest that because Lukas leaped to his feet with a shouted curse. "Who cares about her job. You people don't understand." He wrung his hands so frantically they should be bloody. "*She broke the nightmare demon's bond.*"

Her mother toyed with one of her bracelets. "We've gotten all the luck we need. It's okay."

"No, Mom, it's really not."

"Eva's right." Lukas's wild gaze darted around the room as if he expected an ambush. "When the bond breaks, it reverses the luck. It takes things away." He shoved a trembling hand through his hair. "Sig was conceived after we placed the tattoo."

"*What?*" Tessandra shrieked, rounding on Lukas, a bundle of fury in a floral Hermes blouse, a navy skirt, and Stella McCartney pumps. "You didn't tell us any of that when we came to you for help with Eva's demon. You said you could end her nightmares and make sure it paid for what it had done to her by giving us all good fortune. You didn't say anything about the rest."

Lukas flung his hand out at Eva. "Because she wasn't supposed to have the demon exorcised," he shouted. Swearing, his hand shaking, he grabbed his jacket off the chair. "I-I have to go."

Face dripping with sweat, he took off at a run.

They all sat there, stunned for a moment. Eva realized she was holding her hand over her belly, over the tattoo that had bound her to a demon for over two decades.

Which now might lead to even worse.

"What are we going to do?" her dad asked, his voice pitched high with worry. Eva had never seen him as rattled as he was right now. "This is outrageous, not to mention, dangerous. We could lose everything. I want answers, Hammond."

Hammond stood. "We're going to get our people on this right away. We'll find a solution, I assure you. Eva, you're needed in the Media Affairs office immediately."

Eva should have been thrilled. She'd wanted this since she started work at The Aegis. Yet…the news sat there like a burning coal in her belly.

Had she only gotten where she was because of a demon? Did she deserve the job?

More importantly, did she even want it?

The door to Media Affairs was wide open, and as Eva approached, two Elders exited. Deborah Johnson and Anthony Roffalone both offered their congrats on the new job, but Deborah paused in the doorway to murmur, "Stefani is in there, just FYI. She's pissed that you got the job."

Great. Just what Eva needed on top of everything else. "Thanks for the heads-up."

"No problem. Welcome back. I'm sorry for what you went through, but DART will pay for starting this fight."

Deborah patted Eva on the arm and hurried to catch up with Anthony leaving Eva with a growing headache and increasing unease. Obviously, the video had gotten around.

Inside the office, Jennifer was consulting with the press crew and Stefani. She motioned Eva over. Stefani flashed a fake smile as Eva approached.

"Perfect timing," Jenn said. "We're getting ready to make an official statement about the video."

"Already?" Eva couldn't hide her surprise. And at this point, she didn't give a crap. "Has it been verified?"

Stefani snorted. "Are you for real?"

"Go to hell, Stefani," Eva snapped, so not in the mood to deal with her shit. She didn't give a crap that everyone stared at her. Stefani's eyes bugging out of her little round doll head was worth it.

Jennifer, too busy with her notes to notice anything outside her bubble, gestured for Eva to follow her to the staging area where they recorded both live and pre-recorded broadcasts when no reporters were present.

"We're going live in ten minutes. I'll announce you as my replacement, and then we'll talk about your traumatic experience at DART. The public will want to know how you escaped and what it's been like running from a demon who slaughtered three of our colleagues." She paused and lightly put her hand on Eva's arm. "I'm sorry, I should have asked if you were all right. It must have been a nightmare."

Eva laughed. Jennifer was so wrong, talking like the nightmare was in the past. It was still going on.

Jennifer gave her a funny look and shouted at an intern to fix the glare from the overhead lights.

"After we talk, I'll hand everything over to you, and you can introduce the video. We have a script already loaded." Jennifer gestured to a doorway on the other side of the room. "Now, let's get you into hair and makeup."

Grateful to get away from Jennifer's frantic energy and Stefani's bitter glare, Eva made her escape to the converted office where Aliya, a Guardian who doubled as their hair and makeup person, was cleaning makeup brushes in the bathroom/dressing room.

"I'm almost done," Aliya called out. "Just hop in the chair. I'll be right with you."

Eva sank down, every bone in her body suddenly aching. But her brain sparked with energy. Somehow, she had to get to the bottom of the video's authenticity, and she only had minutes to do it.

Quickly, she pulled the media room's floating desktop close and started parsing through all the data and correspondence that had come into and out of the media office over the last twenty-four hours.

Several news agencies from around the world had called, texted, or emailed. Stefani and Jennifer had recorded six updates on the situation with DART, and one on the Dome of the Rock blood-rain incident, as well as one about an Aegis team in New Delhi that took down two demons after the hellspawn slaughtered a bus full of tourists.

Aliya came over and tugged a brush through Eva's beach-blown hair. "Congratulations on the new job. I'm so glad it didn't go to you know who."

Eva gave an amused snort and clicked into an internal mail file. "Yeah, me too. My ego couldn't have handled it."

Aliya pulled Eva's hair into a bun in the back. "How are you doing? I can't even imagine what you've gone through."

"It's been a weird few days," she said, leaving it there. She was tired of talking about it, but mostly, her attention was fixed on the emails. She opened the most recent one from the Elders, and the video matching Sig's account popped up, along with a message saying that, *under no circumstances are we to acknowledge the video DART sent us. We need to get this one out ASAP.*

The video DART sent?

She started clicking the emails, going backward until a video popped up, along with a message:

We were sent this by DART. We need your team to edit.

She clicked on the video. It was the one Kynan had shown her. He'd obviously sent it to The Aegis to prove that Sig had killed Shanea and Noah not in self-defense, but in cold blood. This first email asked for it to be edited, not fit into an allotted time, but changing it so it looked less like The Aegis started the fight in the cafeteria.

Holy shit.

Her hand shaking a little, she quickly sought out the whistleblower blog, and her gut plummeted. The timestamp on The Aegis's internal mail to alter DART's video was dated several hours before the blog's post.

Which meant The Aegis had doctored and leaked the video themselves and were now planning to publicly address it before DART could release their video. DART would claim theirs was the original and may eventually prove it. But by that time, it would be too late. Public sentiment would be with The Aegis.

Eva felt sick to her stomach.

"Hey." Jennifer popped her head into the room. "You about ready?"

No. No, she wasn't. She couldn't discuss that video, knowing it was fake, knowing The Aegis was manipulating the public.

Knowing that she'd done it herself in the past.

"We can't do the video segment, Jennifer."

"Why not?"

"It's not legitimate. It's been manipulated."

Jennifer rolled her eyes. "What are you talking about?"

"Come look." Eva gestured to the files. "I have proof."

With a huff, Jennifer came over, gave the emails a cursory glance, and then shrugged.

"So what? We don't have time to change the script. The Elders want us to go with the version of the video we have." Jennifer gave her a condescending smile. "I know a lot is happening all at once. Of course, you're confused. But you're a professional, and I have all the faith that you can do this. You gave a presser with a broken ankle once. That's why I recommended you for this job. Don't make me regret it." She glanced down at her comms device. "Let's go. We're on the air in sixty seconds."

Overwhelmed, angry, and so fucking tired of being lied to, manipulated, and forced into situations over which she had no control, she wanted to walk off the job. She wanted to tell Jennifer where she could shove the video.

But that wouldn't right a wrong.

She couldn't stop The Aegis from putting its spin on things, but she *could* slow the spin and give DART a chance to get the truth out.

She'd probably be unemployed by the end of the day and blackballed from the media by tomorrow, but her conscience would be clean.

Too bad clean consciences didn't pay the bills.

Chapter Thirty-Four

By the time Kynan returned to the alcove, Logan had calmed down.

A little.

He was still steamed by the knowledge that he'd been lied to his entire life, but he was willing to hear Kynan out.

So were Scotty, Mace, and Blade, who *just happened* to be gathering in the lobby while Logan was meeting with Kynan.

"I just got off the phone with your dad," Kynan said, taking a stance next to the arched entryway. "I know you're hurt, but you were out of line."

"I don't want to talk about them," Logan said, mainly because he couldn't get the look of utter devastation he saw on his mom's face out of his head. "I want to talk about you. How could you have taken part in of all that?"

Kynan braced his shoulder against the archway wall. "I'm not proud, Logan. I was in The Aegis when Pestilence's Seal broke. We were desperate to avert the Apocalypse."

"Yeah, I know. You sent my mom to seduce my dad because you thought I was the key to keeping his Seal from breaking."

"Exactly. But it wasn't true. We were being manipulated."

Logan really didn't care about their lame reasons right now. "Get to the part where Mom was going to give me up, and you and Gem were going to raise me."

Kynan took issue with Logan's tone and cut him a sharp look

before responding. "That was the plan. It was a stupid one. We know that now." He drove his fingers through his hair and blew out a long breath. "Logan, I have a lot of regrets. We shouldn't have done what we did. But every time I think that, I remember you came of it. And the Apocalypse *was* averted, even if it wasn't in the way we anticipated."

"My parents told me The Aegis tried to kill me." That wasn't in Eva's video. According to The Aegis, they'd attempted to rescue Regan from the evil Horseman's clutches, but he and his vampire servants had killed almost everyone on the rescue team. "Is that true, or just another lie?"

"It's true," Kynan said. "But I didn't know until afterward. Without my knowledge, a team kidnapped your mother, and while your father fought their forces, they tried to rip you from Regan's belly and sacrifice you. Again, they were manipulated by Pestilence's loyalists. When that failed, Pestilence himself tried to kill you. What The Aegis did to your mother and you is why I left. It was something I should have done long before that, but I thought I could save The Aegis and turn it down a better path. I was an idiot, and I was wrong. You and your mother both paid for decisions I took part in, and I'm sorry."

Logan had no idea what to think, feel, or say.

Fortunately, Kynan filled the void.

"You need to talk to your parents."

That was the last thing Logan needed to do right now. Maybe after they got Draven—

A series of beeps screeched through the room.

Logan looked down at his comms device. An Aegis alert popped up, and he suspected everyone was getting the same one.

"Turn on the main viewer," Logan barked at Blade. A heartbeat later, a life-sized color projection of The Aegis's broadcasting room sprang up from the symbol embedded in the floor.

Logan's heart twitched a little at the sight of Eva standing next to The Aegis's Chief Spokesperson. Maybe they were announcing her promotion. Nah. If she'd gotten the job, she'd look less…troubled.

Jennifer started by saying that their people were still looking into the blood rain and insisted there was no reason for alarm.

"Isn't that the same thing we're telling people?" Scotty said, and Kynan nodded.

"I've got every world leader and military general breathing down my neck, but I'm not saying anything until we hear from Reaver."

"Eventually, someone, probably Stryke, is going to figure out that it's angel blood," Logan said. "Then what?"

"I'll call Aleka. If anyone can tell us if there's any historical precedence for angel blood rain, it's my sister," Scotty said. "We need something to tell the people and keep them calm."

"Especially because you know The Aegis will go in the opposite direction. They want to stoke anti-demon sentiment as much as they can, and panic is the way to do it."

"Bastards." That came from Mace.

"Shh!" Scotty hissed. "You guys, they're talking about us."

"…now that you're back from DART, congratulations again on your promotion, Eva. You're going to do The Aegis proud."

Eva's smile didn't reach her eyes. Something was wrong.

"Thank you," she said. "And congratulations to you on your new venture, Jennifer. Morning talk show host at Global News Now is amazing."

Jennifer nodded. "With so much going on in the world right now, I'm sure I'll be busy talking about all the stories. But you…you *are* the story right now. What can you tell us about being ambushed by demons in the DART cafeteria?"

A chorus of "What the fuck?" rose around Logan. Shushing them, he moved closer, his heart pounding in anticipation of hearing Eva's answer. She wouldn't lie…would she?

"I wasn't ambushed. I—and Keeley—actually only got to the cafeteria after the argument started."

Jennifer's mouth twitched in annoyance. "I see." She laid a comforting hand on Eva's arm and gave a dramatic shake of the head. "Well, it's probably a good thing, or you might have been injured or even killed before Sig was able to stop the attack."

"Holy shit, this is worse than I thought," Kynan muttered, and then everyone shouted "Holy shit!" when the feed turned into a video. One that had been altered to show Shanea and Noah as the aggressors.

Kynan swore again and tapped his comms. "Arik! Get our video out to every news source and government that has asked about the incident."

"We have to get ahead of this," Mace said.

"Get ahead of it?" Kynan snapped. "We're so far behind we're looking at our own asses. But we can mitigate the damage. Maybe. Fuck."

"As you can see," Jennifer said, "this video, sent to us by a whistleblower, shows our people under attack. One of DART's vengeance demon employees is still attacking our people. We are appealing to DART to give up the location of this monster—"

"Excuse me." Eva slammed her hand down, and the video cut away. Anger flushed her cheeks, and her dark eyes practically smoked. "DART doesn't know his location. But they *do* know him, and if anyone can find him, it's DART."

"Day-um," Mace said. "Your girl's mad. It's kinda hot."

"You're a dumbass." Scotty kicked him in the shin.

"Shut up, both of you," Logan snapped, gesturing to Jennifer, who shook her head.

"If they know him so well, why haven't they found him yet?" Her demeanor became less *we're friends* and more confrontational. "Three people are dead, and three more are in danger. You are one of them."

Eva looked at Jennifer like she was a dumbass, and Logan nearly laughed. "I'm aware of that." She turned to the camera. "The video circulating about the incident at DART is fake—"

The sound of screams, either distant or muted, echoed through the room where Eva had frozen as if unsure what she'd heard. The screams came again, more of them. Closer.

A man covered in blood stumbled into the room. Air and froth pumped in and out of his mouth in ragged, uneven, gasping breaths as he fell back against the door and held it closed.

"Attack," he croaked.

"Kynan!" Cyan burst out of the elevator, clenching her tablet so hard it turned her knuckles as white as her hair.

"I got it," she shouted, waving the tablet as she ran over. "I know what Draven was after." She took a couple of panting breaths…she must have run from her lab. "He got into Aegis files. Specifically, the DC headquarters."

"Aegis headquarters?" Blade eyed Cy's tablet. "He accessed security files."

"Oh, my God." Logan turned back to the live feed, his voice thick with horror. "He got everything we know about Aegis defenses. He's there."

Another male staggered into the room from another doorway. Clutching his throat, eyes bugging, he fell into the podium.

Mason.

"Eva, run!" Logan shouted, even though she couldn't hear him.

Mason screamed.

And blew apart.

Blood and flesh dripped on the holoscreen, and then it went dark.

Eva.

Ares had literally beaten a never-act-without-a-plan mentality into Logan. *Don't go off half-cocked. Don't panic. Always have a plan.*

Logan had a plan, and his name was Cujo.

He called to the hound in his mind, then darted toward the exit, ignoring Kynan's shouts to stop. Cujo was waiting in his usual spot in the private break area, his head buried in the trash can.

Logan grabbed a fistful of the thick black mane across his neck and shoulders.

"Take me to a gate. Hurry!"

They materialized at a gate Logan didn't know, but they were somewhere rocky and remote.

He gave the canine a fond pat on the shoulder. "Thanks, buddy. I'll call if I need you."

As Cujo dematerialized, Logan stepped inside the Harrowgate, selected the gate nearest The Aegis's DC headquarters, and burst out into an upscale neighborhood. Unfortunately, thanks to the city's planning and its Masonic architecture, no Harrowgates could be constructed within a three-mile radius of the Capitol building.

Which meant he'd have to run a mile to HQ, because Cujo usually couldn't phase to a location he'd never been to.

Logan sprinted, knocking people out of the way and nearly getting hit by half a dozen cars as he dashed across busy streets. If anything happened to Eva...

He put on a burst of speed that got him the rest of the way to The Aegis's official headquarters. He didn't falter until he was through the gate and inside the courtyard. As he approached the entrance, which was usually guarded but was now suspiciously abandoned, he slowed, the hair on the back of his neck standing up in stark warning.

"I know you're not here to help Aegi." Draven's voice, deep and raspy, came from behind Logan.

He spun around, barely resisting the urge to summon a weapon. Cujo phased in next to him and whimpered, clearly not understanding why the guy he'd known for most of his life was now giving off evil vibes.

"Draven. You have to stop this."

Draven grinned. "Only two more to go. The female's gonna be the most fun."

Cujo growled, but his aggression wasn't directed at Draven. Armed

Guardians were closing in from all sides, and Logan was pretty sure they saw all three of them as threats.

Logan held out his hand to his friend. "Take it. Let's get out of here. Your parents are waiting for you."

"I don't need your help to escape these fucks. Killing them has made me so strong." He drew something in the air with his finger, and suddenly, a bolt of crimson fire flew from the glowing symbol to a Guardian armed with a bow, blowing a hole through her throat. "And I brought friends."

Screams and shouts rose as arrows, knives, and bullets flew toward Logan and Cujo. He dove at Draven, catching him in the torso and knocking them both to the ground. Pain speared him in the leg and shoulder, and he heard Cujo's yelp and furious snarl.

Suddenly, Draven disappeared beneath him. Just…disappeared.

And demons from dozens of different species, scores of them, flooded into the courtyard. It was a bloodbath.

"Cujo! The demons! Kill them!"

Cujo gave him a look that said he'd rather kill the Aegi.

"No! Bad dog! The demons!"

Cujo took off in a blur, cutting through the horde of hellspawn like a chainsaw. Summoning a sword, Logan took out demons as he fought his way inside the building. A woman sat against a toppled statue, holding her bleeding ribs. He knelt next to her.

"Where's the media office?"

She pointed down a hall to the right. "At…at the end. Past the fountain. Take a left." Her eyes shot wide. "Behind you!"

He wheeled around in time to decapitate a Croucher demon before its razor-sharp claws did the same to Logan.

Before the body even hit the floor, he scooped the woman up in his arms. "Where can I take you to safety?"

She appeared startled. "Take me with you to the Media Affairs office."

He ran hard, practically skidding around the corner at the fountain. The office door was closed. Locked.

He gently set the female down, leaving an arm around her to keep her from collapsing. Then he used his other arm to pound on the door.

"Open up! Eva! It's Logan."

He heard raised voices from inside. "No! Eva! It's a trick!"

The door opened, and Eva peeked through the crack, her face pale and splattered with blood. When she saw him, tears welled in her eyes.

"Logan." She threw open the door. "Thank God.

"Are you okay? The blood—"

"It's Mason's," she said, the words catching in her throat. She flanked the other woman and helped bring her into the room while an older dude with gray hair and a stand in one hand slammed the door closed and locked it. As if a lock would keep out any of the demons.

They settled the female, whose name was Diana, on the couch. A wide-eyed female with trembling hands skirted around Logan to tend to the other woman.

"Draven's here," Eva said. "How? This entire city is warded against demon violence, and this building is warded against all demons."

"Draven broke into our archives and found a way past all that."

"You sure one of your demon friends didn't just give it to him?" said one of the dudes standing nearby, a blade in his hand and pointed at Logan.

"Don't be a jackass, Sam," Eva snapped before turning back to Logan. "You're hurt."

"It's already healing," he said, a split second before a million pinpricks tore through his right side.

Oh, shit.

He swayed as Cujo's pain became his.

"Logan?" Eva grabbed his arm. "Logan! What's wrong? Talk to me."

But he couldn't. Cujo had fought a thousand battles with thousands of demons, and he'd taken some wounds that had required help from Logan's aunt Cara. But none of them had felt like this.

"It's Cujo," he rasped. Then he shoved everyone out of the way to create a space large enough for a Clydesdale. "Get back. Get way back!"

Cujo.

He sent out the mental call. Pain went through him in a shockwave.

Cujo!

An inky pile of blood, fur, and bones materialized in front of him, taking up almost the entire room and crushing equipment beneath his giant body. Cujo whimpered, huddled on the floor, his crimson eyes glazed with shock and pain.

Logan rushed to the beast's side, his brain barely comprehending the magnitude of Cujo's injuries. Hellhounds were some of the hardest demons to kill, even for other demons. They were the terrors of the underworld.

This can't be happening.

"I have to go," he told Eva, clinging to Cujo's ruff like a lifeline. In a way, it was. If Logan was injured, he drew energy from Cujo. If Cujo was injured, he drew from Logan. An injury this bad…it could kill them both if he didn't get Cujo to Aunt Cara. "I'll come back for you when I can. Is there somewhere secure you can go?"

She took his hand. "I'm going with you."

"No!" one of the guys yelled. "Are you insane?"

Her gaze didn't waver. "I want to be with you."

I want to be with you. Not, *I want to go with you.* Or, *I'll be safer with you.*

His heart swelled even as it flooded with pain for Cujo. He ignored the calls from Eva's colleagues to get away from "the demons" and tightened his grip on Cujo's fur.

"I just hope he has enough juice in him to phase to Ares' place." He placed Eva's hand next to his so she could grip a handful of fur. "Come on, buddy. Take us to Cara."

Cujo shuddered.

"Come on, Cujo. *Cujo!*"

Another shudder and blood streamed from his mouth, flowing down his jaws to puddle on the floor.

Nonononoooo! Panic tore at the edges of Logan's control. He closed his eyes, breathing deeply and recalling his training with Ares, his mother's lessons to rein in his anxiety, and Limos's advice years ago regarding handling their bonded companions.

"Your fear will be his. Your anger will be his. Your stress will be his. And your strength will be his too. Your confidence. Practice control. Our beasts are hard enough to handle without our emotions working them up."

"To Cara," he firmly but calmly commanded. "Now."

Cujo's claws bit into the floor, and wisps of smoke rose from the gashes. His pained whimper became a howl as he gathered his strength and fought the pain.

You can do it, buddy. You got this.

Oh, please let him have this…

The room faded out. Instantly, sunlight stabbed them like a million daggers as they materialized on the steps leading up to Ares and Cara's mansion.

Thank you, Limos!

Logan launched to the top of the steps. "Stay with him," he shouted back at Eva and then burst inside the building. "Aunt Cara! Cara! Help!"

Cara ran into the room from the kitchen, her sandaled feet slapping on the floor. "What is it?"

"It's Cujo. He's hurt. Bad." Nausea and pain made his legs rubbery as he led Cara outside, his heart ripping open at the sight of the canine barely breathing, his mouth gaping as he struggled to take in air.

"Oh, Cujo," she murmured as she ran to him. "What did this?"

"An Aegis weapon. Stryke wouldn't tell me how it works."

"I know," Eva said. "Sort of." She looked up at him. "StryTech created it, but Mason was involved in its development. He said they used a metal found only in Sheoul to form the projectiles. He couldn't tell me what was inside the bullets, but he said he thought it was something holy."

DART was already aware of all that, but it looked like the liquid inside was still a mystery to everyone.

"Could be holy water," Logan suggested.

Cara nodded. "Or even angel blood. That would explain the extreme injuries. These aren't easy to heal."

"But he'll be okay, right?"

The worry in Cara's eyes was a sucker punch. "I don't know." She shouted to a Ramreel demon standing guard nearby. "Get Ares." She turned to Logan. "We'll move Cujo to my workshop. I'm going to need to clean the contaminants out of these wounds, or they won't heal."

He and Eva helped Ares, a couple of Ramreels, and Cara move Cujo to her veterinary clinic, which, thankfully, wasn't used that often. She said she used it more to care for the native island animals than for any of the hellhounds who called her healer or the Horsemen's stallions, including Limos's late hell stallion.

Once the beast was settled on the floor, Cara kicked Logan and Eva out. "I need to concentrate, and I can't do that with you hovering. I'm going to sever the bond between you two if it looks like the worst will happen, but don't worry. I'll take good care of him."

Of course, she would. Cujo literally couldn't be in better hands. But even Cara's extraordinary abilities couldn't save everyone.

Reluctantly, Logan led Eva outside with no particular destination in mind. He was too numb to think about where to go, what to do, or what to say. Although he knew exactly what to say to Stryke and fired off an angry text to do just that.

Your weapon may have just killed Cujo, you asshole. Pray Cara can save him, because if he dies, no one can save you from me.

He stared at his wrist for a second, hoping Stryke would respond, but he should have known better. When he looked up, Eva was speaking with someone through her comms device. As he approached, she turned off the privacy veil, and a hologram of a woman he assumed was her mother was speaking with her.

"Your father and I are fine," she said. "But dozens are injured. More dead. And Sig…" She crossed her arms over her chest and rubbed her bare arms as if she'd gotten a chill. "He's dead."

Good. That was the best news Logan had gotten all day.

"I'm just glad you're both okay," Eva said.

Her mother slid a cold look to him. "That's Logan, I assume." When Eva nodded, her mom inclined her head toward him. "Thank you for saving my daughter. Eva, your father is trying to clean up the mess you made. You need to come back and explain why you sabotaged that press conference. You might have cost yourself the job."

"No, Mom, I'm not going back."

Logan inhaled a stunned breath. Eva wasn't messing around. She was truly giving up a prestigious position with a powerful agency—a move that could cost Eva her entire career.

"Eva—"

"I said no. I'm happy you and Dad are okay, but I don't want the job anymore."

"But that job has been your dream."

"Was it, though?" A thick strand of hair had come free of Eva's bun, and it dangled against her cheek as she cocked her head and studied her mother quizzically. "Or was it yours? Was it part of being tied to that demon? I don't know. And I need time to find it out." The way she looked at Logan as if he was the only thing she could trust right now filled his chest with warmth that had nothing to do with the blazing Greek sun. "I have to go. I'll call later."

"But—"

Eva cut off her mom and turned to Logan, looking exhausted but somehow stronger than ever. She'd given up everything and put her life on a new, strange path, and she faced it the way she did Logan, with strength and determination. "What now?"

Now? Right now, he wanted a break from the insanity. A respite from the pain and confusion. Fortunately, he was in the perfect place to find that.

"I want to show you something." He took her hand and led her down a paved path to an arena complete with weapons lining the walls and stadium seating for viewers.

"What is this?" She took in the combat dummies and sand stained by blood from some of the more intense sessions. "Is it what you wanted to show me?"

"Nah, it's just on the way. It's where my cousins and I train."

"Train for what?"

"Armageddon."

She snorted. And then sobered. "Are you…serious?"

"It's coming, like it or not." He looked around, seeing the thousands of training partners he'd had over the decades, from demons to angels, and even Cujo. The thought of the beast made his heart clench. "I can't lose him."

She squeezed his hand. "Your aunt seems to know what she's doing."

"She does." His confidence in her was the only reason he wasn't climbing the walls right now. Well, her and Eva. "She's basically bonded to every hellhound in existence, and she has a special gift for healing animals."

"Wow. That's definitely not common knowledge in The Aegis." She paused. "What was she talking about when she said she'd sever your bond?"

"My life force is connected to Cujo's. If he dies, I might die too. Until Cara took over, he was draining energy from me to heal his wounds. She draws from all hellhounds and can use that so I don't have to help. But if it looks like Cujo will die, she'll break his bond with me so I'll survive."

He started walking again, because as crappy as things were, there was one place that had always comforted him. And between that and Eva, maybe he could find a few minutes of peace.

Chapter Thirty-Five

Hand in hand, Logan led Eva down a winding, shady path that took them through groves of fragrant trees. It eventually turned rugged until the way through the jagged rocks and brush was little more than a wildlife trail. Finally, they reached a rocky alcove.

A crescent-shaped shoreline of ivory sand, cradled between two cliff outcroppings on either end, created a stunning private beach. Beyond the glistening sands, the sun beat down on calm, crystal-blue water that begged for snorkeling and skinny-dipping.

"Wow," she breathed. "It's beautiful. I was in Greece once for a media conference, but it wasn't like this."

A smile touched his lips, and it took her breath even more than the scenery. He looked so much like his father when he wasn't smiling, had the same hard features and rough-hewn good looks. But when he smiled, her hormones did a crazy little dance. He was a man who could destroy an enemy with efficiency and then charm the panties off his woman to celebrate.

Hot. And Eva had always enjoyed a good celebration.

"When we were younger," he said, "my cousins and I used to explore the island until we knew every tree, ancient ruin, and grain of sand. We all each found a private place to claim as ours. This one is mine. Cujo used to bring me here when I wanted some alone time." He laughed. "I used to think I'd bring chicks here to make out, but then I realized I'd have to use Cujo to get here, and they'd freak. So, it didn't really work out."

She loved that little peek into his past. Maybe not the wanting-to-bring-chicks-here part, but the rest.

"So, you've never brought a girl here?"

"Nope, you're the first. Not even Draven has been here. It was the only thing I ever kept from him." He swallowed. Looked away. Avoided her gaze. "I need to stop him. I can't let anything happen to you. My entire life has gone to shit, and you're the only good thing left right now."

"No, Logan." Heart beating like it wanted to get to him, she captured his face, forcing him to look at her. "You have friends and family. Your parents—"

"My parents? You want to talk about them?" He stepped away from her, breaking contact. "I saw your report."

Oh, shit. That video report had been brutally slanted, and she'd been so sure of her facts that she'd been almost arrogant. Logan must hate her.

"I'm so sorry, Logan." She caught his hand and refused to let go, desperate to show him that things had changed. "I was wrong. And even the things I was right about…weren't exactly as I was told."

He shook his head and let out a bitter sound, but at least he didn't try to get away from her. "But you weren't wrong. Not about all of it, anyway."

"Listen to me, Logan." Her own experience with her parents had changed her perspective a little. "Don't pay any attention to that video. I found out the truth just a couple of hours ago. The Aegis sent your mom with instructions to seduce Thanatos. They always told us she went rogue, but she didn't. They sacrificed her because they thought she was expendable. Then they sent a team to sacrifice you, thinking it would stop the rest of the Seals from breaking." She twined her fingers with his and held his hand in both of hers. "What they did was unforgivable. Editing that DART video was unforgivable too. The Aegis…they aren't what I thought they were. And none of you are either. I'm sorry."

Waves lapping at the beach formed a rhythmic pattern as his silence hung in the air, making her sweat. What was he thinking? *Did* he hate her?

"I know it's not the same thing," she said, "but I've been going through stuff with my parents too."

"Did you get my message about your nightmare demon?"

Obviously, he'd figured it out before she had. "Yeah. And it turns out my parents and Sig's dad thought it would be a great idea to saddle me with a demon in exchange for good fortune for all of us." She let out a frustrated growl. How could they have done that to her without her consent? And why had they kept it from her? "I think my parents' hearts were in the right place...sort of. But Lukas lied to them. He didn't tell them that if the spell binding the demon to me ever became severed, all the luck would pour out like spilled milk."

"I've got Aleka looking into a way to fix it."

"Aleka?" Eva looked up at him. "Why would she be able to find an answer?"

He watched a seabird fly overhead. "She's got a doctorate in ancient demon civilizations and history. She's good at research and has a lot of resources."

Eva hoped his cousin was better than good. So much was at stake right now.

Deep on the horizon, the sun nearly blinded her as she searched Logan's features for a hint of what he was thinking. There was nothing but worry in his expression. Was some of that for her? He didn't need that on top of everything else.

"Logan? Why did you come back for me?"

He seemed surprised, like it was a trick question. "I watched the press conference. I saw you tell the truth before you stopped the video. And I saw Mason."

She shuddered. Seeing him die like that had been one of the most awful things she'd ever witnessed.

"Thank you," she said. "You saved my life."

"You don't have to thank me." Prying one hand away from hers, he cupped her cheek with his palm, and she leaned in, craving his touch. He dropped his arm and let out a long, shaky breath. "Being here with me is enough. If I lose Cujo, I don't know what I'll do. Limos just lost her mount, and I don't want to go through that. Not alone."

The agony in his voice was torture. She wanted to help, wanted to take away his pain. She wished she had something to offer, but nothing short of a cure would help.

"I'm so sorry for what you're going through. For what The Aegis has done to you and your family. What more can I do, Logan?"

He answered with a long pause, his intense stare holding her captive in the sand. Then he answered with his lips. The gentle crash of ocean waves faded into the background as her focus shifted solely to Logan and how his mouth felt against hers. Firm, yet soft. Demanding, yet yielding.

"You feel so good," he whispered against her mouth. "Like you were made for me."

Ha! *Take that, Maja.*

Unless…unless he'd said the same thing to her.

"Logan?" She pulled back, aware that maybe now wasn't the best time for a deep conversation, but everything was so fresh in her mind. "About you and Maja…"

He closed his eyes, and her heart stopped. "I loved her," he admitted, and then he opened his eyes again, and the intensity in those clear depths restarted her heart. "But I was young and dumb. Looking back, I can see we were never right for each other. I spent almost a year pretending to be something I wasn't. I was never *me*. You…you know what I am, and you're still here. My grandma Harvester…she isn't very sentimental, but she once told me that everything happens for a reason. It wasn't one of those eye-roller things people just say to make you feel better. She said not everyone finds their person or soulmate in each of their lives, but when you do find them, you know." He smiled fondly. "She said she'd send me a sign if I was too dense to figure it out. But she doesn't need to. Maja wasn't my person. You are. I don't know how I know that. I just do."

If her clothes had been made of hormones, they'd have melted right off her.

All her life, if she'd wanted something, she went after it. It had worked for her, probably because of the nightmare demon luck. But fighting for what she wanted was also just part of who she was. If Logan was right, and she was his person, he'd better get used to the woman who fought for what she wanted.

And what she wanted was Logan. Right here. Right now.

Logan hadn't laid himself so bare since he confessed to Maja that he wasn't entirely human. His heart hadn't beat for any woman since she broke it.

Now, his heart was in overdrive. And when Eva shimmied out of her dress, bra, and panties right there on the beach, he thought the stupid organ would swell right out of his chest.

Something a little lower also swelled. A lot.

She stood in front of him, naked, a masterpiece of nature that would have made the great artists of the past weep.

Heat swamped him, making a mockery of the baking Greek sun. His blood boiled in his veins as she boldly tugged his T-shirt over his head and unbuttoned his jeans. When he tried to help, she slapped his hands away and gave him a stern wag of the finger.

"Let me do this. It's not a thank you or a way to take your mind off things." She revised her thought. "Okay, it's that. But this is also me making a choice. A real choice for once. Not one influenced by the demon, my parents, or The Aegis. I want you, and I want to show you how much."

Oh, fuck yeah. Speechless, he just nodded. And then he was breathless when she dropped to her knees and took him into her mouth.

Pleasure engulfed him as her tongue swept across the head of his cock, and her fist pumped his shaft. Moaning, he dropped his hand to her hair and fumbled with the pins and band that secured it up high. Ah, yes, her unbound tresses fell in thick waves over his hands and forearms, caressing his skin as her mouth caressed his...oh, yeah.

Throwing back his head, he surrendered to the pleasure. To her.

Nothing had ever felt this good, and it wasn't just what she was doing to him with her magic lips and wicked tongue. He could get a blowjob anywhere. What he couldn't get was a female who trusted him. Who had given up a promotion to do the right thing. Who was willing to step into his world and face it as if she'd always been part of it.

She slid her other hand from his hip to his balls, her touch light and teasing as she skimmed her fingers over the sensitive skin there. Squeezing gently, she applied suction that made him shout as come simmered in his shaft, and his orgasm hovered close, held off by her clever timing.

Suck, lick, pump...pause. Lick, lick, squeeze...pause.

"Holy shit, woman, you're driving me...*ah, yes!*"

She drew hard, applying suction with squeezes and curls of her finger just behind his sac. He came with the force of a hell stallion crashing through the front lines of a battle.

The sea breeze cooled his sunbaked skin as she took everything he had. She made sexy little moans as he pumped into her, and when he became too sensitive for even the lightest flicks of her tongue, he stepped back.

He was still hard. And he wasn't even close to being done. His body recovered from sex like it did from wounds, and as he lifted her to her feet, he was ready to go again.

It was the one benefit of having a sex demon in the family.

"You're amazing," he breathed. "Everything I've ever wanted. Almost."

Her dark eyebrows arched. "Almost? What else do you want?"

"To be inside you."

Her sultry smile matched the heat in her gaze as she took his hands and pulled them both down to the warm sand so he was kneeling between her spread thighs. She gripped his cock and guided it to her center. He let her ease the head into her wet heat, but when she released him, he remained where he was, partially buried, his fingers digging into her toned thighs.

She gripped his shoulders and tried to pull him to her. "What are you doing?"

"I'm watching you."

She gave him a quizzical look. "Watching me? Why?"

Slowly, he eased his hands up her legs, letting his thumb drift closer to her center. Until it found the swollen nub peeking between her smooth, parted flesh.

He stroked slowly, spreading the moisture that seeped from where they were joined until she was slick with desire and starting to roll her hips to meet his touch.

"Logan," she whispered.

Arching his spine, he pressed inside her. Just until the crown disappeared, and the erotic sight nearly sent him over the edge. It was too soon, though. Way too soon.

Besides, he wanted to swallow her orgasm the way she'd swallowed his.

He pulled out, and before she could protest, he covered her core with his mouth. His tongue replaced his cock, thrusting deep and then curling between her folds to flick across her clit.

"I don't know if I told you this," he said against her hot flesh, "but this is my favorite thing."

She made a breathy, greedy sound, and then the only sounds that came from her were whimpers of ecstasy.

Chapter Thirty-Six

Eva lost count of her orgasms after the second one. Mainly because they blended together in one endless peak of pleasure riding on the tip of Logan's tongue.

Finally, mercifully, he lapped gently, the flat of his tongue easing the tender flesh around her clit, leaving the hypersensitive nub to throb from only the warm Greek sea breeze.

With a final, teasing lick through her center, he rose out of the sand like a buried treasure, his cock jutting proudly from his hips, its dusky, veined length making her mouth water. She'd never been one to really enjoy giving oral sex, but Logan was different. The intimacy of it aroused her, and maybe she imagined it, but she swore that after she'd swallowed him, a tingly sensation had overwhelmed her as if every nerve ending was an erogenous zone on its own.

Probably the sex demon DNA.

She waited to be repulsed. Or disgusted. But there was nothing but bliss. Truly, she didn't care about his background or his family tree. What mattered was *him.*

Oh, and the way he slowly covered her, his thickly muscled shoulders rolling as he braced himself in the sand on one elbow and gripped her butt with his other hand, raising her hips to meet his.

His arousal sank deep, stretching and filling her in the best way. Her breasts rubbed against his chest, her nipples sending shocks of electricity to her sex. Everything went electric and wild as he started pumping into her, giving her what Keeley would have called "a proper fucking."

A brief flash of sadness threatened the building passion, but she forced it away. She'd have plenty of time for that later.

As if he knew she'd strayed from the path, he dipped his head and kissed her, bringing her all the way into the moment so nothing else intruded. Everything around them, the ocean waves, the breeze through the trees, the warm sand that shifted under their bodies as they moved…it only enhanced, didn't detract.

She came hard, crying out to the flawless blue sky as Logan peaked too, his shout of ecstasy sending her into another rippling contraction that spread through her body like a current.

Time stopped and started, stretched and contracted, until they lay still, only their chests heaving.

They remained like that for a long time until reality in the form of distant voices made her jackknife into an alarmed sitting position. "What was that?"

He reclined his long body on the sand, not concerned at all. He was still wearing his jeans, his sex lying heavy and spent against his belly, and for some reason, that made her smile despite the fact that she'd heard voices.

"It's the Memitim. When Azagoth destroyed Sheoul-gra, they moved here. Their compound is to the south."

She'd heard of the earthbound angels sired by Azagoth, but people in The Aegis seemed torn on whether their existence was fact or myth.

To the south was a little too general for her, so she reached for her clothes. "Not that I don't want to bask in what we just did, but…what are we going to do now?"

Sitting up, he tucked himself back into his pants and buttoned up. "I've got to find Draven, but I have to keep you safe too. You're going to be his sole focus now. Between him and Lilith, I'm worried nowhere is secure enough."

"Seriously? Not even here?"

"Ares' island is probably the safest place in the world. But Sheoul-gra should have been too, and before Azagoth destroyed it, some of the Memitim were murdered in his realm. Where there's a will, there's a way."

Logan's comms beeped, and a message popped up. She couldn't read it, but she could read him.

It was bad news.

Cujo?

Oh, God. She swallowed dryly, her hand over her mouth as his face drained of blood.

"Logan?"

"We have to go."

"What is it?"

"It's my mom. She's at Underworld General." His voice shattered. "She's losing the baby."

Chapter Thirty-Seven

Logan's first instinct was to summon Cujo to transport him to the hospital. The fact that he couldn't was a sting on top of everything else.

They finished dressing and made it to the island's Harrowgate five minutes later. "You can stay here if you want," he said to Eva. "The hospital is kind of…full of demons."

The look she gave him was pure annoyance. "I can handle it, Logan." Her voice was solemn but firm, her eyes sparking with determination. "I'd rather be with you in hell than without you in paradise."

He drew a breath at the quote she'd taken from the blockbuster movie from last year, a *Beauty and The Beast* retelling in which the Beast was a demon, and Belle was a demon slayer.

Man, Eva just kept getting better and better. "If you're sure." He reached into his pocket and fumbled around the two *decipulas* to find the StryTech coin he hadn't bothered to return to DART. When he found it, he handed it to Eva, and they entered the gate.

He tapped the glowing Underworld General Hospital caduceus symbol, and they stepped out of the gate inside Underworld General's Emergency Department.

Prepared for the usual chaos, he was surprised that only a couple of demons were waiting to be seen, and no one was shouting, screaming, or threatening people.

Miracles do happen.

Right now, though, the miracle he needed was inside the room his father had just walked out of, his expression crestfallen, his pale eyes rimmed with red.

Logan's world wobbled, and the only reason he remained standing was because Eva held him up.

Guilt swamped him, tried to take him to his knees.

This was his fault. If he hadn't confronted his parents, if he hadn't upset his mom, she wouldn't be in that room, and his father wouldn't be on the verge of breaking down.

"Go." Eva squeezed his hand and nudged him. "He needs you. I'll be fine."

Logan had told her that Ares' island was the safest place in the world, but really, it was here. The hospital was warded and defended by the demons who considered this place their home. And they didn't mess around. He squeezed her hand back and went to his dad.

Thanatos watched him approach, his expression carved from ice, his gaze cold and distant.

"Dad." Logan swallowed, willing his voice not to break. They were eye to eye, three feet apart, yet a world away. "I'm so—"

Suddenly, he was engulfed by Thanatos's arms. "Son," he croaked. "Whatever passes between us, I will always love you. I will always be grateful that you are here."

Relief swamped Logan, dulling some of the pain and guilt. If his parents had taught him anything, it was that no matter how much of a jackass he could be, they would always be there for him.

"I know." He pulled back, his eyes stinging. "Mom? The baby?"

Thanatos shook his head. "She started bleeding, and we came straight here, but Eidolon says it's too late."

"That can't be," Logan said as the Harrowgate opened, and Ares stepped out, followed by Limos and Arik. The wagons were circling. "Eidolon can fix…he can fix anything." He looked around wildly for the doctor, but only saw patients and nurses. He was going to lose his mind with remorse.

Thanatos laid his hand on his shoulder, the comforting weight grounding Logan. "Some things are beyond even him."

"But this is my fault. If I hadn't upset her…"

"No." His father released him, his gaze wandering to the room where his mother lay attached to a zillion monitors. "Your mother's pregnancies have always been difficult. This is not on you."

The Harrowgate flashed again, and Reseph and Jillian, both in sweats, ran out, looking like they'd come straight from bed.

"What can we do?" Jillian asked, but Thanatos shook his head.

"Your being here is all we need." He turned back to Logan and pressed something into his hand.

The wooden weapon Thanatos had been working on in the shop when Logan had busted in, full of accusations and bile. His mouth went dry at both the memory and the knowledge that the weapon was meant for Draven.

"Just in case." Thanatos gave Logan's shoulder another comforting squeeze. "No matter if we are at odds or not, I want you to be safe."

Logan wanted that too. He wanted everyone he loved to be safe, but life had taught him that safety wasn't guaranteed, not even for immortals.

Eva had never been comfortable in hospitals. The sounds of pain and illness, the smells of disinfectant and sickness, the sights of blood and suffering. So, she didn't expect to be comfortable in a hospital run by demons.

And boy howdy, she was right.

Underworld General was Bizarro World come to life. Of course, the Four Horsemen of the Apocalypse standing over there with Logan were biblical legends in the flesh so it was hard to be truly shocked. If anything, she was fascinated.

She tried to keep a low profile as she wandered around the Emergency Department, her brain working overtime to process the things she saw.

The Aegis had recorded some of Tayla's accounts, so Eva knew the words written in blood on the gray walls were anti-violence spells. She knew there would be chains and hooks hanging from the ceiling, apparently to help lift or restrain demons. She'd even known about the cages of various sizes and shapes on wheels or tracks, just waiting to be taken to who knew where. But she hadn't known there would be troughs running with blood in the black floor, or skulls perched on shelves, and weird paintings of demonic medical procedures mounted on the walls.

Which, truthfully, didn't look much different from images of what the human race had done to animals and other humans in the name of experimentation, testing, and medical advancements for its entire existence.

She skirted the waiting area where a half-dozen non-humans of various species waited, most bleeding in some way, one holding his severed tentacle. Another guy bounced his eyeball in his palm. It took a second to realize that he hadn't lost it. That was just how his eye worked.

Demons were so damn creepy.

Averting her gaze, she focused on the vending machine across the way. What was inside? Probably not Doritos and Mountain Dew.

"Eva."

Startled, she wheeled around, realizing she was standing in the doorway to the room where Logan's mom lay in a hospital bed, connected to medical equipment and smiling weakly.

"Mrs., ah…"

"Regan." Her voice was raspy but strong, her eyes puffy and sad but sharp. "Come in."

I don't wanna.

Something inside Eva snapped, as if the last few days had finally caught up with her. There was too much to list, too much tragedy, too much truth. And now, the mother of the man Eva had fallen for, the woman who had turned The Aegis upside down and inside out and was now suffering a miscarriage, wanted to talk to her.

Eva had always been confident in any situation. She took control of situations. Situations didn't control her. But what if all of that had been because of the demon her parents and Lukas had tethered to her? Was her confidence a result of her good luck? Now that her fortunes had reversed, so had her faith in herself.

This was all…it was too much.

She looked around wildly for an exit. If she could just catch her breath for a minute—

"Eva." Regan's voice jolted her out of her panic. "Are you okay?"

Am *I* okay? The woman was lying in a hospital bed attached to machines, and she was asking about Eva?

"I didn't mean to intrude…I'll just leave you alone—"

"No, please, I'd like to talk to you."

Unable to come up with a valid excuse to avoid what was bound to be an extremely uncomfortable chat, Eva moved to Regan's bedside.

"I'm really sorry for your loss."

"Thank you." Regan laid her hand on her belly. "It wasn't planned, but we were ready for another baby." She gestured to the television, which ran a clip of the attack at Aegis HQ. "Must have been terrifying. It was a brave thing you did, speaking out against that doctored video."

Eva snorted. "Brave? I was terrified. I knew I was going to lose my job and a lot of friends. Maybe my family too."

"Bravery isn't the absence of fear," Regan said, clearly quoting someone. "That's called stupidity. Bravery is about doing the right thing despite the fear." She let out a weak laugh. "Ares is full of fun sayings like that. You'll see."

You'll see.

As if there was permanence in Eva's relationship with this family.

Warmth flowed through her like syrup. She hadn't been sure how these people would behave around her, given her career and past, but she definitely hadn't expected anything even close to kindness or acceptance.

Regan grimaced, throwing both hands onto her belly. A tear spilled from her eye as she breathed through a wave of what must have been agony.

"I'll get Thanatos." Eva hurried toward the door but drew to a sudden stop at the threshold. The warm, syrupy feeling returned, but stronger. Hotter. Pleasant to the point of pain. A musical hum rang in her ears as a powerful instinct to go to Regan overcame her.

Almost automatically, drawn in a way she couldn't describe, Eva returned to Regan. As if in a dream, she reached out and took the other woman's hand. Something surged inside her, a vibrating tingle, the same as she'd felt at Limos's place when the lightning apparently struck her—if that's what happened.

All around the room, machines beeped and shrieked. People poured inside, expressions ranging from stunned to confused and, in Thanatos's case, terror and fury.

Eva still felt distanced from it all, as if she was only spectating as light exploded from where her hand joined with Regan's and spread to engulf them both.

People shielded their eyes as a sense of peace washed through her, and then…a heartbeat. But not hers. Not Regan's. Strong and sure.

The baby.

Pure joy swept through Eva, and Regan began to laugh.

A doctor whose name tag read EIDOLON reached for Regan, the glyphs on his arm aglow. Before his hand got within six inches, he was thrown backward in a violent lurch, crashing into one of the beeping machines, mercifully destroying the thing.

Abruptly, the light disappeared, and Eva stumbled back a step. Would have gone down if not for a pair of strong arms catching her.

Logan.

"I don't know what just happened," she breathed. "I touched your mom, and I…felt the baby."

"What is happening?" Thanatos bellowed, and then Eidolon was on his feet, his hand on Regan's wrist, his arm glowing again.

"I haven't experienced that since she was pregnant with Logan." His brow furrowed, and then his dark eyes shot wide. "Holy…damn." Eidolon looked at Regan in disbelief. "The baby is…fine. Everything's fine." He glanced over at Thanatos. "I can't explain it."

Logan turned Eva toward him. "What did you do?"

Eva had no idea. She was as confused as everyone else. "Nothing. I mean, I don't know. I had an urge to go to her, and after that, I can't explain it. I wasn't in control."

"Whatever it was," Regan said, her face split in a wide grin, "thank you."

Thanatos's eyes narrowed on the doctor. "You're sure everything is okay?"

"I'm going to run some tests, but yeah, I'm optimistic about the results."

"Logan!" Cara burst into the room, smiling as widely as Regan. "Cujo's going to be fine. I came as soon as I was sure."

Relief flooded Eva, and Logan's entire body loosened, his head falling back as he whispered, "Thank you, Cara."

"It wasn't me," she said, and his head snapped forward again. "Stryke sent the cure for whatever was inside those bullets."

Everyone in the room froze.

"He also said to tell you he had a package delivered to your house. Said it'll help you find Draven."

Thanatos rounded on them. "Go," he said. "I'll be here with your mom. Let us know when you need our help."

Logan nodded and turned to Regan. "Mom…I'm sorry for earlier.

I—"

"It's okay. We'll discuss it all later," she said. "Right now, Draven needs you to stop him. And Eva needs that too."

The well-wishes and thank-yous and hugs were all a blur, and as Logan led her out of his mom's room, all Eva could think about was how incredibly wrong The Aegis had been.

About everything.

Chapter Thirty-Eight

Cujo was waiting for Logan when he got home. The moment he and Eva stepped out of the warehouse that housed the Harrowgate, Cujo tackled Logan to the ground. Pinned beneath the beast's massive paws, Logan could barely breathe as Cujo slapped drooly kisses on his face and head.

"Hey, buddy." Laughing, he made a futile attempt to push the mutt's snout away. "It's good to see you too." He managed to wriggle out from under the canine and, like he used to do as a toddler, wrapped his arms around Cujo's neck and clung to him as the beast lifted him to his feet. "You wanna say hi to Eva?"

Averting her gaze the way he'd told her to, Eva took a hesitant step forward but froze at Cujo's low, throaty growl. Crouching, Cujo eased up to her, sniffed her foot, snarled, and phased out.

Weird. Cujo rarely eased up to people like that. He was more of an in-your-face or watch-from-a-distance-and-then-pounce kind of animal.

"Well, he didn't bite you or piss on you, so we'll call that a win."

Her eyes shot wide. "Piss on me?"

"Yeah." He laughed as they walked toward the house. "Mace brought home a chick a few weeks ago for a barbecue. Cute, red hair, three horns. Anyway, I was tossing Cujo some steak off the grill, and he saw her, ran over, and took a huge, steaming piss on her. And you can smell that stuff for a week on your skin." He took them into the house. "Mace did not get laid that night." He rethought that. "Well, not by her, anyway."

Before they even got to the living room, Crux met them with a box in his skinny arms.

"Logan! You're never gonna believe—"

"I know. It's from Stryke."

The kid nodded and thrust the box at him like a Christmas gift. After everything that had gone down, Crux still hoped Stryke would come around. No one was more affected by Chaos's death than Crux, yet he somehow maintained a childlike innocence about the whole thing. Rade insisted that Crux hadn't dealt with the loss of his twin yet, and he wasn't the only one who had those ideas. Eidolon cautioned that Crux's transition would be difficult without his brother, and that he might not be the same when he came out on the other side of it.

But for now, Crux was a kid who knew how the world worked but wasn't ready to join it.

More power to him.

Logan tossed the weapon his dad gave him onto the table. "Where's everyone?"

"Do I look like a babysitter?" Crux grabbed the box back from him and plopped it onto the dining room table they never used. "I think Mace and Blade are looking for Draven. Sabre's doing lab shit, probably. And last I heard, Rade was interrogating some bad guy for…I dunno, some government."

Crux held up a pair of scissors he must have had up his ass because Logan hadn't seen them lying around anywhere.

Eva's hand came down on his lower back, a gentle reminder that she was there for him, as he cut the tape on the box. Once all four flaps were open, a three-foot-high holovid popped up from inside.

"Hey, asshole." Stryke, wearing a lab coat over a T-shirt with a middle finger printed on the chest, held up what looked like a video game controller. "You can thank me for saving Cujo later. In the box is this device. It's going to send a…spell, of sorts, out to find Draven. I used a combination of physics, herbs, and blood, and some tech shit you won't understand to develop it. I'm sure you're asking why we can't use this same kind of device to find enemies like Lilith, and it's because this technology only works on demons whose body chemistry is in the midst of a major change. I originally designed it to track down Seminus demons going through *s'genesis* who will become evil. When I learned about Draven, I reprogrammed it to seek out his DNA. And yeah, I have his DNA. I have everyone's DNA. Fuck off with your judgmental shit."

Fucking Stryke. The guy was insufferable.

Stryke placed the device in a box. "The A button activates the pilot's comms chip. The B button activates the spell. The joystick guides the spell, but you'll need to use the B and C buttons simultaneously to— Hey, you there?" He knocked on the air as if rapping on a door, being a total giant dickwad. "Have I lost you yet? Thought so. Look, just give the controller to your girlfriend and tell her to press the A button to get started."

Stryke snorted, obviously anticipating Logan's surprise. The bastard.

"Yeah, I researched the fuck out of her," he continued. "Duh. It's like you don't know me at all. So, give it to her, and the instructions will download into her chip implant. She can pilot it. You'll just fuck it up. Crux might be able to handle it too, but only if Eva got smart and told you to fuck off or something. Like I said, Crux, press the A button." He folded the box flaps. "Oh, and one more thing. This is an untested prototype. Use it at your own risk, and don't blame me for whatever shit goes wrong. Because it will. It always does."

The video clicked off.

"Wow," Eva said. "He sounds like a fun guy."

"He's been sad for a long time." Crux stared into the space where his older brother had been standing. "And he's having an episode."

Eva shot Logan a look. "An episode? Like Amber?"

He shook his head. "Amber has visions of sorts. Stryke has moments where his brain gets hyperactive. He'll go for days without eating or sleeping—"

"Or sex," Crux said, and Logan nodded.

"He gets so focused he just...loses himself in work. It's like he's trapped inside his head."

She frowned. "But he's a Seminus demon. How can he go without sex?"

Crux replied as he peered into the box. "Our uncle Eidolon developed a drug that helps us survive for a couple of days."

"Survive," Logan reminded him. "Not thrive."

Logan could recall several times, both before and after Chaos's death, when Stryke had been so deep in an episode they'd had to hold him down and force an injection just to keep him from going insane. Or dying. And several other times when they'd brought him females after the injections stopped working, and he'd become mad with pain and delirium.

Logan had no idea how Stryke was still alive without his family and friends to force injections or bring him females. Masumi, probably. Or maybe he paid someone. That sounded about right. He threw money and insults at everything.

Crux reached into the box and held the controller out to Eva. "He anointed you Pilot Queen."

"Hold on." Logan confiscated the device before Eva could take it. "We still don't know anything about this."

She looked at him. "We know we're out of time. I don't know Stryke personally, but I do know the tech he develops works." She gave a sheepish shrug. "Mostly. There were those few incidents—"

"You mean like when a defective demon detector at the US embassy in Sweden melted the werewolf Australian Ambassador? Or when a half-demon lawyer who represented demon clients was decapitated by a courthouse security system in Argentina?"

"Well, yes, those are the incidents I was talking about." Her annoyed glance amused him. "But what choice do we have?"

She was right, whether he wanted to admit it or not. Draven, paired with Lilith, was a deadly, dangerous combination, and Draven wouldn't stop until Eva was dead, or he was strapped down on a ritual table next to his parents and a demon priest.

But Logan didn't want to risk Eva's life with Stryke's sketchy new tech. "I'll do it," he said, but Crux gave him an are-you-kidding-me look.

"You can't. Only Eva can. Stryke said so. She's The Anointed One."

The kid needed to come down from the clouds. "Crux, man, I know you believe in your brother—"

Eva clamped her hand down on his forearm. "Can I talk to you for a minute? In private?"

"Sure." He let her lead him to the kitchen.

"Look." She turned him, a bundle of strength and determination despite the exhausted shadows in her dark eyes. "I know you want to take all of this on your shoulders, but you're the only one who can handle Draven. Don't worry about piloting the remote. It's something I can do. After everything The Aegis has done, this is something I *need* to do. Let me."

"If anything happens—"

She put a finger to his lips, shutting him up. "Then at least we tried."

Man, this woman was amazing.

Harvester, I know you can't be dead. And I know you said if I was dense, you'd send me a sign when I found the right mate for me. You don't need to send a sign. I've found her.

While Logan contacted his DART people and family to coordinate a battle plan, Eva familiarized herself with the tech Stryke had sent.

Crux took her to the game room, figuring she'd be most comfortable there in a chair designed for piloting a virtual craft. Pretty cool. She'd been so busy with her journalistic life that she'd neglected the part of her that loved playing in virtual reality and losing herself in the flow of another world. It was so, so easy. Because real life was just so awful sometimes.

She sank into the chair meant to simulate the cockpit of anything from a fighter jet or starfighter to a race car. What the guys living here had set up was pretty extraordinary. Sure, virtual and mixed reality was a big thing, making leaps and bounds tech-wise over the past couple of decades, but most people didn't have the kind of space these guys did. This heavily padded room would allow them to play across huge spaces, like a holodeck from *Star Trek*.

But she wasn't playing a game right now, and that realization hit her hard as she gathered the controller in her hands. This was real life. This was *her* life. If this failed, she could die. Draven could die. Heck, for all she knew, she could blow up the entire house.

Well, she'd always loved a challenge.

Determined to win the game, she pushed the A button on the controller. A sudden, mind-numbing jolt snaked through her temple at the site of her comms' chip implant.

Then, standing in front of her in 3D transparency, was Stryke.

"Hey. Whoever you are, you're getting ready to hunt Draven. And for the record, I always liked him, so I hope you're successful. Anyway, here's the deal. You're going to guide a…let's call it a bubble. It's a grain of matter that operates in an alternate dimension, in a space between the demon realm and ours, but that's not important. Your bubble is going to seek out the specific person programmed into the controller. There are limitations, though. It can only find Draven if he's in the human realm. If he's in Sheoul, the bubble will just circle around aimlessly and eventually self-destruct." He hesitated. "Probably."

"What's going on?" Crux asked. "What do you see?"

Eva smiled at Crux's enthusiasm. "It's Stryke. He's explaining how to use the device."

"Oh, cool. I wish I could do it."

"I'll tell you all about it later," she promised.

Stryke went on about how to operate the bubble, mostly how to guide it once it found Draven, operating it like a drone to determine his location. There were a handful of warnings too, like, *Don't press the X and Y buttons at the same time or there might be a bomb-like incident. And, under no circumstances can you allow the bubble to touch Draven. I think doing so might transport him to you. Or maybe cause a rift between the realms and suck us all inside like a black hole. It's truly a mystery.*

So…Stryke was a maniac. Eva was beginning to regret her decision to pilot the device.

"Crux." Logan came into the game room and dismissed Crux with a wave. "Out."

Crux pouted, completely crushed. "But I wanna watch."

"Nope, not this time." Logan cocked his thumb at the doorway. "Scram." Muttering to himself, Crux shuffled out, and Logan turned to her. "Blade, Mace, and Scotty are waiting at a Harrowgate, ready to head to the location the moment you find Draven. The Horsemen are on standby, and they'll go in if Draven isn't alone."

"What about you?"

"I'm staying with you until he's captured. Then I'll help get him to his parents."

"Logan, you really don't need to worry about me."

"Stryke said something could go wrong. I'm not leaving you until your part is done."

Relieved despite what she'd said, she sat back in the chair. "Okay, let's do this, then."

Closing her eyes, she pressed the B button.

Instantly, like a lit match, a tiny flame appeared in front of her. So far, so good. Stryke said to press the same button again to send the spell out into the world.

Press.

The flame spun itself into a little ball and shot through the ceiling. In her mind's eye, she saw it zip down the street, weaving between structures, skimming the ground, and sailing over buildings. It built up speed, bouncing around Australia, checking out vast, uninhabited areas and cities alike in mere seconds.

"Australia's clear." The thing blipped over an expanse of water. "So's New Zealand," she said a few moments later. "Antarctica too. Shocker, there."

The device cleared another dozen countries. And another dozen. And another...no...wait...

The little flame slowed, circling a city somewhere in Africa. The circles grew smaller, homing in on a garbage dump where people were picking through the trash.

The flame skipped around, going from person to person, and then shot like a bullet to a shack on the far side of the massive refuse center. It went through the wall and under the floor, shooting through winding tunnels of earth and rotting wood.

"I'm in some sort of hidden chamber," she breathed, her heart racing the way it did when she piloted a virtual racing vehicle.

"Where?" Logan asked.

"Somewhere in Africa. Hold on...I think we're close." The flame shot into a chamber of horrors that threatened to make her retch. "Oh, shit. There are a lot of demons in there. I don't see Lilith. But the demons are...it's an orgy. There are so many dead things..."

"Demons are fucking disgusting," Logan muttered. "Dammit, Draven."

"There he is!" She spotted Draven near a fire pit, laughing as a fat, ugly demon roasted over the coals, its skin burned, fat dripping into the flames. Quickly, she popped the joystick and spun the flame around. She needed to get out of there to identify the location.

The flame followed her direction, going back through the tunnel, but it glitched before she could guide it out of the hut. The flame flickered, and she shouted in surprise as heat flashed into her face.

Suddenly, it darted back to the chamber, making a beeline for Draven. No amount of button pushing or wrenching on the joystick changed its course until, finally, a split second before it struck him, she employed a dive-hard-yoke-to-the-right move that had won her several competitions in the past.

The flame sputtered and whipped to the side. And then, to her horror, she was looking directly into Draven's eyes. He smiled.

He could *see* her.

"Shit!"

Abort, abort.

Stryke said to press down on the stick and hit the X and A buttons simultaneously, but the moment she did it, the flame exploded into a fireball and plowed into Draven.

Searing heat and stinging pain knocked her backward, throwing her out of the chair. Shouts and grunts filled the air, and then there was a hand around her throat. She couldn't breathe, and her feet were dangling.

Draven!

How did he get in here?

Under no circumstances can you allow the bubble to touch Draven. I think doing so might transport him to you.

A bloodcurdling roar tore through the room, and then Logan was there, a flying punch to the head dropping Draven like a rock. She fell from his grip and gasped for breath. Something wet and warm coated her palm. Blood.

Crimson droplets dotted the floor mat, and she stopped breathing all over again when she saw Logan holding his thigh, his hand pressed against what looked like a splinter of ice.

Draven's eyes, as icy and sharp as the shard in Logan's leg, focused on her, his face a mask of demented hatred.

"Now you die, bitch."

Images of her colleagues—their deaths—flashed in her head. This guy didn't kill with his hands. He killed with his mind. She couldn't give him time to think anything, and she had to buy Logan time to recover.

She launched at him. Caught him by surprise with a powerful uppercut to his sternum. Satisfaction at knocking him backward dulled the pain in her hand, but it only lasted a second. He recovered with a left hook she only dodged because of Logan's training earlier in the week.

Then he followed it up with a right cross and the perfect opening for her special move.

Big mistake, asshole.

She met him in the center of the room. He swung, and she swept low with one arm as she slapped down on the mat with the other. A twist of her legs and—

He caught her calf, spun her, and she was suddenly in his arms. He sliced his right arm down, and pain became her world, clogging her throat so she couldn't even scream. There was nothing but agony and horror as he tossed her aside like a fast-food wrapper.

"Stupid bitch." Draven spat at her as she stumbled backward into the wall. "I saw you try that move in the gym with Logan."

Logan's words that day after he'd sliced through her shirt rang through her head like a death knell.

You try that move with someone who knows it, and instead of a ruined shirt, you'll be cleaning your bowels off the floor.

Looking down, she cried out, warm, sticky blood flowing between her fingers. Her hands were the only things holding her intestines inside. Nausea and dizziness made everything slow and go dark. She felt her legs turn to jelly, and then she was on the ground. She couldn't see, couldn't hear.

And, as one more tsunami of pain crashed down on her, she couldn't hold on to consciousness.

Chapter Thirty-Nine

"*No!*" Logan's entire world tilted as he tore the ice shard from his thigh and watched Eva crumple to the ground, her organs spilling out of her body.

Draven's laughter rang out, high-pitched and deranged.

"I fucking did it!" His body glowed, contorted. Horns erupted from his head as the last pieces of his transformation clicked into place.

Eva was dead.

Logan's chest squeezed tight. He couldn't breathe. Couldn't move.

This can't be happening!

Draven wheeled around to Logan. "I wanted to make her death gorier, but I held back out of respect for you."

Fury and sorrow collided, awakening the dormant demon and angel DNA inside Logan. Everything awesome and terrible about both fed his rage, and he launched himself at his friend. There would be no mercy for this demon. There would only be vengeance—the only thing it would understand.

He whirled, spinning his summoned sword like he was a blender and Draven was the margarita mix.

They'd grown up together, sparred together, hit on females together. Draven knew Logan better than Logan knew himself. And he proved it by avoiding all of Logan's attacks. No matter how hard Logan struck, no matter how fast, Draven dodged. It was as if a barrier surrounded him, making Logan bounce off an undetectable shield without so much as scratching Draven's skin.

Then Draven really put on the pressure. An invisible fist slammed into Logan's head. Heat exploded inside his body, his skin started to blister, and his vision blurred. He shouted in agony, some of it physical but a lot of it mental, as his lifelong friend tortured him.

After killing the female Logan knew was supposed to have been his.

"You gonna call your mutt?" Draven taunted as he hit the mat to avoid Logan's roundhouse kick. "You need help from your puppy?"

Logan wasn't calling Cujo. He wasn't calling his roommates, his family, or his all-powerful grandfather.

He was going to take Draven—or the monster he'd become—down all by himself.

But even as that thought filtered through his mind, he felt Cujo coming. The beast couldn't materialize inside—he had to phase into the backyard and come through a door, and he'd take it down if he had to.

Stay back! Logan ordered. He wouldn't let Draven kill Cujo too.

Cujo's response was a frustrated snarl. The beast would listen, but Logan didn't know for how long.

"Logan!"

Staggering, struggling to keep his balance, Logan spared a glance up at Crux, who leaned precariously over the balcony. He dropped the wooden tool Thanatos had made, the one Logan had left on the table upstairs because he hadn't thought he'd need it.

Logan caught it in one peeling, bleeding hand. What had his father said? That it would deflect mental assaults and send them back to the attacker?

Suddenly, Draven screamed, his skin bubbling and popping. With the mental stream reversed, Logan healed as Draven burned. The stench of blood and seared flesh grew thick enough to taste.

Pocketing the weapon, Logan attacked. He brought to bear every lesson learned during his decades of training with the Horsemen and all the angels, both fallen and Heavenly.

He pressed his advantage, forcing Draven to defend himself with his horns and claws. Logan grunted in pain with every slam of a horn into his chest or shoulder and every tear of his flesh under Draven's serrated talons. But still, Logan pressed harder, his rage fueling his wrath.

Draven must have attempted another mental attack because he screamed again, and the entire left side of his face blew off.

Without Thanatos's weapon, it might have been Logan's entire head.

Through the hellsmoked roar of Draven's misery and rage, Logan heard distant shouts. Familiar shouts. Crux had called for help.

They're going to kill Draven.

Logan's childhood and teen years with his friend flashed in his head. Their college antics. Their laid-back chats about their hopes and dreams. They were going to fight side-by-side in the Apocalypse.

They were always going to have each others' backs.

Their plans for the future weren't going to happen now. But Logan could have his buddy's back one last time.

The second Eva died, Draven had become a full demon without any hope of redemption. He had to die, but Logan wouldn't allow Draven to be hacked apart by the Horsemen or his DART buddies.

Logan would be the one to put his friend down. It's what Draven would have wanted.

Reaching deep, drawing energy at the cellular level, Logan slammed his fist into Draven's throat and power-punched his soul gift into his friend.

Draven's body went limp as his spirit ejected, a screaming, angry wisp. Logan hesitated for only a split-second before he drove a summoned sword deep between Draven's ribs, piercing his heart.

The organ beat a frantic, spastic pulse that flowed down the metal blade and pounded into Logan's palm, connecting them intimately through life and death.

A breeze ruffled his hair as Draven's soul wafted past Logan's head and slipped back into Draven's dying body.

Logan rolled them so Draven was on the floor, Logan hovering above him.

Draven smiled up at him, the mangled flesh on the left side of his face turning the smile into a grimace of bone and teeth.

"Thank you," he rasped. "I didn't—" He coughed, spraying blood. "I didn't want this. Watch...watch out for Lilith. She helped Pestilence try to kill you. And she sent a storm..."

A storm?

Draven reached up and clutched Logan's shirt tight in his trembling fist, using the last of his strength to pull himself close. "She said...said you were going to kill someone you loved. I...laughed because…because I didn't know she meant *me*."

You will be mine, or you will kill someone you love.

Lilith's fateful words ringing in his ears, Logan eased Draven back to the floor, his friend's eyes, once so bright and full of life, growing cloudy.

"Tell…" Draven coughed again. "Tell my parents." He sucked in a rattling breath. "I…I'm sorry."

"No, dammit. Draven? Draven!" he shouted. Felt the tap of his heartbeat against the blade fade, stutter, and then go still.

Everything seemed to go still. Logan had lost his friend and his female in the span of seconds. How was he supposed to move on from this?

He had to go. Had to get away from the pain and the death. Stunned and emotionally drained, he tried to stand, but his legs wouldn't hold him. Someone caught him as his kneecaps hit the floor.

"I've got you, son."

Tears stung his eyes, but through his blurry vision, Logan could make out Draven's spirit swirling toward the ceiling.

"I need a *decipula*," he croaked, and then someone—Mace, he thought—pressed one into his hand and helped Thanatos lift him to his feet.

With a flick of his bruised wrist, he flung the sphere into the air, and as it did its thing, he staggered over to where Eva's body lay in a pool of blood.

Her sightless eyes stared into space as he knelt next to her. She'd been so vibrant, so full of life, and now…

A sob escaped him as he reached for her.

But then…her skin began to glow. Dimly at first, pulsing in slow waves. The light grew brighter with each beat until a radiant sweep of light surrounded her. The blood on the floor poofed away like glitter, the way it had at the beach, and the organs that had spilled out of her torn belly were sucked back in. The gash in her flesh closed, leaving not so much as a scar.

Gasps and shocked curses rippled through the roomful of people.

"Eva?" Gently, Logan gathered her in his arms. The light swelled, swallowing him in its brilliance. A warm, familiar sensation engulfed him, wrapping around him like a blanket of peace. Nothing mattered but the bliss, the calm, and the feeling of Eva's hand gripping his.

She's alive!

Holy shit, she was alive, and as the light faded away, his friends and family gathered around them, asking questions and barking out orders.

Get them some water!

Someone call Eidolon!

Who the hell let the hellhound in?

Then Cujo was there, licking Logan's face, whining and wiggling. Even Eva got a face full of hellhound tongue.

"What happened?" She pulled back enough to see Logan's face as he gently pushed Cujo away to keep from overwhelming her. "Did we win?"

"We won," he said, tugging her to him again, needing to feel her heart beating against his chest. "Somehow, we won."

She clung to him, her face buried in his neck for a moment before she eased away to look down at herself, at her torn...but not bloodstained...dress. "I remember...I thought I was going to die. How am I healed?"

"It was like what happened at the hospital," Thanatos said, a rare note of reverence in his deep voice. "There was a great light." He inclined his head in a respectful bow that Logan suspected was a nod to his Druidic people. "And then there was life."

Eva's dark eyes lifted to Logan, her gaze brimming with wonder. "I have so many questions."

"I think we all do." Logan brushed a lock of hair out of her eyes, wishing they could linger like this, appreciating the miracle and celebrating their victory. But while they'd won the battle, they'd taken heavy losses, and there was more to do. "But they'll have to wait." His heart sat heavy in his chest as he looked over at Draven. His body had already reverted from the monster he'd become to the form in which he'd spent most of his life.

He was Draven again.

Lilith had told Logan he'd have to make a choice, and he'd refused. But his refusal *had* been a choice, and Draven had paid.

"I have to take Draven to his parents."

Chapter Forty

The next two days were a whirlwind.

While Logan and his friends dealt with Draven's parents and the subsequent death ceremonies, Eva remained busy with her own sort of hell.

The strange glow that had saved her and Regan's baby remained an unsolved mystery, although Aleka and Thanatos were both looking into it. Aleka had extensive resources, and Thanatos was a bookworm with a library The Aegis would envy.

Lilith was still out there and remained a threat, so Logan had insisted that Eva have an escort anytime she was outside his Sydney compound or somewhere safe like his parents' place or Ares' island.

She'd been annoyed at first, but her constant companion, Scotty, turned out to be…not so bad. Sure, Ares and Cara's youngest daughter had been a little surly at first, but she'd willingly transported Eva through Harrowgates and even through her own summoned gate once.

Apparently, she could only summon her own gate if she bled on the spot where the gate would open, so she didn't use them often. Eva couldn't blame her. Cutting yourself constantly would suck, even if you healed quickly.

The fallout and bad luck from her nightmare demon removal continued. Eva, as predicted, lost her job, which wasn't a surprise. And she didn't care. She had a resignation letter prepared anyway.

Her parents lost their contract with The Aegis, and their partner left the law firm. The practice, now Tennant & Tennant, was in a death spiral, but her parents were wealthy, and they'd survive anything that came at them.

At least, they would until the next wave of bad luck struck.

Sig's father, Lukas, lost his Elder status and was under Aegis investigation for the unauthorized actions he'd taken when he linked her, him, and her parents to the nightmare demon.

Finally, The Aegis was taking appropriate action.

Still, in Eva's spare time, she'd used her research skills and contacts to find a way to break the demon's negative effects. Before she left Aegis HQ for good, she'd made use of their library and found an interesting text buried deep in the dusty, ancient archives. She'd forwarded it on to Logan's cousin, and just an hour ago, as Eva and Logan were arriving in Greenland for his parents' get-together, Aleka texted that she had something to share and would be joining them shortly.

Eva loved everything about the inside of Logan's childhood home. The castle, hidden from human eyes on the outside, was a page from a fairy tale. According to Amber, Regan had transformed it from what she called a villain's lair to a princess's palace.

A fire blazed in the hearth, and colorful tapestries and cheerful paintings lined the walls. Plush rugs covered the rich wood floors, candles flickered in stone crevices, and pendant lights bathed the rooms in bright warmth. Summery décor created a festive ambiance, and there was even a hint of lemon and berries in the air.

Eva was so busy admiring a medieval suit of armor wearing a sunflower wreath that she jumped at the sound of Logan's voice next to her.

"Bet Sabre won't show up if Aleka's coming," he said in a low voice as he handed Eva a glass of wine.

She watched a vampire walk by with a tray of canapes. "Why do you say that?"

He shrugged. "I have no idea what happened between them after Limos's party, but he's been grumpy and avoiding her."

Eva eyed the buffet and thought about getting a few more of the crab legs. Or the lasagna rolls. Or anything, really. Thanatos's vampire servants had prepared a gourmet feast, and she wasn't going to pass that up. She'd been crazy hungry lately. Probably because she'd been so busy.

Another vampire strolled by with a bottle of champagne, refilling glasses as he went, and she just shook her head at how different things were in Logan's world. Thanks to The Aegis's reports, she'd known about the vampires, but actually seeing them helping around the house, wrangling Cujo when he tried to take a whole roasted suckling pig, and serving drinks still seemed surreal.

Amber came over, a plate full of delicate little pastries in her hand, her curly dark hair pulled back, her pale-yellow eyes focused on Eva.

Eva clenched Logan's hand, unsure how to handle his sister. Clearly, she was something unique even among his kind. For all Eva's experience with people whose positions or money made them important or public figures, she couldn't shake a case of nerves right now.

Amber opened her mouth as if to say something, then snapped it closed and turned to the arched doorway just as four people entered, two of whom Eva recognized.

Aleka and Raika.

But the other two…holy shit. The woman was beautiful, statuesque, and elegant in jeans, jeweled sandals, and a flowing azure blouse.

But the man.

The *man.*

Whatever he was, he wasn't human. Moving like a wraith in heavy black boots, torn black pants, and a hooded leather duster, he sucked every drop of oxygen out of the air as he strode through the great hall. At least, that was how it felt. It felt like one of those gloved hands had clamped around Eva's throat while he decided how to use the scythe in his other hand.

Holy shit.

He took a hard right into Thanatos's library while the three women joined Logan, Eva, and Amber. The slight scent of sulfur lingered in the guy's wake.

Raika gestured to the other woman. "Eva, this is my mom, Lilliana. The hooded guy is my dad, Azagoth."

The Grim Reaper. Of course. Eva just needed to meet an angel now, and she'd totally win Supernatural Bingo.

And that was when she realized that Lilliana, Azagoth's mate, *was* an angel.

Holy shit again.

"Hello," Eva said, proud that her voice didn't crack even a little.

Lilliana inclined her head in greeting and offered her hand. Eva took it, freezing as an instant tingling sensation shot up her spine.

Lilliana gasped softly, her fingers clenching around Eva's.

"Mom?" Raika gripped her mother's wrist. "Mom? What is it?"

Yeah, what is it? The sensation wasn't unpleasant. In a way, it was comforting, as if something inside her recognized a kindred spirit in Lilliana.

"This is…extraordinary." Lilliana blinked at Eva. "I feel something inside you that shouldn't be there." She turned to Logan. "I wasn't at Limos's party, but Raika and Ares told me blood fell from the sky. It was Harvester's?"

Logan nodded. "That's what Reseph said."

"And Eva? You were struck by lightning?"

"I don't know what it was for sure. But it didn't hurt. It was more like a column of light."

"And you saved Regan's baby? And your own body regenerated after you'd died?"

Eva nodded numbly, sensing that Lilliana was about to drop a bombshell on her. But would it be good or bad?

Bombs were usually bad.

Lilliana released Eva's hand. "I sense Grace inside you."

"Grace?" Eva looked between Logan and Lilliana. "As in the energy that fuels angels?"

"It's complicated," Lilliana said. "It's part soul and part energy."

"It all makes sense now," Amber blurted, and Eva was glad it made sense to someone, because she was confused as hell. "I saw Harvester save my brother."

Logan looked over at Eva, as baffled as she was. "But she didn't."

Amber gestured to Regan, standing with Runa near the buffet table, her hand resting protectively over her belly. "You're not the brother I was talking about."

Then it clicked. In the hospital. Regan and the baby.

Smiling, Amber glanced at Eva. "Plot twist."

"Oh, sweet baby Jesus." Abruptly, Eva felt lightheaded. She had a freaking angel's *Grace* inside her. "That explains so much," she breathed, shock making it hard to speak.

"And it means Harvester isn't gone." Lilliana looked at Eva. "I don't know who all was at Limos's, but it's probably a good thing you were there. An angel's Grace can only be stored inside a human. It's likely no one else there was a candidate. If not for you, her Grace might have been lost, and her soul returned to the Creator. She'd have been gone forever. But you can't host it for long. It will eventually burn you out. Have you been hungry lately? You'll need to take in a lot of calories."

Eva eyed the buffet again. "I've been starving." She ignored her growling stomach and turned back to Lilliana. "How much time do I have?"

"I don't know. This isn't something I've studied, and I don't think there are many documented cases. But if I had to guess...a year? Months, perhaps?"

Whew. The way her luck had gone lately, she'd feared the answer would be weeks or even days. Maybe hours.

"So, we have time, especially if we can get rid of the bad-luck mojo." She looked at Aleka. "You said you have news."

"I do." Aleka swiped a glass of sparkling wine from a passing vamp. "To break the luck-reversal spell, the demon needs to be tethered to someone else."

"So, we're just supposed to release it and let it find someone to haunt?" Eva asked. "The answer is to curse someone else? That's not a solution."

Logan seemed to consider it. "What if it was attached to someone it *couldn't* haunt?"

Amber frowned, as confused as Eva, and then she smiled at her brother. "I think I know where you're headed with that." She glanced at a newcomer walking through the gate, and her cheeks bloomed pink.

Eva remembered Raika saying that Amber was in love with the guy, a Seminus demon named Talon. At the beach, he'd been with a slinky fallen angel, but right now, he was alone, and he commanded every drop of Amber's attention.

He waved in their direction and joined Blade, Sabre, and Scotty, who were playing pool on the other side of the great hall. Eva could practically see Amber's heart go with him.

Logan seemed oblivious. Maybe intentionally so. No doubt he didn't want to contemplate the idea of his baby sister with his friend. Who was also a sex demon.

"Come on." Logan squeezed her hand. "Let's find my dad and take care of the nightmare demon once and for all."

Logan started toward the library Azagoth, Ares, and Eidolon had disappeared into, but Eva stopped him.

"Let's do it later. Right now, people need to enjoy themselves and leave some of the hell of the last few days behind them."

She was right. No matter how much he wanted to get it over with so Eva could live without the specter of doom over her head, everyone needed a break and a little fun. Especially since DART would be embroiled in investigations as The World Council on Supernatural Governance attempted to get to the bottom of what had happened between them and The Aegis. Eva would certainly be called to testify too. So, he agreed when she said she wanted to let everyone relax before the next battle.

His uncle Ares would have approved of her tactical acumen.

Logan contacted Kynan and asked him to bring the *decipula* containing the demon's soul when he came, then spent the rest of the evening at Eva's side, helping her navigate the complexities of underworld culture. But truthfully, she fit in like she was born to it. She was an excellent conversationalist and willing to listen and have her preconceptions and beliefs challenged. She truly wanted to learn, and when she found out that something she believed to be true was wrong, she didn't get defensive. She wanted to know more.

She was amazing.

Thank you, Harvester.

Logan hadn't needed a sign that Eva was The One. But Harvester had given him one anyway when her Grace transferred to Eva. Yes, they would need to find a way to bring his grandmother back and return the Grace to her, but in the meantime, Lilliana assured them that Eva was immortal, protected by Heaven's power.

Ares reported some troubling news toward the end of the evening, though. Apparently, the Memitim angels who resided on his island had been blocked from Heaven. And the Memitim in Heaven at the time of the blood event hadn't been seen since.

It appeared that Heaven had closed its borders, and no one was getting in or out. Not even Reaver.

Had Harvester been trying to warn them that something was wrong in Heaven? Had she sacrificed herself to send a message?

So many questions and so few answers, but everyone was ready to start finding them.

"Logan?" Eva placed her third empty dinner plate onto a cart near the kitchen. He loved that she'd taken Lilliana's advice and wasn't shy about eating. "I haven't seen your room yet."

He glanced over at his parents as they said goodbye to the last of the guests. That would probably take forever.

"Let's go. Dad'll be a while."

He led her down the winding stone hallways to the room he'd grown up in, the chamber that had been his sanctuary and second favorite place, right behind the beach on Ares' island.

The spot where he and Eva had made love, which would now forever belong to them. Only them.

And Cujo, because Logan couldn't keep the mutt away.

Eva's arresting smile when she saw his room made Logan's heart stutter. She looked around, her lips parted and eyes wide.

"This is incredible. It's like one of those old *Harry Potter* movies." She walked through the bedroom to the right chamber, an old chapel that had been converted into Logan's playroom first and then a library and game room as he got older.

She circled around and peeked into the left chamber, a huge, round room with a hellhound-sized bed and a feeding trough. She peeked into the bathroom too, and then focused on the wall decorations, which ranged from his high school hockey sticks to a yellowing, sexy poster of Stella Andrews, the first openly werewolf supermodel.

His parents could have at least taken *that* down.

The sound of footsteps announced his parents in the hall.

"Come on in," he called out. They filed inside, his father's hand protectively and lovingly around his mother's waist.

No, she definitely wasn't a hostage, and Logan's harsh words the other day brought fresh shame to the surface. Whatever had happened between them so long ago was exactly that. Between *them*. He knew they'd have a convo eventually, and it would be hard, but their family was strong enough to weather anything.

Eva pointed to a little bow and arrow hanging above his bed. "Was that yours?"

"It was his first bow and arrow set," Regan replied, moving to take it off the wall. She held the tiny weapon, smiling down at the miniature arrow. "Thanatos made it himself. Logan used to hunt apples and pretend he was fighting off waves of demons. He actually did use it against a Tempestus demon once."

He frowned, remembering her saying something about the storm on Limos's beach being a demon. "What are you talking about?"

"You were very little," Thanatos said. "Someone unleashed a Temptestus demon nearby, and it nearly took you and your mother."

"If not for Cujo and your father…" His mother shuddered.

He drew in a sharp breath. "It was Lilith."

"We don't know that—"

"Draven told me," Logan blurted. "Before he died, he said she tried to kill me. He brought up Pestilence. And a storm."

His parents exchanged a glance, and his father nodded. "It makes sense. Only someone extremely powerful could have forced that demon out of Sheoul. If she's stronger now than she was even before she died, she could be behind its attack."

Logan didn't remember any of that, and it sounded like he should be thankful. As he looked at his parents, Eva, the picture of Amber with his grandparents, and even at Cujo, who had managed to slink into the room and plop down on his bed, he was definitely thankful.

He'd had a great life, and Eva would make it even better.

But first, he needed his father's help.

He explained the situation, his heart hammering. What if his father said no?

"I know I have no right to ask," Logan finished, "not after what I put you and Mom through. But—"

"It's okay," Thanatos said. "I've housed countless nightmare demons in my armor. If it will help Eva, I'll do it." He inclined his head at Eva. "You saved my son, and I will forever be in your debt."

Eva shook her head. "It was Harvester's Grace that saved the baby. Not me."

"I wasn't talking about that son." He gestured to Logan. "You didn't know you were hosting Harvester's Grace when you risked yourself to operate Stryke's contraption. Logan told me you distracted Draven, forfeiting your life to buy him time. You," he said, "are welcome in this family."

"Thank you," she whispered, her eyes glistening with tears. Logan wasn't shocked when his mom gave her a hug. His mother had always been, well…a mom.

A great one.

Thanatos's arm came down around Logan's shoulders, tugging him into a brief embrace. "Now, where's this demon soul?"

Grateful for his father's generosity, Logan dug the *decipula* Kynan had brought to the party out of his pocket and handed it to his dad.

"Ready?" Logan asked Eva, and the smile she gave him, so full of trust, made him want to get her home. Soon.

"I'm ready."

"Close the doors." Thanatos skimmed his finger across the crescent scar on his neck, and his armor folded onto his body like a Transformer. Armored for battle, he crushed the little marble in his gauntleted fist.

Screeching at its newfound freedom, the demon's inky spirit bounced around the room, seeking an exit or a new victim, Logan didn't know.

He used his gift to draw it close and keep it from escaping as his father released half a dozen souls from his armor. They shot out and wrapped around the nightmare spirit, circling it over and over until they overwhelmed it and dragged it, screaming and wailing, into the armor.

And there it would reside until Thanatos released it to kill and earn its freedom—something he promised he wouldn't do as long as Eva lived.

"It's done," Thanatos said, and Regan hugged Eva again.

"Congratulations. So, what are you going to do with your life now? I'm sure DART could use you if you need a job."

"Kynan already offered me one," Eva said, and while Logan hadn't known about it, he wasn't surprised.

"He did? When?"

"Just before he and Gem left."

"What did you say?"

"I said I'd think about it." She shrugged. "I want to spend some time figuring out what I'm really meant to do. I had that demon attached to me for so long, bringing me false luck, that I don't know what accomplishments are mine and which belong to it. I kind of want to make some new choices now that I'm in charge of my life and not relying on it for good fortune."

"Well," Regan said, "whatever you decide, if you need help, we're all here for you."

A sense of what Logan could only call destiny, fate, hell, or *fortune*, filled him as they said their goodbyes. Cujo even allowed Eva to pet him for a moment. Afterward, he sent Logan a mental picture of his old stuffed lion, something the beast had always associated with Logan and translated to *affection*.

Cujo had accepted Eva into his life, and unlike most of Logan's other plushie toys, he wouldn't unstuff her. Logan wouldn't tell Eva how Cujo had conveyed *that* part of the communication.

They strolled out of the castle, enjoying the unseasonable warmth on the way to the Harrowgate. But before they stepped inside, Logan pulled Eva aside next to the courtyard wall. He'd always liked this spot, sheltered from the prevailing winds but with a view of the distant mountains and low hills.

"I haven't thanked you for saving me yet."

She rolled her eyes. "You and your father are exaggerating my part in the battle with Draven."

"I wasn't talking about that. It's more about my quality of life." He took her hand and pressed a kiss into her warm palm. "Without you, losing Draven would have been even more devastating." It was still an ache that would be with him for the rest of his life, but with Eva...at least he *had* a life. "And you got me out of a pit I'd been living in for years."

Maja and Chaos had been in that pit with him, ghosts he'd allowed to haunt him. Maja's ghost had been banished, and while he still had to work out his feelings about Chaos and Stryke, at least he had Eva by his side.

She smiled up at him, as much an angel as anyone else in the family. "You freed me from *my* life, Logan. You freed me in so many ways."

"Life with me...with my family...it won't be easy. We have demons after us and apocalypses to train for—"

She silenced him with a look that said he was a dumbass for trying to dissuade her.

"Whatever happens, we do it together," she said. "Family isn't always easy. I'm still not sure how to deal with what my parents did to me with that stupid demon. You're still trying to sort out your feelings about your parents' pasts. It's messy. Life is messy." She shook her head. "A lot messier than I ever would have thought. Everything came to me so easily before."

"You still come easily."

At first, she didn't get his crude joke. Which wasn't a joke. She was responsive as hell, and now that he was thinking about *how* responsive, how she reacted to his touch, whether his finger or his tongue, he wanted to get her home.

He saw the moment she got his meaning in that little wicked twitch of her lips and the flutter of her pulse at the base of her throat.

"So do you," she said in a deep-throated purr. "Why don't we go home and make it a contest?" She gripped his hips and tugged him to her. "And I'm *very* competitive."

Mace and Crux had both mentioned something to that effect. Too bad for her, Logan had a competitive streak too.

But he'd let her win this round. Because no matter what, he'd win too.

He looked out over the harsh landscape where he'd grown up, hunting apples and, apparently, storm demons. He'd lived a life full of adventure and family, but one thing had been missing.

"Eva?"

She looked up at him. "Hmm?"

Dipping his head, he touched his lips to hers, lightly at first, but his depth of feeling for her called for more and more. In a few long, lingering heartbeats, he had her against the great stone wall. They couldn't take it any further, not when the walls crawled with guards and the cameras saw everything.

But his body craved hers, and his heart craved everything else. "I love you," he murmured against her mouth. "I love you so much."

"I love you too," she whispered, tugging him even closer.

Happiness spread through his veins…and then he remembered what she'd said about the false good luck the demon had brought her. He pulled back to look down at her. What if he'd only come into her life because of the demon?

"You said you need to reevaluate your life and the things the demon brought you. Am I part of that?"

"You," she said, "are the reason I'm free to do that. I don't know if I believed in kismet, destiny, or any of that before now, but I feel like this is how my life is supposed to go. It wasn't the nightmare luck demon that put me on Limos's island and turned me into a vessel for an angel's Grace. It was something else. A sign, I guess. That I'm supposed to be here. With you. Always."

Agreed. The signs were there. And they told him that Eva was his. Always.

Epilogue

It was good to be king.

Well, not king, exactly. Zaphkiel's position as Celestial Most High was far more illustrious than any king.

Smiling, he sat in the simple olive wood chair that had recently belonged to the Archangel Michael. The thing needed to be replaced. The last time Zaphkiel was in charge, he'd had a throne of gold and jewels, as befitting his grand position.

He trailed his finger over the worn wood, his gem-encrusted rings glistening in the radiant light that touched all in Heaven. The chair was beautiful in its simplicity, but if Michael thought that an elegant, but plain, wooden seat somehow made him appear humble, he was a fool.

"Are you going to tell me why I'm here?"

Lifting his gaze, Zaphkiel looked at Michael's buddy, Gabriel. The male, draped in a filthy gray smock and chains, kneeled on the pearlescent floor, his multicolor hair matted and hanging in ropes, hatred coming off him in tangible waves.

Zaphkiel was loving it. He gestured to the other angel in the room.

"Tell him, Jophiel."

The senior Throne, standing near the doorway, his gaze hooded, turned to Gabriel. "Your Ordeal date has been set. You'll be tested and tried, and if you're found guilty of collaborating with Azagoth to destroy Sheoul-gra, your punishment will be determined by the Council of Orders."

"And what punishment will you recommend?" Gabriel growled. If glares could turn angels to ash, Jophiel would be a pile of embers.

Zaphkiel would pluck his own wing feathers if it meant he could see Gabriel tossed from Heaven in disgrace. His wings would be breathtaking if mounted on the wall in Throne Hall. Unfortunately, Zaphkiel doubted the Council of Orders would have the balls to give an Archangel the boot. Only one Archangel had ever lost his wings, and that had been thousands of years ago.

But Zaphkiel could live with the next best thing.

"I will recommend nine hundred years hanging in the Holy Grail."

Time ran differently in what was considered angel purgatory, and nine hundred years would feel like nine thousand. Gabriel would probably be insane by the end of it, but that would only make him a fiercer weapon in the Final Battle against Satan.

"First person I'm coming after when I get out is you." Gabriel swung his head to Jophiel. "And you'll be next. You claimed to be Metatron's friend, yet you stand with traitors."

Which was exactly why Jophiel was here. He'd been one of the few voices speaking out against taking control from the Archangels. He'd chosen to side with the Thrones when the time came, but Zaphkiel wanted to keep an eye on him. Just to make sure he remained on their side. The real test would come when Gabriel was found guilty of collaborating with Azagoth to destroy Sheoul-gra. Jophiel headed the punitive council, and he had the authority to change the recommended punishment. Would he go light because of his allegiance to Metatron?

Jophiel's expression was stone, his eyes cold as he strode over to the Archangel and stood before him. "I argued against the takeover, but know this, Gabriel. By helping Azagoth, you put the human world in jeopardy. The humans should never have been forced into accepting demons in their midst. You may have handed Satan the victory in the Final Battle, and you will pay."

Gabriel bared his teeth.

And spit in Jophiel's face.

"Mark my words," Jophiel said in a low, deadly voice, "I will paint Heaven with your blood, and I will enjoy every second of your pain." He wiped his face with the back of his hand before cracking it against Gabriel's cheek.

The sound echoed around the room, fading away just as the door flung open. Metris, a battle angel from the Order of Powers, burst inside. Zaphkiel made a mental note to fire his assistant. No one should have been allowed inside without his permission.

"I have news, Most High." Metris skidded to a stop in front of him, his face flushed, his flaming gold hair unkempt. Which was an unacceptable affront when he could fix it with a mere thought.

"This *better* be important."

Metris nodded vehemently. "We've been assessing the damage to the Gaiaportal."

"Why?" Zaphkiel scowled at Metris's plain orange robes, which again, were unacceptable when facing Heaven's most Divine leader. Clearly, Zaphkiel would have to make it clear that Michael was no longer running this show, and he had standards. "It wasn't operational when Harvester went through it. Did she suddenly make it *more* broken?"

"Of course not," Metris said, his tone bordering on condescension. "But I'm sure you're aware that the Gaiaportal has a Sheoulic counterpart. The Gehennaportal. It was deactivated when the Gaiaportal was shut down. But Harvester's foolish actions…" He trailed off, shifting his weight from foot to foot and sending a twinge of alarm through Zaphkiel.

"Her foolish actions…what? Spit it out. I don't have all eternity to wait."

Metris's eyes snapped up. "She may have opened the Gehennaportal."

All the drama for that? Zaphkiel would have laughed if he wasn't so annoyed. "Who cares? Demons have other ways of getting into the human realm. The Gehennaportal is not important."

"Except that Revenant has been restricted from flashing out of Sheoul or using Harrowgates," Jophiel said, his voice grave. "But we can't stop him from using the Gehennaportal."

Gabriel began to laugh, and as realization set in, Zaphkiel's breath clogged in his throat.

"If Revenant learns that the Gehennaportal is operational," Metris whispered, his voice trembling, "the King of Hell could bring hordes of demons to the gates of Heaven itself…and he will come for all of us."

Also from 1001 Dark Nights and Larissa Ione, discover Bond of Passion, Bond of Destiny, Reaper, Cipher, Dining With Angels, Her Guardian Angel, Hawkyn, Razr, Hades, Z, and Azagoth.

Legacy of Chaos
A Demonica Birthright Novel, Book 2
By Larissa Ione
Coming December 3, 3024

The legacy continues…

It's a gritty new world.

Three decades after the events of REAPER, the world is a different place. The secret is out. The existence of demons, vampires, shapeshifters, and angels has been revealed, and humans are struggling to adapt. Out of the chaos, The Aegis has risen to global power on the promise of containing or exterminating all underworlders, even if that means ushering in the End of Days.

Standing in their way is the next generation of warriors, the children of demons and angels and the Four Horsemen of the Apocalypse.

See how they become legends in their own right.

Legacy of Chaos

Stryke, son of Shade and Runa, grew up a happy, well-adjusted incubus alongside his four brothers. A supergenius, he took an interest in science and technology at an early age, with a dream of joining NASA…until a moment of carelessness resulted in the death of his little brother. Unable to forgive himself and desperate to prevent a similar tragedy from happening to others, he started up his own anti-demon tech company and sequestered himself behind its walls. Now he's a household name and one of the wealthiest people on the planet.

Cyan, a technomancer who works as a cybersecurity expert for DART, lost her best friend to a weapon designed by Stryke's company. She's hurt, angry, and wants revenge. So when an opportunity to work with Stryke on a project arises, she jumps at the chance to help DART and make Stryke's life miserable.

At first, Cyan and Stryke butt heads about everything. But she soon finds that deep down, he's desperately wounded and willing to sacrifice everything, including his family, to achieve his goals. Can she help him heal before he destroys himself—and everyone around him?

* * * *

Read on for a sneak peek!

Legacy of Chaos

PROLOGUE

"Let's go to the merry-go-round, Stryke! C'mon! Hurry!"

Stryke groaned down at his little brother, tugging on his hand. "There's no hurry. The thing runs every three minutes, and no one's in line because it sucks."

The little shit bit him. Right there in the webbing between his thumb and forefinger.

"Ouch. Dammit, Chaos!" He shook his hand out as his seven-year-old twin brothers, Crux and Chaos, darted ahead toward the carousel, their new white sneakers pounding the hot pavement, making the soles light up with every step.

Unbelievable. They were in a theme park filled with loopy rollercoasters, log rides, and race cars, and the little weirdos wanted to ride something they could find at a big city mall. For the third time in an hour.

"Dude, he's a handful." Logan, son of the Horseman known as Death, shook his head. At eighteen, just four years younger than Stryke, he was the spitting image of his father. "How'd you draw the short straw to be their babysitter today?"

The cute blonde popcorn stand girl gave Stryke another seductive smile as they walked by. She'd been flirting with him the entire time he'd been stuck in the lame-ass kid's section of the theme park, and each smile was more suggestive than the last. When he bought popcorn for his brothers, she'd brushed her hip against him in blatant invitation. He'd blame her advances on his sex demon pheromones, and sure, he was probably putting them out there in pulsing clouds, but she'd had her eye on him even before he'd gotten close to her.

And he'd definitely had his eyes on her.

"Blade took them to the San Diego Aquarium last week," he said after they'd passed Popcorn Princess. "Rade took them to a movie before that. Apparently, it's my turn to help out during summer break. My parents don't seem to give a shit that I'm in the middle of working on my doctoral thesis."

"Yeah, yeah, we all know you're working on your second doctorate. How can we forget the boy genius who makes the rest of us look bad?"

Stryke rolled his eyes hard enough to hurt. These guys would never know what it was like for him. His brain was in a constant state of manic sensory input and calculations, focusing on a million things at once. If he couldn't spill some of it out by working on something, his head felt like it would explode. He needed to either organize everything by learning more or release it by creating things, like doctoral theses or rocket engines.

Funny, NASA was happy to accept his designs, but actually hiring him, a demon, turned out to be a hyperdrive too far.

Also, at twenty-two, he was hardly a boy. He'd gone through his first maturation phase over a year ago. Still, in a way, he wished the painful ordeal had never happened. Before the change that made him sexually mature and insatiable, he'd been able to put one hundred percent of his concentration into education, research, and science.

Now, far too much of his brain power got diverted into finding sexual partners. Thankfully, his uncle Eidolon had developed a drug for their kind that allowed them to go a day or two without sex as long as they kept up with the injections. And from the way his dick was pointing at the popcorn girl, it was clear he needed another one.

"I'm gonna go find Sabre and Blade," Logan said. "We want to ride the Ice Tornado."

"Yeah, have fun," Stryke said absently, digging through his pocket for the injector pen. Shit. He must have left it at home. Maybe Blade or Sabre had one on them.

When he got to the carousel, the twins had queued at the head of the line, and the ride hadn't stopped yet. Stryke glanced back at the popcorn girl, hanging a *Be Back in Ten Minutes* sign.

Perfect timing. He might not have to bug his cousin or brother for an injector pen, after all.

He caught Popcorn Princess as she stepped out from behind the cart.

"Hi," she said, her glossy red lips turned into a mischievous smile that made him wonder how they'd feel wrapped around his cock. Depending on the viscosity of her gloss, the friction of her lips on the skin of his shaft could create intense sensations. "I was hoping you'd come over."

He was hoping he'd *come*. "Yeah? What time do you get off work?"

"Not for another four hours." She glanced at her comms unit. First gen. Stryke had just gotten the second gen. Had some cool upgrades. "But I've got ten minutes and a secret spot. You got any juice?"

Juice. Drugs. Stryke wasn't into that shit. His mind was already in a constant spin. "No, but I have a condom."

Not that he needed one. He wouldn't be fertile until his second maturation phase, which wouldn't happen for another eighty years or so. But he couldn't exactly say that, not to a human. At least, he assumed she was human.

She probably assumed he was too.

"S'okay." She started down a winding path off the main pedestrian area, her tight ass swinging under her short white skirt. "I got some J."

He glanced back at the carousel, which had stopped and was unloading. He should have four to five minutes before Crux and Chaos were done with the ride. Perfect.

They passed a sign that said *No Entry*. A small building designed like a tropical hut disguised to blend in with the landscaping loomed ahead. He assumed they were going inside, but Popcorn Girl gave him a flirty look and a *shh* finger against her plump lips before slipping into the brush.

They eased up behind the hut in a little alcove littered with a few candy wrappers and cigarette butts.

"I'm Micha, by the way," she said as she pulled a wadded bit of plastic from behind a tree.

"Stryke." He waved away her offer of one of the tiny pills in the baggie. "And you don't need that shit. You'll like what I'm going to give you way more."

Reaching out, she dragged her finger from his sternum to the button on his jeans. "Oh, yeah?"

"Yeah."

Done flirting, he tore the baggie from her hand and tossed it to the ground. Flirting was an instinctive skill for most Seminus demons, but Stryke somehow lacked that gene. He wrapped his arm around her waist and tugged her to him, his other hand dipping under her skirt. Her cheap panties didn't stand a chance against his probing fingers, and she gasped as he slipped a couple inside her slippery core.

"I don't usually do this," she breathed, hiking one leg up against his hip.

"I'm sure you don't." He hoped he didn't sound sarcastic, and then he realized he didn't give a crap. He'd never see her again.

Except that he liked how willing she was to fuck a complete stranger. Maybe he should get her number afterward and get a sex-only relationship going. No small talk, kissing, or dinner dates. Just pleasure and a see-ya-later. His cousin Mace had about a dozen of those, but Stryke doubted Mace was truly as utilitarian about it as he claimed to be. His cousin liked to flirt. He liked to impress the females. And he loved to be adored.

Stryke couldn't care less about any of it. Sex was a biological necessity for him, as important as breathing or eating. Sure, it was enjoyable, but so was eating. Didn't mean he had to turn every lunch or fuck into a seven-course meal. Who had time for that shit?

"You got a boyfriend?" he asked as he unbuttoned his jeans and backed her up against a tree.

"Not really."

Again, didn't care. But it seemed like a normal question to ask when making small talk.

He guided his cock to her entrance and sank inside her with a groan. He didn't like the build-up to sex, the courtship and then the foreplay, but once he was balls-deep inside a hot female, it was bliss. A few precious seconds for his mind to stop thinking and recharge.

He started pumping, letting his body take over for his brain. He didn't have time to work her up and get her to come before he did, but he had that covered. His semen would trigger a series of powerful orgasms that would last for fifteen minutes or longer.

She would be late getting back to her popcorn stand, and she wouldn't care at all.

His orgasm ramped up quickly, searing bliss that built in his balls and blew up his shaft in wave after wave of ecstasy.

"Ah…yes…" He threw back his head and focused on the tension escaping his body and the sounds of the female's climax.

Around them, the noises from the park grew louder, intruding on

Stryke's precious few moments of mental silence.

So much screaming.

Some ride must be scaring the shit out of people.

Weird. They were in kiddie land. Why would there be so many screams?

He froze. The human was still coming, contracting around his cock and pumping her hips against his. But all around, the gut-wrenching sounds of terror echoed off buildings. Through the gaps in the trees, he caught brief glimpses of people…adults dragging children and strollers, running from the direction of the carousel.

The carousel!

He tore away from the female, leaving her propped against the tree, moaning through multiple orgasms. Heart racing, he scrambled up the path, tripping over roots and his feet as he ran and buttoned up. He burst onto the main drag, colliding with a man whose face dripped with blood. Ahead, the popcorn stand had been turned over. People weren't running now. They were limping. Crawling. Dragging themselves.

"Crux!" he screamed. "Chaos!"

Then he saw the demons. A half-dozen inky nightmarish motherfuckers with jaws full of razor-sharp teeth, Freddy Kreuger claws, and way too many burning red eyes.

Logan, Sabre, and Blade rushed toward the carousel up ahead, Logan armed with the blade he could summon at will. With an agile leap and a smooth swing, he sliced the head clean off one of the demons.

Way to go!

Stryke shouldered past a few stumbling people. There! Crux! His little brother, his tawny hair matted with blood, was scrambling over bodies and dodging a demon's sweeping blows and driving punches.

No! Terror clawed at him as he calculated the distance to his brother and the odds of the demon's next two blows killing Crux. Motherfucker, he wasn't going to make it.

As Stryke threw himself at the demon, knowing he couldn't make it in time, Blade hit the thing from behind. He drove his fist into the back of the monster's head, his *dermoire* glowing with power usually meant for healing but now weaponized. The demon snarled, striking out and knocking Blade away.

Close enough now to smell the beast's rancid, smoky odor, Stryke slammed into him, lighting up his own power and ordering a massive heart attack. The demon screeched as its heart seized. All four fucking chambers of it.

Stryke felt Blade's power join his, causing tears in the bastard's veins and bleeding him out from the inside.

The thing collapsed. Blade instantly went after another demon as Stryke, his body vibrating with adrenaline and fear for his brothers, scooped up Crux.

"Where's Chaos?" he shouted, spinning around in search of the twin boy. Chaos!" he screamed. "*Chaos!*"

Clinging to Crux, he shambled through the ocean of bodies and overturned strollers, as he kept to close to the carousel, hoping to find Chaos hiding nearby. Logan, Blade and Sabre battled the remaining demons, the sounds of slaughter and pain filling the air along with the smell of blood and bowels.

Abruptly, a stab of pain shot through his skull and down his spine, as if he'd been impaled by a rod of white-hot iron. It burned and flashed away, leaving an emptiness inside, as if the rod had taken a core sample of his soul.

And had taken Chaos.

Stryke's gut plummeted to his feet.

Crux screamed as the reality hit him too.

A hand came down on his shoulder, and he wheeled around to Sabre, whose expression conveyed sorrow, trauma, and disbelief. Sabre was a cousin and wouldn't have felt Chaos die.

He probably saw it.

Stryke's brain, which always crackled with energy, went numb. At some point, he must have set Crux down because Sabre had gone to his knees to hug the boy to his chest, shielding his eyes from the massacre around them.

The din of screaming and moaning grew dull as Stryke's sense of hearing became a victim of shock. His balance went next, his legs watery as he stumbled toward Blade.

Blade, who knelt next to a pair of blinking shoes and…*oh, gods.*

Please, no. Please, no! he screamed inside his head. *Take me. Take me instead!*

Blade, his dark head hanging, his shoulders slumped, turned slowly to Stryke. Tears streamed from his eyes and cut paths through the blood splattered on cheeks gone pale with trauma.

"Where were you?" he rasped. "Where the fuck were you?"

The world spun and went gray. The last thing Stryke saw before he lost consciousness was Blade's scorching, accusatory glare, and those brand-new flashing shoes.

Sign up for the Blue Box Press/1001 Dark Nights Newsletter
and be entered to win a Tiffany Lock necklace.

There's a contest every quarter!

Go to www.TheBlueBoxPress.com to subscribe.

As a bonus, all subscribers can download
FIVE FREE exclusive books!

Discover 1001 Dark Nights Collection Eleven

DRAGON KISS by Donna Grant
A Dragon Kings Novella

THE WILD CARD by Dylan Allen
A Rivers Wilde Novella

ROCK CHICK REMATCH by Kristen Ashley
A Rock Chick Novella

JUST ONE SUMMER by Carly Phillips
A Dirty Dare Series Novella

HAPPILY EVER MAYBE by Carrie Ann Ryan
A Montgomery Ink Legacy Novella

BLUE MOON by Skye Warren
A Cirque des Moroirs Novella

A VAMPIRE'S MATE by Rebecca Zanetti
A Dark Protectors/Rebels Novella

LOVE HAZARD by Rachel Van Dyken

BRODIE by Aurora Rose Reynolds
An Until Her Novella

THE BODYGUARD AND THE BOMBSHELL by Lexi Blake
A Masters and Mercenaries: New Recruits Novella

THE SUBSTITUTE by Kristen Proby
A Single in Seattle Novella

CRAVED BY YOU by J. Kenner
A Stark Security Novella

GRAVEYARD DOG by Darynda Jones
A Charley Davidson Novella

A CHRISTMAS AUCTION by Audrey Carlan
A Marriage Auction Novella

THE GHOST OF A CHANCE by Heather Graham
A Krewe of Hunters Novella

Also from Blue Box Press:

LEGACY OF TEMPTATION by Larissa Ione
A Demonica Birthright Novel

VISIONS OF FLESH AND BLOOD by Jennifer L. Armentrout and
Ravyn Salvador
A Blood & Ash and Flesh & Fire Compendium

FORGETTING TO REMEMBER by M.J. Rose

TOUCH ME by J. Kenner
A Stark International Novella

BORN OF BLOOD AND ASH by Jennifer L. Armentrout
A Flesh and Fire Novel

MY ROYAL SHOWMANCE by Lexi Blake
A Park Avenue Promise Novel

SAPPHIRE DAWN by Christopher Rice writing as C. Travis Rice
A Sapphire Cove Noveal

LEGACY OF PLEASURE by Larissa Ione
A Demonica Birthright Novel

Discover More Larissa Ione

Bond of Passion: A Demonica Novella

He was an assassin. She was his lover.
And his victim.
Now, years later, she's back from the dead and looking for vengeance.

Thanks to an unexpected and fortuitous disaster, Tavin's contract with the underworld's Assassin Guild was broken decades early. But instead of freedom, he's suffocated by guilt and regret. In many ways, he's more trapped than he was before. In an attempt to numb his pain, he works at Underworld General Hospital, saving people instead of killing them. But nothing can diminish the memory of assassinating the female he loved…not even the knowledge that he'd done it to spare her an even worse fate.

Deja remembers all of her dozens of former lives, and she knows that she only found love in one of them…until her lover murdered her. As a soul locked inside the nightmarish boundaries of demon hell, she stewed in hatred until a single, fateful event gave her one more shot at life.

And at revenge.

Now another specter from the past is threatening them both. Can two damaged people overcome their history to save not only themselves, but a second chance at love?

Bond of Destiny: A Demonica Novella

Sold into slavery mere hours after his birth to werewolf parents, Tracker spent decades in service to cruel underworlders. Then the fallen angel Harvester transferred his ownership to a human woman who gave him as much freedom as the unbreakable bond would allow. Still, thanks to his traumatic past, he's afraid to trust, let alone feel love. But when an acquaintance shows up at his door, injured and in need of help, he finds himself longing for a connection. For someone to touch. For someone to care.

Stacey Markham has had it bad for Tracker since the day her best friend, Jillian, was forced to hold his slave bond. At first, the fact that he's a werewolf seemed weird to Stacey, but hey, her best friend was married to one of the Four Horsemen of the Apocalypse, so *weird* is definitely a matter of perspective. Stacey knows the depths of Tracker's trauma, and she longs to help him even as he helps her, but breaking through his walls isn't easy.

And it only gets harder when the only blood family he has, the pack that gave him away, lays claim to him...and everything he loves.

Reaper: A Demonica Novel

He is the Keeper of Souls. Judge, jury, and executioner. He is death personified.

He is the Grim Reaper.

A fallen angel who commands the respect of both Heaven and Hell, Azagoth has presided over his own underworld realm for thousands of years. As the overlord of evil souls, he maintains balance crucial to the existence of life on Earth and beyond. But as all the realms gear up for the prophesied End of Days, the ties that bind him to Sheoul-gra have begun to chafe.

Now, with his beloved mate and unborn child the target of an ancient enemy, Azagoth will stop at nothing to save them, even if it means breaking blood oaths and shattering age-old alliances.

Even if it means destroying himself and setting the world on fire...

Hawkyn: A Demonica Novella

As a special class of earthbound guardian angel called Memitim, Hawkyn is charged with protecting those whose lives are woven into the fabric of the future. His success is legendary, so when he's given a serial killer to watch over, he sees no reason for that to change. But Hawkyn's own future is jeopardized after he breaks the rules and rescues a beautiful woman from the killer's clutches, setting off an explosive, demonic game of cat and mouse that pits brother against brother and that won't end until someone dies.

Aurora Mercer is the half-wytch lone survivor of a psychopath who gets off on the sadistic torture of his victims. A psychopath whose obsessive psyche won't let him move on until he kills her. Now she's marked for death, her fate tied to that of a murderer...and to a sexy angel who makes her blood burn with desire...

Cipher: A Demonica Underworld Novella

It's been seven months since Cipher, an Unfallen angel who straddled a razor thin line between good and evil, woke up in hell with a new set of wings, a wicked pair of fangs, and a handler who's as beautiful as she is dangerous. As a laid-back cyber-specialist who once assisted guardian angels, he'd been in a prime position to earn back his halo. But now, as a True Fallen forced to use his talents for malevolence, he must fight not only his captors and his sexy handler, but the growing corruption inside him...before the friends searching for him become his enemies and he becomes his own worst nightmare.

Lyre is a fallen angel with a heart full of hate. When she's assigned to ensure that Cipher carries out their boss's orders, she sees an opportunity to take revenge on those who wronged her. All she has to do is appeal to Cipher's burgeoning dark side. But the devastatingly handsome fellow True Fallen has other ideas — sexy ideas that threaten to derail all Lyre's plans and put them in the path of an approaching hell storm.

Danger and desire explode, even as Cipher and Lyre unravel a sinister plot that will fracture the underworld and send shockwaves into Heaven itself…

Dining with Angels: Bits & Bites from the Demonica Universe by Larissa Ione, Recipes by Suzanne M. Johnson

In a world where humans and supernatural beings coexist — not always peacefully — three things can bring everyone to the table: Love, a mutual enemy, and, of course, food.

With seven brand new stories from the Demonica universe, New York Times bestselling author Larissa Ione has the love and enemies covered, while celebrity Southern food expert Suzanne Johnson brings delicious food to the party.

And who doesn't love a party? (Harvester rolls her eyes and raises her hand, but we know she's lying.)

Join Ares and Cara as they celebrate a new addition to their family. See what Reaver and Harvester are doing to "spice" things up. Find out what trouble Reseph might have gotten himself into with Jillian. You'll love reading about the further adventures of Wraith and Serena, Declan and Suzanne, and Shade and Runa, and you're not going to want to miss the sit down with Eidolon and Tayla.

So pour a glass of the Grim Reaper's finest wine and settle in for slices of life from your favorite characters and the recipes that bring them together. Whether you're dining with angels, drinking with demons, or hanging with humans, you'll find the perfect heavenly bits and sinful bites to suit the occasion.

Happy reading and happy eating!

Her Guardian Angel: A Demonica Underworld/Masters and Mercenaries Novella

After a difficult childhood and a turbulent stint in the military, Declan Burke finally got his act together. Now he's a battle-hardened professional bodyguard who takes his job at McKay-Taggart seriously and his playtime – and his play*mates* – just as seriously. One thing he never does, however, is mix business with pleasure. But when the mysterious, gorgeous Suzanne D'Angelo needs his protection from a stalker, his desire for her burns out of control, tempting him to break all the rules…even as he's drawn into a dark, dangerous world he didn't know existed.

Suzanne is an earthbound angel on her critical first mission: protecting Declan from an emerging supernatural threat at all costs. To keep him close, she hires him as her bodyguard. It doesn't take long for her to realize that she's in over her head, defenseless against this devastatingly sexy human who makes her crave his forbidden touch.

Together they'll have to draw on every ounce of their collective training to resist each other as the enemy closes in, but soon it becomes apparent that nothing could have prepared them for the menace to their lives…or their hearts.

Razr: A Demonica Underworld Novella

A fallen angel with a secret.
An otherworldly elf with an insatiable hunger she doesn't understand.
An enchanted gem.
Meet mortal enemies Razr and Jedda…and the priceless diamond that threatens to destroy them both even as it bonds them together with

sizzling passion.

Welcome back to the Demonica Underworld, where enemies find love...if they're strong enough to survive.

Z: A Demonica Underworld Novella

Zhubaal, fallen angel assistant to the Grim Reaper, has spent decades searching for the angel he loved and lost nearly a century ago. Not even her death can keep him from trying to find her, not when he knows she's been given a second chance at life in a new body. But as time passes, he's losing hope, and he wonders how much longer he can hold to the oath he swore to her so long ago…

As an *emim*, the wingless offspring of two fallen angels, Vex has always felt like a second-class citizen. But if she manages to secure a deal with the Grim Reaper — by any means necessary — she will have earned her place in the world. The only obstacle in the way of her plan is a sexy hardass called Z, who seems determined to thwart her at every turn. Soon it becomes clear that they have a powerful connection rooted in the past…but can any vow stand the test of time?

Hades: A Demonica Underworld Novella

A fallen angel with a mean streak and a mohawk, Hades has spent thousands of years serving as Jailor of the Underworld. The souls he guards are as evil as they come, but few dare to cross him. All of that changes when a sexy fallen angel infiltrates his prison and unintentionally starts a riot. It's easy enough to quell an uprising, but for the first time, Hades is torn between delivering justice — or bestowing mercy — on the beautiful female who could be his salvation...or his undoing.

Thanks to her unwitting participation in another angel's plot to start Armageddon, Cataclysm was kicked out of Heaven and is now a fallen angel in service of Hades's boss, Azagoth. All she wants is to redeem herself and get back where she belongs. But when she gets trapped in Hades's prison domain with only the cocky but irresistible Hades to help her, Cat finds that where she belongs might be in the place she least expected...

Azagoth: A Demonica Underword Novella

Even in the fathomless depths of the underworld and the bleak chambers of a damaged heart, the bonds of love can heal...or destroy.

He holds the ability to annihilate souls in the palm of his hand. He commands the respect of the most dangerous of demons and the most powerful of angels. He can seduce and dominate any female he wants with a mere look. But for all Azagoth's power, he's bound by shackles of his own making, and only an angel with a secret holds the key to his release.

She's an angel with the extraordinary ability to travel through time and space. An angel with a tormented past she can't escape. And when Lilliana is sent to Azagoth's underworld realm, she finds that her past isn't all she can't escape. For the irresistibly sexy fallen angel known as Azagoth is also known as the Grim Reaper, and when he claims a soul, it's forever...

About Larissa Ione

Air Force veteran Larissa Ione traded in a career as a meteorologist to pursue her passion of writing. She has since published dozens of books, hit several bestseller lists, including the New York Times and USA Today, and has been nominated for a RITA award. She now spends her days in pajamas with her computer, strong coffee, and fictional worlds. She believes in celebrating everything, and would never be caught without a bottle of Champagne chilling in the fridge…just in case. After a dozen moves all over the country with her now-retired U.S. Coast Guard spouse, she is now settled in Wisconsin with her husband, a rescue cat named Vegas, and her very own hellhound, a Belgian Malinois named Duvel.

For more information about Larissa, visit:
www.larissaione.com.

On Behalf of 1001 Dark Nights,

Liz Berry, M.J. Rose, and Jillian Stein would like to thank ~

Steve Berry
Doug Scofield
Benjamin Stein
Kim Guidroz
Chelle Olson
Tanaka Kangara
Stacey Tardif
Hang Le
Chris Graham
Jessica Saunders
Anne-Marie Nieves
Trinity Shain
Grace Wenk
Dylan Stockton
Kate Boggs
Richard Blake
and Simon Lipskar